One Million to Die For

One Million to Die For

by

Marlené R. Carter

Laura –
you are a great
inspiration.

Marlené R. Carter

DORRANCE PUBLISHING CO., INC.
PITTSBURGH, PENNSYLVANIA 15222

ISBN # 0-8059-6629-3
Printed in the United States of America

First Printing

For information or to order additional books, please write:
Dorrance Publishing Co., Inc.
701 Smithfield Street
Third Floor
Pittsburgh, Pennsylvania 15222
U.S.A.
1-800-788-7654
Or visit our web site and on-line catalog at www.dorrancepublishing.com

Prologue

When Amara regained consciousness, she found herself sprawled on the cold hard concrete floor in a pool of her own blood. Duke finally caught me, she thought to herself. She slowly lifted her head and then lowered it as the room spun around, out of control. She then lifted her left hand and winced in pain as her fingers gently touched the gash on her forehead. Strands of her hair were mixed in the dried blood that was stuck to her forehead. She looked down at her bloodied arm that continued to throb and ache. Amara tried to steady herself and ignore the ringing in her ears. She said a silent prayer, giving thanks for her life. Amara concentrated hard to overcome the pain she was feeling and remember what had happened. She tried to remember how she had ended up on the floor of an empty warehouse.

Amara began to shiver. I must be going into shock, she thought to herself. She fought the freezing cold that enveloped her entire body, down to her bones. She felt disoriented, as if she had been thrown from a playground merry-go-round. She steadied herself by placing her palms flat on the ground and attempted to raise herself off the ground when she felt another presence in the warehouse.

Amara turned her head slightly and slowly focused her eyes in the direction of a large, dark, luminous figure moving cautiously toward her. She tried hard to focus on the figure that was slowly closing in on her. The room continued to spin and forced Amara to lay down flat on her back and look up at the high warehouse ceiling. The numbness of her body seemed to protect her from the coldness she had originally felt. As the figure moved closer, she smelled the familiar odor that belonged to the man who had tried to harm her twice already.

A red beam penetrated the musty air. Particles of dust floated around the red narrow beam as he aimed it at the middle of her forehead. Amara thought about the irony of her situation and began to laugh so hard tears streamed down her face. Amara slowly lifted her body and sat up. She squinted her eyes as they continued to readjust to the shards of light flowing through the panes of the warehouse windows located high above. Amara placed a blood-ied hand up to her eyes as if to shield them from the excessive light. "So, Dad, are you going to kill your only daughter?" she asked. The red beam suddenly disappeared from her forehead, and the dark figure stood there, jaundiced eyes wide, too stunned to speak.

Chapter 1

*A*mara swayed back and forth in her seat and snapped her fingers as she listened to the live music in the cozy nightclub. LaMont's Club, located in East Seattle, was her favorite hang-out. She and her girlfriend, Tammy, came at least once a month, just to break up the monotony of their lives and listen to some great live music. They both liked LaMont's because it was small and smartly decorated with comfortable wooden chairs that had oversized, soft, maroon velveteen seat covers and soft plush maroon velveteen sofas that were strategically placed throughout the club for easy listening enjoyment.

The crowd that came to LaMont's was more mature and sophisticated than the usual hip-hop crowd. On any given evening you could see young corporate and blue-collar workers sharing an evening meal with friends, co-workers, or a date and later listening to the live music played by one of the up-and-coming bands from the area. The clientele were always dressed to impress. Most men wore coat and tie or an open-collared shirt with a sharp jacket. The women were clad in a business suit or a sexy dress. The club exuded class and subliminally forced everyone to dress and act as such. But LaMont knew how young adults sometimes acted when they had one too many drinks, so he hired bouncers who were discreetly placed inside the club. They were well trained and polite, until you were out of the public eye. Then, all bets were off. You would be shown the back entrance, which was the service entrance and the location of the trash receptacles. Several drunk and unruly patrons found themselves spread-eagled over high mounds of plastic trash bags. The only redeeming part was no one was allowed in the back of the club, so the unruly patrons could return to their cars with their dignity intact.

LaMont, the owner, was a Seattle native. He had attended high school with Amara, though he was two years older than she. At his east side high school he was voted most popular. He was involved in every extracurricular activity imaginable. Everyone knew him and he was a lot of fun to be around. After he graduated, he became frustrated because there weren't many nice places in his neighborhood for up-and-coming young people like himself to hang out and socialize. He thought about all the parties he threw in his basement during high school and got the idea of opening a supper club. His father, a prominent businessman, agreed to provide the financial backing on the condition he attend business courses at the nearby Community College. LaMont successfully completed the necessary courses within one year and developed a comprehensive business proposal. His father loaned him the money to start his business. The following year he opened his club. Two years later he had repaid his father in full. He was really proud of his club. In fact, business was so good he was in the process of expanding. He was adding four large rooms for catered private parties and meetings in the rear of the club. LaMont went out of his way to ensure his club was sophisticated, yet comfortable. When you entered the club you immediately felt comfortable and welcomed. The plush carpet and the strategic arrangement of inviting settees and sofas enabled groups of people to sit cozily and socialize. The walls were red brick. He liked the look so well, he left them it their natural state. He felt it gave the club a sophisticated yet funky atmosphere. His favorite color was maroon; he used that color throughout the club.

To complete his vision, he enlisted the help of one of his retired high school teachers. He happened to find her advertisement on the bulletin board of the Community College he was attending and gave her a call. He struck gold with Mrs. Glenton. He told her what he wanted and she made it come to life. She was really inexpensive, which fit right into his budget since he had very little money to spare. He was her first customer and she wanted to make a good impression and also depended on him to spread the word about her talent. He didn't have to do much work, her designs spoke for themselves and he tossed work to her on a regular basis.

The illumination in the club was provided by soft overhead lights deliberately placed throughout the club and flickering candles nestled in romantic crystal bell-shaped candle holders on each maroon and tan clothed table. Prints of famous jazz musicians hung gracefully on the brick walls. The other walls had autographed photos of famous people who had visited his club when they were in town. LaMont had been so successful at creating an atmosphere that encouraged decorum yet fun and socializing that when people entered his club they felt as if they had entered a large version of a good friend's home.

Tammy had invited her best friend Amara to the club to celebrate the new job she landed a couple weeks ago. They walked through the entrance and stood at the door to look for a place to sit. They had arrived early, so there was plenty of available seating. LaMont spotted them and walked over to greet them. He gave each a friendly hug and personally led them to their table. He joked with them for a couple of moments before leaving to greet another group of customers. Tammy smiled. "You see that's why people keep coming back. LaMont has it going on. He makes sure everyone feels welcome here," she said as she adjusted her seat. Amara shook her head in agreement.

As the waitress approached to take their drink order, two men waved and began to walk in their direction. Tammy smiled and waved back. To help celebrate the occasion, Tammy had invited two male friends she had met while attending a business symposium at the hospital where she did volunteer work on the weekends. Tammy smiled when the gentlemen introduced themselves and sat down in the vacant chairs beside each lady. Tammy leaned in close toward her gentleman friend as he asked her personal questions about herself. Tammy smiled and looked over the handsome man as he spoke to her.

John Glover was six foot three and had the body of a professional weight trainer. The white oxford collar on his shirt gripped his wide neck tightly. His broad shoulders looked as if they were trapped inside his snug-fitting blazer. His slacks flowed freely about his large thighs. He possessed the fine features of a Zulu warrior. His complexion was the rich color of mocha. His dark brown eyes flickered with intrigue as he spoke. His keen nose, chiseled dimpled chin and sultry lips made one think he was a model who had just stepped off a rugged photo shoot. In one word, he was gorgeous. Tammy particularly enjoyed the way women turned to stare at him as they passed their table and how his attention never diverted from her. John waved toward the waitress and ordered a drink while Tammy told him basic information about herself; such as her occupation, marital status, and how long she'd lived in the city—blah, blah, blah.

Amara looked at the man who was sitting next to her. Greg Taylor was a well-groomed man who stood approximately five foot ten. He was dressed in an expensive Brooks Brothers suit with a white tailored button-down-collared shirt and a tie that matched his suit. Very dull, thought Amara. Greg was the color of cocoa butter and had sandy light brown hair that he kept cut in a short conservative style. He had full kissable lips and a very flattering nose. His sexy light brown eyes twinkled as he discussed his passion, which was finance. Amara feigned interest and slowly sipped her mimosa.

When she could stand no more of the dull conversation, she gave Tammy the signal, which was to clear her throat. Tammy nodded and excused herself. Amara did the same. Both men stood up from their chair and watched the women as they walked toward the restroom.

In the restroom, Amara and Tammy stood in front of the mirror refreshing their makeup. As Tammy and Amara applied some face powder to take away the shine, they discussed their dates for the evening. "I don't know how I let you talk me into going out with Greg," said Amara, unhappily. Tammy ignored Amara's sour attitude. "Girl, John is too fine. Did I tell you he's a lawyer?" asked Tammy a bit too loud. Amara rolled her eyes. "Yeah, a lawyer who happens to have motor oil under his nails," she said sarcastically. "You are such a player hater," said Tammy as she quickly applied another coat of lipstick to her lips and matted it with a soft tissue. She looked at her reflection and fluffed her hair.

Tammy was an attractive African American woman, with a caramel brown complexion. She was an expert at accentuating her best qualities. She applied her makeup like a professional, drawing attention to her beautiful round eyes and away from a nose she considered to be rather large. Her full lips were pouty and perfectly shaped. She always wore the right shade of lipstick that accentuated and flattered them. Her hair was always properly coiffed, never a strand out of place. She kept it cut in styles that flattered her heart-shaped face. She usually dressed conservatively, but tonight, she decided to be daring and wore a sexy low-cut midnight blue dress that showed off her perfect breasts and cinched around her petite waist, then flowed out in a layer of sheer material on top of satin, that stopped right above her knees, the exact length to show off her beautiful legs. She wore an attractive sterling silver rope necklace that was tied in a knot and dangled effortlessly in her cleavage. She shook her head and her hair flowed freely from side to side. She smiled at her reflection. "Looking good, girl," she said pointing at herself in the mirror.

Amara laughed. "You are so crazy," she said, giggling. She put the final touches on her lipstick and examined herself in the mirror. Amara was above average height with a medium build. She wore a black form-fitting dress that gave her a slim look and downplayed her full breasts and rested neatly over her curvaceous hips. Amara had been working out and was pleased to see some of the positive effects. She had lost ten pounds in all the right places and firmed up her muscles quite a bit. As usual, she wore very little jewelry, a strand of pearls given to her by her ex-boyfriend and matching pearl earrings she purchased herself. Her flawless skin was the rich color of pecans. Her big eyes and extra long lashes had always been the envy of all the girls throughout her years at school. Her deep dimples appeared whenever she smiled. When she smiled, she exposed perfectly straight teeth thanks to years of forced orthodontist treatments. Her hair flowed down to the middle of her back in natural curly tendrils. She loved experimenting with her hair. She was born with auburn-colored hair and loved how it complemented her skin tone.

Amara frowned at her reflection in the mirror and leaned on the edge of the sink as she spoke. "Greg is so boring! He is a financial planner and you would think that discussing my financial portfolio was like foreplay or something," she said. "Girl, I think he got a hard-on talking about the financial freedom I would experience when my savings bonds and mutual funds matured." Tammy began to laugh uncontrollably. "Mari, I'm going to pee on myself," she said as she scurried into the empty stall, still laughing. Amara laughed aloud at her own little joke.

Tammy came out and washed her hands. Amara was picking something out of her long lashes. Tammy looked over at her friend and smiled. "Anyone who has eyelashes as long and pretty as yours should be shot." Amara grinned and checked to make sure there was no lipstick on her teeth. "Flattery will get you everywhere. Thanks for the compliment," said Amara. "The only compliment Greg has given me is about the how beautiful my bonds will look once they mature," she groaned. Tammy laughed again. "Girl, my bonds are already mature," she said pointing at her seductive cleavage that showed through her low-cut dress. Both women laughed heartily.

"We had better get back out there before my lawyer-mechanic and your financial geek find other fish," said Tammy as she headed for the door. Amara washed her hands and followed. The women exited the restroom and walked side by side down the dim hall that was illuminated by soft recessed lights. The crowd had thickened since they left for the restroom.

Tammy continued to make jokes as they were forced to separate on either side of the hallway in order to allow a group of women to pass. Tammy was still talking as Amara tried to catch up. Amara called out to Tammy and asked her to wait for her at the end of the hall. Tammy acknowledged and slowed at the end of the hall to allow Amara to catch up. Tammy's attention was diverted when she saw a close friend. They began to chat as Tammy waited for Amara to come out of the hallway.

Tammy looked down the hallway and saw Amara heading toward her. She leaned back against the wall and turned her attention back to her friend. Amara could see Tammy leaning against the wall at the end of the hallway and tried to squeeze through the crowd in order to catch up with her. Suddenly, two large calloused hands enveloped her. One hand quickly covered Amara's mouth and the other pulled her with great force into a vacant room located a few doors down from the restroom. It was so fast that she could still hear the faint sound of her friend's voice calling her name and telling her to hurry up.

She felt the skin on her lip tear from the force and roughness of the large hand over her mouth. Amara tried to fight her assailant until she felt a hard metal object against her temple. She stopped fighting and allowed her body to go limp and placed all of her weight on the assailant and forced him to support her. The attacker slammed her limp body against the unfinished wall and placed his large muscular forearm across her throat, causing her to gag. Amara tried to regain her bearings and adjust her eyes to the darkness. Though she couldn't move her neck, she looked up and saw reflections of the nightclub's bright lights that flowed through the high window above her assailant's head.

Her eyes quickly began to adjust to the darkness and she could see her attacker. His eyes narrowed to slits as he glared at her. In a raspy voice, he said, "I am going to kill you. He wants you dead and tonight you are going to die." He adjusted his arm and pulled the soft skin on her neck roughly to one side. She suddenly felt a dull pain but she would not allow herself to panic. Remain focused, she coached herself.

5

Amara's throat began to feel numb. She could feel her legs start to tremble. Amara thought about what he had just said, but made no sound or motion to his statement. She thought it was strange he spoke to her. Most hired killers don't talk, they just kill you, she thought. Maybe whoever hired him, wanted me to know that someone out there hated me enough to kill me, she thought? Her mind began to reel.

He moved closer to her and pressed his weight onto her and pushed his forearm harder against her throat. The sudden pressure gave Amara an urge to gag but she kept her focus and tried not to panic. She began breathing slowly through her nose rather than her mouth. As she breathed through her nose, she smelled his aftershave and felt the damp heat from his breath on her neck as he hissed his final warning to her. Although she was frightened, she opened her eyes and forced herself to look at his face.

Her eyes had fully adjusted to the dark. The slight ray of light flowing through the window was enough for her to make out his facial features clearly. As if she were drawing a portrait, she examined his entire face and upper torso. His skin was black as coal and smooth as a piece of worn wood that had been washed over and over by the ocean waters and sand. His shiny head was clean-shaven with black designer sunglasses perched on top. He had a small diamond stud earring nestled in his left ear. It glistened as it picked up shards of light. His expensive, tailor-made silk shirt clung to his muscular body like a glove. His chest moved up and down as he began to breathe more rapidly.

He gave her a cool grin, exposing deep dimples and pearly white teeth that were naturally straight and even. She guessed he didn't care if she saw him because he intended to kill her. He brought his face close to hers, as if he were going to kiss her. He then took the tip of the barrel of his weapon and traced over her full lips. She was scared, but she didn't flinch. She looked into his eyes, as if she could channel into his soul through them. He had long beautiful lashes like hers, but his eyes were jaundiced and filled with a mixture of hate and sorrow. His breathing was slow and controlled. His breath smelled of stale cigarettes and hard liquor.

As she continued to look into his eyes the look suddenly changed and the grin disappeared. His eyes narrowed as he cocked back the hammer and pushed the weapon deeper into her flesh. She stood perfectly still; her eyes shut tight and unknowingly she held her breath. Amara was too afraid to move.

As he applied pressure to the trigger, a couple burst into the room and switched on the light. They had a bottle of champagne, a couple of champagne flutes, and were laughing loudly. The couple paused at the doorway and gasped. The bright light and sudden appearance of this unexpected and unwelcome company startled him. Reflexively the assailant immediately pulled the gun away from Amara's head and looked in the direction of the doorway. During that split second of distraction, Amara pushed all of her weight onto him and caused him to lose his balance. In an effort to regain his balance, he moved back slightly. Amara took advantage of the opportunity and thrust her full weight onto him. He stumbled back even further and Amara bolted away.

She sprinted toward the door as the attacker reached out to grab her long curly tendrils billowing behind her. She quickly pushed the woman who was holding the champagne bottle toward the assailant and caused her to drop the bottle. He lost his balance and slipped in the spilled liquid. Amara could hear him curse aloud as she ran toward the door of the nightclub into the street. Amara saw Tammy out of her peripheral vision and heard her calling her name but she didn't answer or look in her direction. The adrenaline caused by fear would not allow her to stop running. She continued to run down the poorly lit street. She wanted to make sure she was a safe distance away before she stopped.

It had started to drizzle and then downpour. Amara's hair became matted against her scalp and her running feet splashed in the puddles, ruining her new shoes and pantyhose as she gained momentum and continued down the street. She spotted a crowded restaurant a few blocks down the street and quickly went inside. She smoothed her wet hair and tried to control her heavy breathing. Her wet clothes hugged her body like a second skin.

She wrung out the edges of her dress and calmly walked to the hostesses station and placed her name on the waiting list for a table. The hostess tried to act naturally but couldn't help staring at the fresh blood on her wounded lips and bruised neck. Amara was disheveled, wet, and looked a mess. The woman smiled her best hostess smile and placed Amara's name on the waiting list. Amara tried to smile back but the effort caused excruciating pain to her lips.

She looked down at the ground and walked slowly to the restroom, her feet making sloshing sounds with every step she took. Once she reached the restroom she ran into one of the stalls and threw up into the toilet. When she was finished, she splashed cool water on her face and gently washed the blood from her lips. She patted the rest of her face dry with a rough paper towel. She looked in the mirror and examined the red and purple bruise on her neck and the deep gash across her swollen upper and lower lips. Tears began to stream down her face as she paced the floor and thought about her next move.

Amara stopped pacing. Think, Amara, be calm, she coached herself. She sighed loudly and patted both sides of her dress. She was relieved that her tiny cell phone had not fallen out of her small hidden dress pocket. She removed her phone and dialed Tammy's cell phone number. Amara sent her a text message that read she was safe and would call her later. She instructed her not to call or come by her house. She was afraid if she talked to Tammy, her life might be endangered also. She didn't know if her attacker had seen Tammy when they were together.

Amara thought hard about whom to call next. She searched her electronic phone book and stopped at Paul Whitman's name. She pushed a button and automatically dialed the number beneath the name. Paul Whitman was her ex-boyfriend. She and Paul had broken up nearly a year ago, but had remained good friends.

Paul was seated on a soft faux-fur area rug in front of a blazing fire with his new love interest, a beautiful woman named Shareese, who had recently started working at the Seattle Police Department. Their heads nearly touched as they spoke softly to one another while the fire crackled and the rain beat against the windowpane. This was only their second date, but Paul already knew he wanted to get to know her better. He poured two glasses of wine and handed one glass to Shareese. He leaned in to kiss her when the phone rang.

Inches away from her lips, Paul paused and excused himself. He placed his glass on a nearby end table, slowly stood up from the floor, and grumbled quietly as he picked up the phone. Amara could hear a woman's voice in the background. Paul answered the phone with an impatient, "Hello?" Amara was taken aback by the terseness of his voice and didn't speak right away. Paul responded again. "Hello? Who is this?" he demanded. He looked over at his date and smiled.

"Paul, this is Mari," she said as her voice quivered. "I am in trouble. Someone tried to kill me tonight!" she whispered into the phone. "Can you please come get me? I am scared to ask any of my other friends...please..." she pleaded.

Paul could tell by the sound of her voice that Amara was serious and in trouble. He sighed loudly. "Okay Mari, I'll be right there, where are you?" he asked. Paul grabbed a piece of paper and a pen. Amara told him the name of the restaurant. He didn't have to write the name down. It was a restaurant they had frequented often when they were dating. He looked at his watch before responding. "I'll be there in five minutes," he said and hung up.

Paul gave Shareese a quick peck on the lips and explained the situation. She was very understanding and told him she'd wait until he returned. "Thank you for being so understanding," he said. Shareese smiled and told him it wasn't a problem.

Paul walked to the closet and grabbed his jacket; he then went into the kitchen and removed his car keys from the key holder. "I will be back as soon as I can," he said as he gently closed the door. Shareese held her glass up to him and took a small drink. When the door closed the smile on Shareese's face faded. She sat her drink on the end table and quickly walked over to her purse that lay on the sofa. She pulled out her cell phone and dialed a number. She spoke in a hushed manner and quickly hung up. Shareese paced back and forth nervously as she awaited Paul's return.

Amara's assailant sat in his warm car as it quietly idled in a nearby alley. He watched the restaurant where she was hiding, cloaked by the darkness of the night. He cursed aloud as he lit a cigarette and pulled out his cell phone.

He dialed the number he had been directed to call once the mission was completed. The phone was answered on the first ring. He spoke in the agreed-upon code. "The package will not be delivered tonight. It was lost in the mail," he said. He took another long a long drag from his cigarette. The other man on the line began to yell and curse profusely. "You idiot! How could you mess this up?" he demanded. "I will not pay until the package is delivered!" he shouted. The assailant took another drag of his cigarette and hung up without responding.

Minutes later, Paul pulled his car to the curb at the side door of the restaurant. He kept the car idling and dialed Amara's cell phone number. When she answered, he informed her he was waiting for her at the side entrance of the restaurant. Amara checked her immediate surroundings and walked quickly to the side door of the restaurant. Once outside the restaurant door, she ran to his car. She quickly opened the door, got in, and immediately locked the door and slumped down in the passenger seat. Paul looked at Amara's tear-stained face, wet clothing, cut and swollen lips, and tousled hair. He reached over and gave her hand a quick squeeze of assurance as they drove in silence.

Finally Paul broke the silence. "Where do you want me to drive you, Mari?" he asked. "Downtown to the police station," she responded in a barely audible voice. He drove her to the police station and offered to go in with her. She rejected his offer. "If you don't mind, I will give the police your home number in case they need to talk you," she said as she got out of the car. He nodded. "If you need anything call me," he said as Amara closed the door. Amara thanked him, and quickly walked toward the station. When Paul was sure she was safely inside, he drove away and headed toward home.

A black coupe drove into a space down the street from the police station. He killed the engine. He placed a CD of oldies into the CD player and took out another cigarette. He leaned his seat back and got comfortable. He knew it was going to be a long night.

The police station was relatively quiet. Amara walked up to the officer on duty and explained what had happened. He immediately phoned the back office and requested assistance. A slender Latin American woman in a police uniform came to meet her. Her black hair was slicked back and pulled into a tight bun. The hairstyle gave her oval-shaped face a hardened look and accentuated her high cheekbones. Her thin lips formed an expression that was neither a smile nor a frown. Her dark brown eyes were very round and dull, like puddles of hardened mud. Amara sensed no warmth from this woman and immediately felt defensive. Though strangely, she felt a familiarity about her. She had seen her before, but she didn't know where and was too weary to think about it any further.

The officer extended her hand toward Amara. "Hello, my name is Officer Maria Blanco," she said with a very slight Spanish accent. Amara took her hand in hers. It was smooth and cool like a slab of polished marble. After the introduction, Officer Blanco led Amara to her office and told her she would take her statement. Amara followed the officer into a drab beige office and sat down in an old vinyl gray chair that had a lumpy, gray cushion. The chair legs scraped loudly against the cheap tiled floor as she scooted the chair closer to the cheap pressed-wood desk.

Amara checked her surroundings. The office was sparsely furnished and there were no pictures on the dull beige walls. She had never seen such an awful-looking room. Amara tried to get comfortable on the lumpy chair. She continued to squirm as she tried to find a comfortable spot. It was useless, so she endured the discomfort. Officer Blanco looked up from her computer terminal and apologized for the discomfort. "That chair is over twenty years old, but I promise you, no one has ever fallen asleep while sitting in that chair." She smiled as if she had just told a funny story. Her lips nearly disappeared as she exposed crooked teeth. Amara was so drained she only stared at the police officer.

Officer Blanco then cleared her throat and removed her smile. "I understand that this has been a harrowing experience for you," she said gently. "Let's try to capture all the events while they are still fresh in your mind." Officer Blanco turned on the tape recorder and began typing the information onto the police form as Amara recounted the events of the evening and gave a description of her assailant. Amara's voice was scratchy and sounded hoarse to her own ears. She stopped many times and asked for water to soothe her sore throat.

Several hours later, Amara emerged from the police station flanked by Officer Blanco. The sun had just risen and Amara shielded her eyes with her right hand to deflect the brightness of the light. She moved her left hand and gently touched the bruise across her throat as she swallowed with great difficulty. Amara looked around the area suspiciously as they walked toward the police car. She could feel someone watching them. Perhaps it was just paranoia, she thought. The streets were quiet and desolate except for the few empty parked cars on the opposite side of the street.

Amara brushed off the unsettling feeling and got inside the police sedan. The vinyl seat let out a hiss as she settled in and buckled her seat belt. She looked out the passenger side window in the direction of the parked cars once more as they drove away in the direction of her home.

As the police sedan passed the parked cars on the street, a dark figure slumped deeper into the seat. He remained hidden until the sedan drove past. Once the sedan was a safe distance away he sat up, started the engine, placed his car in gear and followed the police sedan from a safe distance.

Meanwhile, a slender figure dressed entirely in black walked up the steps to Amara's condo. The sun was just cresting over the mountains and the streets in the neighborhood were desolate. The windows of the units next to

Amara's were still darkened with drawn blinds or cloaked with expensive heavy drapes. A sharp object was retrieved from the pocket of the intruder and quickly placed into the lock of Amara's door. The door opened instantly and the intruder walked in without even a backward glance.

Once inside, the intruder pulled out a penlight and immediately began to pull out photo albums and quickly scour through them. The figure then went into the darkroom. Negatives were pulled from shelves and spilled onto the ground. The intruder cursed loudly and continued to rifle through numerous photos and negatives in the darkroom. Expensive equipment was examined and knocked to the floor. Still nothing.

The intruder left the dark room and headed into a small area that was being used as the study. The glow of the computer could be seen throughout the house as the intruder flipped on the switch. The computer was password protected. The intruder cursed and tried a few password ideas, "photo, click, Amara," suddenly the computer automatically shut down. It was a safety mechanism Amara had put on her PC for this very reason. It had cost a lot of money, but she felt it was well worth the extra expense in order to protect the sensitive information she obtained from different sources for the stories she wrote for the newspaper.

Suddenly there was a knock on the door. Startled by the knock, the intruder quickly walked to the back of the house and quietly left through the back door, leaving it ajar. Mrs. Murdock frowned, as she knocked harder on Amara's door. She and Amara had developed a friendly relationship and both agreed to watch the other's home when they were away. Mrs. Murdock was a light sleeper and had heard crashing noises coming from Amara's condo and went to check things out. Amara had not told her she was going out of town, which was unusual because Amara was very good at keeping her abreast of her activities and when she'd be out of town.

Mrs. Murdock pulled Amara's spare key from her housedress pocket and opened the door wide. She placed her hand over her mouth and gasped at the disarray of Amara's apartment. Suddenly, she heard a door in the back of the house slam shut. Mrs. Murdock immediately ran back to her condo and phoned the police.

Amara felt exhausted as she turned names over in her mind of who would want to have her killed. Amara had lived in Seattle her whole life and could not think of anyone who would want to kill her. She had just started her new job as a feature writer with a popular local women's magazine. Prior to that, she had done freelance work for the Seattle Times and Post Intelligencer newspapers. She racked her brain and thought about her latest work. She could think of no one she had angered, betrayed, or brought negative attention by her stories published in the paper.

She then thought about the Cooper infant kidnapping she had covered. That had been an exciting case and her coverage of the event helped her get her current job. Amara shook her head; she didn't think the Coopers would want to kill her. The kidnapper was never found. Amara frowned as she recalled the details of the story. It had a sad ending.

She looked out the car window at the tall evergreen trees that moved slightly in the wind and hid the sun. The road was shaded and Amara could feel the coolness of the air. She hugged herself, unsure if she was cold from her fright or the cool air.

She was quickly jogged from her thoughts as the police sedan's tires rolled over a large pothole and caused her to bump the back of her head against the seat's headrest. It felt as though Officer Blanco had picked up speed. Amara looked over at Officer Blanco. Her lips were pursed and formed a thin straight line. "Someone is following us," she said with her brows furrowed.

Amara glanced into the side view mirror. She saw the person driving some lengths behind them and her stomach turned a flip. "That's him," she shouted hoarsely to Officer Blanco. "That's the man who tried to kill me last night!" Officer Blanco quickly steered the car over to the curb, removed her weapon from its holster, and allowed the black sports coupe vehicle to pass. She read the license plate number of the car as it passed and radioed the information to the police station's radio operator.

Within minutes an unmarked police sedan trailed the car and the driver was forced to pull over. When Officer Blanco heard the radio transmission that the car had been pulled over, she began to steer the car back onto the road. Rocks crunched beneath the tires as she turned the steering wheel hard and drove in the opposite direction. "You'll need to come back to the station to identify him," said Officer Blanco. Amara's chest heaved as she let out a heavy sigh. They returned to the precinct.

Amara was escorted to a private room where she waited for her alleged attacker to be processed. Officer Blanco explained the procedures and waited with Amara while another officer put together the lineup on the other side of the mirrored window.

Several men were escorted into the brightly lit room and told to stand on specified marks. When the lineup was ready, Amara immediately identified her attacker from the lineup of the several men. Even though she was safely behind the bulletproof two-way mirror, Amara immediately tensed her shoulders and shuddered as her assailant stared coldly in her direction through the glass.

Officer Blanco looked at Amara's worried expression and gently patted her hand. "Relax, Amara, he has a long police record and he's done the lineup drill a number of times. He's only trying to intimidate you," she said. Officer Blanco reassured Amara by asking her to move to another position in the small room. When she did, he continued to stare in the same general direction. Amara relaxed a bit and felt slightly relieved. Officer Blanco pulled her lips into a tight line. The expression fell somewhere between a smile and a frown. "See, I told you it was safe here," she said gently.

When the process was over, Officer Blanco stood up. "You did just fine, Amara. He will now be booked and placed in jail until his hearing." Amara looked at Officer Blanco. "Officer Blanco, is there a possibility of him being released on bail?" she asked. Officer Blanco nodded. "Yes, but his bail will be so excessive that it will take someone very wealthy to bail him out and he doesn't look like he rubs shoulders with the rich and famous. I highly doubt that whoever paid him to commit the act would implicate themselves by bailing him out," said Officer Blanco.

Amara took a deep breath and exhaled. "I'd like to leave town for about a week, is that okay?" she asked. Officer Blanco nodded her head. "That should be fine. I will need the address and phone number of where you will be staying in case I need to contact you about a change in the hearing date." Amara nodded and wrote down the address and phone number. Officer Blanco took the address and phone number where Amara would be staying.

"I know there is someone else involved in this and I don't want to return to my house. Can you have someone drive me to the bus station?" asked Amara. Officer Blanco grabbed the keys to the sedan. "Don't worry, Amara, I will have a squad car go by and check your home and I will personally take you to the bus station," she said as she tossed the keys in the air and caught them. Amara thanked her and gathered her belongings.

Officer Blanco and Amara left out the back door of the station and walked straight to her sedan. Officer Blanco drove down a back road, bypassing the front of the police station. Amara rubbed her temples. She was relieved to be out of the police station. A dispatch came in over the radio and Officer Blanco turned the sound down low. Amara leaned her head against the seat and closed her eyes for a moment.

After about five minutes, she opened her eyes and checked her watch. It was close to eight o'clock. and she knew her boss would be in the office early. She pulled out her cell phone and called the editor of the magazine. She explained the circumstances to Margie, her editor, and asked for some time off considering what had occurred last night. Margie was sympathetic to her plight and granted the leave time. "Just be careful," she warned. Margie asked for a number to reach her in case of an emergency. Amara provided the number and ended the call.

She then called her best friend and old college roommate Brianna Barnes. "Hey, Bre…it's Mari," she said. "Can I come down and stay for the week?" she asked. Amara knew Brianna had recently broken up with her live-in boyfriend of six years and was hoping she wouldn't mind the company.

Brianna was excited about the visit. "Your timing is perfect as always," she said. "I just took the week off, so we can pal around for the entire week!" she said in her lively, high-pitched voice. Brianna was from Hawaii, and always spoke quickly with a lot of animation. Amara smiled as she listened to her friend talk about all the activities she had in store for her. Amara chuckled as her friend rattled off all the things she had planned for them. She knew Brianna never stayed in one spot for very long. She was always on the go.

"Hey, can you pick up a couple of things for me?" she interrupted. "I won't have any time to pack anything. So I need everything, okay, Bre?" Brianna frowned into the phone. "'I've got you covered," she said from her mobile car phone. "And why won't you have time to pack any clothes or toiletries? What's going on?" asked Brianna. "I'll explain everything when I get there," she said quietly. Amara also verified Brianna's home phone number and address. She wrote down the new phone number and address and handed it to Officer Blanco. Amara and Brianna ended their conversation and Amara closed her cell phone.

Officer Blanco pulled into the bus depot and remained until Amara boarded the bus to San Francisco, California. Amara cautiously looked around at her surroundings and closely examined the faces on the bus to see if there were any familiar faces. She didn't see any. Everyone seemed to be going through the task of getting their bags in place and settling in for the long ride.

As the bus drove away from the depot, Amara waved goodbye to Officer Blanco. She reclined her seat back, crossed her arms over her chest, and said a silent prayer of thanks. Amara covered her mouth as she yawned. Her eyelids felt very heavy since she had not slept the night before. She looked at her watch and estimated she had approximately thirteen hours on the bus before she would see her friend in San Francisco. Amara yawned again, turned her head toward the window and immediately fell asleep.

Six hours later, Amara was awaken by the loud sound of the hydraulic brakes as the bus slowed into the parking lot of a large buffet restaurant. She looked out the window as her stomach growled loudly. She smiled, patted her stomach and remembered she had not eaten since the prior night when her girlfriend Tammy had taken her out for a celebratory steak dinner before going to LaMont's Club.

The bus driver opened the door and asked everyone to exit. Amara followed the stream of passengers off the bus and looked around for a vacant table. There were no vacant tables left, but she spotted a vacant seat amongst three elderly women. She recognized them from the bus. They were seated three seats ahead of her. Amara walked over to their table and asked the ladies if she could join them. The women warmly welcomed her.

The waitresses bustled around and quickly placed glasses of water on the tables for each occupied seat. They instructed the newly arrived customers to help themselves to the buffet and soft drink fountains. As the crowd stood up en masse and rushed toward the buffet line, one of the women at Amara's table suggested they wait until the crowd thinned.

While they were waiting, the three women introduced themselves and Amara introduced herself. After the introductions the women began to show Amara pictures of their grandchildren and talked non-stop about their upcoming trip on a casino cruise. "Min won five hundred dollars on our last trip," said Eunice, an elderly woman of about seventy. Eunice smiled and Amara noticed that her smile seemed to light up her whole face. She was a trim woman who wore her gray hair in a bob that fell neatly below her ear lobes and flattered her fair, creamy skin.

Min smiled widely. "Sure did, girl. I hope to win five hundred dollars more this time," as she covered her mouth and giggled. Min was a petite woman who also looked to be the same age as Eunice. Her long, predominately gray hair with strands of black was worn in a neat bun at the nape of her neck. Min absently twisted her jade bracelet around her wrist as she spoke. Her family had come over from China nearly a century ago. What Amara found remarkable about Min was her hands. They were delicate and smooth as porcelain.

The third woman, named Elvira, was a full-figured woman with gray and ash blond long corn-rowed braids twisted in a sophisticated chignon. Her coffee-brown complexion had very few wrinkles. She wore turquoise earrings that dangled from side to side when she spoke.

Amara smiled as she listened to the women talk and finish each other's sentences. She was amazed at how each woman seemed to take great care in her health and appearance. All three women sported flattering earth-tone pantsuits and matching soft leather shoes.

Elvira talked excitedly about their upcoming trip. "We have been doing this for fifteen years," she said. "After my Ricardo died, I got my two best friends together and invited them on a cruise."

"We enjoyed it so much we decided to make it an annual event," chimed in Eunice. "We have been friends for over forty years. We used to live in East Seattle, only blocks away from each other," said Min.

Eunice kept staring at Amara. Amara looked at the woman. "I am sorry, sweetie," she said. "You look like so much like this young woman I met almost thirty years ago. You see she had been raped outside a movie theater and...."

One of the other women cut her off. "Eunice, that is such a sad story. I don't know why you tell it so often," said Elvira. Eunice smiled. "I tell it so much because of the strength of the victim. I remember sitting in that hospital room holding her hand until her parents got there. She was a sweet little thing," said Eunice, reminiscing.

Elvira smiled. "I guess you are right. In those days, white women just didn't up and help a black woman, especially if she was being attacked," she said scornfully. Elvira patted Eunice's hand, "But then again, you always did shake up the town. I mean your husband is black, I know that had to be hard for you in those days," Elvira commented. Eunice smiled. "Vira, you know after nearly fifty years of marriage, people still stare at us, and I say let them stare at the happiest married couple in the town!" she said, shaking her fist. All the women laughed.

"I know that's right. Wilmer loves him some Eunice," said Elvira chuckling. Min nodded in agreement. "You should talk, Elvira, your husband was from Puerto Rico," said Min. Elvira smiled widely. "My Latin lover," she said dreamily. "That man treated me good and provided well for our family," she said proudly.

Amara looked at Min. Min smiled shyly. "My husband is Chinese. We met at church," she said quietly.

The lines at the buffet had lessened, so the women got up, prepared their plates, and returned to their seats. Once seated, they continued to make small talk and eat their lunch. Amara ate quietly and was relieved that none of the women had asked about her bruises or any other personal questions. She continued to listen to the exchange of lively banter between the women. Their excitement lifted her spirits.

Amara put her fork down, propped her elbows on the table, and rested her chin on top of her hands. "I sure hope I am as lively and beautiful as you ladies are when I am your age."

The women chuckled. Min looked Amara in the eye and told her, "You are only as young as you feel and act. I walk three miles everyday and also take salsa lessons," she said.

"And I never, ever, date any men my age," interjected Elvira. The other women giggled while Elvira flung her head back and laughed heartily at her own joke.

Amara looked at the women sitting at her table and marveled at their exuberance. Amara extended her hand to resemble the shape of a small notepad and pretended to write inside her palm. "Ms. Elvira, I am taking notes!" she said smiling. The women laughed at her gesture.

The bus driver announced that it was time to return to the bus. The women paid their bills and headed toward the bus. Amara passed the ladies' seats and walked toward her seat when the ladies invited her to join them. Amara happily agreed. She thought the conversation would take her mind off her immediate problems. Amara joined in the laughter as the women told funny stories of their previous adventures. They continued to joke and laugh until they reached San Francisco.

Chapter 2

$\mathcal{T}$he bus pulled into the San Francisco bus depot and stopped. The over-
weight bus driver, who had a jolly face, quickly made annotations in his
travel palm pilot as he opened the door. The passengers were greeted by a
gentle breeze from the ocean as they exited. The breeze ruffled through
Amara's hair as she stepped off the bus. Amara hugged each of the three
women and bade them farewell.

She then heard the sound of a car horn and saw Brianna waving from
a fire engine red BMW sports coupe. Amara waved excitedly as Brianna
waved back. She quickly headed toward Brianna's new car. "Wow! Look at
you, girl! This car is gorgeous," Amara said as she slid onto the soft beige
leather seat. She could still smell the newness of the car as she settled into
her seat. Amara also saw shopping bags in the back seat. She was tempted
to go through them. She knew they contained the items she had asked
Brianna to purchase.

Before Brianna placed the car in gear, Amara gave her a big hug. "Bre—
thank you so much for putting up with me this week!" she said. Brianna
hugged her back. She frowned as she examined the slight cut on her lips and
the large bruise across the front of her neck. Amara self-consciously placed
her hand on her neck. Brianna smiled to reassure her best friend. "Girl, that's
what friends are for. And don't even think about looking in those bags!" she
said as she saw Amara eye the bags in the back seat once more.

"Bre, your car is beautiful! Did you get a raise or a new job?" asked
Amara. Brianna smiled. "I sold that book I worked on for seven years."
Amara turned to look at her friend. She gave her the thumbs up sign.
"Brianna, I am so proud of you!" Brianna smiled at the praise from her best
friend. "My book caught the attention of a big production company and we
are currently in the process of making it into a movie!" she beamed. Amara
smiled. "This is the sci-fi book you were working on in college right?" Amara
asked. Brianna shook her head yes. "I knew you had it in you," Amara said
smiling wide. "I am so proud of you Bre." Brianna smiled. "I am proud of me

too. Good thing I didn't listen to my ex-boyfriend Charles. He said the book was boring and would never sell."

Brianna pushed a button that triggered the sunroof to quietly slide open. The brightness and warmth of the sun poured into the vehicle. Amara tilted her head upward and allowed the sun to wash over her face. A cool mist drifted through the sunroof and gently caressed her face. She smiled and licked her lips. Amara could taste the salt from the water in the air.

As she enjoyed the ride, Amara kept her thoughts about Charles to herself. She had never liked him and hadn't told Brianna he flirted with her during her last visit. Charles had come up from behind and nestled his nose against her neck. He told her he liked the smell of her perfume. Amara smirked as she remembered how she quickly put him in his place and threatened to tell Brianna if he ever tried to pull a stunt like that with her again. Shocked, Charles apologized profusely and avoided her for the rest of her visit.

Amara smiled as she thought of the incident. She was certain no woman had ever turned him down. Charles was a very tall, muscular, and lean man. Most people mistook him for a professional basketball player. His complexion was the shade of honey. His natural curly hair was always professionally cut and styled to reflect the latest fashionable hairstyle. His light brown eyes with amber flecks seemed to invade your very being. Amara took a deep breath. The man was fine and with Brianna at his side, they made the most beautiful couple. People would stare at them as if they were famous movie stars whenever they went out.

Amara looked over at Brianna as she tapped her fingers on her steering wheel to a new hip-hop song. Brianna smiled at Amara, removed her sunglasses from the console and slid them on her face. Amara placed the sun visor down to block the bright sun from her eyes as Brianna expertly steered around the narrow curves that overlooked the ocean.

Brianna stopped tapping her fingers to the music and spoke in a quiet voice. "I caught Charles with another woman in our bed." Amara turned down the music and faced her friend. She tried to act as if she were surprised at what Brianna had just shared. "About three months ago, I came home early from work and heard sounds of love-making coming from our bedroom. I tipped to the kitchen and quietly filled a large pot with very hot water. I burst into the room and threw that pot of hot water on them both while they were right in the middle of the act—on my favorite satin sheets, I might add," said Brianna with a big frown.

Amara faced her friend and gave her a high five. "Girl, you never cease to amaze me." Brianna looked at her and smiled a mischievous grin. "I told them both they had five seconds to get out before I added pool acid to the next pot of hot water." Brianna laughed aloud. "Girl, that is the quickest I ever saw Charles move. The following day, he moved his things out of the condo while I was at work. The following month, I got the book deal and sold the condo, so you get to see my new place!" she said gaily. "I guess that accounts for the new phone number and address. I am glad you didn't change your cell number or I would have been up a creek!" said Amara. Brianna shook her head. "Well, you knew about Charles and me breaking up, and remember I told you I was thinking about moving. Anyway, I've only lived here for a couple of months and you know I was going to call you and tell you. So don't even get an attitude with me, Missy," she said in a joking manner.

As Brianna steered the car onto the long tree-lined driveway, Amara let out a low whistle. "Bre, this house is absolutely beautiful. I am talking Home and Garden, Ladies Home Journal beautiful," she said breathlessly as she took in the beauty of her surroundings. "How much did you make off that book?" asked Amara, still staring at the ranch style five-bedroom stucco home. "Enough," said Brianna smiling.

Brianna chuckled as she stopped the car and placed it in park. She turned to look at Amara. "Charles has been calling like a crazed madman since I sent him a copy of my published novel. I haven't returned any of his calls or spoken with him since the day I threw him out. But I met a really nice man about four months ago. Initially we were both involved with other people and were just friends. When I broke up with Charles, we started dating each other and last month, we began dating exclusively. His name is Clayton Peters," said Brianna, smiling. "He is very handsome and charming. He is a private detective, who owns an exclusive detective agency. He used to serve with the San Francisco police department. I think he may be the one," she said wistfully.

"Bre, I am so happy you've found someone who truly deserves you. Charles didn't deserve you. You know I never liked him," said Amara. There, I said it, she thought to herself.

Brianna frowned and nodded her head. "I know. He must have known how you felt because he acted so uncomfortable the last time you visited," said Brianna.

"So, when do I get to meet your new beau?" asked Amara in an attempt to change the subject from Charles.

"Tonight," said Brianna matter-of-factly. "He plans to take us to a late dinner."

Amara smiled. "That sounds great. I could really use some time to unwind and freshen up. The bus ride was long and my day has been even longer," said Amara, as she stifled a yawn.

Brianna licked her lips and checked her reflection in the mirror. "That will work out great, Mari. Take a few hours to unwind. I will use that time to go to the studio to work out some issues regarding the script with the producer. We are working on the final arrangements for the movie. I will give you a call when I am on my way home, so feel free to use the whirlpool in the master bathroom," said Brianna as she opened the door.

Amara and Brianna gathered the shopping bags from the back seat and walked to the front door. Brianna opened the door and allowed Amara to enter first. The sight of her friend's home took her breath away. "Wow, Bre! Your home is as beautiful inside as it is outside." Amara noted the layout of the house was constructed in the Florida floor plan. The living areas were large and spacious with large windows throughout the house. From the front door you could see to the back of the house, which had a beautiful eye-catching large picture window. Amara looked out to the back yard and saw the manicured Japanese garden. She quickly sat the bags on the floor and walked to the back window to get a closer look at the garden. Its beauty captivated Amara. "Bre, your garden is so beautiful," she exclaimed.

Brianna sat down the bags she was carrying and joined Amara at the window. Placing her arm around her good friend, Brianna explained how her mother helped her put the garden together. "My mom and dad came to visit when I first purchased the house and my mom and I designed the garden together," she said. "You know my mom is very talented in the gardening department and she is always sharing our Japanese culture. It was really special putting this beautiful garden together with her." Amara looked at Brianna and smiled.

Amara looked around Brianna's house. Her furniture was modern and beige with light wood frames. It all looked very expensive. She had beautiful oriental carpets covering hardwood and ceramic tiled floors. Her dining room table was glass with a hand-crafted iron skirt that wrapped around the table. It was pre-set with lively napkins and brightly colored plates and place mats. The flower arrangement was tastefully done with silk flowers in a beautiful brightly colored vase that tied in her placemats, dishes, and napkins.

Amara took a deep breath and walked into her library. It was breathtaking. There was a fireplace and all of her furniture was leather and deep oak. Her books were neatly aligned in recessed bookcases along the walls. They both shared a love of photography, so Amara always checked to see if she could spot any new photos. Brianna had photos throughout the entire house, but in this room there were only photos of family and close friends.

She saw several framed photos she didn't recognize on the fireplace mantle. She walked over to the mantle to take a closer look. She picked up Brianna's recent family portrait framed in a modern bronze frame. "When did you take this one?" Amara asked Brianna as she held up the bronze frame.

Brianna glanced at the frame. "We took that one when they came to visit about five months ago," she said. Amara looked at all the people in the photo. The photo contained Brianna, her mother Kuyono, her father Brian, and her sister Alexis. Amara traced around Brianna's face. "Bre, you truly were blessed with the best from both of your parents." Brianna smiled and nodded in agreement.

Amara looked at her dear friend and smiled. Brianna was a beautiful girl of Japanese and African American heritage. Her color was a deep bronze like her father. Her hair was black and slightly wavy. She had her mother's high cheekbones and a mixture of her mother and father's eyes that were green and the shape of large almonds. She stood almost six feet tall and had the figure of a model. She had gotten the height from her father's side of the family. Men and women alike were tall in his family.

Amara placed the photo back on the mantle and picked up a new picture of herself and Brianna that was taken during her last visit. Amara smiled as she looked at the photo. "I didn't know you had this picture." Brianna walked over and looked at the picture. "I love that picture of us," she said. Amara examined her five-foot-seven medium frame. Her full breasts, narrow waist, and healthy hips seemed to overwhelm her friend's tall, slender body. Her long wavy auburn hair gently framed her round face and full lips and flowed down past her shoulders.

Amara tilted her head as she examined herself in the photo. She chuckled as she recalled the number of women who had asked her what color dye she used in her hair. Amara's pecan complexion was flawless and her deep dimples really showed up in the photograph. Brianna snuck up behind her friend and took the picture from her and set it back on the mantle.

"I know you were analyzing that poor picture to death. So I had to put it back just to take you out of your agony," joked Brianna. Amara glanced at her friend and laughed. "You know me too well, girl."

Brianna smiled and walked back toward the shopping bags. "Mari, I've got some food and your favorite wine in the fridge," she said. "Relax. And later we can talk if you are up to it." Brianna picked up the shopping bags and carried them to the guest bedroom. Amara picked up the remaining bags and followed her. They sat the bags on the beige plush carpeted floor of the bedroom.

Amara sat on the edge of the bed. The oak sleigh bed felt very comfortable. She ran her hand across the beautiful satin hunter green comforter with soft white lily designs. Amara grabbed one of the satin overstuffed hunter green pillows and hugged it to her body. "You know me so well, Bre. I do want to talk to you about what's going on," said Amara in a somber tone.

"Come on, let me show you the rest of the house," said Brianna in a gay tone as she reached for Amara's hand.

After Brianna showed Amara the rest of her home, she retrieved her keys from an antique silver dish that was placed on top of a modern glass-topped table in the foyer.

"Make yourself at home. I've got some medicine in the medicine cabinet for your cuts and bruises," she said casually. "Go out and enjoy the garden! The weather is too beautiful to remain inside," she said as she headed toward the door to leave.

After Brianna closed the front door. Amara locked it and walked to the guest room to put away her new clothes. Amara was pleasantly surprised at all the expensive clothing Brianna had purchased for her. She placed the clothes against her body and twirled in the full-length solid oak mirror. Bre must be doing great, she said to herself and smiled.

Brianna had never been a selfish person. She would give you her last nickel if she thought you needed it more. Amara was tempted to try on the clothes, but she knew she needed to bathe first. Bre has great taste, Amara thought as she carefully hung the expensive outfits in the walk in closet.

Amara selected a pair of beige linen slacks and a soft pastel silk blouse for the late dinner date with Brianna and her new boyfriend, Clayton. Since she had a few hours alone, she decided to dress casually and placed a pair of designer khaki knee-length shorts and a bright cotton blouse on the chest at the foot of the bed. She also set matching leather sandals on the floor beside the outfit.

Amara smiled as she pulled out the expensive lingerie from the shopping bag. She held up the matching pale lavender set and gave a low whistle. It was far better than the lingerie she usually wore. Amara looked around at the beautifully decorated room and chuckled as she spotted her friend's book on the night table. She picked up the book, turned to the first page, and saw an inscription. "To Mari, my best friend, Enjoy! Love Bre."

Amara tucked the book under her arm and headed for the master bath to take a long-awaited bubble bath in the giant marble garden jacuzzi tub. She turned on the water and went to the kitchen and poured herself a glass of wine. Once the tub was filled she turned on the jets and placed her hair in a careless knot on top of her head. She looked in the medicine cabinet and applied some medicine to the cuts on her lips. They had already begun healing. She wanted to make sure there were no scars so she applied the medication liberally. She then settled into the tub of hot water and fragrant bubbles.

Amara was so involved in reading Brianna's book and enjoying the raging bubbles from the whirlpool that she failed to hear the shrill ring of the doorbell. Amara jumped with a start and nearly dropped the book into the bath when she heard a man's voice in the house. At first she panicked. Then she calmed herself and quickly got out of the tub. She put on the soft baby blue terry cloth full-length robe Brianna had purchased for her and quickly padded toward the bedroom door. Her hair fell from its loose knot down her back and into her face. She pushed her hair out of her face and slowly moved toward the door. She placed her ear to the door in order to hear sounds from the other side of the door.

Amara let out a loud yelp as the door opened before she could turn the knob. A tall, muscular man wearing sunglasses, a straw hat, khaki shorts, and white polo shirt stepped back immediately. He removed his sunglasses, stuck his hands up in a surrendering gesture and quickly identified himself. "I am Clayton's younger brother, Sam," he said hurriedly. Amara stared at this man as if he were from another planet and was speaking a foreign language.

She clutched her robe lapels and squeezed them together with one hand. "How did you get in here and why are you here? Is something wrong with Bre?" she asked without taking a breath.

Sam slowly lowered his hands, placed his sunglasses in the opening of his shirt and pulled a single key from his pants pocket. "Brianna always leaves a spare house key under her large flower pot in the back garden and she asked me to come check on you. She said she was a bit worried. Apparently something had happened to you and she was concerned about leaving you alone for a long period of time. She called several times and when you didn't answer, she asked me to come by and check things out," he said.

Amara saw the blinking light on the answering machine and exhaled. Amara took a step back and examined Sam. Since he had removed his sunglasses she could see his warm brown eyes and thick eyebrows. His square-shaped jaw line reminded her of the retired football player and actor, Fred Brown. She could see the softness of his lips as he bit down nervously on his lower lip. He gave Amara a crooked smile as he tilted his head to look at her. He had the physique of an NFL running back. He had a wide chest, washboard stomach, slim waist, and firm thighs that could be seen even through his baggy khaki shorts.

Amara took a deep breath and tried to refocus on the matter at hand. Sam caught her staring and the corner of his mouth rose into a half smile. "What is your brother's name?" she asked suspiciously. "May I?" he asked walking toward the phone. "My brother's name is Clayton," he said. "And if it will make you feel any better, why not call Brianna and check out my story?" he asked. Amara smiled and did just that.

Minutes later she hung up the phone and apologized to Sam. "Sorry about that. Bre is right. I had a bad experience yesterday and I am a bit jumpy. Sorry." Sam smiled again and caused Amara's stomach to do flip-flops. Sam's lips were moving but Amara was having trouble maintaining her concentration. This man was very handsome. "Jumpy and suspicious," Sam joked to lighten the mood.

Amara smiled. "Please sit down and make yourself comfortable. I will be out in a few minutes," she said and rushed into the guest room to get ready.

That evening during shift change Maria looked around to make sure she was the only one left in the office. She quickly took the stack of papers from her desk and walked over to the shredder. She checked the documents over quickly and turned on the machine. As she prepared the papers to go into the shredder she was startled by a familiar voice. "Hey, what 'cha shreddin'?" asked Macey, an officer from the narcotics squad. Maria jumped and dropped the pile of papers. Macey bent down and picked the loose papers off the floor. He began to scan over the first couple of sheets. Maria snatched the papers from his grasp.

She took a moment to regain her composure. "You scared me, Dan!" she said as she playfully hit him with her papers. Macey took his time answering while he looked over her body longingly. He had always wanted to have a relationship with Maria but was afraid to approach her. Instead he hurled insults and harassed her each chance they were alone together.

"Well, well, Miss Goody Two Shoes, what do we have here?" he asked pointing at the top sheet of the papers she was holding. Maria didn't answer. Instead she calmly tried to resume her shredding. Macey walked up close behind her and spoke above a whisper in her ear. "I know you like women, I seen how you get all google-eyed with the chief's secretary when you two have lunch together," he teased.

Maria turned to face Macey with a hardened stare. She shoved him away from her. She then took the offensive and stepped on his newly polished shoes as she spat out her threat. "Mace, you ever try something like that again and I will kick your ass and you know I can, you drunk," she threatened.

Macey threw up his hands in mock surrender. "Hey, just keeping my options open," he said laughing. He then stepped back and looked at her as he openly appraised her body. "If you don't want me to spill the beans on that little number you just did, you gotta come see Papa," he sang as he spread his arms wide.

"You make me sick, you pervert," she snarled.

"Hey, Mace, let's roll," said his partner Rob Sully from the top of the stairs.

Macey frowned, started to walk, and stopped abruptly. He pointed a finger in her face as he walked past. "It ain't over 'till I say so," he said. She bit the tip of his finger hard. Macey quickly pulled back his finger and yelped in pain. "There's more where that came from," she snarled back. "Dammit!" he whined as he attempted to shake the pain from his finger. Sully laughed aloud. "That's what you get!" he said laughing even louder. Macey cursed under his breath and walked away.

"That really hurt," he told his partner as he walked up the stairs to join him. They both walked out of the station. "I told you not to mess with her," said Sully sarcastically. "Everyone knows she's a maneater." They both laughed at his off-colored joke as the station door closed.

Maria was so angry tears welled in her eyes. Now she would have to make nice with that pig. It was bad enough she pretended to be partners with them on this scheme, but now she would have to associate with him even more. She smacked her forehead and continued to shred her papers. Once she was finished, she grabbed her jacket from her desk chair and left the station for the evening.

When Amara returned, she spotted Sam sitting in a shaded part of the garden reading the daily newspaper. She went to the cupboard and took out two tall glasses. She set them in the freezer as she prepared a pitcher of lemonade. She then removed the frosted glasses from the freezer and retrieved a serving tray from the cupboard. She set the pitcher of fresh lemonade and glasses on the tray and took it out to the garden.

"I hope you like lemonade," said Amara as she made her way to where he was seated. Sam stood up, smiled graciously, and took the tray from her hands and set it on the small glass table. "Thanks," he said. Amara smiled appreciatively and sat down next to Sam. "By the way. My name is Amara. Everyone calls me Mari," she said.

"Amara is a beautiful name. If you don't mind, I'd like to call you Amara," said Sam as he sipped his lemonade. Amara shrugged and said it was fine. "The other reason I came over is because Brianna will not be finished with the producer until much later than she expected. She asked me to take you to dinner. That is if you are hungry and feel comfortable going out with me?" he asked.

"As long as I am not putting you out," she said. Sam shook his head. "No problem at all. My girlfriend is out of town on a modeling shoot so I am all yours tonight," he said.

Amara tried to keep her smile from fading. I knew he was too good to be true, she thought to herself. "So where to?" asked Amara.

Sam looked at what they were wearing. "How does pizza sound?" he asked. "There's a nice gourmet pizza restaurant right down the road." Amara gave the thumbs up. "I love pizza, especially Canadian bacon and pineapple pizza. That sounds like a great plan, Sam," she said.

Long after they had finished their Caesar salad and pizza, Sam and Amara became so involved in conversation they didn't notice the time. The manager came over and politely told them it was midnight and time to close the restaurant. Amara blushed and Sam coughed nervously. "Amara, I am so sorry. I didn't pay any attention to the time," he said. The conversation flowed between them effortlessly. They discussed their childhood, college days, and current careers. Amara learned Sam had studied law, but after practicing for two years, found it to be unfulfilling. He was now a partner in his brother's private detective agency whose superior technology and expertise catered to the rich and famous. He and his girlfriend, Franni, had been dating for only a few months, but he really liked her. He told her that Franni was born in America, but her parents were from Africa. The differences in their culture had caused them to work through a few cultural challenges. Sam gave Amara a boyish grin and told her he was certain they could work through their differences.

Amara told him about her new job at the city's popular women's magazine. She also told him that she had not dated seriously since her break up with her ex-boyfriend Paul about one year before. She was telling him funny stories about her and Brianna from college when the waiter quietly walked toward them and placed the check on the table. "I am shocked Brianna hasn't phoned me since I have kept you out so late," said Sam as he took out his cell phone and checked to make sure he hadn't missed any calls. He frowned when he saw that Franni had called and he'd missed it. "Anything wrong?"

asked Amara. "Not really. Franni called and I missed it," he said in a disappointed tone of voice.

Amara placed her napkin on the table and stood up in preparation to leave. Sam noticed the disappointed look on Amara's face and walked over to help her with her sweater. "Don't worry, I'll talk to her tomorrow," he said, smiling.

Amara nodded, adjusted her sweater and forced herself to speak. "Thanks for dinner and the company Sam. I really enjoyed it," she said. Sam paid the bill and walked out beside her and opened the car door for her. She thanked him and slid inside.

Their drive back was quiet, each caught up in their private thoughts. Suddenly Sam broke the silence. "Brianna told me you'd be here for one week. Maybe we can all get together?" he offered.

Amara gave Sam a weak smile. "Sure, Sam," she absently responded as she processed the last days' events.

Sam broke her train of thought. "Amara?" he said for the third time.

"What did you say?" Amara asked absently. "Wow, you must really be deep in thought," said Sam. "I said your name three times before you answered."

Amara looked at him and gave him her full attention. "You're right. I was in deep thought. What were you asking me?" Sam focused his attention on the dark road as he spoke. "I asked if you wanted to go on a picnic with Franni and me tomorrow. She's due back tomorrow morning and she told me she wanted to go on a picnic in the park."

Amara shook her head no. "I think you two should be alone since she's been away for awhile. But I appreciate your thoughtfulness," she said softly.

Amara resigned herself to the fact that she and Sam could only be friends. I can never have too many good friends, she reasoned to herself. Sam smiled as he thought about Franni's arrival and drove the rest of the way to Brianna's home in silence.

Chapter 3

Shareese dialed the number quickly. She had dialed it so often she knew it by heart. "Hey," she said. She listened for a response. "You've got to get him out of there before he says something that may tie us both to that little incident," she said. She rolled her eyes as she listened to the response. "Look, I know you have the money, just do it!" she said sternly. She pulled the phone away from her ear as the person on the other end of the phone began to yell and curse at her. "Calm down, baby. It's my stepdad. I know you can help me," she said sweetly. She smiled as she blew the wet nail polish on her manicured fingernails. "Thanks, baby," she said. "I will make it worth your while," she said seductively and hung up the phone.

An hour later Shareese dressed in a conservative suit and prepared for work. On her way to the office, she stopped by the jail. She asked to talk to one of the inmates. She was granted the visit.

She sat down across from an aging man with jaundiced eyes and skin the color of coal. He looked as if he hadn't slept in weeks. "Hi, Daddy," she said gaily.

His cool grin left his face. "How many times I told you not to call me that!" he hissed. "I ain't got no kids and I don't want any," he snarled. Shareese tried to look like he had hurt her feelings. "That won't work with me either. Your mamma tried that and it didn't work for her so don't waste your time," he spat.

"Look, old man," she hissed back. "You've got a job to do. When you are free, you'd better finish what you started," she warned. He looked at her as if he were bored. His lids hooded over his jaundiced eyes until they were mere slits. She knew from experience it was no use to say anything more. Instead, she smiled sweetly and blew him a kiss through the thick glass. "Bye, Daddy," she mocked and stood up and turned before he had a chance to reply.

He sneered and shook his head. "Just like your mama," he said as a short laugh rumbled in his throat. "Just like your mama," he repeated. He made his hand into the shape of a pistol and pulled the imaginary trigger as

Shareese walked through the thick steel doors. The guard walked up and escorted him back to his cell.

The next morning Brianna and Amara were talking in the garden when Sam and Clayton arrived. Brianna and Amara's heads were almost touching as they spoke in a low whisper. Amara dabbed her eye with a Kleenex. Brianna hugged her tightly and gently rubbed her back in order to comfort her. Sam and Clayton paused for a moment, not wanting to interrupt.

When they heard a nervous laugh from Amara, they walked out into the garden. "Hello, ladies," said Clayton and Sam in unison. Both women looked at the two men. "Bre, you'd better start locking your front door," Amara said as she forced a smile. Amara introduced herself to Clayton and gave Sam a friendly hug.

"Where's Franni?" asked Brianna. "Oh, her flight got delayed in Rome, so she'll be here later tonight," Sam said glumly. Clayton playfully punched his brother's arm. "He's got it bad Bre," he joked. Sam smiled shyly and looked at Amara. "So, Amara, if you are free, would you like to join me this afternoon? A friend of mine is having a showing at an art gallery in town. Since you are into photography, I thought you might enjoy it."

Amara smiled. "That sounds fine, Sam. I didn't want to be a third wheel on Bre's date with Clayton anyway," she said in a teasing manner.

Brianna winked. "Amara, you are welcome to join us and you know it," she said as she playfully hit her shoulder.

Amara smiled. "Yeah, right," she said sarcastically and smiled. "So what time are we going to the gallery?" Amara asked Sam. Sam checked his watch. "In a few hours," he said. "Pick you up at three this afternoon, okay?" Amara smiled. "Sure, that sounds great. See you then." Sam and Amara left Brianna and Clayton in the garden.

Amara went to her room and grabbed her sweater and the keys to Brianna's old car, a VW convertible. She wrapped the sweater casually around her shoulders. "See you later Sam. I am off to the library."

Sam looked in the direction of Amara. She had piqued his interest. "Library? Are you doing some type of research?" he asked. "Because I am the king of research," he boasted. "Do you need any help?" he asked.

Amara shook her head no. "Thanks, Sam. I too am very good at researching information. I appreciate the offer though," she said. Amara didn't need him to be a distraction today. She needed to find out some information on her assailant and the situation at home.

Sam tilted his head to the side and looked at Amara. She looked nervously adjusted the scarf around her neck and looked down at the ground. She wasn't ready to share her predicament with him just yet. Amara had not even told her parents when she called them. All she told them was she planned to spend the week with Brianna. Sam smiled and let himself out the front door. Moments later he returned and took out one of his cards and jotted down his cell phone number. "If you change your mind, give me a call," he said as he handed Amara his card. She took Sam's card, thanked him and placed it inside her front pants pocket.

Amara called out to Brianna to let her know she was leaving and headed out the front door with Sam. Sam walked to his car while Amara went to the garage. She spotted the emerald green VW convertible. Brianna had taken great care of her car. It cranked up with the first turn of the key. She let the roof down, put her sunglasses on and headed toward town.

When Amara reached the research department of the library, she sat down at the computer and brought up a copy of the Seattle newspaper from the Internet and read the small article regarding the man who had tried to kill her. She read the man's name to herself, Duke Ellington. Amara stopped reading the article and frowned. This would be kind of funny if he weren't trying to kill me, she thought. Amara exited out of that site and entered a secured site that belonged to the newspaper. She punched in her old password from the newspaper and looked at the reporter's notes that had covered a past court case involving Duke Ellington.

She scrolled down and smiled. "Bingo!" she said quietly. It was Duke's arrest record. Officer Blanco was right, Amara thought. Duke Ellington was fifty years old and had been in jail over one dozen times. He served fifteen years in prison for raping a woman, whose identity was protected, twenty-seven years ago. He had also served time for attempted murder for shooting his wife in the spine when he caught her in bed with his best friend. Instead of killing her, he left her paralyzed from the waist down. Amara shook her head in disbelief and continued to read the report. He shot his best friend in the head. Lucky for him, the bullet only grazed his skull, but now he suffered seizures and debilitating headaches.

Amara continued to read the reporter's notes. He was also accused but never convicted of five other gangster-style murders in the greater Seattle area. Amara let out a long breath. "This is one demented and dangerous guy," she said under her breath. She scrolled down and found his last known address. Amara jotted down the address.

She quickly closed the site and went to an IRS site. She punched in her old password and entered the information to determine the identity of Duke's last legitimate employer. Seconds later, the information appeared on the screen. She scrolled down and read the name of the employer to herself. She stared at the name for a long time in disbelief. His last employer was her ex-boyfriend's brother, Michael Whitman. Their father Ralph, a widower, was a very prosperous man. He owned a chain of fast food restaurants throughout the city and had recently retired. In anticipation of his upcoming retirement, he had turned the business over to his eldest son Paul four years ago. When Michael completed his graduate studies in business and finance management he joined Paul in the family business. Amara shuddered as she remembered her last encounter with Michael. It had not been pleasant.

They were all at a nightclub together and as usual, Michael had gotten drunk. While Paul and Amara were on the dance floor, dancing close to a popular love song, they noticed Michael and his girlfriend engaged in a heated argument that seemed to be escalating. Paul and Amara walked off the dance floor and headed toward the couple when Michael slapped his date across her face and angrily strode off. Amara recalled Paul ran over to Michael and grabbed his arm in order to talk to him and prevent him from leaving in his current state of mind. Michael jerked his arm out of Paul's grasp and continued out of the club. As Amara walked toward his date, she turned and ran out of the club in tears.

The following day, Michael came to her house looking for Paul. She could tell he was high on some type of drug. When she wouldn't allow him inside her home, he became violent and damaged her door with a crowbar. She called the police and he left without further incident. From that point on, Amara made an effort to stay away from him.

Amara pushed the negative thoughts from her mind and continued to read the information regarding Duke Ellington. Duke had worked odd jobs most of his life. The last entry showed he worked as a janitor at three of the Whitman's food chain restaurants. Amara absently twirled her hair as she thought about this new information. She didn't know what to make of it. She and Paul had remained cordial and she hadn't spoken to Michael since the incident at her home, which was nearly two years ago.

Amara tapped lightly on the computer desk with her pen as she closed the site. She jotted down a few more notes and then went over to the pay phone. She pulled out her phone card and called Officer Blanco. Maria answered the phone right away. "Blanco here," she answered in a gruff voice. Amara could tell by her tone of voice that she was busy and Amara had interrupted whatever she was working on. "Officer Blanco, this is Amara. I was just wondering if you had any news on the man who tried to kill me?" she asked. "Amara, hello, yes, I do have some information for you."

Amara could hear Officer Blanco rifling through some papers. "Mr. Duke Ellington is the man who tried to kill you. He has denied everything. We did not find any weapon on him or in his car. Since we could not locate the witnesses you said came into the room while he was attempting to shoot you, this is going to be a tough case. He has been accused of this type of thing before, but has never been convicted. On another negative note, I must tell you that he was released on bail this afternoon. His employer, Mr. Michael Whitman, paid his bail." Amara drew in a deep breath.

"Amara, one more thing. He provided Duke with an alibi during the time of your alleged assault. He said he was at the LaMont Club with him. Several others have also vouched for his presence and said he only left the table to dance with his date," she said without emotion. Amara was speechless. She felt as if she had been crushed by a ton of cement. Several different thoughts raced through her mind.

As if she sensed Amara's apprehension and fear, Officer Blanco tried to reassure her. "Don't worry, Miss Glenton, we have Mr. Ellington under surveillance. We've also got our eye on Mr. Michael Whitman," she said. "We took a statement from Paul Whitman. He corroborated your statement and said he brought you to the station. He also described the injuries to your face and neck," she said. "But he said he did not see the incident and didn't know exactly what had transpired the night in question. He also didn't know about his brother's relationship with Mr. Ellington."

Officer Blanco smoothed a stand of hair that was out of place and took a deep breath. "Miss Glenton, I need to inform you that your condo was broken into yesterday. Whoever did it searched through every nook and cranny of your condo, including all of your electronic equipment. The greatest damage was sustained in your darkroom. Most of your photos and camera equipment was destroyed.

"Luckily, your neighbor, Mrs. Murdock, called our department when she heard crashing sounds coming from your condo. When the intruder heard Mrs. Murdock knock on the door, we believe he fled out the back door. After we finished with the crime scene, we released the condo to your parents. Your landlady called them while we were at your house. They started cleaning up your house early this morning around six o'clock."

Amara's hand began to tremble as her grip tightened on the phone. "Are my parents still there?" she asked.

"No, we had a patrol drive by an hour ago and there was no one at your place. In fact, I was just finishing up the paperwork on the incident and I was going to call you. Your timing was perfect," said Officer Blanco calmly.

Amara began to pace in the small booth. "Did my parents ask you any questions? What did you tell them?" she asked as her voice quivered.

Officer Blanco's voice remained calm. "I didn't tell them anything about what happened. They think it was random vandalism. I suggested they call you at your friend's house. I am sure they've already left a message."

Amara had turned her cell phone off in the library. She immediately turned it on and saw she had received several text messages. All of the messages were from her parents. She began to read her messages while she listened to Officer Blanco on the telephone. Each text message read more urgently than the prior message. Amara thanked Officer Blanco and hung up the phone.

She quickly left the library and walked to the car. She started the car and drove to a nearby park. In her current state of mind, she didn't trust herself to drive and talk on the cell phone. She pulled into a vacant parking space, parked the car, and called her parents. Her father, Jackson Glenton, a retired lawyer and law professor at the nearby university, answered the phone.

Jackson told Amara what had transpired and began firing off questions in the manner he would during a cross-examination in court. Myra shushed her husband and grabbed the phone. Myra, her mother, was a retired high

31

school math and science teacher. She too began firing off questions, not allowing Amara to answer.

Once Jackson and Myra Glenton calmed down, Amara told them what had happened and her speculation as to Michael's involvement. "He gave him an alibi and bailed him out of jail! Can you believe it?" she asked as her voice wavered. Amara took a deep breath and brushed a tear from her eye. "Why would he do that? I wonder if he was the one who hired Duke to kill me?" she asked. Amara's father pulled his ear from the phone and walked to the next room to talk on an extension phone.

He picked up the phone and spoke to Amara in a calm voice. "Getting hysterical won't solve a thing, honey. What we need is a plan, a good plan. I know some folks down in the old neighborhood that can provide some inside information about Duke Ellington. Last I heard he was out of the country."

Amara looked up at the sky from the Volkswagen convertible. "Dad, do you know Duke Ellington?" Amara asked in a shaky voice.

"Honey, I have lived here all my life. I know a lot of people. Duke Ellington was bad news even back in my day," he said calmly. "You remember Clark, don't you, Mari?" he asked. "He's a tenured professor at the university Michael graduated from. I think I'll have lunch with him tomorrow. Perhaps he can tell me something about Michael."

Amara began to feel herself calm down. "Dad, I appreciate your level head. I'll be home at the end of the week. I have done a bit of research at the library this morning and I will continue to search for information while I'm here."

Amara's mother got into the conversation. "Mari, baby, we took the liberty of packing up your things at your condo. You are not safe at that place. The movers are coming tomorrow. We'll put most of your stuff in storage and you can stay in the little apartment over the garage until this is all over," she said sensibly.

Amara smiled. She remembered when she had begged her parents to allow her to stay in the apartment while attending college and they had told her she needed to stay in the dorm and meet new people. When she earned her college degree, she asked to use the apartment until she found a job and got on her feet. Her parents had encouraged her to get a small apartment close to town, which in hindsight was very smart. Living close to downtown had allowed her to walk the six blocks to work and save enough money to live in the nice condo she was currently renting. Amara knew the last occupant recently moved south to live with her grandchildren. She was very neat and kept everything in working order. Amara knew she would not have to do any work to the place.

She had not seen the inside of the apartment for five years. She wondered how her mother, who had become quite good at interior decorating, had decorated the apartment. Amara smiled again before responding to her mother. "Oh, so it takes someone trying to kill me to move into the apartment huh?" joked Amara.

"Don't get smart with me, young lady. You are never toe big...."

Amara broke in, "That's a great idea, Mom. Thank you. And thanks for taking care of my things."

Amara's mom breathed a huge sigh of relief. "Now that we have that all settled, how is Brianna?" asked her mother, changing to a lighter subject. Jackson told his daughter goodbye and hung up the extension phone in order to allow Amara and Myra to talk. Amara told her mother about her beautiful new home and Japanese garden and about her new novel and pending movie deal. "She was always such a sweet and talented child," said Myra. Amara agreed with her mom.

She glanced at her watch and told her parents she needed to get off the phone. She made sure they had her email address so they could send her any pertinent information before hanging up the phone. Myra jotted down the information and they both said goodbye and hung up the phone. Amara hung up her cell phone, slipped on her sunglasses, and headed back to Brianna's house.

Jackson walked back into the kitchen where Myra stood staring at the phone. Her brave front quickly faded when she hung up the phone. Jackson walked over to her and hugged her close. Myra began to weep. "Dear God. When will this all be over?" she pleaded. Myra rested her tear-stained face on Jackson's chest. "Amara is our only child," she whispered. Jackson held his wife tight and gently stroked her hair as she continued to sob.

Sam appeared at Brianna's house at three o'clock sharp. He was whistling a catchy tune as he rang the doorbell. Amara answered the door and let Sam inside. Sam smiled widely and looked at Amara appreciatively. "Amara you look really nice," he said. Amara grinned widely and grabbed her shawl. She had chosen to wear her hair down. Her soft wavy curls framed her face and cascaded down her back. She had carefully put on her makeup and chosen a colorful silk skirt and matching blouse that looked sophisticated, but was comfortable. The fine lines in the fabric made the outfit look as if it were made especially for her.

Sam stuck out his elbow and Amara slid her arm through. Sam laughed aloud as he told Brianna and Clayton not to wait up. "I just might take this woman dancing," he said cheerfully. Brianna lifted an eyebrow and looked at Clayton. Clayton pretended to read the paper and gave no response.

Amara and Sam arrived at an upscale art gallery downtown. When they walked through the door, she looked at the photography and sculptures and immediately recognized the work of Harry Bellamy. It turned out that Amara had done a great feature story on his work a couple of years ago when he had his first exhibit in Seattle. Her article had brought him a lot of business and notoriety. When Harry saw Amara he remembered her right away and gave her a big hug and a light kiss on the cheek. "Are you covering this show as well?" he asked anxiously. She told him she was not, but was there as a guest of Sam, who had been invited to the show. Harry and Sam shook hands like old friends and Harry gave them a personal tour until he was asked to meet a buyer interested in one of his art pieces.

As they came to the end of the show, Amara's stomach growled loudly. Sam chuckled and placed his hand in the small of her back and led her toward the door. "Let's go get you something to eat," he said. "I know just the place." Before they left, Amara took a picture of Sam standing outside the gallery. Sam stopped one of the patrons leaving the gallery and asked him to take a picture of him and Amara. Sam placed his arm around Amara's waist and they both smiled widely. The patron took the picture and handed the camera back to Sam. Sam handed Amara her camera. "I want a copy," he said. Amara smiled and promised to send him a copy.

Sam took Amara to a nice seafood restaurant that overlooked the ocean. Since it was slightly before the dinner hour, the restaurant had only a few patrons eating a late lunch. Amara stared out into the ocean lost in thought as the waiter left to get their drinks. "Hello? Come back to earth," said Sam good-naturedly as he waved his hand in front of Amara's face.

Amara shook her head and brought her attention back to Sam. "What? Oh, I'm sorry, I got some news earlier today and I was thinking about it," she answered cryptically. "I'm a good listener if you'd like to share your news," he said as he gave her his undivided attention.

Amara took a deep breath and began to tell Sam about the attempted murder, her house being ransacked, and the possibility of her ex-boyfriend's brother, Michael, being involved. Sam let out a low whistle. Just then the waiter returned with their drinks and appetizers.

Sam picked up one of the fried oysters from the platter and popped it into his mouth. He then looked at Amara. "Do you really think Michael had anything to do with the attempt on your life?" he asked as he removed the grilled shrimp and vegetables from its skewer. Amara dipped her shrimp in the cocktail sauce and took a bite. "I'm really not sure, but I suspect he is," she said thoughtfully as she chewed her shrimp.

Sam smiled and made a suggestion. "I think I can help you find some of the answers you are searching for," he said. "If you don't need to go home right away, I'd like to take you to my office. Electronics are a passion of mine, and our office has the latest state of the art electronic equipment. I also have the ability to tap into a couple of top-notch secure information web sites." Amara readily agreed and quickly finished the last of the grilled shrimp from her skewer. "That's sounds great, Sam. Let's go!"

Sam slowed his car as he pulled into the sloping parking garage of a very modern five-story office plaza. Amara looked at the rich architecture of the building. "Sam, this building is fantastic!" said Amara. She continued to check out the building as Sam pulled the car into his reserved parking space.

The security guard walked toward them and Sam greeted him by name. "Hey, Todd, how are you this afternoon?" he asked. Todd smiled. "Hey, Mr. Peters, I'm great, how about you?" Sam looked at Todd's leg. "How's that knee holding up?" Todd rotated his new kneecap with ease and gave the thumbs up sign as Sam and Amara walked toward the elevator. "This new rotator cup works like a gem," he said. Amara looked at Sam as if to ask about Todd's injury. "Skiing accident," Sam replied. Amara smiled and nodded her head.

Both waved at Todd and faced the elevator. Sam then placed his hand inside a handprint imbedded in the wall. An infrared light scanned the inside of his hand and a green light appeared. "I enjoy skiing. Do you ski, Sam?" Amara asked. "Yep, every winter," he said. The elevator immediately opened and automatically traveled upward to the floor where Sam's office was located. Amara looked at Sam in amazement. "Wow, I am impressed. Only one question, what if you want to go to a floor other than the one programmed?" she asked.

"You just manually select the floor and it will change," he said.

When they arrived on the correct floor, Amara continued to be amazed. Everything looked very modern and comfortable. Each office was painted a different color. The modular furniture was made of beautiful teak wood. Large oil paintings and prints by popular African American artists hung throughout the offices and in the foyer. The effect was a very soothing and comfortable atmosphere. The décor in the offices was pastel colors with matching soft upholstered furniture.

"Who was your decorator?" asked Amara, truly impressed. Sam laughed. "An old girlfriend who happened to be a graduate of one of the most prestigious interior decorating schools in Europe. This was her first project. Since she was in love with me at the time, her services were very reasonable. Now, I couldn't even afford a consultation," he joked. "She has even done some work for Oprah," he said. Amara laughed.

"When you choose your women, you pick them beautiful and talented don't you?" she teased. Sam cleared his throat and changed the subject.

He led her to his office. As soon as he entered the office, the lights automatically came on. "Heat sensored," he said. Amara lifted her eyebrow. "Impressive," she said. His computer rose from the desk console and automatically began to boot up. He walked over and slipped a coded signature card into its drive. A voice greeted him and a site automatically popped onto his screen. Amara was in awe of the high level of technology in his office.

Sam sat down and asked Amara how to spell Michael's full name. Amara gave him the proper spelling of his name. He typed the information into the database and a series of data information screens appeared. Sam frowned as he read the information on the screen. "Amara, you may want to come around the desk and look at this," he said in a serious tone. Amara got up from her chair and walked over to his side of the desk and looked at the screen. She wrinkled her nose as she read the information.

"Sam, I don't know who Amelia Hernandez is," replied Amara. Sam smiled and replied, "I cross-indexed it with information from the IRS. Scroll down on that screen, Amara." She looked at him with a puzzled look on her face and scrolled down the computer screen. "Wow, this shows that up until two years ago, Amelia Hernandez paid the taxes and now it shows Maria Blanco is paying these same taxes. She changed her name," said Amara.

Amara became agitated. "Sam, Officer Blanco is the woman who helped me through this crisis," she said. Sam could see she was visibly concerned and rightfully so.

Amara closed her eyes for a few moments and began to remember where she had seen Maria Blanco. "Sam, a couple years ago, I was at a night-club and Michael was there also. He and his date got into a loud argument in the club. Michael slapped his date and immediately left the club after he and Paul had words. The more I think about it, I believe Officer Blanco was that woman!" she said. Sam scrolled down the computer images. "Bingo!" he said aloud.

Amara leaned over his shoulder to get a better view of the computer screen. "What is it?" she asked excitedly. Sam turned and looked at Amara. He examined her soft lips and thought about kissing her. The cut on her lips had begun to heal nicely. Amara could feel him staring at her. She tried to act natural as tiny beads of sweat formed above her upper lip. Sam leaned over toward Amara as she continued to read over the birth certificate on the screen.

Sam moved his chair closer to Amara until their bodies were nearly touching. He looked at the silhouette of her face and felt his heart racing. He wanted to touch her soft skin. Amara's long lashes nearly touched her cheek as she closed her eyes. She could feel his hot breath on the side of her face. Sam continued to stare and slowly leaned toward her when his cell phone rang.

Amara's eyes popped open and she stood up and walked away from Sam's desk. Sam nervously cleared his throat and answered the phone. Amara walked to the large window at the other side of the office and stared out at the city. She hugged herself as she stood perfectly still in an attempt to become invisible. She tried not to listen, but she could hear his conversation.

"Hi, honey! I am glad you made it back! I've missed you too. Yes. I am at the office helping a friend find some information. I can't wait to see you either. Yes, I will be right over. Love you too! Bye." Amara walked back over to the desk and clicked the mouse and made a copy of the birth certificate. She pulled the copy from the printer as Sam removed his card from the computer. The shutdown procedure on his computer was automatically initiated.

"This is really interesting," said Amara as she read the copy.

Sam had a huge grin on his face, oblivious to Amara's last comment. "Franni is home. I am sorry we have to cut this short, but we can start again tomorrow afternoon all right?" he asked.

Amara looked at Sam. "Of course, Sam. Thanks for your help. I am now curious about Officer Blanco's motive in all of this. I can't wait to see what else we find out," she said.

Sam quickly walked toward the door, leaving Amara standing in the middle of the office. She quickly followed Sam to the door. "I will let the front desk know you have an appointment with me," said Sam, not breaking his stride. He scanned his automated schedule on his telephone. "I have an appointment with a client tomorrow morning at nine o'clock. Let's shoot for one-thirty in the afternoon, okay? Franni and I plan to have lunch tomorrow and I'd love for you to meet her," he said. "I know you two will hit it off right away."

Amara smiled again. "I am sure we will," she said nervously.

Wasn't this man about to kiss me a couple of seconds ago? she thought to herself. She immediately pushed the thought from her mind. Amara wet her lips nervously. "That sounds great," she stammered. "I am really interested in what other information you have. I am not sure how all of this ties together, but I think I might want to consult a lawyer. Surely there is a conflict of interest here with Officer Blanco?" she asked. Without responding, Sam pushed placed his hand at the small of Amara's back and ushered her into the elevator.

The elevator automatically went down to the parking garage. Once out of the elevator, Amara pulled out her cell phone and called for a cab. Sam frowned. "I can take you home."

Amara laughed. "Hey, if I keep you from Franni one minute longer, I think you are going to burst!" she joked. Sam smiled awkwardly and gave Amara a peck on the cheek. "Thanks, Amara." Sam walked Amara to the street and offered to wait with her until the cab arrived; Amara assured him it wasn't necessary. She just wanted to get away from him and his mixed signals.

A cab quickly drove up to the curb and paused while they were talking. Amara got into the cab and let out a sigh filled with relief and frustration. After making sure Amara was safely in the cab, Sam patted the trunk of the cab and trotted to his car in the parking garage. Once inside he let out a nervous breath. What was I thinking, he thought to himself. He chastised himself more as he quickly got into his car and drove out of the parking garage toward Franni's apartment.

Amara was so busy reassuring Sam that he didn't need to stay that she hadn't paid any attention to the cab driver. The cab pulled away from the curb and merged into the heavy late afternoon bumper-to-bumper traffic. She leaned into the seat and closed her eyes. She decided to call Brianna and let her know she was on her way to her place.

She began to dig in her purse for her cell phone when it hit her. She smelled a familiar odor. Goose bumps appeared on her arms and she suddenly felt nauseous. It was the strong odor of the familiar aftershave she smelled on Duke Ellington when they were at the club. Visions of that fateful night began to flow through her head. As the scent continued to waft through the cab her heart beat so fast and hard it felt as if it were beating outside of her chest. Amara continued to keep her head down and look into her purse and hummed a tune. A friend of hers who was in the Army had taught her how to regulate her breathing by singing cadence. The tune forced her to regulate her breathing so she wouldn't hyperventilate.

The cab slowed down for a stoplight. Duke had a sly grin on his face. He believed Amara had no clue he was at the wheel. Amara continued to hum. Without lifting her head, Amara burst out of the cab door and fell hard to the ground. Blood spurted from her scraped elbow and knee. Ignoring her pain, Amara grabbed her small handbag, got up, and ran down the street in the opposite direction of the traffic. Duke slammed his fist angrily on the dashboard and cursed Amara as she ran in the opposite direction.

He followed her direction through the rear view mirror, but the heavy traffic prevented him from pursuing her. Duke couldn't leave the cab in the middle of street because it would draw too much attention to him. He was out on bail and had been instructed not to leave Seattle. He knew the authorities would put him back in jail if he were caught in San Francisco.

Amara ran as fast as her legs would take her. She said a silent prayer of thanks that she was wearing flat shoes. She ran into a shopping mall and began to walk at a normal pace. She went to the public restroom and cleaned the blood away from her cut knee and elbow. She winced as the water stung when she rinsed out the dirt and blood. Luckily neither cut was too deep.

She then went to several stores and purchased different clothes, a hat, and sunglasses. She went back to the public restroom and put bandages she had purchased from the drug store on her wounds and changed her clothes. She tucked her long hair into the hat and placed the sunglasses on. She made sure she departed out of a different exit.

From her vantage point, she saw Duke Ellington sitting in the cab at the other end of the mall and prayed he would not recognize her. She quickly blended in with a crowd of people and casually walked with the wave of people to the next block. She waved down another cab and got in. She looked back at Duke's cab and was relieved to see someone had gotten into his cab and he had driven off in the opposite direction. Amara breathed a sigh of relief and gave instructions for the new cab driver to take her to her friend's house.

When Amara reached Brianna's house, she quickly paid the cab driver and ran toward the door. As usual, the door was unlocked. When she entered the house, she saw Brianna kneeling on the ground, picking up shards of glass. Amara ran over to Brianna and kneeled down, so they were face to face. "What happened?" asked Amara. Brianna gulped back her tears. "About an half hour ago, I was carrying a glass of lemonade out to the garden when I saw this tall, bald-headed black man standing in the middle of my garden! I dropped the glass of lemonade and screamed as loud as I could. Luckily, Clayton was in the other room and as soon as the guy saw Clayton, he ran away," said Brianna through her tears.

Amara rubbed Brianna's back as she angrily pushed her hair out of her face. Her face was streaked with tears. Amara took the shards of glass from Brianna's hands and pulled her up from the floor and held her close. Clayton entered the room, swept up the remaining shards of glass, and tossed them into the wastebasket in the kitchen.

Amara guided Brianna to the sofa in the den. She went into the kitchen and joined Clayton. "I think this is my fault," said Amara. "The guy who tried to kill me in Seattle is here. He picked me up in a cab and I got away. I also found out that he and the police officer that helped capture him are indirectly related through my ex-boyfriend's brother.

"When I was in Sam's office, we found a birth certificate verifying Officer Blanco had a baby by Michael Whitman. Duke Ellington, the man hired to kill me, was jailed and released on bail the same day by Michael Whitman and somehow located me. The funny thing is, Officer Blanco was the only person who knew my exact whereabouts. Even my parents don't know since Brianna recently moved."

Clayton rubbed his chin thoughtfully. Brianna stood up from the sofa, went to the bathroom, splashed water on her face, and fixed her hair. She then joined Amara and Clayton in the kitchen. Clayton walked over to Brianna and placed his arm around her. Brianna smiled at him and placed her head against his chest. "I want you both to pack a bag and stay at my place for tonight. I will call an old buddy at the local police station and ask him to put out an APB—all points bulletin—for Duke Ellington. I will also call an old friend of mine at the Seattle Police Department and report Mr. Ellington leaving the state, thereby disobeying the restrictions set by the terms of his bail. I know a great bounty hunter, named Blake Hunter, who will pick this jerk up quickly and place him in our jail until we can contact someone other than Officer Blanco. I plan to report her conflict of interest to a friend of mine in Seattle's Police Department Internal Affairs." Amara looked at Brianna and felt a wave of comfort come over her.

She walked over and clasped Brianna's hand. "Your man is well connected," whispered Amara. Brianna smiled, turned her face up toward Clayton, and kissed him. "I know," she beamed.

Brianna looked at Amara and gasped. "Amara, you're bleeding!" she said.

Amara looked at the blood flowing through the flimsy bandages from the gash on her knee and elbow. "Yes, I fell getting out of the cab," she said.

Brianna walked over and put her arm around Amara. "Let's go get you cleaned and patched up. Then we'll pack some clothes. I am ready to get out of here," she said as they walked toward the guestroom. Clayton grabbed a cold beverage from the refrigerator, walked into the den, and turned on the television. He flipped the station to a baseball game and watched television while the two women packed.

True to his word Blake, who had the reputation of being one of the best bounty hunters in the state, combed the streets for Duke Ellington. Word spread quickly about Duke. In his effort to get out of town quickly, Duke left a sloppy trail. Blake captured Duke on the outskirts of town as he drove a stolen nondescript Lincoln Continental toward the state border in an attempt to reenter Washington State. Blake brought him back to San Francisco and turned him over to the authorities to be held in jail. After Clayton called the district attorney in Seattle and explained the situation, Maria Blanco was visited by Internal Affairs and suspended without pay until her hearing date. All of this happened within hours of Clayton making a few strategic phone calls.

The following morning Amara sat at the edge of the heated pool with her feet immersed in the water. She watched the ripples in the water slowly form and spread across the width of the pool. Amara tilted her head up toward the sun and took advantage of the quietness of the morning. It gave her a chance to think about her next move and reflect on the events of the past few days. Clayton and Brianna had gone to the grocery store to pick up groceries for breakfast and Amara took full advantage of being left alone. She stood up, dried off her legs and feet, and returned to Clayton's guest room.

Amara rummaged through the designer tote bag and found the swimsuit, swim cap, and goggles she had packed. She put the on the swimsuit and swim cap, grabbed a towel from the guest bathroom, and ran out to the pool. She threw the towel on the nearby chaise lounge, pulled the goggles over her eyes, and jumped into the pool. The water felt cool and invigorating against her skin as she swam lap after lap and cleared her mind of all negative thoughts. As she finished her final lap, she got out of the pool, removed the goggles and cap, and wrapped the soft towel around her body.

She was startled when she saw Sam standing in front of her with his balled fists on his hips and his jaw rippled in anger. Sam continued to clench his jaw as he stood glaring in Amara's direction. Sam spoke in measured tones. "Why didn't you call me? My brother called me and told me you and Brianna were staying at his house because Duke Ellington tried to kidnap you. Why didn't you call?" he demanded.

Amara looked at Sam as if he had lost his mind. "Sam, you were in a rush to see Franni, remember?" she responded coolly. "Anyway, Clayton had the situation under control and I didn't see a reason to bother you about this," she said exasperated. "And why are you so angry with me?" she asked. Sam couldn't answer her question.

Just then Franni walked onto the patio, accompanied by Brianna and Clayton. "Yes, Sam, why are you so angry when it seems Clayton has everything under control?" asked Franni. Embarrassed over his outburst, Sam relaxed his stance and walked over to Franni. He gave her a quick kiss and a hug. He appreciated the fact they had an open and honest relationship.

"I am angry because I felt partially responsible. I was in such a rush to see you that I didn't bother to take Amara home or even make sure she made it to Brianna's safely," he said. Sam took Franni's hand and intertwined his fingers with hers. He gently kissed her fingertips and led her by the hand over to Amara.

"Franni, I would like you to meet Amara. Amara, this is my girlfriend Franni." Franni gave Amara a brilliant smile and released Sam's hand. She shook Amara's hand and said with a slight French accent, "It is wonderful to meet you. Sam told me about your situation and how he is trying to help you."

Amara let out the breath she was not aware she had been holding. She smiled genuinely and covered Franni's hand with her own. "I feel as if I already know you. Sam has told me a lot about you," she said.

Amara quickly appraised Franni. She was breathtakingly beautiful. Her deep cocoa skin was flawless. Her facial features were keen. Her short-cropped hairstyle immediately drew your attention to her large fawn-like eyes. Her appearance was impeccable. Amara smiled as she imagined her sauntering down the walkway.

Amara was quickly brought back to reality by Franni's laughter. "He is something else. He told me he has been entertaining you during your short stay here." Amara nodded. "He has been great," she said releasing Franni's hand. Brianna brought Amara a cup of her favorite natural brewed Berry Zinger tea. Amara thanked her friend and sipped her tea appreciatively. It felt good going down after her swim. Brianna offered beverages to everyone else. "It was nice meeting you, Franni," said Amara. Franni smiled and nodded. Amara excused herself and went to the guestroom to change clothes.

When Amara returned she saw everyone was seated around the large patio table. They were discussing her situation. She felt self-conscious and yet honored that she had people who were supportive during this tenuous time. Amara quietly walked to the table and sat down in the vacant seat beside Brianna. She placed the napkin on her lap and spoke. "I want to thank you all for your support. This has been a very scary experience and I don't know why Duke Ellington wants to kill me or exactly who else is involved. I am confused and a bit afraid," she confessed. Brianna immediately leaned over in her seat and hugged her friend. Amara bit her lower lip in an effort not to cry in front of everyone. "Can I talk to you?" she asked Brianna. Brianna nodded yes and both ladies excused themselves and went into the guestroom where Amara was staying.

Amara explained it was time for her to return to Seattle. She needed to find out what was going on. She felt as if she were hiding out in San Francisco. She informed Brianna she would be leaving the next morning. Brianna looked sad, but understood. They hugged once more and Amara returned to the patio. Amara thanked everyone for their concern and under-standing and announced she'd be leaving first thing in the morning. Franni released a sigh of relief as Sam caressed her fingers beneath the table.

When Brianna returned to the table she told Amara she had pur-chased a nonstop plane ticket for her. The plane departed at ten o'clock the next day. Amara hugged and thanked her. Franni looked at Sam and he gave her a reassuring smile and brought her fingertips to his lips and light-ly kissed them.

The women excused themselves and went to the kitchen and placed croissants, meat, cheese, and fruit on platters while the men set the table. Once they had finished their chore, Clayton asked Sam to join him by the pool. When both were out of earshot from the women, Clayton placed his hands on Sam's shoulders. "Bro, what's going on with you and Amara?"

Sam looked down at his feet. He then looked his brother in the eyes and responded. "I really don't know Clayton. I love Franni. But I am drawn to Amara and I don't know why. I don't know if it is her, or her situation. She needs someone and I like that. Franni is so independent that it seems she never really needs me," he said.

Clayton held his brother's gaze. "What happens when this is all over and Amara doesn't need you anymore? It is apparent that she is as attracted to you as you are to her. Then what?"

Sam's jaw twitched nervously. "What does it matter, Clay? She is leaving tomorrow morning and I don't plan to do anything stupid to jeopardize what I have with Franni," he said. "And just for the record, nothing has happened between Amara and me. She has treated me like a good friend. I was the one out of bounds this morning," he said quietly.

Clayton slapped his brother playfully on his back. "It's all right. I think you have your head on straight. I just wanted to make sure you knew what you were doing," he said. "Remember I was in the same situation with Vida?"

"Yes," Sam responded in a barely audible tone.

"I had met Brianna a couple months before she broke up with her boyfriend of six years, remember? Brianna was everything I wanted, but I was afraid to give up Vida. I knew her. We were comfortable, but I wasn't in love with her. Too much history between us," he said nonchalantly. Sam looked at his brother and expected him to say more about the history that was between him and Vida, but he didn't.

"Anyway, when Brianna broke up with Charles, I wanted to take our relationship to another level. I felt she did also. I was so drawn to Brianna's warmth and openness I kept coming around under the pretense of being 'just a friend' until Brianna gave me an ultimatum. She told me how she felt about me and that I had to choose either to date her or Vida, but not both. She told me to stop coming around under the pretense of being just a friend when we both knew we felt more.

"Vida was such a class act. We talked about it and she admitted that we had grown apart through the years and that she knew we weren't in love with each other anymore. Vida had found someone she wanted to start a serious relationship with as well and was trying to find a way to talk to me about it. We were honest about our feelings toward one another and split on great terms and are still good friends," said Clayton.

"You and Vida had been together for over five years," said Sam. He then looked at his older brother and smiled shyly. "I understand and I choose my relationship with Franni," he said. Clayton smiled and lightly punched him on the shoulder. Both laughed and walked over and sat down on a bench in the garden and talked about yesterday's events.

"Breakfast is ready!" the women called as they brought the food and juice to the table. After breakfast Brianna and Amara packed their belongings and prepared to return to Brianna's house. Clayton walked Brianna to the door and asked if she wanted to meet later for lunch and a game of tennis. Brianna gave Clayton a deep kiss, told him she'd meet him at noon, and thanked him for everything he had done for her friend, Amara. Amara hugged Franni, Clayton, and Sam and joined Brianna at the door. Brianna wrapped her arm around Amara and they walked out to the car and slowly drove away.

Once on the road, Brianna turned down the CD player and looked over at Amara, who seemed distant as she stared out the car window. "Okay, Mari, what is going on with you and Sam?" she asked. "If I were Franni I would have been pretty angry at the little scene by the pool," she said accusingly. Amara looked at her friend. She opened her mouth to say something and then closed it. "Well?" asked Brianna. Amara took a deep breath. "I don't know. I was just swimming, taking advantage of being alone and there he was, chastising me for not calling him last night. I'm not going to lie. I am attracted to the brother. But he's got a girlfriend whom he really seems to love. I swear, Bre; I never stepped over the line. And I never came on to him," she said. "That is the honest truth."

Amara laid her head against the headrest and smiled. She was glad it was all out in the open. She was leaving and wouldn't see Sam again until her next visit. By then, he and Franni would probably be even closer. Amara sighed heavily and looked out the window. They drove the rest of the way in silence.

The following morning Brianna took Amara to the airport. As she prepared to board the aircraft Sam quickly walked down the aisle and stopped in front of her. Amara smiled and showed off her dimples. She asked him what he was doing there. Sam gave her a soft kiss on the lips and handed her a card. "I am still here to help you solve this situation. I have the technology you need. I will continue to search for information. Call me if you need me. Okay?" he pleaded. Amara shook her head, not trusting herself to answer.

Brianna frowned and shook her head. She placed her hands up in a gesture of surrender. "You are both adults," she said in mock defeat.

Amara and Brianna hugged and Amara kissed her on the cheek. "Thanks for everything. Hopefully the next time I see you this will all be over," she said. Brianna assured her it would be over soon. Amara walked through the detectors toward her gate. Brianna slipped her arm through Sam's and led him away. "Come on, Sam, before you get yourself in trouble," she said wearily.

Chapter 4

$\mathcal{S}$ hareese paced back and forth in the bathroom angrily. "Dammit!" she yelled as she kicked at a stool that was positioned under her vanity mirror. She looked at her reflection in the mirror. She saw the frown lines and immediately relaxed her facial features. "Now what are we going to do?" she asked anxiously. She listened to the voice on the other end of the phone and cut the person off in mid-sentence. "Don't give me empty promises!' she yelled. She continued to pace the floor, trying to think of what to do next.

"Honey," she said sweetly, "let's just take the money and go," she said impatiently. She listened to the response. "Who cares about your partners? I am to be your wife. Just tell me where you stashed the money and we can go get it and leave the country," she pleaded. She listened to the laughter from the voice on the other end and grew angrier.

Without saying another word, she hung up the phone abruptly. She screamed in frustration and threw her cell phone across the room. It crashed against the wall and broke into pieces. She rubbed her aching temples as she tried to figure out her next move. She needed money. She had bills to pay and had squandered the meager thousands Michael had given her.

She picked up the paper and saw an article about Duke's capture. She used her manicured nail and traced around the photo in the paper. "Well, you've done it again. You are right back where you started and I can't get you out this time," she scoffed. Shareese threw the paper across the room, grabbed her purse, and stomped out of the house.

Amara's parents spotted her as she walked down the long hall toward the baggage claim area. She had a small duffel bag draped over her shoulder. She looked tired and her eyes were red and puffy. Her parents ran up to her and hugged her tightly. She told them she had no other luggage and they quickly walked to the car and headed home. They rode back to the house in silence. Her parents wanted to give her some time to collect her thoughts before they asked her more questions about the attempt on her life.

Amara felt weary as she got out of the car. Jackson asked her to come inside before going to the apartment. "I have something to show you," he said. Amara walked inside the house and sat down at the kitchen table. Myra began fixing some tea for Amara and coffee for herself and Jackson.

Jackson slowly opened a huge scrapbook and set it on the kitchen table. "We pulled all of your old articles and this one caught our attention," he said, pointing to an article about an infant kidnapping. "It seems as though Michael is somehow involved. I am not sure how, but word on the street is he was engaged in some illegal activity with some of Seattle's finest. He handed the scrapbook over to Amara.

She reread her article. "This article has to do with drugs, Dad, not the kidnapping," she said. Jackson pointed to the other page. She read the article. Her face paled as she read. "Mom, Dad, don't you remember this article? I wrote the first article two years ago and the follow-up story almost six months ago. This piece of investigative writing got me my break into the magazine where I am currently working," she said excitedly. She began to recount the events of the article to her parents.

"This whole thing began with an affluent African American and Latino couple, named the Coopers, who had their newborn baby boy kidnapped from the hospital right after he was born. The Coopers paid a one million dollar ransom and their baby was returned to them. When they requested DNA tests to be conducted to make sure the child was theirs, they discovered the infant was not theirs.

"An investigation was immediately conducted at the hospital and it was discovered their baby had died shortly after being born and somehow their infant was swapped with another in the hospital.

"The body of the dead infant was exhumed and was verified to be the corpse of the Cooper's son. The one million dollar ransom was never retrieved. The biological mother of the infant was located and notified. She was a Latino woman who had recently separated from her husband, named Amelia Hernandez.

"The Coopers and Ms. Hernandez went to court in order for the newborn to be legally returned to his mother. The court ordered the Coopers to return the infant to Ms. Hernandez, "Amara paraphrased. "Two days later, Ms. Hernandez' infant son died of Sudden Infant Death Syndrome. After the death of her son, Ms. Hernandez was hospitalized and treated for a nervous breakdown," she said. "Last I heard, she divorced her husband, left Seattle and changed her identity, and started a new life. Mrs. Cooper got pregnant later that year and delivered a healthy infant boy at a private facility on the outskirts of the city."

Jackson rubbed his face and looked at his daughter. "So, what do you think is in this article that would cause someone to want to kill you?" he asked.

46

"I don't know, Dad. But I found out that Michael fathered a child with Amelia, who is now known as Maria Blanco, the police officer who has been handling the case.

"Do you remember the two hospital security guards who got fired because it was discovered during the investigation of the swapped infants that these security guards had obtained illegal access the main computer and had altered prescriptions for narcotic drugs and went to small pharmacies?" she asked. Jackson shook his head.

"I remember that case, they took the prescriptions to pharmacies that did not have the electronic capability to check the validity of the prescription or verify that the prescription had not already been filled by a different pharmacy," said Jackson.

"I later found out the security guards blamed my article for their dismissal. Actually, it was the video tapes that nailed them," she said. "The video cameras captured the two guards breaking into the facility. Their faces were never shown on the camera, but they were wearing their security uniforms. After they were fired, the hospital brought this to the attention of the police department. But since the guards' identity could not be verified, the police officers gave them a warning and monitored them closely.

"To top things off, a wealthy hypochondriac almost died when he overdosed on some pills he purchased off the street. Unfortunately, it could never be proven that these guards were dealing illegal drugs, but I think the police chief always suspected them.

"How do you think Michael is involved?" she asked.

Her dad looked at her. "Do you still have the photos you took the day of the ransom exchange?" he asked.

Amara shook her head. "In fact, they are tucked safely away in a security box at the bank," she said.

"I think you should take a look at those photos more closely. Who knows you have the photos?" he asked.

Amara thought hard and snapped her fingers. "Dad, I only told you, mom, my good friend Shirley from the newspaper, and Paul."

Jackson rubbed his chin. "What are you getting at, Jackson?" asked Myra.

"I think one of those people told someone else who might be involved in the kidnapping of the Cooper's, uh, Amelia's baby. I think you should look at those photos more closely," he said cryptically.

Amara looked at her father. "Thank God I never took any of photos from my articles home. That was the best advice you gave me, Dad," she said, smiling. "Remember, when I first started writing articles independently, you advised me to open a safe deposit box and store all film, photos, tapes, and materials regarding any of my stories there?"

Jackson smiled. "It's the lawyer in me. I can't help myself. Never show your full deck to anyone. Always have a backup plan," he, Amara, and Myra said in unison. Jackson smiled.

Amara kissed her parents and went to her apartment. She made a mental note to go to her deposit box to retrieve the photos that went with the article. "Perhaps the photos will reveal why someone was trying to kill me and how Michael is implicated in all of this?" she said aloud.

Shareese looked at her reflection in her car mirror, smoothed her hair, and repaired her makeup. She got out of the car and walked upstairs and knocked on the door. Paul answered the door and smiled wide with a look of surprise and pleasure. He opened the door and invited Shareese in. "What a nice surprise," he said in a sultry voice. He was shirtless and exposed his muscular chest that was spattered with curly chest hair. His drawstring flannel pajama bottoms clung loosely about his slender waist. Shareese looked him over appreciatively.

"I brought some breakfast," she said gaily as she waved the bag of pastries. Paul smiled and followed her into the kitchen. She set down the bag and gave Paul a quick peck on the lips. Paul spied the duffel bag hanging on her shoulder and looked at her. Shareese smiled and asked, "Did you forget we were suppose to work out together this morning?" Paul slapped his forehead. "I'm sorry, I sure did," he said.

Shareese looked up and saw someone who was a shorter version of Paul standing in the kitchen doorway. He glared at Shareese without speaking. Shareese stopped talking abruptly. "Oh," was all she could muster.

Paul turned and saw his brother enter the room. "Hey, Mike, come on over and meet the woman I've been telling you about," he said. Paul clasped Michael's shoulder and introduced him to Shareese. "Mike, this is my girl Shareese. Shareese, this is my brother, Michael," he said smiling. Shareese shook Michael's hand but avoided his piercing eyes. He shook her hand and quickly released it as if her hand was hot as fire.

Paul, oblivious to the cool exchange, snapped his fingers. "Hey, Mike and I had planned to go to the gym in about half an hour. Why don't we all go together?" he suggested.

Shareese smiled uneasily. "Sure," she stammered. "Where can I change?" she asked.

Paul looked at his brother. "Mike, do you mind if she uses the guest bath?"

Mike nodded. "Not at all. Let me go with you and clean up a bit," he offered.

Michael and Shareese walked into the bedroom and then into the adjoining bath. "Let me clean the sink before you use it," he suggested. Mike began running water into the sink at full force. Paul announced he was going to take a quick shower and change into his workout clothes. He walked into his bedroom, closed the door, and turned on the water in the bathtub for a quick shower.

When Michael saw his brother go into his bedroom, he quickly closed the door to the bathroom. He cupped his hand under her chin and shoved Shareese's body against the bathroom wall. The force jarred her body and nearly knocked the wind out of her. "What the hell are you doing with my brother?" he demanded.

Michael placed his knee between her legs and kept her pinned to the wall. His eyes roamed over her breasts. He began to get hard with desire.

Shareese pushed him away and stared straight into his eyes. "I am using him to get information on those photos you told me about. Remember?" she hissed.

Michael backed away slowly. His eyes softened. "Hey, I'm sorry. When I saw you here, I got a little crazy," he said as he rubbed his head nervously.

Shareese looked into his eyes. She could tell he had recently taken drugs. His eyes were glazed and he was easily agitated. She needed Michael's money. She had spent all the money he had given her and needed more. She knew Paul would not give her any money. He had already told her all of his money was invested in the future of the business. He was useless.

Shareese looked at Michael again. Probably cocaine, she surmised. She smiled. She knew she had the upper hand and took advantage of the situation. She knew his weakness and knew how to get what she wanted from him. She moved her hands down the front of his loose-fitting pajama pants and fondled him. She crushed her body against his, kissed him hard on the mouth, and bit his lip, nearly drawing blood.

"You know he is the one who drove her to the police station," she said in a sultry voice. Michael didn't answer her comment. Instead he unzipped the jacket she was wearing. He knew she was not wearing a shirt underneath. He jerked her bra away from her breasts and roughly sucked on her nipples.

He then hungrily kissed her lips. "How do you know that?" he growled suspiciously. Shareese smiled wickedly and pulled down his pants. She hoisted herself on the counter and he pulled her body onto the edge of the sink as she wrapped her legs around his waist. Michael roughly pushed her legs apart, removed her shorts, and yanked her panties to one side. He opened the drawer under the sink and pulled out a condom. He placed it on his erect penis. She arched her back as he roughly pulled her body toward his and allowed him to take her. The sex was rough and fast. Shareese closed her eyes as Michael grabbed her buttocks and thrust himself in and out of her. He stared at her as she closed her eyes, tilted her head back, and felt a mixture of sexual pleasure and pain.

Now that she knew she would get the money she wanted, she began thinking about how she was going to find out more information from Paul about the photos. She had to get those photos before it was too late. Michael grabbed a handful of her hair and pulled her head toward him and kissed her hard.

Shareese was jerked from her thoughts. She quickly came back to reality. She opened her eyes and looked at Michael. The look on her face was passionless and held no expression. He grinned and kept gyrating. He wanted her to know that this was all about him and his needs. He needed to feel he was in total control of her, the situation, and the sexual encounter. Within minutes he was spent. He pulled out of her, removed the condom, grabbed a towel and turned to wash himself. Without saying a word, he left her disheveled half naked body on the counter and walked out of the bathroom.

The water had filled the sink basin and was beginning to run over. Shareese turned off the water and released a breath of relief. She slowly scooted off the counter, carefully washed herself, and changed into her work-out clothes. When she walked out of the bedroom into the kitchen, Michael roughly grabbed her wrist and pulled her close to his body and whispered, "You may think you are smart, but if you are fucking my brother, consider yourself a dead woman." Shareese snatched her arm away and rubbed the slight bruise on her wrist.

Before she could respond, Paul came in humming a catchy tune and began getting plates for the Danish pastries. Shareese placed a phony smile on her face and busied herself by getting the glasses while Michael took the juice out of the refrigerator. They all sat down and had a quick breakfast.

Paul began telling funny stories of his and Michael's childhood. Shareese laughed so hard, tears streamed down her face. After breakfast, Paul walked over to Shareese and pulled her close. "I am glad you came over," he whispered as he gently kissed her lips. He then pulled her arms up around his neck and Shareese winced in pain. Paul slowly pulled her arms down and examined them. When he saw the small bruise on her wrist he looked at her in surprise. "What happened, Shareese?" he asked.

Shareese tried to hide the pain. "Oh, I accidentally bumped my wrist on the bathroom counter while I was changing," she casually answered.

Paul gently kissed her wrist and went to the freezer and placed a couple of ice cubes in a paper towel. He covered the bruise with the paper towel and enclosed her hand over her wrist. "I think the ice will take down the swelling," he said softly.

"Thank you, sweetheart," she said as she brushed her lips against his. Paul pulled her close and whispered something in her ear. Shareese let out a slight giggle and shooed him away.

Michael slowly sipped his juice while he jealously watched the close interaction between Shareese and Paul. Uh-huh, I will pay Shareese a visit later to make sure she is alone tonight, he thought to himself. He also wanted to find out what was going on between his brother and Shareese, his girlfriend. He nodded his head and smiled. He would talk to his brother and try to dissuade him from dating Shareese. Shareese needed to get information, not sleep with his brother. He didn't understand why she needed to develop a relationship with Paul just to find out about those photos. I'll nip that relationship in the bud quickly, he thought to himself as he finished his Danish.

After their workout at the gym, Paul offered to follow Shareese home, so they could spend some quality time together. Shareese readily agreed.

Michael frowned and shook his head no, but she ignored him and they made plans to go to the movie theater. Shareese looked at Paul and sweetly suggested they return to their respective homes, change and shower, and he pick her up in two hours. Paul agreed and told her he'd check the paper for the show times of the movie they had talked about seeing together. Paul kissed her tenderly and walked her to her car. She turned back and looked at Michael. "It was nice meeting you Michael," she said in a pleasant voice as she waved in his direction. Michael stood at the doorway and tilted his chin in the air as an acknowledgment.

As Shareese drove away, Paul headed into the house. Michael stood at the entrance with his arms crossed. He began asking Paul questions about Shareese. "Paul, man, what do you know about Shareese?" he asked. Paul looked at his brother and took his time answering. Michael always seemed to be jealous of any woman he dated.

Paul sighed and asked pleasantly, "Why do you ask, Mike?"

Michael took a deep breath in order to keep his temper under control. "I just wanted to know. She really doesn't seem like your type," he said. Paul looked at his brother and lifted his eyebrow. He formulated in his mind what he was going to say before he said anything. Paul knew each time they had this discussion it turned into an argument. He didn't want to have an argument with his brother, but he would not allow his brother to question him about who he was seeing. He had gone through the same question and answer issue with Michael when he dated Amara. And he really liked Shareese. She was sweet and thoughtful.

Michael's raised voice broke through his thoughts. He was demanding an answer to his question. Paul shook his head and would not allow his brother to bait him into an argument. "Mike, I have a date in a couple hours and I'm going to take a shower. I really like Shareese and I plan to keep dating her." Paul walked over to the door and held it open for his brother. "Good workout, man, see you later," he said calmly. Michael stomped back to the guestroom and snatched his overnight bag of clothes off the bed. "You will regret your decision," he announced. Paul refused to be baited. Without saying a word, he closed the door and locked it.

"Get a life and a woman," Paul grumbled. He strode over to the stereo and turned on some soothing music. He then checked the clock on the living room wall and smiled in anticipation of seeing Shareese later that day. He whistled to the tunes of the music emanating from his speakers and went to take a shower.

Michael pulled away from the curb in front of his brother's home and drove fast and wildly down the street. Driving fast seemed to clear his head. Luckily there was no traffic on the road. His erratic driving would definitely have caused an accident. He stopped abruptly in front of a nice Tudor home with a neatly trimmed lawn and flowers. He stomped up the stairs and banged on the door with his fist. Shareese opened the door wearing a very short red satin robe. Michael immediately grew excited and grabbed her around the waist as he pushed her further inside the house and kicked the door closed.

Shareese broke away and looked at him. "What do you want Michael," she demanded in an irritating tone. "More rough sex?" she asked sarcastically. Michael looked at his shoes and then into her eyes. He gently pulled her toward him and kissed her softly, first on her bruised wrist and then her lips. "How was that?" he asked in a soothing voice.

Shareese stared at him, her eyes void of all emotion. Michael began to fidget. "Look, I'm sorry. When I saw you with Paul, I just lost it. Forgive me?" he asked as he kissed her tenderly once more.

Shareese smiled and kissed him back. "Just don't ever treat me like that again," she said in a serious tone. "Never," he said as he led her back to the bedroom.

As Michael began to undress, Shareese went to the kitchen and got two glasses of wine. She poured a powdered mixture into Michael's glass and swished the liquid around to dissolve the powder. She then filled her glass with the same fruity red wine. Shareese made sure they drank the wine first.

Michael smiled as he began to feel really mellow and relaxed. He loved the way he felt when he was around Shareese. She always makes me feel so relaxed, he thought as his body sank deeper into her soft mattress. He watched Shareese seductively remove her short satin robe. She was naked underneath. She knew he would come straight over from Paul's house and what he would want. His eyes grew wide with desire. She stepped away from her robe and walked over to the bed. She straddled his body and began to place little kisses all over him.

Michael chuckled as if he were inebriated. "Damn, you've got me drunk with your love, baby," he joked as Shareese initiated the sex. Shareese leaned over to her nightstand and removed a condom from the drawer. She stretched the condom over his hard member. She placed him inside of her and began to rapidly move up and down. She looked down at him as he released a loud yell as he began to climax. The bed seemed to whirl in circles as he lay there. Shareese quickly pulled him out of her, tore off the condom, and carefully placed a plastic vial over his penis as he ejaculated. He couldn't remember ever coming so hard or fast. The feeling consumed him to the point where he was forced to close his eyes and enjoy the climax. Michael was so exhausted he immediately fell asleep.

After she ensured Michael was asleep, Shareese ran into the kitchen and placed a top on the vial. She immediately placed the vial in the freezer. She picked up the phone and pushed the speed dial for Maria's number. When Maria answered the phone she whispered and told her to come over quick and collect the vial. Shareese hung up the phone and quietly went back in the room to get her robe.

She spied on Michael as walked into the living room toward the window. She moved her drapes slightly as she watched for Maria's arrival. Maria arrived at Shareese's house within ten minutes. Shareese saw Maria walk up the steps to her door. She ran and grabbed the vial from the freezer and quietly opened the door. Shareese handed the vial to Maria and kissed her gently on the lips. As they hugged one another Shareese whispered, "Good luck." Maria smiled and placed the vial in a cold padded container and quietly left.

Shareese crossed her fingers. Hopefully, this time Maria will become pregnant, she thought. Shareese then called Paul and told him she would not be able to make their date. She gave an excuse about having to go into the office to help the police chief with some important documents. Paul was very disappointed and did not hide it. "Wow. Okay, I guess. Talk to you later," he said and abruptly hung up the phone before she could respond. Shareese looked at the phone as the dial tone sounded. She shrugged and went back into the bedroom.

She removed her robe and sat naked by Michael. She checked her watch. The drug should be wearing off soon, she thought. "Michael," she cooed softly as she played with his chest hair. She knew from previous times that he really enjoyed it when she played with his chest hair. It seemed to relax him. Once she felt he was lucid she calmly brought up the topic of the hidden money.

"Michael, you were so smart to hide that money where no one would suspect," she said gently. Michael made a sound of acknowledgment. "I mean, who would ever think that you hid the money in your house," she said just above a whisper. "That was really smart, honey," she rattled on. "At first I thought maybe you hid it on your new boat, docked in Puget Sound, but that would be too easy. It's in your house, isn't it?" she whispered. Michael rolled over on top of her and pinned her arms above her head. He kissed her deeply. "I'll never tell," he said in a seductive voice.

He looked into her eyes and drew away from her. "Why all the questions about the money, Shareese? I told you I'd share it with you when the time is right," he said abruptly. Shareese stroked his chest gently and got him to relax again. "I know, honey. I'm on your side, remember?" she asked sweetly. Michael looked at her again and smiled. "I guess you are," he said quietly. Shareese looked him in the eyes before speaking. "Michael, you can trust me. You know I love only you. It was your idea for me to get to know your brother and find out more about the photos his ex-girlfriend had, right?"

Michael nodded his head. "You are right," he said sheepishly. "In fact, you didn't want anything to do with all of this," he said huskily. "I just got so jealous when I saw you two together," he said helplessly. "I really love you and want to marry you," he said.

"Soon, baby, soon we can get married. Paul and I have not been together in that way, Michael. If you like, I will break it off with Paul right away, okay?" she asked.

Michael shook his head and tried to get his bearings. "No, don't do that. He will become suspicious and blame me," he said. Reluctantly Shareese agreed to continue seeing Paul.

Michael sat up in the bed and rubbed his face. Things were coming back into focus and he began to feel much better. Perhaps he was catching the flu, he thought. He bent down and pulled a package out of his pants pocket. It was a ring box. Shareese looked at him, and tried to prepare herself for what she anticipated would come next. Michael got down on one knee and gave her the box. Her hand trembled as she opened it. She held her breath as she slowly opened the box.

She looked inside and saw a one hundred dollar bill shaped in the shape of a ring. Shareese laughed heartily with delight and relief. Michael gazed into her eyes. In a serious tone he said, "Baby, this is my pledge to you that we will spend the rest of our lives enjoying the benefits of one million dollars. I will tell you that you guessed where the money is, but I will not tell you the exact location." Her eyes lit up. Michael thought it was because of his proposal.

Shareese grabbed his face and kissed his lips. "How about a hint?" she pleaded in a small voice.

Michael smiled. "Let's just say, it gets as hot as I do whenever I am around you," he chuckled.

Shareese tried to act calm. She traced the hairs on his chest once again. "Honey, I know you are going to take care of me when we get married, but I need you to take care of now," she said softly. "I need more money. I need to pay my bills," she said as she looked deep into his eyes.

Michael looked annoyed and ran his fingers through his hair. "All right, all right," he said absently. Shareese cooed softly and kissed his lips once more. "Thank you for taking such good care of me," she said in a baby voice. Shareese kissed Michael passionately. Michael groaned and pulled her body on top of his and they made love once again.

Chapter 5

*T*he sounds of crashing waves echoed throughout the quiet office as Sam busily worked to close out some of his cases. He enjoyed coming to work early. There was no one else in the office except him. Clayton and his secretary wouldn't be in for another couple of hours. It gave him time to catch up on cases and to work at his own pace without the nuisance of a ringing phone.

He had completed the update on his latest case and decided to log onto the site he and Amara were on the previous day. As Sam scrolled down he reviewed the charge sheet where Duke Ellington had been convicted of rape twenty-seven years ago. He continued to read down the page and suddenly stopped. He punched in his password into the protected site to reveal the victim's name. The victim's name appeared on the screen. He thought about a conversation he had shared with Amara at the restaurant last week. He read the victim's name again and his mouth fell open.

He printed the page on the screen and escaped out of the site. As he paced back and forth with the pages in his hand, he snapped his fingers. He set the papers on the desk and picked up the phone to call his brother Clayton. The phone rang but there was no answer. Sam cursed under his breath. Clayton must be at Brianna's place, he thought as he checked his watch. It was too early to call her place. He would have to wait and address the issue with him when he got to work.

He stood up and looked outside his window. The city was still asleep. There were few cars on the road and even fewer pedestrians. His heavy breathing fogged the window. He stepped back and watched the moisture from his breath dissipate.

He tapped his head as he tried to think of a resolution to the problem. Do I tell her? he thought to himself. He sat down at his computer and wrote Amara an email note. He read the email to himself and then erased it. If I do tell her, it needs to be in person, he thought. He decided he wouldn't do anything until he discussed the matter with Clayton. He checked his watch again. Clayton would arrive in two more hours. He pulled out some of his unfinished paperwork and busied himself until his brother arrived.

Amara got up early that morning and was first in line at the bank. Her mother stood staunchly by her side, not willing to allow her go anywhere alone until this incident involving Michael Whitman and Duke Ellington was resolved.

Amara looked around and noticed a vehicle with two men sitting inside. It was the same vehicle that had been behind them a couple of miles back. Amara had a strange feeling about these men. Perhaps they are waiting for the bank to open also, she thought. But she realized they were parked on the street instead of in the bank parking lot. She thought it strange that two men were just sitting in a parked car, one was reading a newspaper and the other was eating a breakfast sandwich.

Her instincts took over and she returned to her car parked in the lot and removed her camera. She attached her zoom lens and snapped their picture. The man eating the breakfast sandwich tapped his partner reading the newspaper. The man sitting in the driver's seat immediately put the newspaper down and started the car. Amara focused her camera and snapped again. As they zoomed past, she snapped a picture of their license plate.

Amara's mother looked at her with worry in her eyes. Amara rubbed her mom's back. "Don't worry, Mom. That was just for some insurance. I will send these pictures to a friend of mine and see what she can find out." Myra relaxed and smiled at her daughter. When the bank opened, they both went inside. Amara opened her security deposit box and removed the photos that were related to the kidnapping and ransom article she had written.

She took out her magnifying glass and carefully went over the photos. As she looked at one of the photos more closely she spotted four figures but they were too far away to ascertain their identity. The second photo was of someone either taking something or leaving something at the ransom drop-off point and the last photo had five figures scattered in different positions and a lone figure by a car farther in the distance.

She placed the photos and the disk in an envelope. She also removed the small disk out of her camera and carefully placed it in her pocket. "I want to have these blown up," Amara said. "I am glad I made extra prints of this photo. "She counted them out on the counter. I have two sets."

Myra smiled at her daughter. "Give me one set and take me by my bank. I will put this one in my security deposit box. Mine is fire proof, you know," said Myra as she placed the photos inside her jacket pocket. Amara smiled at her mother and gave her a quick hug. Amara placed the small envelope containing the photos and the disk into her purse. "Let's get out of here," she said.

The women wasted no time getting into the car. Amara called her close friend Shirley and explained that all of her photo developing equipment had been destroyed. She asked her if she would enlarge some photos for her.

Shirley readily agreed and told her to drop it by her home. "Someone may be following us. I will leave it in our secret place like the old days," said Amara. She and Shirley used to cover stories together. Shirley was a professional journalist and photographer as well. Shirley laughed. "High adventure, huh? Got it. I will pick it up soon," she said.

Amara thanked her and drove to her mother's bank. Myra placed the photos in her security box and resealed it. She returned it to its shelf and left the private room. Amara waited in the lobby to ensure the gentlemen in the car had not followed them. Myra came out and walked toward her daughter. "Hungry?" she asked her daughter. Amara shook her head yes. "Let's go get something to eat," she said. "Hey, how about lunch at your aunt's restaurant? It is walking distance from here. It has a huge picture window so we can enjoy the view," she said.

Amara laughed aloud. "I think you are getting into this too much Mom. This could be dangerous you know. If Michael was willing to have me killed and my home ransacked, then he is capable of doing anything," she said.

Myra smiled. "We will be safe at Sarah's," she said.

On the way to the restaurant, Amara asked her mother to stop at the neighborhood video store. Amara went to the comedy section and pulled out her favorite comedy video. She inconspicuously slipped the items into the video jacket and took the video up to the front counter and requested the video be placed on hold for two hours. The cashier smiled and placed the video under the counter with the other video holds for the day. "Have a great day, Amara!" said the clerk, smiling.

Myra looked at her daughter. "Come here often?" she asked. Amara smiled. "I used to," she answered.

When Myra and Amara opened the door to the café, the breeze caused the colorfully potted ferns hanging from the ceiling to swing lazily to and fro. A hostess greeted them with a polite smile and led them to their seats. She was dressed in a bright multicolored shirt with "Sarah's" embroidered in white on the front pocket with khaki slacks. Amara looked at her mother and they both smiled. They both enjoyed eating at Sarah's because of the wonderful atmosphere. The restaurant was bright and airy and the food was delicious. Each meal was made to look attractive on the brightly colored plate and the taste was even better. Sarah showcased different artists' pottery in the form of plates. The artist's work would be placed in the small glass showcase with a small placard bearing the artist's name in the small foyer at the entrance. Customers could purchase the plate their food was served on and others if they chose to.

The natural light from the skylights made the entire restaurant seem bright and yet tranquil. The large picture windows strategically placed throughout the place, along with fresh ferns that hung freely, added to the relaxed atmosphere and easy conversation. Sarah's staff was painstakingly selected and specially trained to make each patron feel as if they were the only ones in the restaurant. The service was rated superb in all the local newspapers. Sarah had succeeded in creating an atmosphere of relaxation and eating pleasure.

Sarah came out of the kitchen and greeted them both with big hugs and kisses. "Hey, Auntie Sarah," said Amara. Sarah Miles was Myra's younger sister. "It is so good to see you both!" Sarah said happily. Amara smiled at her aunt. Sarah had no children of her own and she treated Amara as if she were her daughter. They were very close and for as long as she could remember Sarah had always been a pleasant and positive person.

She had opened her restaurant five years ago on the south side of Seattle and it had done very well from the day she opened the front doors. Sarah was genuinely nice and charismatic. She was an excellent listener who was non-judgmental. People from all walks of life frequented her establishment, from the wealthy to the homeless. All were welcome and somehow she made the combination work.

Amara smiled as she looked around the restaurant. Nowhere else would you find one women dressed in Gucci and another dressed in old rags, sitting only tables apart, each enjoying an affordable yet exquisite meal. She served a variety of food from quiche to collard greens. She also experimented with different types of ethnic foods from different countries. Her theme nights were renowned and the line would stretch around the restaurant on those nights.

Her tableware was colorful and gay to match her personality. She had even been featured in the popular Seattle newspaper, written up by none other than her niece, Amara. Amara examined a new photo that was colorfully framed and hanging on the wall. The photo was of Sarah and a famous actress who had recently visited her restaurant.

Once their order had been taken, Sarah poured herself a glass of water, placed a wedge of lemon on the side of the glass, and joined her niece and sister. "So ladies, what's new?" Myra pursed her lips but said nothing. Amara bent her head toward her aunt and spoke in a hushed voice. Sarah's eyes grew wide when Amara told her who was trying to kill her. Her eyes filled with tears and she promptly excused herself.

Amara looked at her mom. "She is taking this a lot harder than I thought," Amara said as she sipped her diet cola. Myra remained silent, twirling her straw in her root beer, but not taking a sip. Out of the corner of her eye, Myra saw her sister signaling for her to meet her. Myra excused herself and walked over to her sister. They began talking simultaneously in hushed voices.

Amara looked over at them and didn't like the facial expressions she saw. She got up and walked over to them. "You need to tell her," Sarah whispered.

"No, it's better that we say nothing," retorted Myra.

Amara walked over to her mom. "Say nothing about what, Mom?" she asked. Amara looked at her mother and aunt and folded her arms over her chest.

Myra took a deep breath. "Look, honey, our food is ready. Let's go eat," she suggested.

Sarah smiled and hugged her niece. "Don't worry about me. I am just really worried about you. Please take care of yourself. All right?" she asked. Amara said she would and gave her aunt a big hug. She then took her mother's hand and went back to the table. Sarah rejoined them and had everyone laughing about a funny story involving one of her regular customers.

After lunch Amara and her mother left and headed back to the video store. The clerk handed her the tape and told her to enjoy the movie. Two gentlemen in the back watched Amara leave and began to follow her. As the men reached the door, the clerk pushed the button that caused the door to beep noisily. She walked over to the two men and asked them if they had mistakenly taken a video. Both denied taking a video. She held them in conversation a bit longer, giving Amara and her mother time to get to their vehicle and drive away. Frustrated, the two men walked past the clerk, who apologized profusely for the delay. By the time they got outside the video shop Amara and her mother were no longer in the area.

One of the men stomped his foot and walked to their vehicle, clearly agitated. He made a phone call and left the area.

The clerk smiled, retracted the portable antenna, and replayed the tape. "We lost her, boss. We will check her residence," said the voice on the tape. The clerk blew on her knuckles. "Shirley, you haven't lost your touch," she bragged to herself. She then phoned Amara's cell phone and spoke in code. "Did you already take the roasted chicken home for dinner?" she asked.

Amara caught on immediately. It was a game they used to play when they covered stories together and thought someone was listening to their conversation. "Not yet. I need to stop and get some pudding first," she responded.

Shirley laughed. "Well, make sure it's chocolate," she said with a slight southern lilt.

"Hey, since you are coming to dinner, can you bring a bigger roast than you did last time?" asked Amara.

"I could, but you'd have to delay your dinner party for a couple of nights," she said cryptically. Amara agreed to reschedule the dinner party for a couple of days and hung up the phone.

"We are either being followed, or those guys we saw today are hanging around the house. We need to stall for awhile and let Dad know to be alert," she said.

"No problem," smiled her mother.

"Shirley should have my photos blown up in a couple of days. I'd like to get a better look at the figure by the ransom location and by the car. I think it may be Michael, but I want to be sure," said Amara as she dialed her dad's cell phone. She left a text message and hung up.

Her father heard the phone ring, read the text message, and went into action. The message read, "Beware, two guys might be snooping around the house. Be careful." Jackson quietly went around his house with a baseball bat when he saw two gentlemen bent over the phone line that was attached to his house.

Myra continued to drive as Amara pulled the photos from the enveloped and examined them closer. She chastised herself for not using a better lens that would have photographed the people and the objects larger and clearer. She couldn't take all the lenses she needed because she had had to climb that darn tree. She sighed and leaned her head back fully onto the headrest.

Myra looked over at Amara and quickly placed her full attention back on the road. "So what do you think Michael has to do with this?" asked Myra. "Do you think he had something to do with that poor baby's disappearance?" she asked fretfully.

Amara turned her head and looked at her mother. "I don't know, Mom," she responded. "I am glad I asked Shirley to develop all the pictures on the disk," said Amara, deep in thought.

"So am I, honey," said her mother in a sorrowful tone of voice. She was thinking of the circumstances surrounding the kidnapping of the infant from the hospital and the death of the couple's real baby.

Amara fell silent as she tried to piece the story together while her mother concentrated on driving. Amara turned the radio on and they listened to the mellow sounds of Nat King Cole as he serenaded them the rest of the way home.

Jackson tapped his bat loudly against his open palm. "May I help you, gentlemen?" asked Jackson. "I have already called the police," he announced. Jackson continued to tap his bat against his hand as held his stare on their bent bodies. The two men stood nervously. Even though Jackson was in his mid-fifties, he was still muscular and stood six foot four. His large hand made the end of the bat disappear as he continued to slap the bat against his palm and look at the two men with anger and disgust in his eyes.

"Take whatever you have on my phone line off," he demanded in a steady voice. "You have messed with the wrong man this time. I have already called the police department and you have no authorization to be here." The two men removed the bug as their phone rang. One of the gentlemen answered the phone. The officer spent the entire time on the phone responding to the captain's litany of questions. "Yes, sir. No, sir. Will do, Captain. Yes, sir. Goodbye, sir." When the officer hung up the phone, his face was beet red. Although he didn't apologize, he asked Jackson to excuse the intrusion. It was a case of mistaken residence, he replied. Jackson shook his head and glared at them in disbelief. He escorted the two men off his property and told them he planned to file a formal complaint tomorrow. They quickly got into their vehicle and drove away.

Once the car was out of sight, Jackson went back and checked his phone line for any other foreign objects that could be a detection device. He knelt down and traced the line into the dirt, about three inches into the soft soil. He felt something on the line and quickly dug around it. After examining the object that was clamped on his line, he pulled it away, taking care not to damage the line. He carefully placed it in a Kleenex and stuck it inside his pant pocket. He walked into the house and retrieved his keys and sports jacket. He got into his car and drove over to the police station to visit Chief Chaddam.

By the time he reached the police station, Jackson had calmed down considerably. He walked up to the desk and they phoned the chief's office. "He is expecting you. Go right up," said the police officer. Jackson thanked him and walked over to the elevator. He pushed the button and the elevator immediately opened. Jackson walked inside and pushed the button for the tenth floor. As the door closed and the elevator began to rise, he released an anxious breath. He wanted this whole ordeal to be over with. He did not appreciate anyone messing with him or his family. He knew the law and he wasn't going to let these police officers get away with tapping his line. He was confident he would get support from Chief Chaddam.

He looked up as the number ten lit up on the top panel and the elevator doors quietly slid open. Jackson walked down the hall and stopped at the secretary's desk. Shareese looked up and smiled. "Mr. Glenton, the chief is expecting you. Please go in," she said. Jackson nodded politely and walked over to the opened door. Tom Chaddam saw Jackson and waved him in. "Come on in, Jackson," he said. Jackson walked inside and closed the office door.

Once the door closed. Shareese's smiled faded. She got nervous. Michael's plan hadn't worked. She hated amateurs. Those bozos he was working with were total amateurs. She tried to eavesdrop, but she couldn't hear anything. She turned on the intercom and listened intently. "Shareese, you've hit the intercom button. Could you please turn it off?" asked the chief. Shareese stopped typing. "Sorry, sir," she said and switched off the intercom as instructed.

Jackson dug into his pocket and pulled out the gadget he had taken off his phone wire. He handed it to the chief. The chief slipped his reading glasses on and got a closer look. "This isn't one of ours. But that doesn't mean they just didn't go out and buy one off the street," he said as he continued to examine it.

"I plan to make a formal complaint against those two officers," said Jackson sternly.

Chief Chaddam looked at his friend. "That is certainly within your rights. I am really sorry about this, Jackson," he said. Jackson didn't know how much to tell him about what was going on, so he kept quiet. Chaddam interrupted the silence. "I know exactly who these police officers are and I will personally take corrective action," said Chaddam.

Satisfied with his response, Jackson rose to leave. Chaddam rose and shook his hand. "I am glad you came by," he said. Chaddam held the small device in the palm of his hand. "May I keep this?" he asked.

"Sure," said Jackson as he headed for the door.

Chaddam opened the door and the two men shook hands. "Thanks for seeing me on such short notice, Tom," said Jackson.

"Anytime, Jackson. Hey, you still owe me a game of golf. When are we going to play?" he asked.

Jackson smiled. "Whenever you are ready for another whipping on the course," he joked.

Chaddam laughed. "I will give you a call soon. We had a bizarre murder a few days ago and it has been really crazy around here," he said.

Jackson shook his head in acknowledgment. "I read a little bit about it in the newspaper," said Jackson. "Were the hands of the victim really severed?" he asked.

The chief shook his head yes. "Have a good evening, Jackson," said Chaddam. The two men shook hands again and Jackson left the office.

Shareese continued to type at her desk. She didn't look up. Chaddam frowned. He placed his glasses on top of his head and looked at Shareese. "Make sure you submit a work request to get that darn intercom repaired today," he growled.

"Yes sir," said Shareese as her fingers continued to swiftly move across her keyboard.

Chaddam walked back into his office and closed the door. He sat down at his desk and looked at the small device Jackson had given him. He thought about the two officers involved. He had had problems with these two officers in the past. This would be enough to suspend them and possibly get them off the force for good. The police chief smiled, leaned back in his seat, and placed his hands behind his head. "Two bad apples on their way out," he said aloud.

Jackson exited the elevator and walked into the lobby area. Before he left the station he filled out a formal complaint on the two police officers. After he had completed the form, he submitted it to the appropriate office and left. He walked to his car, got in, and drove toward home.

Sam gathered the papers he had printed earlier that morning. He read the information once more. He stacked the pages neatly and walked to his brother's office. Clayton was finishing up an appointment with a client when he saw Sam standing outside of his glass door. Sam was pacing back and forth nervously. Clayton shook his client's hand and walked him to the door.

When his client had left, Clayton motioned for Sam to come inside his office. Sam walked in past Clayton and stood uneasily in the middle of his office. Clayton came and stood beside him. Sam handed Clayton the papers he was holding and began pacing around the office. Clayton quickly scanned the papers and stopped reading abruptly and stared at his brother. Sam had a worried look on his face. "What do I do, bro?" he asked.

Clayton blew out his breath nervously. He then reread the paper. "I think you should notify Amara," he said.

Sam looked down at the carpet. "I don't think I can. This information would devastate her, Clay. I don't think she knows."

Clayton looked at his brother. His brow was furrowed with concern. Clayton placed his hand on his brother's shoulder. "Let's have a seat and develop a plan of action," he said gently. Sam's head hung in frustration as he followed his brother to the sofa.

When Myra and Amara walked into the house they saw Jackson pacing back and forth in the kitchen. It was clear that he was agitated. Myra walked up to Jackson. "Jack, honey what happened?" she asked.

"After I chased those yahoos off our property I found another device on our line. I went and talked to the chief about it. He said he'd take care of it. If I didn't know any better, he seemed happy that I caught them. Like he wanted to get rid of them," he said.

Myra hugged her husband. She saw the bat in the corner. "Jackson! You took that bat out with you?" she asked, with annoyance in her voice.

Jackson shook his head like a small child who had just been chastised. "Yeah, I know, that was not a smart move. I allowed my anger to get the best of me," he said quietly.

"I am just glad you weren't hurt," she said as she hugged him close.

"I made a formal complaint when I went down to the station," he said calmly.

He looked at his wife and daughter. He was glad they were home safe. He smiled.

"What are you smiling at?" asked Amara.

"I am just glad you two are home safe," he said.

"Group hug!" yelled Amara as she rushed upon her parents and gave them both a hug.

Chapter 6

$\mathcal{M}$ ichael cut his engine and coasted toward the curb and stopped at Shareese's house. It was close to midnight. He opened a vial that contained a white powdery substance and quickly took a snort. He then stared at the house. It appeared to be quiet. He got out of his car and quietly walked to Shareese's backyard. He stooped his body and walked gingerly over to her bedroom window and peered inside.

Shareese heard the shrill beep of her motion detector and asked her lover to check it out. She heard the rustling of grass in the backyard and attempted to ignore the intrusion and act normally. "It's Michael," her mate whispered loudly. Her mate tiptoed back into the living room where she could keep an eye on Michael's car.

When Michael peered in the window, he saw Shareese on her bed, partially naked, with a towel wrapped around her hair and another covering her lap as she painted her toenails and watched a video on television. After she finished polishing the last toe on her right foot, she stopped and took a sip of her sweet wine from a chilled crystal wine goblet.

Satisfied that she was home alone, Michael walked back to the front yard and got into his car. He started the engine and immediately drove off. Shareese heard the car pull away. Her mate walked over to the window and closed her bedroom drapes. Shareese put the polish away and finished the last of her wine. "He's gone," said her lover and padded over to the bed wearing an oversized bath towel.

She walked over to the nightstand and poured herself a glass of wine and kissed Shareese on the lips. "Smart move getting the motion detectors for your yard and house," she said as she placed her body against Shareese. Shareese smiled and gently rubbed her nose against hers. She stroked Shareese's face and spoke quietly. "Well, did you find out where he hid the money?" she asked in a slight whisper.

Shareese shook her head. Next she opened her drawer and pulled out a velvet ring box. She opened the ring box and placed the one hundred dollar ring on her lover's finger. "That man owes me more than a measly hundred bucks! He owes me the child he stole from me!" she said angrily. She began to curse in Spanish. Shareese stroked her face softly. "It's okay, honey. I have an idea where the money is and I have a plan to get to it. When we finally get the money we can leave this place for good!" she said triumphantly. The woman happily agreed. Shareese spread travel brochures over the bed and ran her fingers through them.

"We are too close to stop now," Shareese told her. "We need to start planning our getaway," she said in a deliberate tone. "I was thinking about Europe. How do you feel about living in Europe?" Shareese asked. Her lover looked at her with doubt in her eyes. "That is too far. I don't want to be that far from my sister," she said nervously.

Shareese tried to reassure her so that she wouldn't panic and ruin everything. "Don't worry, baby. We will decide together where we want to live and I will find out what we need to know. Michael is too stupid to realize anything," she said flippantly. "I have him under total control. He is wrapped around this little finger," she laughed as she held up her pinky finger.

Her lover joined her in laughter. "Yeah, except for his explosive temper, he is pretty easy to handle," she reminisced. Shareese kissed her passionately.

"Now all we have to do is get you pregnant by Michael so you can claim your child's trust fund from his dear old dad," said Shareese quietly.

Her lover shook her head. "Those last two inseminations didn't work and I am waiting for the results of the most recent insemination. I really want a baby," she said disappointedly.

"This is going to work. Trust me. You will get your baby and we will have more money than we ever dreamed of. Trust me," said Shareese seductively.

They set their wine glasses on the nightstand and turned off the lamp. Her lover pushed the brochures to the floor. Shareese caressed her lover's toned body gently and whispered her name softly into her ear, "Amelia," until she was fully relaxed. Her lover whispered back into her ear and said, "Call me Maria. Amelia is dead." Shareese giggled and they held each other close and made sweet, gentle love throughout the night.

Amara examined her reflection in the mirror as she dressed for work. She had decided it was time for her to return. Keeping busy would take her mind off her current situation. Her father had insisted on taking her to work and her mother insisted on picking her up after work. She was angry at first, but now the idea didn't seem so bad. Amara smiled as she brushed her hair into place. Her navy suit was a bit conservative, but it looked very nice with the beautiful new fuchsia blouse her mother had purchased for her. As she placed her earrings in her ear lobes, Amara's cell phone rang. She pulled her cell phone out of her purse and answered it. Amara smiled when she recognized the voice on the phone. It was her good friend Shirley, who she had given the photo and the disk that contained the film.

"Hey, Shirley. Were you able to get everything accomplished?" she asked cryptically.

"Yes," Shirley answered. "Are you free for lunch? I'd like to talk to you about the roast I am making. I'll bring my cookbook and we can catch up on old times," she said. Shirley and Amara made a lunch date for Sarah's Café. "See you there," said Shirley. "Okay, see you for lunch," responded Amara.

Amara canceled the call with Shirley and dialed her friend Tammy's number. The phone rang several times and then she received a recorded message that her phone had been disconnected. Concerned that she couldn't contact her friend, Amara made a mental note to stop by Tammy's apartment on her way to work.

Jackson knocked on the door. Amara answered it. "You ready to go to work, Pumpkin?" he asked. Amara nodded yes and grabbed her briefcase and cell phone. "Dad, could we stop by Tammy's on the way?" she asked. Jackson looked at his watch and told her that would be fine.

When they got to Tammy's apartment, they saw a big moving truck and Tammy was standing on the lawn dressed casually in jeans and a t-shirt. Tammy spotted Amara and ran over to her. "Thank God you are okay," she said with tears in her eyes.

"What's wrong? Where are you moving to?" asked Amara. Tammy took a deep breath. "I got a new job in Ohio and will be transferring there next month. I thought I'd go ahead and make the move early. Mari, I started getting a lot of threatening calls and my car was vandalized two days ago," she said sadly. "Someone also broke into my house, but all that was stolen was my camera and photo albums. Things you can't quickly replace," she said fighting back the tears.

Amara hugged her friend tightly. Tammy continued, "I was going to call you but I have been very busy and honestly scared. So, I will be at my mom's tonight and I will fly to Ohio tomorrow."

Amara began to cry as she hugged her friend once more. "You have been my lifeline here. I am really going to miss you."

Tammy's tears slid down her cheeks as she hugged Amara back. "Mari, I will call and give you my new number and address soon, all right?"

Amara noticed a man carrying some of Tammy's belongings to the van. He stood out because he was wearing a white dress shirt, tie, and slacks. He nodded in Amara's direction as he walked to the van carrying an oversized box. Amara smiled. She remembered he was the man who was at the club with them that night.

She hung her head low and slowly turned to walk toward her father's car. She got in and dried her tears with the Kleenex her father always kept in the glove box. Jackson looked at his daughter and waited for her to speak. "Someone broke into her house and vandalized her car. She also got a new job in Ohio. She's leaving tomorrow," sniffed Amara.

Jackson patted his daughter's hand. "I know you will miss Tammy, Mari. But, be happy that she has found a better job and she'll feel safer also," he said.

"Dad, it's because of me that all this happened," Amara cried.

Jackson shook his head. "You don't know that, Mari. Let's get you to work. I don't want you to be late your first day back," said Jackson as he put the car in gear and drove away.

Amara's first day at work was pretty uneventful. Several of the staff members stopped by her cubicle to check on her. She was glad she didn't have a lot to do because she was terribly distracted by everything that was going on. She continued to search for more information on the Internet. She pulled out Sam's card and sent him an email, so he could contact her in case he needed to send her some new information regarding her situation.

She didn't want to talk to or see Sam anytime soon. Her emotions were too raw and the mixed signals she received from him didn't help matters. She still didn't know why he had met her at the airport after he had openly professed his love for Franni. She chastised herself for allowing him to kiss her. "Men," she scoffed aloud.

Amara checked her watch and saw it was time for lunch. She called a cab and waited for it in front of the building. Amara arrived at the restaurant first. Sarah had reserved a small table in the corner where they could talk and not be disturbed. Amara sipped hot tea while she waited. Shirley spotted Amara when she walked into the restaurant and joined her at the table.

Shirley was a short woman who barely cleared five feet. She was slightly plump and had light freckles sprinkled across the bridge of her nose. Her wavy strawberry blond hair fell loosely about her shoulders. Shirley's large blue eyes sparkled when she saw Amara sitting in the corner. "Hey, Mari! It's great to see you again. It's been quite a while," said Shirley as she sat down.

"It sure has, Shirley," said Amara. "How's work going?" asked Amara.

Shirley adjusted her glasses. "Though I really miss you, it is going great! I have been doing some investigative pieces and I am having a lot of fun!" she said, with her voice full of excitement.

"That's great," said Amara smiling.

She was really happy for her friend. Shirley was an extremely hard worker and deserved the challenging assignments she had been given. "I loved that piece you did on the fugitive last week," said Amara. Shirley blushed and quietly thanked Amara for the compliment.

Shirley leaned forward in her seat and told Amara she had the photos. Amara looked at her anxiously. She pulled a large envelope out of her handbag and handed it to Amara. Amara opened the envelope and pulled the photos out one by one. She examined each photo closely. "I was right," she whispered. "Look at this picture. How could I have overlooked this!" she exclaimed. "Remember the drop-off for the ransom?" she whispered to Shirley.

"Yes I do," said Shirley quietly. "I wasn't suppose to be there, but I picked up the location off the scanner and used my weakest telephoto lens because I had to climb that darn tree," she said.

Shirley pushed her wavy strawberry blond hair out of her face and smiled. "Amara, I swear, you are such a tomboy," she joked as she picked up the menu and read the specials for the day. The waitress approached and Amara quickly put the photos back in the envelope and placed the envelope on her lap. They gave the waitress their order and she left the table to get their drinks.

Amara picked up one photo and set it on the table. She opened her purse and removed a mini-magnifying glass that was shaped like a pot of lip-gloss. She took off the cap and placed the glass over one of the figures in the photo in order to examine the photo more closely. "Shirley, there is no doubt about it. That is Michael taking the briefcase with the money while the jogger," she said as she pointed at the other figure in the photo, "provided a distraction."

"Didn't they arrest that guy?" asked Shirley.

"Yes," answered Amara. "In fact, it turned out that he was an actor. I did a bit of research and discovered someone had made arrangements through his agent and paid him one thousand dollars to participate in what he thought was a screen test for an upcoming movie," said Amara. Amara turned the pictures over as the waitress walked to their table and set down their drinks. She smiled and quietly walked back to the kitchen.

"Wow," said Shirley as she took a sip of her diet soda, "For one thousand dollars, I would jog amongst police and knock over a garbage can too!" Amara laughed and picked up one of the other photos and examined it. The photo contained several people and two police officers in uniform.

"One of those cops had to be in on it," said Amara skeptically. "Michael should have never been allowed to be at the drop-off point. I can't believe none of those police officers noticed the swap of the briefcase," she said.

Shirley looked at Amara and provided another point of view. "Mari, if you recall, you didn't notice the briefcase swap either. And you were taking pictures," she pointed out.

Amara sighed. "Yes, you're right. It happened so fast, that I never even noticed, especially when that actor caused the distraction," she said. "Luckily I kept my eye on this guy," she said pointing at Michael's figure in the photo. "No one else saw him during all the confusion. And look at this," she said pushing the third photo toward Shirley. "Who is that person over there in the dark outfit?" Shirley picked up the photo and placed the small magnifying piece to her eye in order to get a closer look.

Shirley shrugged. "Don't know, Mari. It is definitely a woman, but with the glasses and scarf, it's hard to make out her facial features. The glasses and scarf look out of place with the oversized shirt and pants she's wearing," she said as she handed the photo back to Amara.

Amara examined the photo again. "Those baggy clothes really make it hard to tell how big or small she is," sighed Amara.

Amara placed the photo back in the envelope and pulled out another photo. "Look!" Amara said excitedly.

Shirley leaned over and examined the photo. "It looks as if one of the officers is placing something in his pocket," said Shirley. "He was the officer closest to the man who I think is Michael," said Amara as she flipped to the next photo. "Here is an earlier picture of the Coopers at a press conference. That also looks like Michael standing in the background and it looks like he was placing something in the police officer's hand or shaking it. I really can't tell," she said, frustrated by the whole ordeal.

Amara then tried to surmise the chain of events based on the pictures she had. "So, this plainclothes police officer drops off the money at the appointed time. The actor somehow gets through the tight security and jogs toward the garbage can and tips it over," said Amara.

"During the confusion, a man resembling Michael appears, picks up the briefcase, and leaves a similar one in the exact location where the original briefcase was placed," said Shirley as she flipped to the next photo.

"Somehow this woman is involved," said Amara pointing at the mysterious figure.

"Perhaps she's there to help Michael's getaway," speculated Shirley.

Amara nodded in agreement. "You may be on to something," said Amara, smiling.

"This photo needs to be enlarged more in order to see the license plate number," said Shirley.

"Can you do that without distorting the photo more than it already is?" asked Amara.

Shirley shook her head. "I'm not sure, Mari. They are already blown up quite a bit. I think if they are enlarged anymore, you won't get any more detail from the photos, in fact, it may distort them," she stated. Amara nodded in agreement.

Just then Amara's eyes brightened. "I can take these photos to the Chief Chaddam first thing tomorrow," she said as she tucked them back in the envelope.

"At least we will know who the vehicle belongs to," said Shirley.

"If it's not a rental or stolen," remarked Amara pessimistically. Both women went silent as the smiling waitress approached their table with their food and refreshed their drinks.

As they ate their food Amara continued to mull over the chain of events that transpired while she was taking photos. She munched on her salad and posed a question to Shirley. "Shirley, how on earth did Michael get through all the tight security? How did the actor get in close enough to knock over a garbage can? Why weren't the police on the other side of the park where the lady and the car were located?" Shirley thought about the questions Amara asked as she continued to eat.

Shirley waved a french fry in Amara's direction. "How on earth did they get away undetected? If it hadn't been for your photos, none of this could be proven," she said as she chomped down on her fry. Shirley wiped her greasy hands with a towelette and asked to see the photos. Amara handed her the envelope containing the photos.

Shirley pulled out one of the photos and pointed at the two police officers. "Don't these officers resemble the two police officers who were fired from the hospital and suspended from the force because of your article?" she asked.

Amara turned the photo over when the waitress returned to refresh their drinks. Once the waitress departed, Amara turned the picture over and examined it closer. "You are right, Shirley!" she said in a hushed voice. "Look how they are standing. If you were standing in front of them like those police were, the view would be obstructed," she said.

Shirley grabbed another french fry and took a small bite. "Didn't you tell me the kidnapper demanded everyone stay on one side of the park?" she asked.

"Your memory is phenomenal," said Amara.

"Because of that demand, no one had a complete view of the area," Shirley said deductively. "Except you, Amara. You were high enough in the tree to have a clear view of the whole area and be totally unnoticed. Since the extortionist demanded no one be on that side of the park, there was really no way anyone could see Michael or this woman. And you were camouflaged in the tree, so no one ever noticed you. I mean you were about fifty feet up in that tree. You were really brave," said Shirley.

Amara smiled. "I wasn't brave, just desperate, and I could have jeopardized the whole deal if I had been seen," she said sadly.

Shirley patted her hand. "Stop beating yourself up," she said.

Amara nodded in agreement. "You're right, Shirley. I think the police chief will know what to do with these photos. He's also a friend of my dad's," she said absently. Amara was still thinking about the photos and what actually took place at the park. She looked at the other photos and examined the men closest to the briefcase and sighed. "What am I missing?" she asked aloud. Shirley shrugged her shoulders.

Shirley then frowned and posed another question. "Hey, didn't you tell me these guys worked in narcotics?" asked Shirley.

"Yeah, so?" asked Amara.

Shirley bit another French fry and took a sip of her soft drink before responding. "Why would narcotics police officers be involved in a kidnapping case?" she asked. Amara stared at her without responding. "Perhaps they weren't suppose to be there in the first place," she said grinning.

"This is getting better every moment," Amara said as she took another bite of her salad. Shirley stacked the photos in a neat pile and placed them all in the envelope. Amara placed the envelope inside her purse. She then looked at her friend Shirley and began to chat about the recent events in their lives and enjoyed the rest of their lunch.

After work, Amara called the police chief and asked if she could see him. He told her to come right away because he had a big meeting to attend with the mayor. Amara walked the few blocks to the police station. She rode the elevator up to the tenth floor. She walked into the executive area toward the police chief's office. Amara told the secretary who she was and she told her to go right in.

Amara walked into his office and asked if she could close the door. Chief Chaddam stopped and looked at her. "Sure, close the door, Mari. This must be serious."

"Sir, I have some photos I'd like to show you," Amara said, as she pulled the envelope from her soft leather briefcase. She held the envelope out to the police chief. The police chief quickly took the envelope that contained the photos. He glanced at his watch and stood up and apologized for not having the time to go over them with her. "I will review them after my meeting and give you a call," he said. Amara looked anxious, but told him she understood.

Chief Chaddam placed the sealed envelope on his desk and walked out of his office. His secretary was standing by her desk straightening some papers. He told his secretary to lock his door and he'd be back in one hour, after the meeting. He instructed her to allow no one in his office while he was away. Shareese acknowledged his order and handed him the notes for his next meeting. Amara smiled at the secretary and shook Police Chief Chaddam's hand. "Thank you sir," she said as she left the office with the police chief.

After they had departed, Shareese walked to her boss's office to lock the door as instructed. Curiosity got the best of her. She opened the door, walked over to the desk and saw the sealed envelope. Her hand shook as she picked up the envelope from the Chief's desk and held it up to the light. These might be the photos Paul told me about, she thought. She had to check them out to make sure. Shareese went to the door and looked around. She quietly stepped back into the chief's office and walked over to his desk. She picked up the envelope containing the photos and placed them inside her suit jacket. She gently closed and locked the door and walked over to her desk. She looked around once more to make sure no one was in her area. She pulled the envelope out of her jacket and slipped it into a manila file folder. She retrieved her sharp letter opener from her desk drawer and cut along the sealed portion of the envelope.

She slowly removed the photos and examined them closely. She flipped through the first two and suddenly stopped at the third photo. "That sneaky little witch," she spat under her breath. This photo is very incriminating, she thought as she closely examined the somewhat blurred photo. She pulled the photo from the manila folder and took a closer look.

She got up from her desk and casually closed the folder that contained the photos. She placed some papers on top of the folder and walked over to the compact shredder in her office. She turned on the shredder. The machine quietly idled as she programmed in the type of paper to be shredded. She selected photos. The size of the teeth changed to accommodate the choice made.

Shareese quickly opened the folder and started shredding the photos. She held her breath as the sharp teeth ground the paper into fine particles. She began to place the last photo in the shredder and stopped. Instead, she quickly folded the photo in half and stuck it in her pocket.

She shredded the blank sheets she had placed on top of the photos for good measure. When the job was completed, she turned off the shredder, reset the settings, and calmly walked back to her desk with a smile on her face. No one messes with me or my man, she thought to herself as she returned to her desk. She pulled out her notebook and began to type one of the chief's memos he had dictated earlier that day.

Mr. Jenkins, the janitor quietly wheeled his cart across the floor. "Hey, Ms. Miller, how are ya doing today?" he asked.

Startled, Shareese jumped and grabbed her heart. She glared at the man who spoke and then broke out in a sweet smile when she recognized who it was. "Hey, Mr. Jenkins! I have something for you," she said sweetly.

Mr. Jenkins smiled. "Shareese, girl, you take such good care of me. I love those padded socks you gave me. You don't have to give me nothing. I just enjoy your company at night when I am on my rounds," he said sincerely.

Shareese pulled out a bag of homemade cookies and a tube of ointment to relax his muscles. Mr. Jenkins smiled his toothless grin. "You sure know how to spoil a man," he said. He took the items and bit into one of the soft cookies with one of his side teeth. "Mm, this is real good. Are these cookies from Sarah's place?" he asked.

She smiled. "You found me out. I wanted you to think I baked them," she teased. Mr. Jenkins chuckled.

"Hey, we still on for tonight?" he asked. Shareese smiled and nodded yes. "Tonight I will show you part of the station most folks don't know about," he bragged.

Shareese stopped typing and looked at him. "You are so sweet. This building is so fascinating! I enjoy learning the layout of where I work. You know what I mean, Mr. Jenkins?" He nodded and took her trash and dumped it. Shareese got up and unlocked the chief's door so Mr. Jenkins could clean it. "I will see you tonight at eight," she said and returned to her desk and resumed her typing. Mr. Jenkins waved and quietly went about his task of cleaning the executive office suites.

When the police chief returned from his meeting, he asked Shareese about the envelope that he had placed on his desk before he left earlier that afternoon. Shareese stopped typing and faced the chief. "Sir, Ms. Glenton returned shortly after you left and retrieved the photos," she said crisply. She turned and continued to type on her word processor. Shareese felt the Captain's gaze remain on her.

She continued to type as she thought of something else to say that would pacify him. "She said something about bringing the wrong envelope." The police chief looked at his secretary and grunted as he walked to his office and shut the door behind him. He felt something was not right and made a mental note to call Amara and determine why she had retrieved the photos.

He also made a mental note that Shareese had mentioned the envelope contained photos. He had not told her what was in the envelope, only that Amara was bringing by some materials for him to examine. Before he could think about it any further, Shareese knocked softly on the door before opening it. She informed him of a gruesome murder that just occurred. Chief Chaddam groaned and turned his full attention to the latest murder. He never remembered to call Amara.

Later that evening while sitting on the sofa with Michael, Shareese pulled out the folded photo. Before she could show it to Michael, they were interrupted by a loud knock on the door. Shareese quickly refolded the photo and walked to the door. She looked through the peephole to see who was at her door. "It's Paul," she whispered to Michael. Shareese had forgotten Paul was coming by tonight. Since she had the photo, she had no more need for Paul. She sighed loudly.

Michael gave her a nod to open the door. Before she opened the door, they kissed each other and Michael went into the guest bedroom. Shareese hid the picture in a safe place and smoothed her hair. She smiled widely as she opened the door. "Hey, good lookin'," said Paul. "I rented a couple of videos and got some pizza!" he said in a cheery voice. Paul's smile faded when he saw what he thought was a look of disdain in Shareese's eyes. "Did I come at a bad time, Shareese?" he asked.

Shareese gave Paul a warm kiss and invited him in. "No, I was really busy going over some dictation for the chief and I lost track of time," she said, smiling. Michael quietly put on his shoes and jacket and crept out of the door onto the small patio and out of the backyard.

Shareese excused herself and went into the kitchen to get some wine and snacks. Paul placed the pizza box on the coffee table and made himself comfortable on her sofa. He removed the video from its jacket and placed it into the VCR. Shareese saw Michael slip out of the backyard gate and breathed a sigh of relief. With all the energy she could muster, she grabbed a tray and placed plates, glasses, and soft drinks on top of the tray. She carried the tray into the living room where Paul was relaxing and waiting for her to return.

She placed the tray on the table and gave him a chaste kiss on the lips. Paul smiled and held her close.

"What was that for?" he asked.

Shareese forced herself to smile. "Just for being the kind and thoughtful man that you are," she said sweetly.

Paul grinned at her compliment and said, "I do try, Ms. Miller." Shareese fed Paul a bite of pizza, got up to push the VCR tape all the way inside the slot, and grabbed the VCR remote control. She sat next to Paul on the sofa and started the movie. They snuggled together and enjoyed the video for the remainder of the evening.

Amara paced back and forth in her office. She was surprised the police chief had not contacted her about the photos she gave him. She sat down at her desk and dialed his number at work. His secretary answered, using a very official tone, "Seattle Police, Chief Chaddam's office, Ms. Miller speaking."

"Hi Shareese," said Amara. "This is Mari Glenton. May I speak with Chief Chaddam please?" she asked.

There was a brief pause. "Oh, hello, Mari, Chief Chaddam is in meetings all day. May I take a message?" she asked in a very official tone.

"If you would, please," responded Amara. "Please let him know I called about the envelope I dropped off," she said.

"Will do, Mari," said Shareese in a gentle tone. "I will make sure he gets your message and have a great day!" she said with false enthusiasm.

Amara looked at the phone as if she could see Shareese's phony expression. "Thanks," said Amara hesitantly and hung up.

Amara's successive calls for the next three days met with the same result. Finally, Amara spoke to her dad and got Chief Chaddam's home number. She waited until the evening when she anticipated he'd be home and dialed his number. "Chaddam," he answered.

Amara shifted the position of the phone and began to speak. "Chief Chaddam, this is Mari Glenton. I apologize for the intrusion at your home but I was wondering if you had a chance to review the photos I left at your office a few days ago?" she asked.

Chief Chaddam scratched his head. "Oh, yes, the pictures you dropped by last week, right?" he asked.

Amara breathed a sigh of relief. "Yes sir. Can you help me at all?" "I believe Michael Whitman had something to do with the kidnapping of the Coopers' infant last year," she said.

"Whoa, slow down, Mari," said the chief. "I never saw the photos. Shareese said you came by and picked them up the same day. She said you had changed your mind," he said.

Amara became frustrated. "Sir, I have been trying for the past three days to contact you at your office and Shareese said you've been in meetings and were unavailable. Did you get any of my messages this week?" she asked.

Chief Chaddam had a worried look on his face. "Mari, I have been in meetings most of the day for the past three days, but I haven't received any of your messages. This really concerns me," he said. "Shareese has performed flawlessly," he said.

As he said that, he recalled his conversation with Shareese concerning the photos. He also noticed that the files involving the Cooper kidnapping case were missing. Those files had been secured in his desk. He made a mental note to have the locks on his desk changed. Tom began to pace the floor as he spoke to Amara. He had been so busy that he hadn't thought about all the inconsistencies that had occurred during the past week.

Amara invaded his thoughts and brought him back to the present. "Sir, if you aren't busy, I'd like to drop the photos by your home tonight," she said. He knew she didn't trust Shareese and at this point, neither did he. Chief Chaddam readily agreed and Amara arranged to come over at eight in the evening.

Shortly before eight, Amara walked up the stone walkway and knocked on the chief's door. Chief Chaddam answered the door. "Hi, Chief, I brought over the photos for you to look at," she said. Tom smiled and invited Amara in. She walked through the threshold and handed him the photos. The chief led her into the den and offered her one of the stiff leather oversized chairs.

He walked behind his large desk and sat down in his well-worn leather office chair. Amara sat down in the chair and smiled as she equated the experience with being called to the principal's office. Lena, the police chief's wife, entered the den and greeted Amara. She had a tray with a soft drink, a glass of ice, and a cup of iced coffee for her husband. She served them refreshments and left the room, quietly closing the door behind her.

The chief took a drink of his coffee, pulled out a letter opener, and opened the envelope containing the three photos. He looked at the first photo and frowned. "Well, I know who these two gentlemen are," he said of the two police officers. "What were they doing there?" he asked rhetorically. He looked at the third picture and grabbed a magnifying glass. "This one is a bit fuzzy, Mari," he said as he tried to get a closer look by using the magnifying glass. "This is the Cooper kidnapping case, isn't it?" he said.

He looked up at Amara with a perturbed look on his face. "This area was prohibited for all photographers and journalists," he said. "How did you come across these pictures?" he asked in a concerned tone.

Amara cleared her throat and took her time answering. "Well, Chief, you might recall that I was doing the investigative piece on the kidnapping and baby swapping?" she asked. The chief shook his head in acknowledgment and waited for her to continue. "Well, um, you see, Chief, I was in a tall tree about fifty feet above the park, approximately fifty yards back in the dense tree line behind all the security," she answered nervously.

The chief took another look at the photos and decided not to chastise her. "Mari, it's too fuzzy really to see who that person is. But he does have what looks like the briefcase the Coopers left with the ransom. Also, it looks like there is a woman right here," he said, pointing to the far right side of the photo.

Amara quickly went to stand beside the chief. "Yes sir, but she's wearing sunglasses, a scarf, and with those baggy clothes, she could be anyone," she said. She was dressed from head to toe in what looked like forest green or black, which helped her to blend in. As Amara focused the magnifying glass to the next power, she had to agree with the chief.

The chief picked up the photo showing the man picking up the briefcase and examined it closely. Amara thought for sure the man was Michael, though without proof she didn't dare mention it to the chief. The chief invaded her thoughts by handing her the photo and making a recommendation. "Could you drop the negatives of these photos off at the police lab? I will let them know you are coming. I don't want anyone else to know about this yet," he said.

Amara smiled and promised to bring the negatives in the next day. "This may take a few days," said Chief Chaddam. "One of my photo techs had a family emergency and won't return until next week, so the production and analysis will be bit slow," he said. Amara thanked him and walked to the door. Chief Chaddam thanked her for her persistence and opened the door for her. As Amara left the chief's home she felt relieved. Perhaps she was closer to confirming who was behind ordering her death and who the mystery woman in the photo was.

Chapter 7

$\mathcal{T}$he following day, the chief of security called Chief Chaddam's direct phone line and asked him to come to the security viewing room to watch the videotape. The chief of security looked very nervous. "Sir, I have no explanation why this wasn't brought to my attention sooner, but I think you need to take a look at this video. This video was taken about four days ago," he said nervously. Chief Chaddam looked at him with concern in his eyes.

"What is it, Walt?" he asked.

"It involves your employee and your office. So just take a look at the tape and you decide what needs to happen after that," he said nervously.

Chief Chaddam stared at him. "Okay," he said as he took the tape and sat down at one of the television/video recorder combination sets. The chief placed the video in the recorder and began to watch the footage caught by the security camera. When the tape was complete, he placed his face in his hands and said nothing.

The chief of security waited nervously for a response. The chief's face was red with anger and disappointment. "I want a full report on my desk as to why this took so long to uncover," he demanded.

"Yes, sir," said the chief of security, clearly flustered and embarrassed.

Chief Chaddam handed the tape back to the chief of security. "Walt, make a copy for me and place the original in a safe place," he said quietly.

"Yes, sir," said the chief of security as he took the tape from Chief Chaddam. The chief got up without saying another word and quietly walked out of the viewing room.

The following week Chief Chaddam called Shareese into his office.

Shareese entered his office with pencil and steno notebook in hand in order to take a memo for him. She sat down in her usual chair and prepared to take notes. Chief Chaddam leaned forward and placed his crossed hands on top of his massive oak desk. "Shareese, what happened to the envelope Ms. Glenton left last week?" he asked calmly.

Shareese avoided eye contact and shrugged nonchalantly. "Sir, as I said before, she returned the same day and picked it up."

Chief Chaddam squinted at her and did not say anything for several seconds. He removed a pencil from his pencil holder and slowly tapped the pencil on his desk. Chief Chaddam replaced the pencil in its holder and rubbed his temples as if he were suffering from a headache.

"Shareese, you have done a fantastic job for me. You are professional and you are an asset to this office and the station. You have been an excellent executive assistant," he said in a business-like tone.

Shareese smiled. "Thank you, sir. I try to uphold the level of professionalism I think this office deserves," she said, as she made eye contact.

Chief Chaddam shifted his bulky frame in his large leather chair. "Shareese, one thing I cannot tolerate from my staff is lying. I am going to give you one more chance. What happened to the photos that were left on my desk from Ms. Glenton?" he asked sternly.

Shareese began to fidget and broke eye contact. "Sir, it's like I said...."

Chief Chaddam held his hand up in order to stop her from speaking. "Shareese, I know she didn't take them back because she called me at home after trying to reach me several times at the office. Why didn't I ever receive her messages?" he asked.

Shareese continued to look down at the floor. "Well, sir, It was very busy and perhaps...."

The chief cut her off again. "Shareese, did you take the envelope that contained photos from my desk?" he asked. Shareese maintained eye contact and told him, "No." Chief Chaddam released a long sigh. "Shareese, you are the only person who had access to my office. Clara over in personnel saw you at the shredder, shredding an envelope that resembled the one left by Ms. Glenton," he said sternly. "Do you wish to change your story?" he asked wearily.

"No, sir," she said defiantly.

The chief crossed his arms over his wide chest. "I have no alternative but to fire you. Integrity is a must for this office. Integrity is something you can't lose. You have to give it away. Shareese, you've given away your integrity by taking those photos and lying about it.

"Just so you know, there are hidden video cameras throughout this office for safety and security reasons. You were caught on one camera at the shredding machine and later as you folded one of the photos and placed it in your pocket. Based upon this information and your inability to tell the truth, I must ask you to please clear your desk of all personal belongings and turn in your keys and identification badge at the front desk. I will have Scott escort you off the premises.

"I am really sorry, Shareese. I truly like you and thought you were a great asset to this office," he said with finality.

Shareese glared at Chief Chaddam but said nothing. She turned on her heel and walked quickly back to her desk. She loaded her personal items in the small box Scott, the security guard, had placed by her desk. She placed the office keys on the desk. Scott took inventory and asked her for her badge. She tried to remove it from her suit jacket, but it was tangled in the weave of the jacket.

Shareese looked at Scott and explained the situation. "Scott, my badge is tangled in the weave of my suit. If I force it, I will tear my favorite jacket. May I bring it in tomorrow?" she asked sweetly. Scott smiled. He had always been fond of Shareese because she was kind and treated him with respect, unlike many of the others who worked on the executive floor.

Shareese knew Scott was interested in her and felt he could be of use to her. She knew he wanted to ask her out on a date. She needed something he had and she needed to get closer to him. Scott nodded his head in agreement. Then he looked at her and pointed his finger. "Don't let me down, Shareese. Make sure you turn your badge in tomorrow. I don't want to come looking for you," he threatened.

Shareese smiled sweetly and gave Scott a big hug. The gesture immediately excited him. He quickly stepped away from her embrace, embarrassed. Shareese looked down at the silver ring on his belt and smiled. "I promise, Scott," she said as she made the boy scouts' honor sign with her fingers.

Two days passed and Shareese had not returned her badge. Scott smiled. She was interested, he thought to himself. He went to the Human Resources department on the fifteenth floor and walked into the office. He explained the circumstances to the young receptionist and she eagerly allowed him to look up Shareese's home address and phone number. He smiled as he wrote down the information. He thought this was the perfect excuse for him to make contact with her one more time. Something in her eyes led him to believe she might be a little interested in him as well. He thanked the young girl and walked out of the office.

He went to the security office and picked up the phone in one of the vacant viewing rooms. He dialed her number and she answered on the second ring. Scott took a deep breath. "Hey, Shareese, this is Scott from the police department," he said nervously.

"Hi, Scott," said Shareese in a sexy voice.

Scott swallowed hard. "Um, the reason I am calling is because you have not returned your badge and you had promised to do so yesterday," he said in an official tone.

Shareese laughed into the phone. "What time do you get off from work?" she asked.

Scott began to perspire. "What...I mean, I get off at eight, Shareese," he said nervously.

"Well, if it's not too much trouble, why don't you stop by and pick it up? That way you can return it for me and I won't be embarrassed by having to come back to the office," she suggested.

Scott released a hard breath. "Well, okay, what is your address?" he asked.

Shareese laughed again. "If you got my phone number, then you can find my home address," she said in a sultry voice. "I'll see you at nine," she said and hung up the phone.

Scott hung up the phone and wiped the sweat from his brow. One of his co-workers looked at him and laughed. "Man, what is wrong with you? You look like you've been asked to go to the principal's office," he joked.

Scott loosened his top button. "I have," he said nervously. "I have."

Scott looked at his watch. He had two more hours until quitting time. He jotted down Shareese's address and placed it into his pocket. He worked through his security tasks with zeal. He wanted to keep his mind off Shareese. He didn't know what was going to happen, but he thought this might be his chance to ask her for a date. Scott looked at his watch a second time and he had five minutes remaining on shift. He was glad he had kept busy. The time flew by and he didn't have time to think about Shareese.

He quickly changed out of his security outfit and took a shower in the locker room before putting on his street clothes. He combed his hair and allowed it to dry naturally. Large blond curls formed all over his crown. His hazel eyes sparkled with excitement. He hurriedly brushed his teeth and neatly hung his uniform in his assigned locker. He clipped his key ring to his belt.

He walked out of the building and onto the street. He climbed into his used Ford pick-up truck and drove slowly to Shareese's address. Shareese heard the knock on the door and peeked through her security hole in the door. She unlatched the lock and opened the door. Scott looked at Shareese and immediately began to blush. He stuck his hands in his pockets and looked up at her shyly. Shareese smiled warmly and invited him in. She offered him a seat and brought in a can of cold beer and a wine for herself from the kitchen. Scott exhaled as he gladly took the beer.

He looked around the interior of her house. It was spotless and everything was in its place. He tried hard not to stare at her scantily clothed body. She was wearing a very short cream-colored satin gown with a matching sheer robe that was tied together with a cream-colored satin belt. Her hair was loose and fell neatly around her shoulders. Her breasts moved freely as she leaned over to place his cold beer on a nearby coaster. Her expensive perfume seemed to intoxicate him. She sat close beside him.

Scott felt an uncomfortable bulge in the small of his back. Without thinking, he unhooked the key ring from his belt loop and set it on the table. Shareese eyed the key ring and smiled like a cat that had cornered a mouse and was going in for the kill.

"So," she said. "You came all this way to get my badge?" she asked innocently. Scott took a large gulp of beer and shook his head. Shareese moved closer. "Is that all you came for, Scott?" she asked as she ran her hand through his thick mane of blond curls. Scott shook his head, unable to speak. Shareese leaned even closer, allowing the tip of her breast to brush against his bare arm through the thin garments.

Scott sucked in his breath as he felt the cool, smooth material flow across his arm. She found an excuse to move back and forth against his arm until her nipple became taut against the material. Scott wanted to touch her breast, but he refrained. Shareese took a sip of wine and laughed. Scott took another large gulp of beer and began to feel more relaxed. He leaned back comfortably in the sofa and allowed his fingertips to rub gently the material across her nipple that was pressed slightly against his arm. Shareese moaned softly. Scott smiled and took another sip of his beer.

Shareese moved closer until she was practically sitting on his lap. She crossed her legs and the scant material fell away, allowing him to see her shapely thighs. His breath caught in his throat when he noticed she was not wearing any panties. Scott quickly stood up and felt the blood rush to his head. "Easy, big fella, be careful, Scott," said Shareese playfully. Scott sat back down. This time Shareese sat on his lap.

He began to feel very relaxed and mellow. He placed his hand high on her thigh and traveled upward and didn't stop until he heard her moan once more. He laced his hands through her long hair and gently pulled her face toward his. She allowed him to kiss her and she returned his kiss with the same amount of passion.

Scott stood up again. This time he took his time. He ran his hands through his hair.

"Shareese, what are we doing here? What do you want from me?" he asked. His voice sounded hoarse. He took another swig of his beer and cleared his throat. Shareese stood up and placed her body against his. "I want the same thing you want," she said as she ran her fingertips over the bulge in his pants.

"Are you sure?" he asked. Shareese nodded her head and began to unbutton his shirt.

As Shareese undressed him, he spotted his keys on the table and placed them inside his pocket. "I never let these babies outta my sight," he said. Shareese frowned and then looked at him and smiled. She continued to undress him. "Let's take this to my room," she said seductively. Scott finished his beer and followed her into the room.

When they got to the room, Shareese excused herself and went into the kitchen. She returned with another can of beer and a glass of wine for herself. She gave Scott the can of beer and placed the glass of wine on the nightstand. She continued to kiss and undress Scott as held onto his beer.

He leaned over to put the beer on the nightstand when Shareese stopped his hand. "Don't you want to take a quick drink first?" she asked.

Scott shook his head. "I have had enough already. I don't need any more to drink," he said. His head felt light. He looked at Shareese and smiled mischievously. "Did you put something in my beer, Shareese?" he asked as he shook his finger at her. "Naughty, naughty," he chastised. "Two can play at that game," he said as he moved toward the nightstand and placed his beer beside the glass of wine. He accidentally spilled the wine.

He cursed aloud as he pulled several sheets of tissue from the nearby Kleenex box to sop up the mess. He grabbed her wastebasket and threw the saturated tissues away. "I am so sorry, Shareese," he said. "Let me get you another glass of wine." Shareese quickly picked up her glass and headed toward the kitchen. Scott gently took the glass from her hand. "It's the least I can do since I spilled it," he said. She told him the wine was in the refrigerator.

As Scott left, Shareese followed him to the kitchen. As Scott opened the refrigerator, Shareese placed her arms around his body and began to unbutton his shirt. As she got a few buttons undone, she pulled his shirt off his shoulders and covered his back with little kisses. Scott told her to let him get her wine before she started to undress him. He told her he didn't want to make a mess in her spotless kitchen.

Shareese allowed him to pour her glass of wine. She grabbed her wine glass from the counter once it was full. "I'll carry this for you," he said. He picked up the wine glass and walked very cautiously back to the bedroom. Shareese walked past him and went into the bedroom. She sat on the bed and waited for him to join her. He carried her glass to the bedroom and swirled the liquid as he continued his slow walk to the bed. Shareese got up and took her glass. She took a sip of the sweet cool liquid and gave him a kiss. "Thank you," she said. "This tastes cold and sweet, exactly how I like it," she said.

Scott continued to stand at the edge of the bed. "Are you having second thoughts?" she asked. He tilted his head and watched her. Shareese took several sips of her wine and set it down. She stood up and pulled him to the bed.

"Look, this isn't a good idea," he said, nervously. "I like it kind of rough and I don't think you could handle it," he said. He stuck his hands in his pockets.

Shareese smiled as she looked at his exposed muscular chest through his opened shirt. "No marks on the face, neck, or arms," she said as she began to unbutton his shirt once again.

He caught her hands. "I can do that myself," he said as he began to unbutton his shirt. "Why don't you get out of that?" he suggested as he pulled her satin sash. She stood in front of him and began to disrobe. He smiled as watched her untie her satin belt and allow her robe to float slowly to the ground. She then pushed the skinny straps off her shoulders and wiggled her body in a provocative manner and allowed the thin garment to fall to the ground. She stepped out of the clothing on the floor and stood naked in front of Scott.

He sucked in his breath. She was absolutely gorgeous. Her body was perfect. He had never seen a woman more perfect. He was mesmerized.

Shareese smiled at his reaction. "So you like what you see?" she asked. Scott nodded his head and quickly removed his clothing.

Shareese pushed his naked body down hard on the bed and lay on top of him. He quickly flipped her over and got on top. "Uh-uh," he admonished. "This time I'm in charge," he said boldly.

Shareese's eyes grew wide. "Well, then," she said, "Take charge!" He laughed and pulled the thin cover over their bodies. He pinned her hands above her head. "This will be a night you won't forget for a long time," he said, laughing ruefully.

Shareese grabbed her head as she felt herself fading in and out. She was aware of everything that was happening to her. She could feel the roughness of his hands as he pulled her nipples and the force of his lips and teeth as he sucked and bit her breasts. He bit and slapped her on the buttocks several times. She let out a yell and bit him on the chest. Their intercourse was more like a rugby tournament. It was fast and very rough.

Shareese tried to focus. She did not like the feeling of not being in full control of the sexual encounter. She had always been in control. "What did you put in my wine!" she demanded.

Scott laughed coarsely. "The same stuff you put in my beer," he yelled as he readied himself to enter her a second time. She looked at him with complete surprise and laughed.

Sweat glistened on their bodies. The sheets were contorted and ripped on the bed. He looked down at her with a gleam in his eyes as he held her legs over her head and entered her again. She grabbed him by the hair and pulled his face down to hers. She kissed him hungrily. She then bit him on his chest and clawed his back. He screamed with pleasure as she slapped him hard on his thigh. She grabbed her sheets and cried out savagely as she felt slight pangs of pain followed by excruciating pleasure. Scott let out a low moan as he climaxed. Moments later Shareese's body convulsed from the orgasm she experienced. When it was over she lay still atop of rumpled soiled, and torn sheets.

Several hours later, Shareese awoke and found herself alone in bed. She gained her bearings and looked around the room. It was completely dark and quiet. The red digital lights on the clock read midnight. Scott was gone. She sat up and winced in pain. She walked to the bathroom and surveyed her body. "Dammit!" she said as she looked at the welts over her entire left buttock where he had slapped her hard with his hands or perhaps his belt. She even had a few bite marks on her left breast where the skin was not broken, but slightly bruised.

How was she going to explain this to Michael? she thought. She remembered him telling her he knew she had drugged him and he had done the same to her. "That bastard!" she screamed at the mirror. She pushed her hair out of her face and smiled. She remembered her multiple orgasms and the extreme sensations she felt when he tugged and pulled on her breast and slapped her buttocks. She was aware of everything he did and all that transpired. She just didn't like the few times it felt as if she were fading in and out during the night. She had never experienced sex so intense. She had to admit to herself, she actually enjoyed it. He was a challenge. That sweet demeanor was just a façade. He was a total animal in bed.

She frowned as she opened her medicine cabinet and pulled out two bottles. She didn't like being outsmarted. She had underestimated him completely. And to make matters worse, it was all for nothing. She didn't get the keys! She needed those office keys to get back into certain offices to complete her plan.

"So he likes it rough," she said, ruefully. "I guess he had his fun this time," she said aloud to the reflection in the mirror. "Round two will belong to me," she smirked as she grabbed the witch hazel and aloe vera ointment off the bathroom counter and returned to her bedroom.

Chapter 8

*T*hree weeks passed without incident and Amara had gotten back into her regular routine. She really enjoyed her new job and was working on an article about one of the premier chefs who worked at one of the most exclusive Seattle restaurants, who happened to be a woman and a native of Seattle. She checked her watch to make sure she gave herself enough time to navigate through Seattle's hectic downtown traffic in order to make the interview. It was still early. She had nearly an hour before she needed to leave.

She looked around her small apartment and started some of the dreaded chores she'd put off for the past couple of weeks. Amara dusted the furniture throughout her apartment and filed the personal paperwork that was piled high on her small desk. She smiled with relief as she filed the voided contract for her condo lease. The owner, Mrs. Kuntz, was an elderly woman who seemed relieved when Amara requested to break her lease. She told Amara that she didn't need the extra excitement in her building. Amara knew she was worried that a repeat performance of someone breaking into her home would devalue the three other units she had in the building.

Amara enjoyed living in the apartment above her parents' garage. It was the perfect size for her and she felt the arrangement helped her become closer to her parents. Amara sprayed special furniture polish on her antique coffee table and straightened all the magazines. She carefully displayed all the new magazines on top and placed the older ones on the bottom. She stopped when she came across a fitness magazine with Franni's picture on it. Amara examined the beautiful woman in the photo and sighed.

She placed the magazine back on the table and checked her watch. It was about time for her to leave. She put away her cleaning supplies and washed her hands. She retrieved her jacket from the hall closet. Amara checked her reflection in the hall mirror and furrowed her brow. She recalled the last conversation she had with Brianna a few days back.

She had tried to ask about Sam indirectly and Brianna had laughed and teased her. Brianna told Amara that things were not so great in paradise for

Sam and Franni. Franni was at the peak of her modeling career and continued to travel all over the world modeling for the top designers and magazines. She was rarely in the city and was thinking about moving to New York.

Brianna also told her that they were spending a lot less time together and the possibility of Franni moving to New York had put a strain on their relationship. She told her that Sam was at her house often and always asked about her. Amara listened but didn't know how she felt about what Brianna was telling her.

Amara checked her watch once and dashed out to her car. She started up her car and sat there gripping the steering wheel a little too tightly. She relaxed her grip and sighed loudly. She put the car in gear and drove down the street toward the interstate. Using her hands free car phone, she dialed Sam's office number. She took a deep breath as the phone connected to the number she dialed and began to ring.

Sam was concentrating heavily on a new case when his cell phone rang. He cursed aloud, grabbed his cell phone, and read the number. He didn't recognize the number, so he allowed the cell phone to continue to ring. After a few more rings he answered. "Yes?" he said, without taking his eyes off the document. There was a pause. Sam stopped reading the document and responded again. "Hello?" he said.

"Hi," replied the voice from the other end of the phone. Sam did not reply. He continued to read the document in front of him.

Amara broke the silence. "Sam, this is Mari. I hope you aren't too busy," she said quietly.

Sam put the file down and smiled. He picked up a rubber ball from his desk and began squeezing it. "Amara, how have you been?" he asked excitedly. "I've missed you," he said spontaneously.

Amara was surprised by his last remark. She hesitated and said, "I've missed you too." There was a longer pause.

"So, to what do I owe this call after nearly two months?" he asked.

Amara laughed. "I spoke with Bre a couple of days ago and I mentioned you and I thought it had been a long while since we've talked, so I decided to call."

Sam smiled. "I am glad you did. I have been a workaholic lately," he said. "Franni has been traveling since you left and I use work to keep my mind off being lonely."

Amara could feel her heart beating faster. "Well, that just means it will be that much better when you see her," she said diplomatically.

Sam laughed. "Oh, you are good. Always the noble one," he teased. "Why don't you say what you really feel?" he asked in a sensuous tone.

Amara swallowed hard. "Because I don't have the right to. We agreed to remain friends. You made it clear that you were in love with Franni and wanted to make it work," she said defensively. "I don't believe in taking another woman's man during a time of weakness in the relationship. I don't want some rebound relationship," she said. "I want a man who wants to be with me because of who and what I am. Not to replace another woman or to fill a void. That's where I think you are right now," she said barely above a whisper. There, she thought, I've told him how I truly feel.

"Amara, why are you whispering?" asked Sam. "Because I am opening myself up to you and it's a bit scary," she said.

Sam smiled. "I appreciate your honesty. And you are right on target. I haven't broken up with Franni. I keep hoping we can work it out.

"When we became serious we had a long talk about what we expected from this relationship and she was honest with me from the beginning. She told me she loved me but her career came first at this point in her life. And when she was with me, I would be number one. We both agreed to total honesty and a monogamous relationship.

"But after spending those couple of days with you, I knew I was missing out. I tried to create that with Franni, but it didn't work. My thoughts kept coming back to you, Amara. How's that for honesty?" he asked.

Amara felt as if she had a huge lump in her throat. She made a sound as if she were clearing her throat. "Sam, I need to go now. It was great talking with you. I hope you and Franni can work things out. I wish I could say that I was here for you if you needed to talk, but I would be lying. I hope I continue to stay on your mind. And when Franni is totally out of your system, give me a call. Okay?" she said, and hung up before Sam could respond.

Sam looked at his cell phone with disbelief and disconnected the call. He pulled out his desk drawer and stared at a picture of him and Amara together at the art gallery. Coward, he thought to himself as he gently closed the drawer. Sam picked up the file he was reading before Amara called and began reading where he left off.

Clayton walked into his brother's office. He was worried because Sam had been working so hard in the past couple months. He had overheard Sam's conversation with Amara a few moments ago. He cleared his throat in order to get Sam's attention. Sam looked up and smiled. "Clayton, what are you doing here? I didn't even hear you come in," he said as he closed the file he was reading. Clayton grinned at his brother but said nothing.

Sam looked at his brother. "What?" he asked, smiling.

"Why don't you go see her?" asked Clayton as he leaned against the edge of Sam's desk. Sam stopped smiling and became serious. "What?"

Sam asked as he laid the file on his desk.

Clayton rolled his eyes. "You heard me. Why don't you stop this nonsense and go see Mari."

Sam opened his mouth to deny what his brother was saying but he couldn't. "You overheard our conversation, didn't you?" he asked.

Clayton folded his muscular arms across his chest and shook his head. "Yep," he said.

Sam broke eye contact with his brother and stared down at the folder. "I can't do that until I resolve things with Franni."

Clayton laughed. "I was hoping you'd say that. It just so happens that Franni is on her way up right this moment."

Sam jumped out of his seat. "What are you talking about, Clayton? She is not due back in town until next month." Clayton jerked his head in the opposite direction and Franni walked into the office holding two suitcases and a small duffel bag. Franni smiled and dropped her bags. She quickly walked over to Sam and gave him a big kiss. Clayton quietly excused himself and left the office.

"Wow, what a great surprise!" Sam said excitedly. He was grinning ear to ear as he rubbed Franni's shoulders and caressed her face.

Franni laughed. "Perhaps I should go away more often if this is the reception I receive when I return," she joked.

Sam continued to smile widely. "How long do I have you all to myself?" he asked as he nuzzled her neck. Franni giggled and pushed him back.

"Three days, then I am off to Europe again," she said breathlessly. Sam's smile faded. "Oh, three days, I see," he said without emotion. Franni frowned and tilted his chin up. "Honey, you knew my priorities when we decided to become serious," she said, unapologetic. Sam refused to look into her eyes because he knew what she was saying was true. He forced himself to smile and hugged her tightly.

"Well then, let's go out and get something to eat and then how about going to a live jazz concert tonight?" he asked with all the enthusiasm he could muster. Franni moved in closer and leaned her body against his. "How about an intimate dinner at my place and we just see what happens after that?" she purred. Sam felt himself getting excited. "That sounds just fine," he whispered into her ear.

She kissed him passionately, stepped back, and grabbed her luggage. "See you at six tonight!" she said brightly. "And don't be late or you might miss dessert," she teased. Sam looked at his watch. "Oh, I won't be late," he stammered.

Sam walked her to the elevator and kissed her once more. "Welcome home, honey," he whispered. "See you at six tonight," he said as he held the elevator door open for her. Franni blew him a kiss and headed to the front of the building to catch a cab home. Sam sat at his desk and quickly went about completing his work, so he'd be free by the evening.

Amara pulled her car into the large parking lot of the restaurant. She felt foolish for calling Sam and even more foolish for telling him that she missed him. "Gosh, he must think I am desperate," she mumbled to herself. She shifted her car into park and leaned her head against the seat headrest. She needed to focus on her interview, not on Sam.

She pulled out her notes for the interview and pushed all thoughts of Sam out of her mind. Amara grabbed her camera, notebook, and recorder from the back seat. She checked her makeup in her mirror and got out of the car. She walked toward the restaurant and opened the door. The restaurant was still closed to customers. Amara smiled as the chef appeared in the waiting area to greet her. They shook hands and the chef took her to the kitchen in the back of the restaurant.

Shareese lay across his bed naked as she watched him put on his clothes. "Do you have to leave so soon?" she cooed. He looked at his watch and smiled. He placed his security officer's uniform on a chair and walked toward her. "I have a few more minutes before I go on shift," he said as he firmly bit the flesh alongside her back and gently bit her on the buttocks. He was totally enamored with her. He had never been with a woman who allowed him to do all the things she had allowed him to do to her.

She wiggled her index finger at him and signaled for him to get back in the bed. He readily complied. He lay on top of her as she wrapped her legs around him. This time she made sure he left no marks on her buttocks or breasts. All the marks were made in discreet places where Michael would never look. He was usually high from some drug most of the time they had sex anyway, so she wasn't very worried about him detecting any of her love bites or passion bruises.

She dug her nails into his flesh as he entered her and moved inside her at a rapid speed. He didn't have a lot of time and he wanted to climax one more time. He exploded with such force that it writhed through his body. "Wow!" he said breathless. "I have never come like this before in my life!" he said.

She giggled and lay beside him. "That is the least I could do since you've allowed me to keep my badge and gave me a little money to tide me over while I look for a new job," she said.

Scott turned red with embarrassment. "Is that the only reason?" he asked as he kissed her lips and bit the tip of her breast. Shareese looked into his eyes and said, "I think you are the most exciting man I have ever met. And you are a great lay." Scott laughed. He looked at his watch once more. "I feel so tired," he said. She laid his head on her shoulder and gently stroked his hair. In a matter of seconds Scott was fast asleep.

Once she ensured he was asleep, Shareese got out of the bed and walked over to his uniform. She removed the keys from his belt and made wax impressions of them. He had keys to the jail portion as well as the executive offices and file rooms. She labeled them and quickly put his keys back on his belt. She dumped out the juice he had drunk and thoroughly rinsed the glass to remove any traces of the powder she had added.

She went back into the room where he lay and rolled him over on his stomach. As a parting gesture, she took his belt and gave him a hard swat on his buttock and bit him on the other cheek, causing a substantial bruise. He squirmed and whimpered, but never woke up.

Twenty minutes later, fully showered and dressed, she walked out of his bedroom. She slammed the front door as she left. The loud noise from the door caused Scott to wake up with a start. He was disoriented and felt panicked. He looked at his watch and quickly got out of bed. He stumbled over to the chair and reached for his pressed uniform. He quickly put on his uniform without bothering to take a shower. He winced as he pulled his underwear and pants over his buttocks. He smiled as he put on his shirt and quickly buttoned it. "You will pay for that, you little minx," he hissed. He put on his socks and shoes and ran out of the door.

Shareese drove down the road singing a happy tune. "Mission accomplished," she sang and patted her purse that contained the wax impressions of the office keys. She then picked up her cell phone and placed a call to her lover.

Michael slammed down the phone. No answer. He was frustrated. It was early in the morning and she wasn't home. He called her cell phone and it was busy. They talked every day on the phone and she left sexy little messages on his machine whenever she needed money wired to her account, but he had not seen her. He had been trying to see Shareese for over three weeks and had not been successful. The past two weeks she had complained of having the flu and she didn't want him to catch it. She knew he was deathly afraid of hospitals and abhorred getting sick, so he was glad she had told him before he showed up at her place.

Could she be seeing someone else he wondered? "Nah," he said to himself. He smiled smugly and relaxed in his chair. He had all the money. She wasn't going anywhere, especially since she got fired from her job. He pulled out his wallet and looked at the miniature calendar he kept. Yep, it was going on three weeks since he had seen her last. That was certainly long enough, even if she did have to care for a silly virus, he thought. He would just surprise her and go by her house later that night and see for himself how she was feeling.

He imagined her naked body and became excited. He needed to relax and he knew just the thing, his favorite wine and his favorite music. He got up and turned on the stereo and slipped the disk of his favorite jazz artist inside the CD player. He then walked down stairs to his wine cellar to get a bottle of his favorite wine. He knew that winning combination would help him relax and take his mind off of Shareese.

The three police officers sat in a small desolate bar off the dusty highway. They huddled around a tall lacquered wooden table with tall matching stools and drank beer from large glass mugs. It was early in the morning and the bar was nearly empty. They dipped their heads in toward the table and talked in hushed tones. "That little bastard has cost us our jobs," said one of the officers as he reviewed the paperwork concerning their suspension and possible dismissal from the force. The other two remained silent.

Then the other spoke up. "And he needs to pay our pensions that we would have received if we were still on the force. I only had two more years until retirement," said Macey, the older police officer.

"I had three years left until retirement," said Sully.

"I was just getting started. I was to pin on sergeant next year," said Blanco.

Macey began to laugh. "Well, I guess it's time to pay dear old Mikey a visit." Scully let out a grunt in agreement and Blanco, the youngest officer, spoke up. "He definitely owes me."

"Yeah," they all said in unison. They slapped each other high fives and paid their tab. They gathered their belongings and prepared to leave the bar.

As they got to the door, Maria got a call on her personal cell phone. It was Shareese. She told Maria that Michael had all the money hidden somewhere in his home. She asked Maria to plan to go over to Michael's later that evening. She and the other two cops could search the place after she lured Michael over to her house. All she had to do was promise him sex and he'd be there in a flash. She continued to emphasize to Maria that she wanted the burglary to take place later that evening while he was away. They could ransack his home and look for the missing money. She would have no problem keeping Michael busy.

Shareese told Maria everyone would think it was a random burglary, and he couldn't report the money missing because he wasn't supposed to have it in the first place. Maria smiled, agreed with the plan, and hung up. She clapped her hands loudly and said, "I think I know where the missing money is located! It's at Michael's house." Both Sully and Macey's eyes brightened. "Well, then let's go get it!" they said.

"Wait guys, let me tell you…." Before she could finish, they grabbed her arm and all piled into one vehicle. "Guys, there's more, I am trying to tell you that…."

Sully cut her off. "Don't worry about a thing. We've got this under control. Right, Macey?" he asked.

Macey didn't answer right away. He kept his focus on the road. "Yeah, sure," he said. Macey stepped on the gas and the car skidded around the corner.

"Easy guys," said Maria nervously. They only laughed and continued to drive fast down the narrow neighborhood road toward Michael's home.

Maria quickly called Shareese and told her there was a change in plans. They were headed to Michael's house right now. Shareese cursed aloud. She would have to go home and pick up her duffel bag and her police radio scanner. Shareese told Maria she needed to get Michael out of the house. Maria warned her not to call him. Her companions were drunk and she could get hurt if she interfered.

Shareese quickly hung up the phone and tried to call Michael. There was no answer. "Pick up, pick up!" she yelled into the phone. When no one answered, she cursed aloud and threw her phone onto the passenger seat in her car. She pressed down on the gas pedal and sped home.

Michael ran up the steps from the wine cellar in order to answer the ringing phone but didn't get there in time. He looked at the caller ID and smiled. It was Shareese. "It's about time!" he said, grinning. He took his bottle of wine into the kitchen and poured a little into a glass. He sniffed the bouquet and placed a little in his mouth and swished it around. "Excellent!" he said as he poured more wine into the glass. He returned to his leather easy chair and began to relax as he got into the music. The tunes permeated his spacious home while he slowly sipped his expensive imported chardonnay.

He grew serious as he took another sip of wine. It was time to focus on his problem. He had to come up with another plan. Duke Ellington was back in jail and those dummies at the police station got caught placing the phone tap on the Glentons' phone line. His plans were in such disarray. Luckily, he could not be tied to any of those incidents.

He had to find a way to get back in the police chief's office and get those photos. Amara must have a copy too, he thought to himself. Since Shareese had been fired, he could no longer use her. And he knew Amara would never agree to see him alone. He would think of some clever way to lure her away and put her in a vulnerable position. Perhaps even threaten to kill her parents. He knew she was close to them. The wine was not helping him concentrate. Michael needed something stronger. He thought about snorting some coke. That usually helped him concentrate better.

The ringing of his doorbell interrupted his thoughts. He smiled. Perhaps that is my girl Shareese? he thought as he stood up from his comfortable chair. He hadn't seen her in awhile and she had just called a few minutes ago. He sat his glass of wine on his expensive imported glass end table and turned down the music that played from his high tech stereo. He checked the small video screen mounted on his wall. The camera showed the area in front of his door. He smiled to himself, pleased that he had had the foresight to install the security camera.

After Duke was jailed, he had become paranoid and hired a security company to install the hidden camera and place a monitor inside so he would know who was coming to visit him at his home. His eyes lit up when he recognized his brother Paul on the monitor and he quickly opened the door.

"Hey, brother, what a great surprise!" he said happily. He hadn't spoken with his brother since the incident involving Shareese and he was glad to see him. Michael opened the door wider and walked toward Paul in order to hug him. The startled look on his brother's face caused him to pause momentarily. Before he could react, a violent blow knocked him to the floor. His brother was pushed from behind and landed on top of him. Michael grunted as his brother's body fell on top of him. Michael tried to push Paul off and get up but it was too late. Paul was instantly shot in the back. "Lucy, you got some 'splainin' to do," snickered Sully as he holstered his weapon. Michael looked in horror at his brother as he rolled onto his side and convulsed on the floor. The bloodstain quickly grew below his body.

Michael swallowed hard. "Look guys, Sully, Macey, Maria," Michael was in mid-sentence when all three intruders began to take turns beating him with hard rubber sticks and kicking him. Each time he tried to get up and defend himself, the blows to his body grew in frequency and level of pain. The only thing he could do was contort his body into a tight ball to protect himself from the blows and kicks.

When the blows slowed, he looked over at his brother, who was sprawled face down on the floor. A large puddle of blood surrounded his body. Michael raised his head and glared at the three police intruders. "Why did you shoot my brother? He had nothing to do with any of this," he asked. A swift kick met his lips and broke his front tooth. He grabbed his mouth in pain.

"Well, well, sugar daddy," said Maria as she placed her foot back on the floor. "We want to get paid and…."

"We know you have all the money right here," interrupted Sully as he unholstered his gun and waved it around, pointing at various possible hiding spots inside Michael's home.

Michael slowly got to his feet and immediately brought his hands to his mouth. He stared angrily at the three intruders and spit out the broken tooth. The tooth, mixed with blood and spittle, hit the floor with a loud thud. He looked drunkenly at all of them. He raised his hand in defeat and asked if he could call an ambulance for his brother. They laughed at his request.

The oldest veteran, Macey, pulled out his gun and aimed for Michael's leg. "You've got two minutes to get us the money, or I will start shooting those little arms and legs of yours." To prove his point, he aimed the weapon at Michael's right leg. "I'll start with that leg, go to the other, and then…."

Suddenly, Sully butted in. "Look, we want some of that ransom money. We all lost our pensions because of you. So now you need to pay up," he said in a harsh tone.

Tears streamed down Michael's face. He looked at his brother in shock and prayed he was still alive. "Look, guys—Sully, Macey, Maria, please listen to me," mumbled Michael as his mouth throbbed with pain.

Sully, who was the most angry, began to yell at Michael as he charged his weapon. "No more games, Michael. Give us our cut of the money or we will kill you!" he screamed.

Michael had to think fast and stall for time. He could hear the faint sounds of police sirens in the distance. "If you kill me you'll never get any of the money because I am the only one who has access to it," he said calmly, feeling a bit in control. Sully growled in anger and shot Michael in the right leg. Michael fell to the floor and howled in pain. Maria unholstered her pistol and both she and Macey kept their guns pointed at Michael, but did not fire.

Suddenly, four police officers burst through the front door and shouted out a warning for all of them to place their weapons on the ground and put their hands on top of their heads. Ex-police officers Dan Macey and Maria Blanco immediately complied with the instructions, but Rob Sully pointed his weapon at the police officers in an attempt to shoot them and was shot several times before he could fire a round. He fell to the floor in a crumpled heap and died instantly.

A paramedic ran into the house and kneeled next to Paul. "He has a weak pulse," he yelled into his radio. "I need a stretcher now!" Instantly two emergency medical technicians ran into the house with a stretcher and immediately hooked Paul up to an IV and oxygen. They wheeled him into the ambulance and drove away. The paramedic then looked at Michael's wounds and requested another stretcher. The coroner's office was called for Sully's body.

As the medical technician wheeled Michael out the door, Michael looked over at Maria Blanco and said, "I'm sorry, Amelia." Maria did not look at him. Instead she turned her head in the opposite direction as the police officer read her Miranda rights and placed handcuffs on her wrists.

"Please be careful, I am pregnant," she said quietly to the police officer who placed the cuffs on her wrists. The police officer acknowledged her statement and gently placed her into a separate police car. "Make sure you do a pregnancy test on this one," said the arresting officer to the police officer driving. "Got it, boss," he said as he drove away with Maria handcuffed in the back seat.

Shareese turned up the volume on her police scanner and took a deep breath. She picked up her binoculars and watched the police take Maria and Macey out of the house and place them into separate police cars. She then gasped when she saw one man being carted off on a stretcher. She had heard on the scanner that three men had been shot, two were alive and in critical condition, and one was dead. She was relieved to see that Michael was being escorted into the ambulance and seemed semi-conscious. "Thank God he is alive," she said aloud. She then saw the coroner drive around the corner and run into the house. He returned with a dark colored bag and placed the corpse in the vehicle.

Once she was sure everyone had left and the neighbors had returned to their homes, Shareese placed the binoculars under the seat and slowly drove down the road. She parked in front of Michael's house, pulled out her workout duffel bag and her designer suitcase from the back seat, and casually walked to the front door. Michael had given her a key to his house and many of his neighbors had seen her around, so she drew very little attention when she went in.

Once inside, Shareese nervously paced up and down the foyer as she tried to solve the riddle Michael had given her. "Someplace hot," she said aloud. She averted her eyes from the large bloodstains in the foyer and walked into the bedroom. She placed the suitcase in a special hideaway Michael had recently installed. "For a rainy day," she whispered.

She kept her duffel bag and walked into the kitchen. Shareese walked over to the stove and pulled it away from the wall. She found nothing behind the stove, so she checked the oven and the small drawer beneath. She cursed softly under her breath when she did not find the money. She walked into the laundry room and checked the dryer. Nothing. Shareese snapped her fingers and ran to his backyard, where he had recently purchased a portable solar sauna and jacuzzi. She walked onto the patio deck in his back yard. She checked inside the sauna and didn't find the money. She took off her shoes and rolled her pants legs up above her knees and climbed into the jacuzzi.

Slowly she felt along the walls inside the tub. Suddenly she felt a spot that was lumpy and softer than the other spots she had checked. Totally focused on getting the money, she ran inside the house and found a long sharp knife. She made a neat incision across the spot that felt strange. She stuck her hand inside and pulled out a handful of bundled twenty-dollar bills.

Shareese smiled and ran to get her duffel bag. She filled her bag full of the money and replaced the money with white paper she had cut into the size of the dollar bills. She went in the house once more, pulled out a drawer, and removed a bag of rubber bands. In front of each paper bundle, Shareese placed an actual bill and banded them as close as she could to resemble the money she had removed from the jacuzzi. She checked her watch and called the pool supply shop and made an appointment for the lining to be repaired early the following morning. She also called a cleaning service to clean up the blood and broken glass in the living room and foyer.

Clayton smiled as he stuck his head in his brother's office and overheard him humming a catchy tune as he filed some past cases. "I guess everything is fine between you and Franni?" he asked.

Sam let out a chuckle. "Don't bug me, bro, I have be out of here by five-thirty tonight."

Clayton laughed. "Well I guess I'd better stop bothering you, so you can get your work completed," he said as he placed another file on his brother's desk.

Sam picked up the file and groaned. "Not Mrs. Holloway," he whined.

Clayton grinned widely. "She's on her way up right now." Sam rolled his eyes. Mrs. Holloway was a very high maintenance woman. She paid very well for the service she received, but she expected every penny's worth. She would have a litany of questions. Then she'd have to talk about her Pomeranian poodle, Dixie, and her digestive problems. Sam slapped his head. He picked up the file from his desk and quickly began to read over her case.

"Knock, knock," she called in a shrill voice.

"Mrs. Holloway, please come in," he said as he pulled out a bottle of mineral water for her and plain bottled water for Dixie. Mrs. Holloway smiled and walked into his office. Dixie was dressed in a pink and black plaid doggie outfit with a matching beret. Mrs. Holloway was dressed in the same outfit. Sam bit down on his lip to keep from laughing.

Mrs. Holloway sat down and glared at Sam. "Is something funny, Mr. Peters?" Sam removed the smile from his face. "Oh, no, ma'am. I just received some very good news right before you arrived," he said, truthfully. And five-thirty can't come soon enough, he thought to himself. Mrs. Holloway grunted a response and sat Dixie in her lap. She removed her beret and Dixie's.

Sam sat down in the chair next to Mrs. Holloway and opened the file. He removed some photos and notes from the inner pocket of the file and handed them to her. "Now, let's get started," he said as he turned to the appropriate sheets in the file.

Mrs. Holloway dabbed her eyes with her handkerchief. She had Dixie, her dog, tucked under her arm. "This is great work," she sniffed, "Thank you very much."

Sam escorted her out of his office and continued to walk with her to the elevator. "I am glad you are pleased, Mrs. Holloway," he said as he pushed the elevator button. Mrs. Holloway blew her nose into her handkerchief and stuffed it into her pocket. "This is the best work you and your brother have done for me yet!" she said smiling. Sam smiled back. "I am glad we were able to meet your needs." The elevator sounded off with a low "ding" and the doors swished open. Mrs. Holloway stepped in and the doors quickly shut and whisked her to the lobby without even a push of a button. Sam checked his watch. It was five-fifteen in the evening. "Yes!" he said as he rushed back into his office and prepared to leave for the day.

Clayton hummed as he finished the last of his work for the day. He handed his secretary several letters to type and send out. He filed his cases and cleared his desk. Tonight he was going to spend a relaxing evening with Brianna.

When Sam arrived at Franni's he knocked on the door. He was so excited about the prospect of being alone with Franni he was beside himself. "It's open," she yelled from inside. Sam quickly opened the door and stepped inside. His eyes quickly adjusted to the candle-lit room. Franni had lit at least fifty candles and placed them all around the living room. Dinner was on the table. Soft music played low in the background. Franni stood beside the table as if she were posing for a fashion layout. She looked terribly sexy in a black teddy, matching garter belt, and black stockings. She was wearing high-heeled shoes that made her legs seem to go on for days. Sam was literally drooling.

He wiped his mouth and stepped toward her. "Ready for dinner?" she whispered. Sam didn't wait for any further invitation. In one swoop he lifted Franni off the ground and into his arms. Franni squealed and giggled with delight as he walked toward the bedroom. "What about dinner?" she asked.

"Let's work on building up our appetites," he said as he kissed her lips.

"Yes, let's" she said breathlessly as he gently placed her on the bed.

Brianna sat on the sofa in Clayton's den reading a book when he walked through the door. "Hey, you!" she said and stood to give him a kiss on the lips. Clayton gave her a kiss and a hug and sat down beside her. She sat her book in her lap and looked over at Clayton. "You look like a cat that just swallowed a mouse," she joked.

Clayton smiled. "Franni arrived today," he said. "You should have seen Sam at work today. He was went through his work like a man possessed," he joked.

"Was he rushing to finish, so he could see her?" she asked.

"Let me just put it this way. Sam's been on the desert for two months without any water and Franni is the water."

Brianna covered her mouth. "Clayton, you are so bad!" she said as she swatted his thigh with her hand.

Clayton put his hand around her waist and pulled her onto his lap. "You know," he said clutching his throat. "I could use some water too."

Brianna laughed heartily. "Well, let's see what I can do," she said in a sexy tone of voice. She got up and went to the kitchen to prepare him a glass of water. She signaled for him to come close. When he walked into the kitchen, he stuck out his hand to take the water. Brianna pulled the glass toward her and drank the contents.

Clayton roared in laughter. "I can't believe you did that!" He picked her up and carried her outside to the patio by the pool. She was kicking and screaming. "Put me down!" she yelled.

Clayton smiled. "As you wish." Clayton dropped her into the pool fully clothed. While she was in the air, she grabbed Clayton's shirt pocket and pulled him in with her. He let out a loud yell as he fell into the water spread-eagled. The water was cold. It took his breath away. Brianna swam over to him and kissed his lips. "That will teach you to throw me into the pool," she teased.

"Oh hush, and give me another kiss," he said as he pulled her body close.

Sam did not get the three days he was promised. Franni received a call from her agent late that evening requesting she leave early the next morning. The shoot had been pushed up because of an incoming storm front. Sam took her to the airport. "I won't be gone long," she said as she gave him a goodbye kiss. Sam didn't respond. He helped her place her bags on the scale. After she got her ticket, she turned and gave Sam a hug. She looked into his eyes. He had been unusually quiet. Sam forced himself to smile. "Take care and I will see you when you get back." Franni smiled nervously and headed toward her gate.

Sam put on his sunglasses and walked to the airport parking lot. Sam got into his car but did not start the engine. He didn't feel like going to the office. He really needed to resolve the issue involving the information he found out about Amara's aunt. He would do it while Franni was away. He thought it would only take one day and he could return the following day.

He took out his cell phone and called the travel agent for a flight out. There was one available in three hours. He made the reservation over the phone.

He then called Mr. Glenton and told him he was coming for a visit. "Sir, I found out some information regarding a your wife's sister that I would like to discuss with you and Mrs. Glenton in person. If you don't mind, I'd like to fly down in the next few hours?" Jackson agreed. "I'll see you then, sir," said Sam as he closed his cell phone and drove home.

Sam thought about Duke and the latest news he had on him. He needed to take protection. He would take his pistol and bulletproof vest. He called his buddy Ted in airport security and explained the circumstances. "No problem, come early and bring your weapons permit and I will do the rest," he said. Sam thanked him and hung up. He looked at his watch. He needed to go home and pack some clothes. He had to be back at the airport in one hour. Sam started his car and headed home. On his way home, he called his brother Clayton and left a message that he would be in Seattle overnight on business.

Chapter 9

*E*arly that morning, Amara sat at her parents' kitchen table, sipped her favorite tea, and read the feature story of the morning newspaper in disbelief. The incident involving Michael and Paul was on the front page. Tears streamed down her face as she completed the article. "Mom!" she wailed.

Myra ran into the kitchen. "What's the matter, honey?" she asked her daughter. Amara stood up and ran over to her mother and hugged her tightly.

"Mom," she cried. "Paul was shot and nearly died yesterday." Her mother covered her mouth in shock. "Oh my God." Amara looked up at her mother. "Michael was shot also. Those two police officers who were in the photo I took were involved. One of them died. They are also the same ones Dad described when he caught them placing the bug on our phone line in the back yard. And they arrested Maria Blanco, the police officer who initially helped me when Duke Ellington attacked me," said Amara as she continued to cry.

Myra held Amara close and comforted her. "Shh, it's okay, Mari baby," she said softly. Amara's body shook as she continued to sob. "Let's go to the hospital and see how Paul is doing," suggested Myra as she wiped Amara's tears away with the back of her hand. Amara shook her head and clutched her mother's hand.

It was well into the afternoon before Paul was permitted to have visitors other than his immediate family. When Myra and Amara were finally allowed to see him, the nurse escorted them into his room. Paul was lying in the hospital bed with plastic tubes connected to his nose, mouth, and wrist and faint beeps monitored his heartbeat, blood pressure, and breathing. His face looked swollen and pale. "Please don't stay long, he is not very strong," said the attending nurse. Amara and Myra both nodded and walked quietly toward his bed.

"He's a lucky man. If that bullet had been two centimeters closer he would have been dead. Currently he is experiencing temporary paralysis. He should make a full recovery after some intense sessions of physical therapy," said the nurse in a voice a little above a whisper. Both Myra and Amara breathed a sigh of relief. Paul made a great effort to turn his head. He was still feeling the effects of the sedatives from his emergency operation the previous night.

"Hey," he said in a raspy voice. Amara and her mother moved closer to Paul. Amara took his hand and held it gently. "How are you feeling, Paul?" Myra and Amara asked in unison.

Paul gave a slight smile. "I am alive. That is a blessing," he whispered.

"Do you know what happened?" asked Amara.

Paul tried to talk, but it was too painful. Instead he nodded his head to answer yes. "Wrong place, wrong time," he mumbled softly.

Amara and Myra looked at each other but said nothing. "We plan to visit your brother Michael as well," said Myra. "The nurse said he is scheduled to be released today." Paul smiled and shook his head in acknowledgment. Amara placed some magazines, audio tapes of some of his favorite books, and a small tape cassette player on the table beside his bed. She handed him a small pad and pencil so they could communicate. "Thanks, Amara," he wrote on the pad.

"Well, the nurse said we couldn't stay long, so we will leave now," said Myra and kissed him softly on his forehead.

"I will call your momma tonight and will see if she needs a ride to come see you tomorrow." Myra and Estelle had been childhood friends. Estelle refused to drive, so they carpooled a lot during the week.

"Thanks, Myra," he wrote. "Mom came last night. She caught a cab. She stayed most of the night and left early this morning," he jotted on the paper and gave it to them both to read. Both women smiled.

"You take care Paul. I will be back to visit tomorrow," said Amara.

Paul tapped Amara lightly on the arm and handed her a note. The note read, "Amara, could you contact Shareese Miller, my girlfriend, and let her know that I am okay?" But before Amara could assure him she would contact Shareese, Paul quickly fell asleep.

The nurse returned from her station and walked them to the hallway. "Michael's room is on the next floor, room one hundred seventeen," said the nurse. Myra and Amara thanked the nurse and headed down to the next floor.

Amara had a perplexed look on her face. "I didn't know he was dating Shareese, the police chief's secretary," she said. "She was the only one who had access to Chief Chaddam's office when those photos I delivered disappeared. Remember when I followed up with the chief and he said Shareese told him I came back and retrieved my photos when I had not?"

Myra shook her head. "I remember, honey. She also said the police chief must have misplaced them when you asked her about the photos. Luckily, you gave me those extra sets and took them by his home. I always thought something was suspicious about that whole situation," said Myra. Amara nodded her head in agreement.

"Don't you think it's odd that Paul still thinks she works for the police chief when he fired her a few weeks ago?" she asked. Myra agreed with her daughter. When the two women reached Michael's room, Amara stopped abruptly at the doorway. Her mouth fell open as she witnessed Shareese kissing Michael passionately on his swollen lips. Myra cleared her throat and entered Michael's room.

Shareese looked nervous and picked up her jacket and purse in an effort to leave. "I will wait down in the lobby for you, Michael," she said nervously. Shareese would not make eye contact with Amara as she left the room.

Amara placed her hand firmly on Shareese's arm and stopped her as she stepped across the threshold into the hallway. "Shareese, Paul told me to let you know that he was upstairs and that he was okay," she said in a deadpan tone as she stared Shareese down. Shareese jerked her arm out of Amara's reach, glared at her angrily, and walked swiftly to the elevator. She shoved the button hard and as soon as the doors opened, she got in without looking back.

Myra spoke briefly to Michael and joined Amara in the hallway. "Aren't you going to visit Michael?" she asked.

"No, Mom," she said. "I still think he had something to do with the attempt on my life," she said coolly. "In fact, those photos I gave Chief Chaddam should be fully analyzed next week if not sooner. I also think Miss Shareese is somehow involved as well. Maybe she was the one dressed in the dark suit in that park that day," she said, using her investigative tone.

Myra smiled. "Oh Lord, I know that tone of voice," she said. She slid her arm through her daughter's. "Let's get you home before you interrogate poor Michael," said Myra.

Amara looked at her mother and laughed. "You know me too well," she said.

"Like a book," said her mother. They both looked at each other and laughed aloud as they left the hospital.

Shareese removed the magazine from in front of her face and stared angrily at Amara and her mother as they walked through the hospital's mechanical glass doors. That woman could mess up all the hard work I've done to get Michael where I want him, she thought to herself. Within moments, her manicured fingers began to dial Duke Ellington's phone number. I own that man since I got his silly case thrown out of court, she thought to herself.

Duke looked at his caller ID display and read Shareese Miller's name. "Damn," he said and took a deep breath. "Hello?" he answered as if he were already bored with the conversation.

"Look, Daddy, I don't have long to talk, so listen up," she said in a bossy manner.

Duke sighed loudly. "Girl, how many times I got to tell you that I ain't your daddy," he said harshly.

Shareese clicked her tongue. "Whatever. After you put my mamma in that wheelchair and she couldn't earn us a decent living, you owe me, Duke," she said nastily.

Duke rolled his eyes. "Here we go again. I provided for you and your mamma just fine. Trouble was she couldn't keep her legs shut," he stated matter-of-factly. Shareese cleared her throat. She knew what he said was true. Her mother slept with plenty of men during her marriage to Duke and mostly for money. They paid her bills, bought her things…her mother had taught her all she needed to know about using her body for what she wanted from a man, which was lots of money. Her mother always had money stashed away for a rainy day, as she would call it.

"What do you want, girl?" said Duke as he intruded into her thoughts.

Shareese cleared her head. "I want you to do what you can't seem to finish. Get rid of that Amara bitch. Do it now!" she demanded.

"Gonna cost you," said Duke in a nonchalant manner as he flicked a speck of dirt from his tailor-made trousers.

"Whatever it takes," she said in an all-business tone.

Duke smiled. "Now we're talking, baby girl. I want a hundred grand up front and another hundred grand when the job is done," he said. Shareese agreed. "Let's meet at Donny's Tavern on the east side to work out the details," he said. Donny's Tavern was a dilapidated shack where petty criminals frequented. No one would recognize her there, she thought.

They agreed to meet in one hour. Shareese assured him she would have the money for him. Without saying another word, Duke hung up the phone and sat down in his single room apartment to work out the details. This time he wouldn't fail.

Shareese hung up her phone and headed to Michael's place to make sure the cleaning team she hired had completed all the work. She wanted everything to be perfect when she brought him home from the hospital later that day.

When Myra and Amara got home that evening, there was a rental car in the driveway. Amara felt a nervous pang in the pit of her stomach as they walked to the porch. Her father met them at the door. He had a strained look on his face. "Daddy, what's wrong?" asked Amara in a panic. Jackson nervously cleared his voice. Amara was trembling. She had never seen her father in this state. "Dad, what's wrong?" she again asked.

Myra came and stood beside Amara. "Jack, honey, what's the matter? You are pale as a ghost," she said, opening the screen door.

Jackson slowly stepped aside and allowed the ladies in. He then placed his hands in his pocket to prevent his wife and daughter from seeing them tremble. Tears welled in his eyes.

"Amara, honey, why don't you make some coffee and tea?" he asked. Amara looked at her father with fear in her eyes. "All right," she answered softly. "Do I need to make any for our guest as well?" she asked. Jackson nodded yes. "That would be nice. One extra coffee please." When Amara walked down the hall, Jackson led Myra into the formal living room. Myra walked into her own living room slowly, not knowing what to expect.

"Myra, this is Sam Peters from California," he said. "He is a private detective and a friend of Amara's," he said cautiously.

Myra looked at her husband quizzically. Myra relaxed and walked over and shook Sam's hand. "Nice to meet you, Sam," she said, smiling warmly. "How long have you've known Mari?" she asked.

"Not very long, Mrs. Glenton," he answered.

"Please call me Myra," she responded. "So are you hear to see Mari?" she asked.

Jackson walked over to the love seat and sat down. He patted the cushion and motioned Myra to sit beside him. When she sat down, he grabbed her hand and kissed it gently. Myra looked at her husband. "What's going on?" she asked.

Sam opened a folder. "Amara asked me to look into the past of Duke Ellington. She wanted to know more information about him. I was able to obtain his police record. He was charged and went to prison for rape," he said steadily. He opened the file slowly and pulled out the record and handed it to Jackson. Myra closed her eyes in an attempt to shut out the tears that began to fall. "Yes," she answered softly.

"I found out some other information about Amara. Does she know about any of this?" he asked cryptically. Both Jackson and Myra shook their heads no. "I won't say anything if you don't want me to but I...."

Amara walked into the living room holding a tray with mugs of coffee and tea. "Won't say anything about what?" she asked. Amara's eyes grew wide as she spotted Sam sitting in one of the cream-colored high-backed chairs. "Sam, what are you doing here?" she asked as she set the tray on the table.

Jackson looked at Myra and asked if he could tell Amara. Myra closed her eyes and whispered "Yes."

"Mari honey, Sam discovered some information regarding Duke Ellington and he wasn't sure how much of the information he should share with you," said Jackson. "Son, I appreciate you coming in person and talking to us first before sharing this painful information," he said.

Amara picked up her tea and sipped it slowly. "Dad, you sound like you are trying a case in the courtroom," she joked. Jackson didn't smile at her joke. Amara blew on her tea. "Sorry, I always joke when I get nervous," she said. "What is it, Dad?" she asked as she continued to blow the hot steam from her tea.

Jackson cleared his throat. "Duke Ellington was charged with rape almost twenty-seven years ago," he said.

Amara looked at her father and wondered where this conversation was going. "Yes, Dad, I know. I found that out at the library. So?" she asked.

"Mari, the woman who was raped nearly twenty-seven years ago was your Aunt Sarah," he said. Amara's hand shook as she sat her cup on the coffee table. The liquid swished around the rim and spilled onto the highly polished wooden table. Amara cursed under her breath as she mopped up the spilled contents with her napkin. She then looked at her father, waiting for him to continue.

Jackson gave a loud sigh as he grappled for the right words to explain further. Myra interrupted before he could begin. "Mari, when your aunt Sarah was raped, she became pregnant and she was not married. She was in college at the time and did not want to keep a child conceived in such hate, so she went to get an abortion," she said as she twisted her napkin.

"She went to some lady who lived in a back alley on the east side of town. Sarah had left a note for me and I returned home hours earlier than she had intended. I raced to the woman's house and pounded on the door. I got there just in time. I took Sarah out of that awful place and told her I would take her child when it was born and raise it as my own. You see, I could never have children and Jack and I wanted a child so badly. That child was part of my sister's blood. That child was you, Mari," she said quietly.

Amara covered her mouth and gasped. She stared at her parents and tried to comprehend what she had just been told. "When Sarah married your uncle Raymond, they tried to have children, but each time Sarah miscarried. This happened five times. The sixth time, she went past the first trimester. When she lost that child, she had a surgical procedure performed so that she would not bear any more children. It was just too painful," said Myra.

"I have always been close to my aunt," said Amara looking at Sam. She went and sat by her mother and held her hand. "But you are my mother. You are the only mother and father I know. I am just so thankful that you didn't allow the abortion to happen," she said as tears formed in her eyes. "Then I would never have had the chance to enjoy this full wonderful life that I have been blessed with," she said tearfully. Both of her parents hugged her close.

Sam remained seated and said nothing until everyone had regained their composure. "Amara, there is more. Duke Ellington is dying. I obtained records from his latest stint at prison and he has AIDS," he said. "To my knowledge, he is not taking any medication. It is just a matter of time." Amara shook her head. "I guess I should be angry for what he did to my aunt and to me, but I only feel sorrow for him. That night, when I looked into his eyes, I saw such anger and sorrow in them," she said quietly.

"Well, it's not over, Amara," said Sam.

"I know that," said Amara. "I am supposed to testify at his trial," she said.

"There won't be a trial, Amara," said Sam wearily. "Officer Blanco destroyed your statement, tampered with Duke's paperwork, and bribed some of the jurors prior to her arrest. The judge presiding over the case received an anonymous tip and called for a mistrial. Duke was released late yesterday evening."

Jackson was furious. "Why weren't we notified?" he asked.

"I don't know," said Sam. "Someone should have notified you. The mistrial was declared late yesterday." As Sam was finished his sentence, the phone rang. It was Police Chief Chaddam.

"Hey, Jackson, Tom here. I just wanted you to know that Duke Ellington is going to walk. The judge ruled the case a mistrial because of some illegal actions by one of my police officers. All I can say to you and your family is that I am sorry and we will keep tabs on Mr. Ellington for a while."

Jackson's jaw twitched as he listened to Tom. "Well, Tom, I appreciate you calling and notifying us personally," he said.

Tom apologized once more and asked to speak to Amara. Chief Chaddam told Amara he had the photos back and wanted to talk to her about them. She made plans to come to his office and asked if she could bring Sam with her. Chief Chaddam agreed and made arrangements for them to meet the following morning. Jackson invited Sam to stay at their home during his stay in Seattle. Sam graciously accepted the offer. He wanted to be close to Amara in case Duke Ellington came around and tried to finish the job.

Amara calmly picked up the coffee mugs and placed them on the tray. She excused herself and went to the kitchen to be alone and think. She rinsed the mugs, placed them in the dishwasher, and wiped down the already spotless sink. The phone rang and Amara answered. It was her aunt Sarah. "Hey, Aunt Sarah," she said cheerfully. She smiled with pride when she thought about her feelings toward her biological mother. She wasn't angry that she had given her up. Instead, knowing her aunt as well as she did, she was happy she had decided to go through the pregnancy. Her mother Myra was a wonderful mom, and she loved her more than anything.

Amara relayed to her aunt what she had just discovered and she and Sarah talked and cried for over an hour. Amara made sure Sarah knew she loved her and was not resentful. She also made it clear that she wanted their close relationship as aunt and niece to continue unchanged. Sarah gave a nervous giggle and agreed. She had no desire to change anything. They ended with their familiar "I love you" and hung up.

Myra came in and hugged her daughter. She held her tightly and gave her a big kiss. "I love you, Mari," she said with tears in her eyes.

"I love you too, Mom," said Amara, hugging her tightly. Myra looked at her daughter and wiped her wet eyes with the back of her hand, something she had done since Amara was a small child. Amara laughed at the gesture. "Mom," she said playfully as she got a Kleenex and dabbed her eyes. Myra smirked at her daughter and changed the subject.

"Sam is really cute. Do you like him?" Myra asked.

Amara shrugged. "I do, but he is involved in a serious relationship with someone else and Mom, she's drop dead gorgeous," she said.

Myra hugged her daughter and laughed. "If you want him, go for it," she said matter-of-factly.

Amara looked at her mother, surprised. "Mom, you never cease to amaze me," said Amara laughing playfully with her mother.

"Well let me get our guest comfortable in the guest bedroom," Myra said. "You go in there and say goodnight and give your daddy a big kiss," she said. Amara kissed her mother again and walked into the living room where Sam and her father were in deep discussion.

Amara walked over and gave her father a big kiss. He smiled and hugged her tightly. "You going to bed?" he asked.

"Yes, I think I will turn in for the night," said Amara as she gave her dad a big hug. Jackson smiled widely as he hugged her back. Amara walked over to Sam. "Sam, thanks for coming and letting me know about Duke," she said. "I'll meet you for breakfast tomorrow and we can go see Chief Chaddam about those photos I gave him," said Amara.

"Sounds great, Amara," he said. "See you tomorrow."

Myra walked in and offered to show Sam to his bedroom. She had already changed the linens on the bed and laid out clean towels for him. Sam shook hands with Jackson and excused himself. He followed Myra into the guest room. He set his duffel bag on the floor and marveled at how much he felt as if he were home in his own mother's house. He thanked Myra and told her that her guest room was so warm and comfortable it reminded him of his mother's home. Myra smiled and asked if he needed anything else. He smiled and told her she had already provided everything he needed. She told him that there was some hot chocolate, tea, and home-baked pound cake in the kitchen and for him to help himself. He patted his stomach, thanked her, and told her he was watching his weight. She smiled, said goodnight, and closed the door softly behind her.

Sam looked around the spacious room and adjoining bath. Both room and bath were decorated with old-fashioned wallpaper. There were thick blue and white throw rugs on the highly polished wooden floor and thick royal blue shaggy carpets on the spotless white-tiled bathroom floor. The dark oak bed was masculine and stood high off the ground. An oversized antique handmade blue and white quilt adorned the bed with matching throw pillows. White doilies covered the oversized dresser that still had its original smoky mirror. An antique porcelain pitcher and washbowl sat on top of the doilies. A comfortable overstuffed blue chair with a blue and white crocheted afghan blanket draped over one of its arms sat in the corner. There was also a matching footrest and a sturdy small table with a white doily set snugly against the chair in the corner. Oil paintings by famous African American artists hung on the walls. The paintings depicted scenes of country farms and small town activities. Sam noticed the guest room did not contain a TV, but had a well-stocked bookcase that contained hardback novels written by famous African American authors and a beautifully bound book of photography by Van Der Zee on the small table beside the chair. He smiled and knew who had placed that book in the room.

Sam took off his shoes and sat in the overstuffed chair. His body seemed to float on top of the cushion. He was surprised how comfortable the chair actually was. He sank into the chair and covered his legs with the afghan throw. He lifted his socked feet and rested them on the soft footrest. "Ah," said Sam as he felt his body sink to a comfortable position. Sam reached over and got the Van Der Zee book of photography. He flipped through the pages and examined the black and white photos of glamorous African Americans during the early 1900s in Harlem.

Sam continued to look at the photos and thought about Amara's love for photography. He also thought about Franni's love for being in front of the camera. He thought about how each woman was equally skilled in her craft. When he had looked at all the photographs, he placed the book back on the small table. As he placed the book back on the table, he noticed neatly displayed magazines sitting on the corner of the table. One magazine caught his eye immediately. It was an African American health magazine where Franni and another beautiful model adorned the cover. He looked at her beautiful profile. Her dark chocolate skin glistened beneath the white scant bikini. Her perfectly toned body looked very elegant in the photographed pose. Her close-cropped curls accentuated her beautiful facial features. He examined her flawless complexion that showed off high cheekbones, a small nose, full luscious lips, and wide eyes that were warm and brown like a baby doe's. He thought about how much care she took with what she ate, her daily beauty and work-out routines. He absently rubbed his chin in thought.

He thought about the direction of their relationship. Except for the time they had shared last night, they had not seen each other for several weeks. The calls from Franni had become infrequent, and each time he called her, she seemed too busy to talk. She always promised to return his call, but it usually took two to three days after the initial call. A sad feeling came over him. He felt as if Franni was slipping away. Sam thought about Amara and smiled. He had feelings for Amara, but had not acted on them because of the unresolved issues with Franni. Sam continued to muse about Franni when his cell phone rang. He answered the phone. It was Franni.

Amara couldn't sleep. She grabbed her keys and headed for the door. She checked her watch. It was nearly eight in the evening, but visiting hours were still open and she had to talk to Paul. She went into the den and kissed her parents on the cheek. "Mom, I have to go see Paul. There is something I need to tell him about his girlfriend."

Myra nodded her head while Jackson went back to reading the newspaper. "Just be safe," he said as he folded the paper to another section. Amara said she would and quietly closed the front door behind her.

Amara noticed an unmarked police car parked across the street with two police officers inside. She smiled and walked toward her car. One of the officers looked really cute, she thought to herself. She got in her car, started the engine, and drove down the familiar road of older homes with manicured lawns and tall trees. As she drove, she rehearsed what she would say to Paul. She didn't want to upset him, but she felt she owed him the truth.

Amara pulled into the hospital parking lot and parked her car. She walked quickly toward the automatic glass doors while constantly keeping an eye on her surroundings. She walked to the elevator and pushed the button. The doors slid noisily open. She got inside and absently pushed the floor number and rode quietly upward. The elevator bounced as it halted at the desired floor. The jolt made her stomach feel queasy, or perhaps it was her nerves? As she exited the elevator she saw Paul's nurse. The nurse recognized her and smiled. "Hi, hon," she said. The nurse looked down at her watch. "Only stay a few minutes okay? He needs his rest," she said protectively.

Amara nodded and quietly tiptoed in. Paul was trying to sip from a cup but was having a problem balancing it. Amara rushed over and helped him balance the cup. "Thanks, Mari," he responded groggily. Amara smiled and held the cup until he had drunk enough. Paul pulled his head back from the straw and lay against his pillow. She placed the cup on the tray connected to his bed.

"Hey, Paul," she said. She sat in the short vinyl covered chair next to the bed. Her hands brushed over the cotton blanket and she picked lint from the blanket. Paul rested his hand on hers. "Mari, what is it?" he asked.

Amara smiled and took a deep breath. "Paul, there's no easy way to tell you this. But I wanted to talk to you about Shareese," she said carefully. Paul exhaled. "What did you want to tell me?" he asked as if he already dreaded the answer.

"Paul, Shareese has been seeing Michael." Paul looked at her as if he couldn't believe what he just heard. "I saw them together today. She was kissing him passionately in his hospital room. She also took him home." Paul looked away and stared at the wall. He was upset by Amara's news and tried hard to process it. Amara stopped talking and stroked his hand.

He took a deep breath and drew his hand away. "Are you sure Mari? Michael and Shareese together? Are you sure?" he asked desperately. Mari nodded her head yes. Paul groaned and stared at the ceiling to keep tears from falling. He didn't know which hurt worse, the betrayal by his girlfriend or by his own brother. "Mari, I think you should leave now," he said barely above a whisper. Amara nodded. "I just need to be alone right now."

Amara gently kissed his forehead and walked to the door. "I am here if you need to talk," she said.

"I know. Thanks, Mari." There was silence and Amara walked out of the room and quietly shut the door behind her. She walked to her car and wondered if she had done the right thing. She sighed and started her car and headed for home.

Sam adjusted his feet on the matching footrest and sank into an even more comfortable position. "Hi, Sam!" said Franni in a cheerful voice.

"Hey," answered Sam absently. He was still thinking about the direction of their relationship. "Well, I am happy to hear from you too!" said Franni in a joking manner.

"Huh? Oh, I am sorry, honey. How are you? Did you make it in okay?" he asked, focusing totally on their conversation.

Franni gave a slight chuckle. "The storm hit sooner than we anticipated. I will be home tomorrow. I was hoping you'd pick me up from the airport," she said in a gay voice. Sam sat up straight in the chair. "That's wonderful," he said as he sat up in the chair.

Franni let a few seconds elapse before she responded. "Sam, you don't sound very happy that I'm coming home," she said slowly.

Sam sighed into the phone. "Franni, we haven't had a real conversation in about one month. Last night was the first real quality time we've had in I don't know how long. I will be glad to see you, but I feel that things have changed and I really want to discuss that with you," he said evenly.

"I know, Sam," said Franni. "I have been really busy, but I had a lot of time to think about us during my flight and I would like to discuss our relationship too," she said. "How about we go out to our favorite little bistro and talk over a good plate of broiled fish and...."

Sam cut Franni off before she could complete her sentence. "Franni, I am at Amara's. I found out some information about the man who tried to kill her and I came up to Seattle to discuss it," he said.

"I see," said Franni. "Couldn't you have discussed the information on the phone?" she asked in a strained voice.

Sam looked up at the ceiling. "No I couldn't, Franni. It was very personal information that I needed to discuss with Amara and her parents," he said.

"So what hotel are you staying at?" she asked.

Sam set down the magazine and traced Franni's face with his forefinger. "I am staying with Amara's parents," he said.

"And where is Amara staying?" she asked. Sam refused to answer.

"Franni, look. I will be home in about three days. The man who tried to kill Amara has been released from jail due to a mistrial and she and I are going to talk to the police chief tomorrow about some possible incriminating evidence," he said.

Franni rolled her eyes upward. She puckered her lips in disappointment. "I see," she said unemotionally. "So when will I get to see you?" she asked in an even tone of voice.

Sam smiled. "You sound like you miss me. Do you?" he asked seductively.

Franni couldn't help but smile because she really had missed him. "Yes, I do. I want you home soon," she said.

Sam smiled. "Give me two days and I will be back in your arms," he whispered. "Did I tell you that I missed you too?" he asked.

Franni smiled into the phone. "No you didn't. I can't wait to show you how much I missed you," she sang.

Sam laughed. All right, sweetheart, we'd better stop. You are getting me excited!" he said breathlessly.

Franni laughed. "See you in two days. Bye now," she said.

"Goodbye, honey," he said. Sam hung up the phone, grabbed the magazine that had Franni's photo on the cover, and kissed it. He then went into the guest bath and took a quick cold shower before retiring to bed.

Michael leaned on Shareese for support as he limped into the house. He was still very weak. Shareese had already set up the couch for him and led him over to it. He sat down gingerly and leaned against the soft pillows. A small smile appeared on his swollen face. It felt good to be back in his own home. Shareese had cleaned up the blood in the foyer and put everything back in its place. "Thank you for standing by me and doing all of this," he said as he gestured around the room. Shareese smiled and told him she was going to fix some soup.

Michael picked up the remote and began flipping through the channels. By the time Shareese returned with a mug of hot soup, Michael was fast asleep. Shareese covered him up and tenderly kissed him on the cheek. She placed the soup in a warmer and wrote him a note that said she would return later that evening. Shareese got into her car and returned to the hospital.

Shareese walked into Paul's room with a bundle of brightly colored balloons. The largest one read, "Get Well Soon."

His eyes sparkled. He was very happy to see her. "I see you got my message," he mumbled. Shareese looked at him, puzzled, and just smiled. She sat next to him and held his hand. She told him about Michael and that she had taken him home where he was resting quietly.

Paul remained quiet. He thought about his conversation with Amara. He then thought about how his brother had tried to dissuade him from dating Shareese. He became angry and hurt. Shareese was chattering on in a gay voice, but Paul didn't hear a word she was saying.

"Shareese, I am really tired. Would you mind leaving?" he asked abruptly. Shocked, Shareese gathered her things and tried to kiss his forehead. Paul turned his head away. A tear rolled down his face as she quietly closed the door behind her.

Shareese strode to her car at a quick pace. She got in and smacked the steering wheel with her fist. How stupid of me to tell Paul how much I had been helping his brother. Now he knows that I went to see Michael before coming to see him. She shrugged her shoulders carelessly. She never really cared for Paul anyway. He had nothing to offer her. She had learned a long time ago that all of his money was tied up in long-term investments and bonds. She also had the photo she needed, so she didn't have to waste anymore of her time on him. He was so boring and not her type.

She hummed a tune to the song on the radio and headed off to the city jail where Maria was being held. She had to find a way to get her out of jail, at least for the baby's sake. Nothing could happen to this baby. It was her other meal ticket. Once this little one was born and the DNA test conducted, they would both be rolling in the dough. Shareese smiled an evil grin as drove to the city police department.

Shareese walked into the office where she used to work. She smiled at familiar faces as she walked toward the chief's office. The chief always went out to lunch at the same time and he usually allowed the secretary to transfer the phones, so she could enjoy lunch too. She hummed a catchy tune and sashayed down the corridor to the chief's foyer. She stopped in mid-step when she spotted Scott.

"Where do you think you are going?" he asked as he backed her toward the wall, out of the main thoroughfare. Shareese regained her composure and walked back into the middle of the hallway. She looked at Scott and smiled sweetly. "Scott, how are you?" she said in a falsetto voice. Scott squinted his eyes. "My butt is much better, thank you for asking. Shareese smiled a catlike smile. "You enjoyed it and you know it," she said confidently. Scott backed away.

"When will I see you again?" he asked. "I miss you, us being together," he said shyly.

Shareese smiled. "Soon. Is the chief out? I left some paperwork for him to sign for my next job," she lied.

Scott squinted at her again. "My bullshit meter is going off a mile a minute," he said with suspicion in his voice.

Shareese cleared her throat and flung back her hair. "Well it's true," she pouted. "He said I was one of the most professional people to ever work for him," she said. Scott had overheard their conversation and knew that to be true.

"Hey, I start at the police academy next month," he said excitedly. She gave him a thumbs up.

"Well deserved, Scott. I wish you well," she said as she continued to walk slowly down the hall toward the chief's office. She stopped and turned to face Scott. "Hey, once you graduate, come on over to my place so we can celebrate!"

Scott smiled widely and tossed his keys in the air. "You've got a date!" he said as he went about his rounds humming one of his favorite country western tunes.

Shareese gave a sigh of relief and went to the chief's office. Bingo! No one was there. She remembered the hidden cameras and decided to step out of the view of any camera and place her scarf and glasses on. She walked up to the chief's door, inserted the key, and pulled it out of the lock. She breathed a sigh of relief as the door clicked open.

Shareese nearly fell inside the chief's office as the door jerked open. A woman was standing there adjusting her shirt and carrying a small padded bag by its handle. Both women gasped in surprise. The other woman regained her composure first.

"May I help you?" asked the sharply dressed black woman.

"What?" asked Shareese as she tried to bargain for time in order to think of an explanation.

"May I help you, Ms. Miller?" asked the woman impatiently. Shareese puckered her lips and slipped the key back in her pocket. She pushed up her sunglass and glared at the other woman. She allowed her glasses to fall into place on the bridge of her nose and turned on her heels and walked away.

The new secretary pushed a button and summoned Scott. Scott appeared immediately. "Scott, could you please escort Ms. Miller to the lobby and remove her badge," she said authoritatively.

Scott smiled. "Yes, Ms. Samuels, I will," he said as he gently took Shareese by the elbow and escorted her to the lobby.

Shareese snatched off her glasses and scarf when she got into the elevator. "Cow!" she spat.

Scott shook his head and t'sked. "You should have known better, Shareese," he said. "I guess I forgot to tell you that the chief allows his new secretary to expel her breast milk in his private bathroom while he's away for lunch," he chuckled. Shareese kept looking straight ahead and did not respond. Scott led her to the door. "Remember our celebration," he teased. Shareese glared at him.

Scott held out his hand. "Aren't you forgetting something?" he asked. Shareese smiled sweetly and walked up close to him. "Can't I keep it just a little while longer? I need to go see my sister who is in jail," she asked. Scott had heard about her twin sister Charlene. He had also heard that she was on the road to recovery. Officer Riley had discussed it during one of their breaks.

Scott grinned. "On one condition," he said. Shareese waited to hear the condition. "You let me come see you tonight and bring some of my new toys," he said softly.

Shareese smiled. "Sounds like fun. Come over at the usual time," she said. "See you at nine," he said. He watched her walk out of the door and smiled wide. He still owed her for those scratches and bruises she had left on his butt. He had something for her all right.

Scott made a quick call to the jail and said a few words to his cousin who was working at the front desk. They exchanged pleasantries and then Scott said something in a low tone of voice. He thanked his cousin and quickly hung up the phone. He began whistling his favorite tune as he took the elevator back up to the executive floor.

Shareese sauntered out of the door and headed toward the city jail. She entered the front door and walked to the front desk where a police officer was sitting and requested to speak with Maria Blanco. The police sergeant on duty was a muscular man with a clean-shaven face and blond hair cut short on the sides and trimmed flat on the top. His sky blue eyes seem to pierce through her as he glowered down. Without any pleasantries, he handed her a clipboard and instructed her to fill out the appropriate forms.

Shareese took the clipboard from the officer and filled out the forms. Once finished, she returned the clipboard to the desk. The sergeant took the forms and checked the list of names he had on another sheet. He shook his head. "Ma'am, I am sorry, but you must be a relative or a lawyer in order to see this detainee," he said.

"What? Why?" demanded Shareese.

"Chief's orders. Sorry, ma'am," he said abruptly. He went back to working on his paperwork.

Shareese opened her purse and pulled out her Seattle Police Department identification. "I work for Chief Chaddam," she huffed in an official tone of voice. The sergeant asked to see her identification. Shareese handed him her identification. He took the identification and placed it on the desk. He compared the identification with the roster from his word processor. The officer frowned and opened his desk drawer. He held the card up in the air, pulled out a pair of scissors, and cut her identification badge in half. "You were released from the police department several weeks ago, Ms. Miller," he admonished. "In accordance with our regulations I must confiscate your badge."

Shareese fumed with anger. "How dare you!" she shouted. Without saying a word, the sergeant pushed a button beneath his desk and a muscular young police officer calmly took her by the arm and escorted her off the premises. Embarrassed, Shareese got into her car and sped away.

Chapter 10

*A*mara knocked softly on Sam's door. Sam opened the door after the first knock and smiled at Amara. Amara smiled back shyly. "Hey, Mom has breakfast ready," she said. "I thought we could eat a quick breakfast and head over to the chief's office," she said.

"Let me put on my shoes and I will meet you in the kitchen," he said.

Amara stole a look at Sam as he bent over to retrieve his shoes. She thought he looked really sexy in the baby blue cotton polo shirt that hugged his muscular upper torso. His slacks hugged his lean waist and flowed about his thick thighs. Amara also noticed his protective vest and his weapon on the dresser. She took a deep breath but said nothing. As he stood up Amara turned quickly and blew out a nervous breath as she headed for the kitchen.

Sam smiled as he walked over to the chair, sat down, and put on his shoes. He had felt Amara's eyes roam over his body. He liked the idea of her getting frustrated by looking at his physique. He thought she looked very pretty in her soft cotton dress that accentuated her full breasts, even though the cut was modest. He liked the way her skirt flowed graciously about her hips and showed off her firm calves as she strode away from the doorway. Her hair looked so soft. The curls seemed to caress her face and give her a soft feminine look. He liked her sensible shoes, leather sandals with low heels. Franni hardly ever wore sensible shoes. They were always high heeled and glamorous.

Sam cleared his head and walked into the kitchen. He saw Myra standing over the stove and walked over and gave her a hug. "Good morning!" he said.

Myra smiled and hugged him back. "Good morning. You sleep okay, Sam?" she asked. Sam grabbed a plate from the counter and told her he had.

He walked over to the stove and put some breakfast on his plate and sat down across from Amara. They both ate in silence and stole looks at the other when they thought the other wasn't looking. Myra shook her head and chuckled. She prepared two plates for Jackson and herself and walked toward the patio where Jackson was reading the newspaper in the early morning sun. "Enjoy breakfast," she said as she stepped out onto the patio.

Sam looked over at Amara and cleared his throat. "Do you have copies of the photos that you gave the police chief?" he asked. Amara shook her head as she finished her toast and sipped her tea. "No, but I really hope the enlargements of the photos will help us identify some of the people in the photos. There were two people in the distance that we couldn't quite make out from the original photo. I have my suspicions but I want to be sure before I say anything that might incriminate someone who might be innocent. Chief Chaddam had all the photos enlarged and segregated by the people in the shots," she said as she took the last sip of her tea.

Amara looked at Sam and smiled. Sam couldn't help but smile back. He felt her smile was infectious. "Ready?" she asked.

Sam shook his head. "Just let me put these dishes away and thank your mom," he said. Amara helped him put the dishes in the dishwasher and they both went out to say goodbye to her parents.

As they drove off Sam told Amara he would be leaving tomorrow. Amara shook her head in acknowledgment as she navigated through the traffic. "Is Franni returning soon?" she asked. Sam stared straight ahead through the windshield. "Yes," he said.

"That's great, Sam," she said. "I know you really miss her," she said cheerfully.

Sam looked over at Amara and smiled. "I really do miss her," he confided. "We haven't been able to spend a lot of time together," he said glumly.

"Hey, Sam, you don't need to hang around here."

She steered the car into the Seattle Police Department parking garage. She handed a card the chief had provided to the attendant and was allowed access. "I will be around until tomorrow. I want to make sure you are safe," he said. Amara looked over at him and smiled. "Okay," she said. They got out of the car and walked to the garage elevator. Amara pushed the button for the police chief's office.

When they got out of the elevator and walked through the reception area, Chief Chaddam was waiting for them. Both shook the chief's hand. He introduced his new secretary, Mrs. Samuels, and escorted them into his office. He removed several photos from a large interoffice envelope. He handed each of them a copy.

Amara examined the photo. "That is definitely Michael with the briefcase and the woman looks like Shareese, your old secretary," she said to the chief.

Chief Chaddam shook his head in disappointment. "My sources tell me that Shareese and Michael have been an item for some time now. Even while he was married to Amelia—I mean Maria," he said.

Amara began to ask a question and the chief held up his hand, so he could explain further. "Amelia worked in the administrative section of the police department about three years ago. From what I can gather, Amelia Hernandez became pregnant by Michael Whitman before they were married. Apparently she broke the news to him and he deserted her during her pregnancy.

"I also discovered Michael fell on hard times. He skimmed money from his father's business to support his growing cocaine habit. Although the theft was never reported, Paul corroborates that part of the story with a written statement," he said and handed copies of Paul's statement to Sam and Amara.

"During college, Michael was close friends with Mr. Don Cooper, but their friendship waned after Cooper became a multimillionaire while working in a Fortune 500 finance company. It seems he developed a procedure to streamline the information about their clients. The simple software saved the company millions of dollars. Luckily, Cooper had the software patented. He quit his high paying job and sold the software to other institutions. Shortly afterwards, he married an affluent Latino woman from Spain and she became pregnant five years later.

"When Michael found out through a mutual friend that Mrs. Sonya Cooper was going to have a baby around the same time as Amelia, he renewed his ties with Don Cooper and mended his relationship with Amelia Hernandez. He became the doting father-to-be and caring mate.

"The story goes, after an ultrasound that determined the sex of their unborn child, he asked Amelia to marry him. The word around the station was that Amelia was relieved to be married before the baby was born. His friendship with Don was quickly rekindled and Amelia's friendship took off with Don's wife.

"They discovered many of their relatives were from the same hometown in Spain. Their pregnancy also drew them closer," said the chief.

He flipped to the next page of the report he was reading aloud. "Amelia delivered on the same date and at the same hospital as Mrs. Cooper. When her baby was born stillborn, Amelia was devastated," said the police chief. "She experienced a minor breakdown around the time of the ransom and baby fiasco with the Coopers.

"Amelia quit her job at the station and immediately requested a divorce from Michael. She then left town and changed her name from Amelia Hernandez to Maria Blanco. Once Amelia left town, Michael began to date Shareese openly. One year later, Maria returned and joined the force," said the chief as he shook his head in dismay. "She really seemed to have her life together," he said and set the file down on his desk.

"Shareese also dated Michael's brother, Paul," said Amara. "I later found out she was at his house the night Duke Ellington tried to kill me. She could have phoned Duke and told him where I was hiding." The chief nodded his head in agreement. "Apparently Michael Whitman concocted the scheme of

116

Shareese dating his brother in order to get information about the photos you took. He thought she could find out where you had hidden them. According to Paul, you had mentioned that you were there when the ransom was paid and took some pictures. Unfortunately Paul shared this in confidence with his brother," said the chief.

The chief opened his desk drawer and popped a couple of antacids into his mouth. "Miserable breakfast at the diner," the chief complained.

"Chief, I have a bit of information on Shareese Miller," interjected Sam. The chief shifted his attention toward Sam.

"Her mother was married to Duke Ellington for several years until he caught her with another man and shot them both. Shareese was the first to leave home. Her mother kicked her out when she became pregnant at the age of fourteen. Shareese ended up having two children and both were taken away and placed in foster care when she was seventeen years old because of her neglect.

"She also has a twin sister named Charlene, and a younger sister named Charity, who is autistic and has lived in a state run assisted living community home outside of Seattle for most of her life. According to the reports, both sisters visit Charity often. Charlene has been in and out of correctional facilities most of her life."

Sam showed them a picture of Charlene and Charity. He also had a picture of Shareese. The police chief took the three photos and examined them closely. "Uncanny," said the chief about the resemblance.

"When Shareese was twenty, she married a very wealthy man twenty years her senior who succumbed to heart failure two years later. He left her a small fortune of an inheritance and she squandered all of her inheritance in less than five years.

"Three years after her husband's death she met Michael Whitman, son of business magnate Ralph Whitman. Shareese and Michael have had a relationship for over four years. When her money was nearly gone, she took a job as a bookkeeper in one of Ralph Whitman's fast food restaurants. She recognized early on that Michael had a serious drug problem and thought him to be an easy prey.

"Michael's father learned that his business was losing money shortly after Michael became fully involved in the business. It was later determined that Shareese was skimming money from the accounts. Though they couldn't prove it, Ralph quietly fired her.

"After she was fired, Shareese latched onto Michael and persuaded him to continue to skim funds from his family's business and threatened to tell his father he was using drugs and stealing money, a prison offense, unless he paid her a monthly stipend equivalent to what she had earned when she was employed at the business," said Sam.

"Unfortunately, unbeknownst to Michael, his father already knew he had been skimming money from the business and was taking drugs. Ralph began to take responsibilities away from Michael and give more responsibility to his brother, Paul. Michael didn't mind the loss of responsibility, because he didn't lose any of the money he was earning."

Sam went through his notes and found the page he needed. He skimmed the document with his finger until he located the information. "According to a reliable source, Michael's father discussed his relationship with Shareese and his concern about a scandal since he had just learned his son had gotten his longtime girlfriend Amelia pregnant. Michael refused to stop seeing Shareese or take responsibility for Amelia's—or rather Maria's—pregnancy.

"Out of concern for his son and his business, Mr. Whitman placed Michael's stipend into a trust and forced Michael to live off his salary and he set up a trust fund for Amelia's baby to be used and managed by her until the baby reached the age of eighteen. He allowed Maria to manage a monthly stipend of fifteen thousand dollars to provide her son with everything he needed growing up and another two hundred thousand dollars for his college fund when he turned eighteen.

"Stunned, Michael felt he should manage the baby's fund and continue to get his stipend as he had in the past. Without the extra cash, he could not continue to live in the same manner and support his drug habit. Shareese continued to spend money and live in the manner they'd grown accustomed. Soon, they were both nearly broke.

"When Michael learned from a mutual friend that Mrs. Cooper was pregnant, he repaired his relationship with Amelia, and married her, but continued to see Shareese. So I guess they came up with the scheme of kidnapping the Cooper baby when all the money dried up," said Sam.

Chief Chaddam picked up the story where Sam left off. "Throughout the pregnancy Michael made every attempt for Amelia and Mrs. Cooper to get acquainted. Fortunately for Michael, the women got along very well and began to form a close friendship. In fact, Michael and Amelia even dined with the Coopers at their home on several occasions," said the chief.

"How did they get the child out of the hospital?" asked Amara.

The police chief smiled. "That was courtesy of Dan Macey and Rob Sully, two of Seattle's finest who were moonlighting at the hospital as security guards. They cased the place, reset two important video cameras while on duty the night before, and took the baby in the early hours before the security guards coming on shift realized something was wrong with the cameras.

"What they didn't plan on was one baby dying and the mix-up of the infants by the hospital staff. Shareese had spotted those two rotten apples and they were only too happy to comply with her scheme," said the chief.

Sam exhaled loudly. "Shareese is some piece of work," he said. "To make matters worse Michael schemed for Shareese to meet Paul and begin to date him. Paul had slipped and told Michael the story about your photos from the ransom and he wanted Shareese to find out more," he said. Amara massaged her temples.

"Paul is a very nice guy and a bit gullible," she said.

"Shareese could put on the charm when she wanted to. She had me fooled," said the chief. He then picked up the photo again. "And this whole thing would have gone off pretty much without a hitch, if you," he said, pointing at Amara, "had not taken this photo or told Paul about the photo," he said.

Amara shook her head guiltily. "You are right. I was so concerned about my investigative piece that I totally forgot about the innocent lives involved," she said.

"To make matters worse," said Sam, "the kidnapped infant was not even the Cooper's but the kidnapper's own child," said Sam. Amara shook her head in disbelief.

"And to add salt to the wound, Amelia, who up to this point was clueless about the whole ordeal, found out the Coopers had her child. She went to court and got her child back from one of her best friends, only to lose him two days later to SIDS," said Sam. Amara was astounded by this information.

"Yes, Amelia was never the same after that. Once the child died, Michael's father stopped the monthly stipend and withdrew the college fund. He told her he would continue it only if she had another child by Michael. This left Amelia totally dependent on getting a job for her continued survival. She went away for a while and worked odd administrative jobs. Then she returned and successfully went through the police academy training.

"A short time after she was on the force, Sully and Macey confronted Amelia about not getting their cut of the money. She didn't know anything about her ex-husband's participation in the kidnapping or the ransom money. When she discovered what had happened, her hatred grew so great that she readily agreed to join Macey and Sully in their blackmail scheme," said Chief Chaddam.

"When the blackmail money ran out, they wanted part of the ransom money," said Chief Chaddam. "I don't know why Paul was coming over to visit Michael," said Chaddam. "From what I hear, their relationship was pretty strained. I think Paul was beginning to really like Shareese and all Shareese wanted was part of the ransom money," said Chief Chaddam.

"And Michael hid the money as insurance, so the blackmailers wouldn't murder him," said Amara.

"I believe you are right Mari," said Chaddam.

"Even now, no one knows where the money is hidden," said Chief Chaddam. "But I can tell you that Sully, Macey, and Blanco are in jail and we have an all points bulletin for Shareese to bring her in for questioning." Chaddam scratched his head. "Something odd occurred yesterday," he said. "Shareese tried to use her old police identification to get in to see Maria."

Amara and Sam looked at one another. "Why would she do that?" they asked in unison.

The chief shook his head. "I don't know," he said thoughtfully. "But I do know that Maria is pregnant. She claims it is Michael's child." Both Sam and Amara looked at him, astonished. He shut the file completely and clapped his hands once. "As soon as Michael is well enough, he will go to jail also," said Chaddam.

"What about Duke Ellington?" asked Amara.

"As you know, he was released. We have intelligence that he is hiding out on the east side of town with relatives," said Chaddam. "Don't worry, Mari, we will find him. Until we do, I have put a patrol team at your home," said Chaddam.

Amara smiled. "I saw them yesterday, thanks, Chief," she said. Chief Chaddam covered her hand with his. "Anytime, Mari," said Chief Chaddam.

Sam smiled. "Anything else we should know?" asked Sam. Chief Chaddam shook his head no. Sam got up and shook Chief Chaddam's hand. "Thank you, sir, and it was good to meet you," said Sam. Chief Chaddam smiled. Amara gave him a hug and thanked him as well.

Sam and Amara left the office and headed to the elevator. Sam pushed the elevator button. The elevator opened swiftly. They both got in and Amara pushed the button for the parking garage. "Sam, why don't you leave this afternoon?" she suggested. "I have a patrol at the house and my parents won't allow me to go anywhere alone," she said. "Anyway, Franni needs you more than I," she said looking into his eyes.

Sam looked back into her eyes and couldn't decipher what he saw. She was keeping her emotions hidden. Sam smiled and hugged Amara. "Thanks, I think I will," he said. They got in the car and rode back in silence. Sam thought about seeing Franni and Amara thought about Duke, Paul, and Michael and how they were all connected.

When they reached her home, Amara parked the car and they both got out and headed for the door. Myra had made lunch. Sam smiled. "Mmm," he said aloud, "something smells really good!" he said.

Myra met them in the hall and invited them to share lunch with her and Jackson on the patio. They had not realized the amount of time spent with Chief Chaddam. It was already well after noon. As they prepared their plates and headed to the screened-in patio, Sam's cell phone rang. He immediately excused himself and went back into the house to take the call. It was Franni.

"Hi, honey," she said in a dull voice.

"Hey," said Sam. "You sound down. What's the matter?" he asked.

Franni explained that her agent had booked her for another photo shoot in the Caribbean. She would leave in two days and would not return for three weeks. After that she was going to Maui for another shoot and would be there for two weeks. Sam did the math and took a deep breath. "Franni, it will be nearly two months before I will get to see you," he said glumly. Franni kept silent and braced herself for his next comment.

"Franni, I plan to come back tonight. Would you make reservations at the bistro and meet me there at seven tonight?" he asked.

Franni calculated the time it would take her to pack. "Let's make it eight," she said.

"That's fine," he agreed. "I will see you at eight." The phone disconnected and he placed the phone back in its holder. By the time he joined the Glentons on the patio, they had finished their lunch and were laughing about a private joke.

Sam quietly walked onto the patio and looked for his luncheon plate. Myra smiled. "Your plate is in the oven, baby," she said. Sam thanked her and went to retrieve his plate from the oven. He placed his plate on the mat on the glass table and sat down to eat his lunch. Myra and Jackson excused themselves and took their dishes into the kitchen.

Amara drank the last of her lemonade turned her attention to Sam. "So, what time do you fly out tonight?" she asked.

"I made flight reservations for five," he said between chews.

"Well hopefully you and Franni will have some quality time," Amara said diplomatically. Amara then checked her watch. "Well we have about three hours before you need to be at the airport. Let's go down to Pike Place Market," she said smiling. "I want to have a little fun before you take off," she said. Sam smiled widely. "Sounds like a plan!"

He placed the last portion of chicken into his mouth and took his plate into the kitchen. "Give me five minutes to put my stuff in my duffel bag and I'll be ready to go," he said excitedly. Amara rushed into her room to change into jeans and one of her favorite designer t-shirts. She combed her hair and put a band around her thick mane. A single ponytail trailed down her back. She then added fresh lipstick to her lips.

She grabbed her keys and met him out in the driveway. He was placing his duffel bag and bulletproof vest in the trunk. He carefully placed his gun in the glove box. Amara wrinkled her nose. "Why did you bring your vest and your gun?" she asked.

"I wanted to be prepared for anything Duke Ellington has to offer," he said confidently. He shut the passenger door.

Amara suggested they take separate cars so he could go straight to the airport after the market. Sam agreed and returned to the house to thank both Myra and Jackson for their hospitality. Myra hugged him and gave him a big kiss. Jackson shook his hand and slapped him on the back. "Don't be a stranger now," said Jackson. Sam assured them both he wouldn't.

Amara spotted the two on duty police officers and smiled. She recognized Officer Riley and waved. He smiled and waved back. Myra went over and asked if they wanted coffee or sandwiches. As Myra conversed with the officers, Sam ran to his car and followed Amara, who was backing out of the driveway. They both headed downtown to the Pike Place Market.

Sam grabbed Amara's hand and held it as they walked through the market. They laughed at the men throwing fish back and forth. Amara bought fresh fruit and vegetables for her apartment and they looked at the sterling silver jewelry and unique gifts specifically made in the Pacific Northwest. Sam bought a t-shirt that had a funny saying about rusting in the rain. Amara suggested he buy Franni something fun from the market. He decided to get her an oversized t-shirt that had PIKE PLACE MARKET on it and two men tossing fish in a pastel yellow. "She will love it," said Amara. Sam smiled. "Something for her to sleep in on the road," he said, smiling.

Amara looked into Sam's eyes and though he was smiling his eyes looked sad. Amara walked toward him. "Want to talk about it?" she asked as she led him to a table in the back of the market. Sam shook his head no and took a deep breath. He looked at his watch and gave her a forced smile. Amara didn't press any further. Instead they got up from the table and walked through the rest of the market.

Sam checked his watch once more. He grabbed her hand and they headed to their cars, which were sandwiched with dozens of other cars. Amara gave him a hug and asked him to keep in touch. Sam promised he would.

As Amara was walking away, Sam called her name. She stopped walking and turned to face him. He walked to her and gently kissed her on the lips. The sensation shocked them both. Amara pulled away and looked nervously at the ground. Sam took the crook of his forefinger and lifted her chin. "Thank you," he said and kissed her again on the forehead. Amara hugged him tight. "You are welcome," she whispered in his ear. She dared not speak any louder for fear of crying. She felt so mixed up. Her control over the situation fled with the kiss on the lips.

Amara stepped back and walked to her car. Unsure of her willpower, she got in her car without looking back. She started her car and waved as she drove off. Sam smiled, waved back, and got into his car and headed toward the airport to catch his flight. He rehearsed in his mind what he wanted to say to Franni when he saw her that evening. He smiled when he thought of seeing his beautiful girlfriend. He hummed quietly and drove with the heavy traffic on Interstate 5 to the airport.

Tears streamed down Amara's face, nearly blinding her. She wiped them away and focused on the task at hand. Why did he kiss me? she asked herself. Even more important, why did I kiss him back and then allow him to kiss me a second time on the forehead, when I knew he was leaving me to be with Franni? I must be the biggest idiot, she thought to herself.

Just then a car rammed her from behind, causing her to swerve off the interstate. Her tires skidded as she tried to gain control of her car. She continued to career across the road and crashed into a guardrail. Amara's forehead suffered a deep gash from her steering wheel when her vehicle finally came to a stop. She felt herself falling into darkness, into a restful sleep.

She never felt him yank open the door and grab her as her car ignited in flames. She never felt him shove her into the back seat and drive away. And he never saw Sam slow down and watch the whole interaction.

Sam followed the vehicle expertly. He picked up his cell phone and immediately dialed Chief Chaddam's office and told him what had transpired. Chief Chaddam told him to keep in touch and he'd dispatch police cars to their vicinity. Sam's pulse raced, because he knew that the driver could only be one person, Duke Ellington.

Chapter 11

*M*ichael limped to his jacuzzi with the assistance of a cane. He needed something to relax him. He had called the nurse but was denied permission to sit in the jacuzzi. So he gingerly stepped into the warm water and sat on top of the padded bench, allowing only his feet and ankles to be immersed in the bubbling water. He tried to relax as the bubbles massaged his tired feet.

Michael moved his feet slowly and felt along the lining of the Jacuzzi where he had hidden the money. He closed his eyes as his feet felt along the familiar contours. Abruptly he stopped. His eyes popped open and he nervously felt the area again. Something was wrong. Something had changed. Michael could feel his heart beating faster.

He got up and slowly moved toward the knob to turn off the bubbles. He bent down and examined the spot more closely with his hands. He cursed aloud when he spotted the place that had been repaired and tucked under the lip of the Jacuzzi. He got his cane, limped slowly into the kitchen, and got a sharp knife. He returned to the pool and sliced open the plastic lining. Bundles of dollar bills tumbled into the hot water.

Michael breathed a sigh of relief. Everything looked fine. He picked up a bundle and unwrapped it. He removed the top bill in order to count the bundle and stopped. He threw bills across the length of the jacuzzi. White paper in the shape of dollar bills littered his tub. He limped to his bedroom. His heart felt as if it would beat out of his chest. He dried himself off and quickly got dressed. He called a cab. When the cab arrived Michael got in and gave the cab driver the address where he wanted to go.

Duke picked up the unconscious body of Amara from the back seat and carried her into the deserted warehouse. He placed her limp body on the cold concrete floor. He took out his pistol and placed a silencer over the muzzle. On top of his pistol he had placed a red laser sight. He smiled as he admired the work of his close friend.

124

He began to step back into the shadow when he noticed Amara making slight movements. He could see her begin to shiver from the coldness of the concrete. He grinned as he saw her try to orient herself. She looked like a small child who had just gotten off a fast merry-go-round. Her body swayed as she attempted to sit up. The bump on her head must have caused her to lose her equilibrium, he thought.

She then slowly lowered herself back onto the ground. Duke watched, amused, as Amara slowly attempted to pull her body into a sitting position once again. Dried blood was still on her forehead. She gently raised her hand to her head and gingerly touched the gash on her forehead with the tips of her fingers. She cringed in pain when her fingers touched a sensitive area. She tried to pull her matted hair from the gash, but gave up. It was too painful.

Duke's grin disappeared when Amara began to laugh hysterically. He turned on the laser sight and pointed it at her forehead. What came next seemed to make Duke's world stand still. Amara finally raised her body into a sitting position and glared at Duke like a caged animal. She then said, "So, Dad, are you going to kill your only daughter?" Duke's hand began to tremble for a slight second. He turned the laser sight off Amara. "What the hell did you say?" he asked nervously. Amara took advantage of his state of surprise and vied for more time. As Amara spoke the next words, she tried to sound more confident than she felt. "Do you remember a Sarah Miller?" she asked. "She was raped twenty-seven years ago," she spat.

Duke rubbed the smoothness of his bald head; the memories flooded back to him. He had adored Sarah for years. He asked her for a date every time he saw her, and each time she would refuse. One night after a movie, he saw her walking alone and followed. As she attempted to cross the street, Duke grabbed Sarah's arm.

When she looked into his eyes, she was afraid. She told him that the look of hate and contempt in his eyes scared her and that she didn't want to end up like his other girlfriends. She told him she knew he beat and disrespected women and she wanted a man who would love her and treat her with respect.

He had laughed in her face. He knew he could get any woman he wanted. No other woman had ever turned him down. They were too scared to turn down Duke Ellington. He found Sarah's confidence and self-assuredness to be a challenge. He wanted to break her like he had broken all of his other women. He wanted to take away her confidence and arrogance.

She quietly asked him to let go of her arm. He looked into her eyes and saw she truly did not want to be with him. He became angry and he slapped her hard, knocking her to the ground. Blood spewed from her busted lip, but she made no sound. Sarah tried to pick herself up from the ground and run away, but Duke punched her in the stomach. She doubled over in pain and threw up. Without saying a word, he dragged her to the alley behind the theater and violently raped her. His mind was on automatic pilot, he didn't even comprehend what he was doing, he saw only red.

Then suddenly his anger subsided and he saw a frail woman, bloodied, with ripped clothing, laying on the ground, her body contorted from the pain he had forced on her. He felt ashamed about what he had done. He tried to make amends by trying to pull her up and make her stand. But when he attempted to touch her in order to pick her up, Sarah let out a loud scream that attracted movie patrons to the back of the theater. Afraid, Duke ran away.

A middle-aged white woman parted the crowd and quickly covered Sarah's half-naked body with her coat. She knelt down and looked in the direction where she had seen the dark figure run. As she looked down the dimly lit alley, Duke slowed to look back. That was his terrible mistake. He and the middle aged woman's eyes locked in contact.

The woman yelled into the crowd for someone to call the police. She accompanied Sarah to the hospital and ensured her mother was contacted. When Sarah's parents arrived, they found the woman holding Sarah's hand and talking to her gently. The woman then volunteered to go to the police station where she provided a statement and a full description of Duke Ellington. He was immediately arrested and later sentenced to fifteen years in prison.

When he was released from prison, he never approached Sarah, though he had seen her on the street from time to time. Of all the bad things he had done, he was truly ashamed of what he'd done to Sarah. He couldn't believe Sarah had a child, his child, he mused.

A noise brought Duke's attention back to the present. He saw Amara running in a zigzag pattern toward the door. He aimed his gun at her back and pulled the trigger. The bullet sped through the air as Amara continued to zigzag toward the door. The bullet impacted Amara's arm, and she screamed in pain and fell to the ground.

At the same moment, Duke felt the strong force of another person restraining his movements. A second gunshot echoed through the air and landed in one of the wooden pillars of the warehouse. Duke used his elbow to jab the person in the ribs; that allowed him the space he needed. He turned and fired another shot. The bullet hit the man directly in the chest and he fell hard to the ground.

He turned his attention back to Amara. She was about one hundred feet away. She had her arm outstretched in an attempt to grab the large steel door handle. Duke lifted his weapon again and pointed the laser beam at her head and another gunshot rang through the air. Fearing for her life, Amara fell to the ground.

This time the bullet impacted into Duke's back. The force of the bullet caused Duke's body to lunge forward. On the ground, Amara inspected her wounded arm. The bullet had only grazed her outstretched arm. Duke's body convulsed momentarily before it became perfectly still. Sam got up from the ground. Thank God for bulletproof vests, he thought.

He looked down and saw where the bullet had lodged in the vest. His chest was bruised and ached from the impact. His breathing was labored. He slowly walked over to Duke's limp body, knelt down on one knee and felt for a pulse. He did not feel one. Duke Ellington was dead.

Sam walked slowly to where Amara lay and held her close. Her breathing was shallow. He looked at her wound and was relieved to see the bullet had only grazed her forearm. Her forehead was no longer bleeding, but the gash looked pretty deep. "You'll need stitches," he said to Amara in a calm voice.

Amara opened her eyes. Her arm felt as if tiny needles were shooting through it. Her head ached even more than before. She slowly turned her head and was relieved to see Duke lying on the ground.

Just then Police Chief Chaddam and several Seattle police officers burst into the warehouse. The chief began to bark instructions at the emergency medical teams as they ran toward Amara. They quickly placed her on an emergency stretcher and wheeled her toward the door. They also checked on Sam.

A police officer walked over to Duke and snapped pictures of his lifeless body and the surrounding area from every angle. The other officers continued to mark the crime scene and document the evidence retrieved.

Chief Chaddam walked quickly toward Amara and held her hand. "Thank God Sam called me," he said. Amara gave him a weak smile.

The chief continued to talk quickly as he walked alongside the stretcher. "We have police pursuing Michael Whitman. We found his business card and some money in Duke's car. The serial numbers on the bills match the ransom money from the Cooper kidnapping. It is almost as if he was setting Duke up to get caught by giving him this marked money," said the Chief. "He definitely wouldn't have gotten far." Amara still felt woozy. She couldn't understand why Michael wanted her dead.

Chief Chaddam seemed to read her thoughts and continued to talk. "Michael panicked. We checked out Duke's apartment and found written instructions and a dollar amount for killing you. Apparently Michael offered to pay Duke a large sum of money to kill you when he found out about the photos.

"After Duke bungled the first attempt on your life and Shareese recognized herself in one of the photos you provided me, she paid Duke to kill you in order to keep you quiet. As you know, Duke was her stepfather."

Amara was trying to comprehend what the chief was saying but couldn't.

The chief continued to ramble on. "Duke didn't trust Michael and had him tailed by a friend of his. Fortunately for us, his friend was an undercover officer," he said. "The undercover officer is at Michael's house right now, keeping surveillance on him."

"The doctor stated Michael was not strong enough to go to jail and our infirmary is full, so Michael is being held under house arrest until his wounds heal." Amara looked at Chief Chaddam, still trying to take it all in. The medical technician had given her something for the pain and she began to feel very sleepy. By the time they lifted the stretcher into the back of the ambulance she was fast asleep.

At the hospital, Myra and Jackson waited nervously for their daughter to come out of the emergency room. When they wheeled her out she had a few stitches in her forehead that was heavily bandaged and a bandage covering the wound on her arm where the bullet grazed her, but overall she was fine. The nurse had Amara's parents sign the release form and Amara was told she could she could go home.

The doctor advised her mother that she should not be left alone for the first night because of the gash she sustained when she bumped her head, but she would be fine. She handed Myra the prescriptions for Amara. Myra took them and walked behind the wheelchair and pushed her toward the hospital exit.

Myra smiled as she spotted Sam walking stiffly toward them. He looked as if he was in great pain. Myra rushed up to him and immediately told him that he was not leaving town tonight. He needed to call his lady friend and tell her he'd be there tomorrow.

Sam winced. "I have to go back, Myra," he said. "Franni is leaving in two days for the Caribbean," he said wearily. Myra smiled. "Have her come stay with us. We have another guest room," she said with finality. Amara rolled her eyes. Jackson saw her and admonished her with a stern look. She looked down at the ground, ashamed that her father had seen her react so selfishly.

"She's right, Sam," said Amara. "Call her and tell her to come up before she flies," she said. Sam agreed and called her. Franni agreed and Sam told her he would pick her up from the airport. Everyone piled into Jackson and Myra's Volvo and headed to Sam's car. Jackson dropped Sam off at his car, which had been left at the warehouse. Franni was already packed and was able to get on the next flight that would arrive in two hours. Sam sped toward the airport, while the Glenton family headed home.

Shareese smiled as she quickly packed the last of her belongings in her designer luggage. She slipped her ticket to Europe in her pocket. She heard the taxi honk outside and grabbed her luggage. She checked her watch. "Well, Duke should have done the deed," she said aloud to herself nonchalantly. She opened the door and struggled with all of her luggage. She had four large suitcases. She saw the taxi as she backed out of the door with two large pieces with her.

"Excuse me, sir," she called over her shoulder, "can you help me, please?" She felt someone grip the luggage and answer, "Sure thing, Shareese." She froze in her tracks. She dared not turn around. She regained her composure and turned with a big phony smile plastered on her face.

"Michael, baby, what are you doing here?" she asked. "I thought the doctor gave you another week of bed rest?" she asked, with concern. Michael limped toward her with a huge scowl on his face. Before she could move, he struck her hard across the face with his cane. He connected with her cheekbone and continued until he reached the corner of her mouth. Shareese fell backward and hit her head on the cement stair. Her hand immediately went up to her face as blood trickled from her cheek. She howled in pain and knew that blow would leave an unflattering scar and cause permanent damage to her beautiful face.

Shareese began to curse Michael while he ripped open each piece of luggage and threw her clothing about the front yard. Shareese tried hard to focus but couldn't. As she sat up, more blood streamed from her face. She swore she could see white dots in front of her eyes as she tried to focus. She grabbed hold of the stair rail to steady her and used the stair to support the weight of her body. She tried to speak as blood continued to pour from her face and busted lip.

"Michael, why did you do this to me?" she screamed. "What is the matter with you?" she cried. After he had gone through the last piece of luggage, he ran over to Shareese and placed his large hands around her neck and began to choke her. Shareese gagged and could no longer speak. She felt herself lose consciousness as her air was cut off.

The taxi driver, who had been waiting by the curb, sped off. His wheels squealed on the cement as he quickly turned the corner. The cab driver immediately got on his radio, requested 911, and gave Shareese's address. Suddenly a sedan door quickly closed and as Michael continued to choke Shareese and demanded to know where she had hidden his money. A strong hand grabbed Michael's collar and threw him to the ground. Michael landed hard on his injured leg and was unable to get up.

The gentleman showed his badge and identified himself as a Seattle police officer. Michael lay flat on the ground in pain. Shareese clutched her bloodied, swollen face and remained on the step.

The officer summoned back-up and both Michael and Shareese were arrested. To her dismay, all of her luggage was taken into custody as evidence. As the officer removed the last suitcase from the house, the suitcase latch gave way, and bundles of money fell to the ground. Both Shareese and Michael looked at all the money and hung their heads low. They were put in separate cars and driven to the police station.

Franni got off the plane and anxiously looked around. She smiled as she saw Sam holding a beautiful bouquet of flowers. She strode over to him and gave him a passionate kiss on the lips. "Wow," he said, nearly breathless. "I should buy you flowers at the airport more often." Sam looked at her ticket. "How much luggage did you bring?" he asked. She patted her small duffel and told him she had two large suitcases at the baggage claim. "I travel light," she said smiling. Sam rolled his eyes and smiled. "Considering you are going on a big photo shoot, you really did travel light," he joked.

They smiled at each other and went to pick up her luggage, Sam led her to the rental car. Sam and Franni chatted easily on the way to the house.

Franni told him about her next photo shoot and how excited she was to be doing the layout for one of the top magazines in the country.

Sam told her he was happy for her, and glad they could spend a little time together before she left. He also told her about the incident with Amara, the Glentons, and their beautiful home and warm hospitality.

As Sam turned the corner onto the Glenton's block, Franni looked out the window and admired the manicured lawns and older traditionally styled homes in the established neighborhood. "Maybe one day we will live in a neighborhood like this," she mused.

Sam chuckled. "That's if I can keep you in one spot long enough to marry you," he said jokingly. Franni gave him a serious look, but said nothing. They had never discussed marriage.

Sam pulled into the drive and saw Myra and Jackson, arm in arm, standing at the door. Franni walked quickly up the stairs. Sam introduced Franni to Myra and Jackson. Myra smiled and gave Franni a warm hug. "Let me show you to your room and then you can join us on the patio for some refreshments," she said. Sam took her duffel bag and other pieces of luggage out of the car and carried them to the room. He set her things on the floor and headed out to the patio. He knew Franni was in good hands with Myra.

Sam spotted Amara propped up with pillows on the cushioned chaise lounge slowly sipping juice from an iced mug. He smiled and told her that Franni would be out in a moment. He sat down beside Jackson and poured himself a drink in one of the frosted mugs and took a big gulp.

Franni followed Myra into the bedroom. She looked around the room and liked it right away. "Mrs. Glenton, this room is beautiful! It looks likes one of those rooms shown in those popular home decorating magazines," said Franni.

Myra blushed at the compliment. "I bet, as a model, you've been in many fabulous rooms," said Myra. "And please call me Myra," she said giving Franni a slight hug.

The room was decorated in white and mauve. It looked very feminine. She placed her duffel on the polished wood floor. She was immediately drawn to the small white wood dressing table with its delicate antique glass perfume bottles. She moved over and touched the canopied white bed. She admired the mauve net canopy that delicately cascaded down on three sides of the bed like a teepee. The white chenille bedspread and white pillows with mauve ruffles adorned the oversized bed. She smiled when she saw the crackle whitewashed small stepstool with a paisley cushion that matched the pattern of the duvet by the window. There was an antique white armoire placed in the corner. Several black, brown, and tan rag dolls were perched on an antique duvet painted in a white crackle finish. A sturdy high-backed chair in a white and mauve paisley pattern was adorned with a crocheted mauve throw made with soft, rich-colored yarn.

"Mrs. Glenton—I mean Myra, this room is simply fabulous!" exclaimed Franni, truly in awe. Myra smiled. "Did you have a designer decorate this room?" she asked.

Myra chuckled. "No, child, I did this room by thinking about what I really liked and about the things that I liked in my momma and grandmamma's homes. We've always been a creative bunch. I think that's why Mari likes photography so much. She comes from a line of creatively inspired people," bragged Myra.

Franni shook her head in agreement. She asked Myra questions about the patterns and the crackle painted furniture. "Wow, I can't believe you did this all yourself!" said Franni.

Myra smiled. "Now let's get you freshened up and out on the patio with Sam," she said as she showed her the guest bathroom.

Franni gasped at the beauty of the bathroom. It looked small from the outside, but once you walked in it was huge. There was a dressing table inside the bathroom, an oversized tub with gold bear claws supporting its frame, and an old-fashioned porcelain sink with antique white hot and cold knobs that looked like daisy petals. Myra smiled and handed her thick, fluffy mauve towels.

She gently closed the door and walked into the kitchen to join the rest of the family. Myra went to the kitchen and took out a tray of hors d'oevers and placed them on the table. She poured herself a glass of juice and relaxed beside Jackson. "Franni will be out in just a moment," she said to Sam. Sam smiled nervously. He hadn't seen Franni in such a long time. He felt selfish and just wanted to take her away and be alone, but he knew that would be unkind to the Glentons.

"Mari, honey, do you need anything?" asked Myra. Amara shook her head and patted the spot beside her. Myra walked over and sat down beside her daughter and gently smoothed back her hair.

"Mom, I feel so jealous right now," she whispered in a low voice. "What do I do? How do I act?" she asked in a desperate tone.

Myra smiled, and whispered in her ear as she continued to stroke her hair. "Just continue to be the decent person that you are and allow those two to work things out. If it is meant to be, it will happen. I am proud of how you are acting, and how you have conducted yourself around Sam. You just watch, whatever the outcome, it will be for the best," she said. Amara began to pout. What happened to, "go for it?" she thought to herself.

Myra smiled as she sensed what Amara was going through. "Things will work out, trust me," she said lovingly. Amara nodded. Just then Franni walked into the room and sat down by Sam. She greeted Amara and asked how she was feeling. Amara smiled slightly and told her she was doing better. Amara also welcomed her to her parents' home. Franni smiled.

Amara noticed that Franni was wearing a beautiful powder blue silk lounging outfit that went perfectly with her mocha complexion and curly short-cropped hair. Her flawless skin glistened and looked as if she had put a little powdered glitter on it. "Your outfit is beautiful, Franni. Where did you get it?" she asked. Franni smiled and told her she had purchased it when she did her latest photo shoot in Europe.

Everyone made small talk and Sam poured Franni a cool glass of juice. Jackson gave Myra the cue and both went to help Amara get comfortable in the den. "You all don't have to leave," said Franni nervously. Jackson smiled. "It has been a hectic day and we are all pretty tired. We are going to get Amara set up in the den and allow you two to have some quality time before you leave tomorrow," he said. "It was nice meeting you all," said Franni graciously. They smiled and nodded.

"Maybe next time you visit I can really show you around, Franni," said Amara.

"That would be really great," said Franni. They left the room and closed the sliding door behind them.

Franni felt so welcomed in the Glenton's home and told Sam how she felt. Sam looked into her eyes and kissed her passionately. Franni returned the kiss. "Franni, there is something I need to talk to you about," he said, in an unsteady voice. Franni held her breath, expecting Sam to break off the relationship with her. "Sam," she interrupted. "Look, I know we haven't spent much time together and my career has taken me away from you but...."

Sam placed his forefinger gently on her lips in order to silence her. He then took a deep breath and continued with what he was saying. "What I was going to say is that I love you, Franni, and I want to spend the rest of my life with you. I know it won't be easy but after this episode with Amara, I know I don't ever want to leave your side," he said.

"Are you sure?" she asked. "I was concerned about you and Mari. I was afraid she could give you something I can't right now, her undivided attention and time," she said, honestly.

Sam smiled. "We've always been honest with one another. That has been the cornerstone of our relationship. I was attracted to Amara and flattered that she had so much time to spend with me, but my heart and thoughts were always of you. Even when I was with her," he said earnestly.

He got down on one knee. "Franni, will you marry me?" he asked. He presented a beautiful three-carat diamond ring and placed it on her finger. Her hand trembled and the tears began to flow. "Yes, I will marry you!" she yelled.

Myra ran to the patio when she heard Franni yell. "Everything all right?" she asked cautiously. Sam and Franni were holding hands. Franni was crying. Myra's face filled with worry until she looked down at Franni's finger. "Oh my gosh! Congratulations, you two!" she exclaimed. She yelled for her husband.

Jackson came back and joined the celebration. He went into the kitchen and got four champagne glasses and a bottle of expensive champagne from his wine rack. He poured ice into the champagne bucket and brought it out onto the patio. "This calls for a celebration!" he said excitedly. They allowed the champagne to chill while they discussed the upcoming wedding. Franni asked permission to use the phone to call her parents. Myra showed her where the phone was and she left her to make her call in private.

Franni returned and was handed a glass of champagne and Jackson made a toast to the newly engaged couple. "To Franni and Sam, may your marriage be blessed with longevity and happiness." Sam and Franni smiled as they looked at one another. They each clinked their glass against the other's and took a sip of the champagne.

When they had finished the glass of champagne and talked about some of the wedding arrangements they'd have to make, Sam excused himself and politely told Jackson and Myra that he and Franni were going for a short ride and would be back soon. Myra and Jackson hugged the couple and remained on the patio for a while and discussed the days' events.

A couple hours later Franni and Sam returned and walked in the house holding hands and talking quietly to one another. Myra smiled at both of them. "Mari's awake if you'd like to share your wonderful news with her.

Sam and Franni looked at each other and smiled. "We'd like that," they said in unison. Franni knocked softly on to the den and peeked in. Amara asked her to come in.

As soon as Franni walked into the room, Amara saw the large diamond in her ring glisten. Her stomach turned flip-flops, but she managed a smile. "Wow, I guess congratulations are in order?" she asked, genuinely happy for the couple. They both smiled and were relieved by her comment. Franni walked closer, so that Amara could see her ring. "Franni, your ring is so beautiful," she said, as she held her hand. "I am so happy for you both," she said smiling.

Amara began to feel tired and yawned. "Mari, thank you for welcoming me into your beautiful home," said Franni.

Amara smiled sleepily. "I am glad that you were able to make it," she said. "Sam really missed you. He really wanted to see you before you left on your photo shoot. If it hadn't been for me, you'd both be in California instead of here," she said glumly.

Franni laughed. "Then I wouldn't have had the chance to meet your wonderful family. Mari, you are so blessed to have such a wonderful and loving family. There is warmth everywhere in this house," she said. Amara knew Franni's comment was heartfelt.

Amara held out her hand and Franni gently took it into hers. "I am glad you are here too," she said honestly. Sam walked over and gently kissed Amara's swollen forehead. "You take care of her now!" she said jokingly to Sam. Sam smiled and said he would. Amara yawned once more, mumbled something, and drifted back to sleep.

Sam and Franni quietly tiptoed out of the room and went to sit on the patio. They enjoyed another glass of champagne and discussed dates for their wedding. Franni pulled out her planner and they decided on a December wedding. That would give them eight months to plan the perfect wedding.

Sam rose and gave Franni a big hug and a kiss. "Baby, I missed you so much!" he said as he continued to hug her.

Franni hugged him back. "I missed you too," she said. Sam took her hands and sat with her on the settee.

"What would you say if I joined you in the Caribbean on the last day of your shoot and perhaps we could stay over a couple of days?" he asked.

Franni smiled. "That is very sweet, but I am not going to have any personal time," she said.

"How about I meet you in Maui and we spend some quality time together?" he suggested as he ran his hand through her short-cropped curls.

Franni's head reeled back in complete pleasure. "Sam, stop, you know how much that turns me on," she said in a naughty tone of voice.

Sam laughed out loud. "Well, how about Maui?"

Franni looked Sam in the eyes and held both his hands. "Sam, I need to be totally focused and I won't be if I am thinking about you coming to visit," she said. Sam took his hands from hers as if they had suddenly turned poker hot. He bit down hard and caused his jaw to ripple. Franni tried to tease him. "Sam, stop biting down on your jaw. You only bite down hard like that when you are angry. Are you angry with me?" she cooed.

Sam shook his head no. "I am just very disappointed, Franni," he said.

Franni sighed and moved closer to Sam. "Well, how about we go on a little vacation when I return?" she asked.

"That would be fine, if I didn't think you were going to pick up another shoot after Maui," he said defensively. Franni started to speak and Sam cut her off. "I know, I know, your job is the most important thing right now," he mimicked.

Sam guzzled down his champagne and bade Franni goodnight. He walked to the door and left her alone on the screened patio. Franni wiped the tears from her eyes. She cursed Sam aloud. She couldn't afford to have puffy eyes for her next day's shoot. Franni got up and picked up the tray that held light snacks and drinks and carried them into the kitchen. She took a few of the sliced cucumbers and placed them in a small dish.

She left the kitchen and headed toward the guest room. She went into the room, closed the door quietly, and set the bowl of cucumbers on the dressing table. She walked over to the stereo and pushed the power button. Franni pressed the digital tuner until she found a soft jazz station. Humming softly to herself, she set the volume on low, pulled off her shoes, and went to the bathroom to shower. When she finished, she went through her beauty regime.

She saw an oversized yellow t-shirt with a tiny note placed on her bed. She read the note aloud, "Think of me when you are in this t-shirt." She took off her clothes and put on the large t-shirt and looked at herself in the mirror. The t-shirt had two men tossing fish at one another. She covered her mouth to stifle a giggle.

She picked up the small bowl of cucumbers and stepped on the small paisley stool and climbed onto the bed. She fluffed the pillows, reclined back, and looked at her ring once more before she placed the cucumber over her eyes. Franni sighed loudly. She thought about her relationship with Sam. She had no idea how she was going to make it up to him, but she would try. They were going to be married soon. She had some serious decisions to make about her career. Franni pushed all negative thoughts from her mind and began her breathing exercise. Soon she drifted off to sleep.

Sam grabbed a book from the shelf and walked over to the comfortable chair and sat down. His body sank down into the chair until he was completely comfortable. He felt so frustrated. I just proposed to Franni and she is still putting her career first, he thought. Sam continued to stare at the same page for five minutes before he discovered he wasn't reading. He closed the book and set it on the table. He grabbed the magazine with Franni's face on the cover. He traced her face. Exasperated, he set the magazine back on the table and prepared for bed.

Amara woke up with a start. She sat up in her bed and yelled out into the darkness. Perspiration dripped from her forehead. Her heart was beating rapidly. She picked up the glass of water her mother had placed on the small table and took a sip. It was also time for her to take another pill for her pain. They would help her sleep as well. She removed the top from her pill bottle and popped one into her mouth and chased it with water. What a terrible dream, she thought.

Myra, who had been lounging in the recliner in the back of the den sat quickly up from the chair and stood to go over to Amara.

Amara tried to calm her breathing, so that she could go back to sleep. Just then a voice startled her. "Are you all right?" he asked. Amara jumped when she heard Sam's voice. She could barely make out his figure as he stood in the shadows of the dark room. She had been totally unaware that Sam was in the room until he spoke.

Amara was annoyed. "I just had a bad dream," she snapped. Myra quietly sat down in the shadows. Amara checked her watch. "What are you doing here?" she asked. "It's three in the morning," she stated.

Sam began to stutter. "I—I wa—was just checking on you to make sure you were all right," he said. "And?" she asked. "Franni and I had a little argument earlier and I was hoping I could talk to you about it," he said warily.

Amara pointed at the overstuffed chair near the sofa where she was lying. Sam walked over to it, sat down in the darkness, and pulled it close to the sofa, so he could talk quietly. Amara leaned back on her pillow and closed her eyes for a moment. She reached for his hands and held them firmly. "Sam, you need to get a grip. I can guess the fight was about her career. Franni is not going to drop everything just because you asked her to marry you. Her career is important and it fulfills her. She loves you and she has been honest and up front with you from the beginning of the relationship. You told me that many times. I suggest you try to understand her position and be patient. Her career is short-lived. Let her live it without any regrets. Franni's yours for a lifetime," she said.

Sam smiled and kissed her hands. "Thanks. I needed a kick in the butt," he said lightheartedly.

Amara looked at him and tilted her head. She pulled her hand away from his. "Sam, stop straddling the fence. I am attracted to you and that is something I will have to deal with. I need some space from you. Time to adjust to this engagement. Okay?" she asked earnestly.

Sam shook his head. "You are right. I am sorry I put you in such a position. I am truly sorry." Sam got up and quietly left the room.

Amara sighed and turned her head as the tears dripped onto her pillow. Moments later, there was a knock on the front door. Amara wiped her eyes and got up from the sofa bed and walked slowly to the front door. She turned on the hall light and looked through the small glass window to see who it was. The porch light illuminated a tall handsome man dressed in a police uniform standing at the door. She could barely read his badge, but she recognized his face. It was the same officer she had seen parked outside the front of her parent's house earlier.

She opened the door. Tony looked at her and smiled. "Ma'am, I am Officer Tony Riley. I was assigned to your house yesterday, but we've just been notified that we are no longer on this detail. I apologize for the inconvenience and the lateness of this notification, but I wanted to inform you that we were departing and make sure everything was okay."

Amara smiled and winced in pain. "I am fine, Officer Riley. Thank you for your concern. "He smiled and exposed white even teeth. He tilted his police cap and walked away from the porch.

Sam had also heard the doorbell and stood in the background with his hands on his hips just in case there was any trouble. When he saw the silly grin on Amara's face he quietly walked back to the guestroom. Amara felt a jolt as she quietly closed the door. "Who on earth was that?" she asked aloud as she walked back to the sofa bed. She faintly remembered seeing him earlier in the day and smiled at the recollection. She got in bed and pulled the covers up to her chin.

Minutes later her mother got up from the recliner and checked on her. She pulled the covers down and tucked them around her as she heard soft snores coming from Amara. Her mother looked down at her and gently caressed her mussed hair. She had already fallen into a drug-induced slumber.

Chapter 12

After being on bed rest for one week and taking it easy an extra week, Amara was ready to get back into the swing of things. She also decided it was time to look for another place to live. The threat on her life was over and it was time for her to get back out there on her own. Her new job and higher salary meant she could afford to look at some single-family homes in a nearby suburb. She had already decided she didn't want to live far from her parents. Since her ordeal and finding out about her adoption, she had grown even closer to her parents and her Aunt Sarah.

Amara examined her reflection of her face in the mirror. She timidly touched the area where her stitches once were. They had dissolved and all that remained was a light scar that seemed to fade more and more with each days passing. She had almost full movement of the arm that bore a slight scar where the bullet had grazed her. She smiled at the prospect of regaining her normal life. She had purposely not made any contact with Sam since their discussion the night before he and Franni left. He had sent her a bouquet of get-well flowers and a quick email wishing her a speedy recovery. She thanked him for the flowers with a return email and had not corresponded with him since.

She really needed space from him so she could sort out her life and move on. She was not jealous of Franni. In fact, she knew he loved her, but her absence had definitely made his eyes wander. Amara smiled. She would find the right person for herself. She knew he was out there somewhere.

She placed a small amount of makeup concealer on her forehead and carefully blended it in. Once she was satisfied, she added lipstick and styled her hair. She examined her forehead in the mirror. She liked what she saw. She was just happy to be alive. She shuddered to think what would have happened if Sam had not shown up. For that she would always be grateful. She checked her watch and quickly left the bathroom and retrieved her coat from the small hall closet. "New beginnings!" she said as she grabbed her purse and strutted out the front door.

Amara walked briskly up the steps to the local real estate agent. She double-checked her watch to make sure she wasn't late. She was told this new agency was really good. It had a strange name, but the co-manager, Angelique, sounded very professional and told her she had a lot of homes that fell into her price range and the desired areas where she wanted to live. DeCar Real Estate Agency was a small store-front operation that was located only minutes from her home in East Seattle.

Once she walked into the brightly lit room, she was greeted with a firm handshake from Angelique. "Hi, I am Angelique. Welcome to our agency," she said in a cheerful tone. She asked her to take a seat and told Amara that her partner, who was her father, would be right with her.

Several seconds later, a slightly balding middle-aged man with a bushy mustache and twinkling, mischievous eyes walked briskly toward her. He stuck out his hand and introduced himself as Mr. Dern. Although his hands were soft, his handshake was very firm and businesslike. She liked him right away. Amara smiled as she thought of the bright and professional attitude of DeCar agency.

Mr. Dern walked over to his desk and asked Amara to follow and take a seat. He pulled out a list of homes he wanted to show her and assured her that by the end of the appointment she would fall in love with one of them. Amara laughed at his confidence. "All right," she said hesitantly as she looked over the list of homes and the small photos that accompanied them. He placed his reading glasses on the tip of his nose and reread the questionnaire she had filled out earlier in the week. He went over a few areas with her to ensure he had the correct information. Once that was complete, he grabbed his jacket and told his daughter he would be on his cell phone. She waved in acknowledgment as she spoke with another client on the phone.

After seeing three homes, that she didn't care for at all, Amara became a bit discouraged. As if to read her mind, Mr. Dern, the real estate agent, gently patted her on the hand. "Don't get discouraged, Amara, I think you will really like this next one. My daughter showed it to a newlywed couple yesterday, but they didn't make a bid on it, so you are in luck. I believe it will have everything you said you were looking for."

Amara smiled at the encouragement as they drove down the street filled with new homes and freshly sodded yards. When they approached the house, Amara was breathless. "Oh Mr. Dern, you were so right!" she exclaimed. Before he could put the car in park, Amara was out of the car and walked swiftly up the walkway. Mr. Dern shook his head and smiled and slowly walked up the walkway and told her about the yard, the current and future neighbors.

"The neighbor over there is on the police force and is single. The neighbor to your left are a newly married couple. The ones across the street...." Amara stopped listening. She fell in love with the house immediately. It was a ranch style home with three bedrooms. The front of the house had a man-icured lawn and newly planted shrubbery. The house was a beautiful sand color with burgundy shutters. It had an old-fashioned wrap-around porch. The fenced back yard was perfect for entertaining guests. There would be plenty of privacy back there.

Mr. Dern opened the door and allowed Amara to enter. Amara let out a sound of marvel. "Oh, Mr. Dern, this is exactly what I have been looking for!" she said excitedly. The front door opened into a small stone tiled foyer. The family room had a cozy fireplace. There was also a formal living and dining room off to the left. The kitchen was large and contained skylights that engulfed the whole area with natural light. He had an island with a small sink and cutting boards as counters. She marveled at all the new appli-ances. She loved the stove. She squealed with delight as she opened the oven door. "Two ovens!"

Mr. Dern crossed his arms across his chest and leaned against the door jamb. "This home is a bit special. It was supposed to be a wedding gift for a loving couple, but unfortunately, the bride had other plans and ran off with the plumber the night before the wedding."

Amara looked astounded. "You are kidding," she said breathlessly.

Mr. Dern laughed. "Yes, I am," he said chuckling at his own little joke. "The home was originally intended for an elderly couple. Their only son had it built for them. At the last minute, the parents decided they wanted to live with him and his family. He was overjoyed and immediately placed the home back on the market. So it has a lot of special amenities most of the other homes do not have," he said.

Amara laughed and shook her finger at Mr. Dern. "You really had me going," she said as she headed for the master bedroom. She let out a sigh of pleasure when she entered the master bedroom. The master bedroom was more like a master suite. It had its own fireplace, a sitting area, and also a door that led out to the back yard. The master bath had a garden tub and a separate shower. There were two sinks and lots of cabinet space. The bed-room had two walk-in closets. The carpet was a rich beige color. The tile in the bathroom was breathtaking. It was sand colored but looked like marble. My mom is going to love decorating this house, she thought to herself and smiled. The other bedrooms were also fairly large.

"This house also has solar panels," said Mr. Dern authoritatively. Amara was sold. She didn't even need to look anymore, but Mr. Dern insisted on showing her the formal living and dining room, the family room with fire-place, and the other bathroom and half guest bath.

She went back into the kitchen. All the cabinets had lots of space and there was a walk-in pantry. She revisited the island in the middle of the kitchen. She rubbed her hand across the smooth wooden counter and pulled up the handle to the faucet in the sink. She sighed. Bre will love this island, she thought to herself. Mr. Dern saw the big smile on her face. "So I gather you like this place?" he said. Amara shook her head. "I'd like to make a bid," she said anxiously.

Mr. Dern shook his head and called back to the office. Once they returned back to the office, Amara filled out all of the requisite paperwork and waited on the owner's answer to her bid. She shook Mr. Dern and Angelique's hands and left with one of their business cards. "I will definitely tell my friends about your agency," she said happily.

When she left, Angelique gave her father a high five. "Do you know who that was?" she asked. Her dad shook his head no. "She was the woman that guy Duke Ellington was trying to kill. Don't you remember reading about it in the newspaper?" she asked incredulously. Her father didn't remember.

"Well, she has lots of friends from the newspaper, perhaps they will do a little piece on us?" she suggested in a hopeful tone. Mr. Dern wasn't quite as enthused. "Maybe," he said absently as he placed his reading glasses on the tip of his nose and began completing the paperwork for the day.

When Amara returned home, she ran into the den and told her parents about her soon-to-be new home. "So, you bought it already?" asked Jackson. Amara smiled. "No, but it's mine, Dad, I can just feel it. I placed a bid and I should know by tomorrow. There were a couple of other families bidding for the same home. Grab your coat, I want to show you this place. It is not too far from here!" she said excitedly.

Myra spoke up first. "Honey, don't you think we should wait to see if you get the place first?" she asked. Jackson nodded his head in agreement.

Amara looked at them both and frowned. "Don't you have any faith?" she asked exasperated. "Come on! You've got to see this place. Myra and Jackson shrugged and got their jackets.

They piled into Amara's Volvo sedan and drove to the house. When they pulled up to the house, Mr. Dern was placing the key in the key holder. When he saw Amara he smiled. "Ah, Amara, how are you? Are these your parents?" he asked. Amara told him yes and introduced everyone.

"Would you all like to take a look at the place?" he asked. Amara told him they would. Mr. Dern checked his watch. "You have to make it quick, okay?" he asked.

"We'll be quick, Mr. Dern," said Amara. He unlocked the door and stood outside while they looked around. Jackson and Myra were impressed with the house. "Mari, honey, this house is simply beautiful!" exclaimed Myra. She walked into the master bedroom and she started jotting notes on a notepad.

Amara laughed. "Getting ideas already, huh, Mom?" she said jokingly.

Myra giggled. "Just a few," she said as she jotted down a few more notes. "Mari, I've got a border that would look great in this guest room," said Myra. Jackson walked to the back and looked at the backyard. "Nice size yard. We could do cookouts back here nicely," he said, as he envisioned the nice grill he planned to buy Amara as a housewarming gift. "If I only had a grill," hinted Amara as she placed her hand around her dad's waist.

Jackson grunted as they stood together and looked out into the back yard, each person thinking of different possibilities. "You could also use a patio," said Jackson. "You know your Aunt Sarah's husband, Raymond, is really good at that kind of stuff," he said.

Mr. Dern walked in and told them he needed to leave in order to meet another client. "We should hear something about your bid first thing tomorrow," he told Amara. Amara beamed. "Thanks, Mr. Dern, this place is perfect!" she exclaimed. They all left together and the Glentons headed home. All the way home they talked about the exciting changes and decorating they planned to do once Amara got the house.

The following morning, Mr. Dern contacted Amara at work and told her the house was hers. He asked her to come to the office and start the paperwork for the financing, and she could move in the first of the month. Amara looked at her calendar. That was in two weeks! She decided she wanted to have a big housewarming party for her first home. She clapped her hands and stomped her feet with excitement. After Mr. Dern's phone call she could barely concentrate on her work.

When the clock struck quitting time, she raced out of the building, and headed to the real estate office. She filled out all the pertinent paperwork and wrote a check for all the required fees. Mr. Dern shook her hand and told her he'd have to process all the paperwork and, barring any problems, the house was hers in two weeks.

Amara rushed home, burst into the house, and announced the house would be hers in two weeks! Her parents yelled and gave her a big hug. Amara looked at them and said, "I don't know if you are happy I got the house, or happy that I am leaving that apartment." Jackson and Myra laughed.

"That place is perfect for you. I had the neighborhood checked out and though it is fairly new, the surrounding area has a very low crime rate," said Jackson. "I am way ahead of you, Dad!" said Amara. "I checked that out at work today," she said proudly.

Amara looked at her mother. "Mom, I want to have a big housewarming party. Will you help me?" she asked.

Myra rubbed her hands together. "Girl, that's right up my alley," she said. Myra pulled a piece of paper out of her pocket. "I thought you might want to do something like that since this is your first home and all, so I took the liberty of setting up the menu. Sarah said she'd cater the whole thing," said Myra.

Amara hugged her mother tightly. "Mom, you are the best," she said.

"Now, I have a few ideas for your guest room," she said as she pulled out some swatches of material and paint samples. Amara sat down at the kitchen table with her mother to discuss her ideas.

Jackson looked at his wife and daughter in deep conversation and made them some hot chocolate. He had already ordered the grill, and it would be delivered the day she moved in. He smiled at his good fortune in finding a grill that was more than 75 percent marked off its original price and the free shipping that worked well into his plans.

"What are you smiling about, Dad?" asked Amara.

Jackson quickly removed the smile from his face. "Oh, just something I picked up today," he said elusively. Amara squinted at him as he placed the cups of hot cocoa on the table. They each sipped and talked about the house-warming party that would take place in two weeks. "We have a lot of work to do," said Myra excitedly. Amara smiled widely. "With you two and Aunt Sarah helping out, everything will be just perfect," she said brightly.

Amara called Brianna and told all about her new house. Brianna was excited and happy for her friend. "I know you are excited about my house, Bre, but is there something else going on with you? I mean you always sound happy, but there's something else in your voice. Did something happen with your movie deal or with Clayton that you are really excited about?"

Brianna smiled through the phone. "You know me better than my own sister!" she exclaimed.

Brianna took a deep breath. "Mari, I am getting married in December!" she screamed into the phone. Mari screamed through the phone as well. Her parents stopped what they were doing and looked at her quizzically. Amara mouthed to her parents that Brianna was getting married. They both said, "Oh! Good for her!"

Mari turned her attention back to the phone conversation. "I knew it wouldn't be long before you and Clayton would tie the knot!" she said happily.

"I want you to be my maid of honor," she said, in a serious tone.

Amara was touched. "Sure, Bre, but why all the seriousness?" she asked. "Well," she stammered. "It's going to be a double wedding, Amara. I didn't know how you'd feel about being in the wedding. Sam and Franni had planned to get married on the same day, so we decided to have a double wedding.

Amara smiled. "Franni is a wonderful person. I got to see another side of her during her visit after I got shot," she said. "I can understand why Sam is so in love with her," she said without any sarcasm or remorse in her voice.

"Wow, Mari, I am really impressed by how you are handling all of this," she said earnestly.

"My prince is out there too!" said Amara wistfully.

"So, can you and Clayton make it to my housewarming party?" she asked excitedly. Brianna checked her calendar and asked Clayton, who was standing beside her. "We are both free and wouldn't miss it for the world," she said. "I also plan to invite Sam and Franni," she said. Brianna smiled into the phone.

"Great, then we can all come together. I can't wait to see your mom. I know she is going to do something spectacular to the rooms in your house," said Brianna.

"You know my mom well. She already has the menu prepared and we were just looking over swatches of material and paint colors before I broke away to call you. So look for your invitation in the mail!" she said. "Also, do you have Franni's address, I want to send the invitation to her house," she said.

"Good choice, since Sam moved into her place last week," she said as she gave her the address.

"I will see you guys in a couple of weeks, okay?" she asked.

"Right!" said Brianna in an excited tone.

"And then you can tell me all about your gown and your wedding plans," said Amara.

"Girl, I can't wait to show you my Tanaka knock-off," she said giggling.

Amara frowned. "Tanaka what off?" she asked.

"Oh, you will see," she said.

Amara smiled. "Are you talking about Danny Tanaka from college?" she asked.

"Uh-huh," said Brianna. "He has his own dress shop now. His gowns are lovely. Many of them are remakes or redesigns of famous designer gowns as well as his original designs. You are going to love this dress. I fell in love with it the moment I laid eyes on it," she said dreamily.

Amara looked at her watch. "Well, sweetie, gotta go. Thank you so much for including me in your wedding. We need to talk bridal shower and about the bachelorette party!" said Amara. "I've got some great ideas and if you don't mind, I'd like to include your mom to help me with the planning," she said.

Brianna smiled widely. "You are so thoughtful. That's why you are my best friend. My mom will be honored. Trust me," said Brianna, as she cradled the phone with her shoulder while she chopped tomatoes for their dinner salad. "See you soon! Bye," said Amara as she hung up the phone.

One week later, as Angelique had predicted, Amara did a feature story on their up-and-coming real estate agency in her magazine. Amara had mailed them a copy of the magazine that had hit the newsstands that morning. She also included an invitation to her housewarming party. Angelique stuck the invitation on the bulletin board and quickly read through the article. She smiled at the picture of her and her dad standing outside their business. She sighed with relief when she saw that Amara had used the photo that had their new awning. The first photos she took did not have the new awning and Angelique thought the lack of the awning made their building look drab.

Angelique read the article and nodded with approval. Amara had expertly highlighted their professionalism and the personal touch they used with each client. She spoke about the friendliness of the small staff and their efforts to find her the perfect house, she wrote all about in the magazine.

Angelique screamed when she had completed the article. She ran to the back room to show her father. He stopped stocking the shelves with brochures and read the article. A smile came across his face. "Not bad," he said, "Not bad at all."

Before Angelique could return to the front desk, her phone was ringing. Within one hour, they were booked for the day with appointments. As her father grabbed the car keys and master key to meet a client, Angelique smiled and said, "Told you so."

Mr. Dern looked at her and smiled. "That you did, now get to work!" he joked. Angelique laughed and grabbed the other set of keys for her morning appointments.

Shareese stood in front of the scratched aluminum mirror and examined the two-inch scar on her cheek. She took a deep breath as she thought about how her once flawless skin was now marred and disfigured. She thought about reestablishing her relationship with Maria. She had heard Maria was pregnant with Michael's child, so that meant she was going to get paid. Shareese planned to use some of that money to get the scar on her face removed and get back to high society living when she got out of jail. She frowned about Duke and then shrugged her shoulders as she checked cheekbone. The doctor had done a wonderful job. You couldn't even tell it had been broken.

Shareese sighed loudly. She had to find a way to get out on bail. She needed to check on her money she had stashed away for a rainy day. It was about one hundred thousand dollars. But that chump change wouldn't last for long. She needed to get more money. She needed to get out of jail but how? Shareese walked back to the bench.

The police officer on shift had allowed them to read magazines while she stood and watched. Several of the women used the magazines to pass messages. She didn't have anyone to pass a message to. Her sister was a dope addict and in jail more than out. Her other sister was autistic and could not be relied upon. Her thoughts went back to Charlene, her twin sister. She had sounded strange the last time they spoke on the phone. For the first time in a decade, she sounded as if she was sober.

She laughed at people who said twins could sense what was going on with each other when they were apart. She and her sister Charlene had never had that type of connection. They had traveled down two distinct paths. Shareese would never take drugs. Not after she saw what it did to her mother and most of her friends back home. She liked to be in full control and she couldn't be if she was loaded.

Shareese flipped through one of the local magazines and stopped at one of the articles. "Well, well, what do we have here?" she asked aloud. One of the other jail mates snatched the magazine from her and read the article aloud. A third jail mate smiled and asked, "Ain't that where Tony Riley lives?"

Shareese perked up. She knew Tony Riley had helped her sister. Her sister told her Tony was very handsome and single. She was sure Amara had already been to his house and was throwing herself at him.

Shareese thought Amara was a bit plain and boring. She wondered why she and Paul had broken up. They seemed made for each other. She definitely didn't know how to enhance her best assets, not from what she had seen of her when she came by the chief's office. But, she was single, Paul had told her that.

Perhaps Tony Riley needed to be paid a visit and convinced that it was in his best interests to release her on her own recognizance. She chuckled to herself as one of the inmates tossed the magazine back in her lap. Shareese made a mental note to call her sister the next time they were afforded time.

Two weeks flew by and Amara was waiting nervously in her new home for her guests to arrive. Sarah had done a great job with the food and her dad's gift had arrived and was out on the patio her uncle Raymond had built two days ago. She had purchased new lawn furniture as well. She wasn't financially able to buy any new furniture for the inside of the house yet, but her mother had made some really nice slip covers for her furniture and it really livened up her den and living room.

For the first time Amara had enough room to display most of her photography. She had framed and hung several pieces throughout the house. She had given her mother total license on her master and guest bedrooms and was very pleased with the results. Her master bedroom had a very ladylike and mature look to it. Her mother stuck to tan and deep maroon. It gave the room a really rich feeling. She added some of her silk plants and refinished her dresser and chest of drawer in a deep dark wood color.

The guest bedrooms were done in gay colors that made one feel back home in the country. It made people want to just kick their shoes off and relax. Myra gave Amara many of the antique pieces she had in the garage and mixed it with the furniture she already had. The final look was simply captivating.

Brianna and Clayton were staying with her, while Franni and Sam planned to stay with her parents. Amara felt a bit nervous seeing Sam after their last exchange, but she felt she was over him and was sincerely happy he had found his soul mate.

Her doorbell rang and Amara panicked. She wasn't dressed yet and her first guest was forty-five minutes early. Amara ran to the door and opened it. She smiled as she saw Tony Riley standing there with a large plant adorned with a bright blue bow. "Hi," he said shyly. "I am your next door neighbor and I wanted to welcome you to the neighborhood," he said as he handed her the oversized plant.

Amara smiled widely and invited him in. "Officer Riley, it's good to see you again!" she said, smiling.

Tony smiled. "You remember me, I'd hoped you would," he said quietly. How could I forget a hunk like you? she thought to herself with a silly smile plastered on her face.

Tony looked around in amazement. "Amara, this looks like a totally different house. The decorations are breathtaking. This looks like a professional job. If you don't mind me asking, who decorated your home? I would love to have them come look at my home's interior and give some suggestions on how I can make my home as beautiful as yours," he said earnestly.

Amara grabbed her mother. "This is my interior decorator. She is very expensive but worth it," she said, hugging her mother.

Myra blushed. "Hi, I'm Mari's mom, Myra. And I would love to take a look at your place," she said.

Tony shook her hand. "Myra, would tomorrow be too soon?" he asked.

Myra laughed. "You sure know how to make a woman feel good, son," she said.

"Well," he stammered. "I don't have to go to work until tomorrow evening, so whatever time is convenient for you, I'd be happy to meet with you, Myra," he said.

Myra reached in her pocket and handed him her business card. She winked at her daughter. "I had some extra cards made up today for this very reason," she said laughing. Amara laughed also.

"Let's shoot for ten o'clock. Is that all right with you?" asked Myra.

Tony smiled. "Yes ma'am. That would be perfect," he said smiling widely. "You need to think about how much you'd like to spend, and I will bring my little questionnaire and my fabric and color samples so I can better assist you," she said.

Amara was impressed with her mother. She had not seen her in action with others when she talked about her new business. She was really proud of her mother's savvy business sense. Tony stuck out his hand for Myra to shake. "Ten tomorrow morning it is, I will see you then."

Myra shook his hand and Tony turned to leave. "I can see you are expecting guests and I don't want to intrude."

Myra nudged Amara. "Would you like to come back in about forty-five minutes? It's just a few of my friends. I'd really like you to join us," she said.

Tony looked at his watch. "I don't have to go to work for another four hours. I'd love to come back. Should I take my plant and bring it back later?" he joked.

Both Myra and Amara laughed. "No, just bring yourself and a big appetite," she said, pointing at the food that was being arranged by her aunt Sarah on the long cloth-covered table. Amara walked him to the door and thanked him once again for the plant. After she closed the door, she could feel her cheeks getting hot. She was attracted to him, but didn't want to rush into anything. She had had the same feeling the first time they met.

Myra came over and placed her arm around her daughter's waist. "He is really cute and such a gentleman!" said Myra.

"I know," said Amara absently. Amara excused herself and went to change. She had planned to wear one of the designer outfits Brianna had

146

purchased for her. She was really excited about her evening and getting together with all of her friends.

One hour later, Amara had a house full of well-wishers. Everyone had found seats and was eating, talking, and laughing. Amara grabbed her camera and snapped photos of all of her friends. Just then the doorbell rang again. Amara opened the door and her face brightened. She smiled widely as she gently pulled him across the threshold. "Paul, I am so glad you made it!" she said happily. Paul had a lovely woman by his side. He introduced his date for the evening and Amara shook her hand and invited them both in. She showed them where the food was located and took their housewarming gift. "Thank you both," she said.

Paul kissed her on the cheek and led his date to the buffet table. Amara noticed he still needed the extra support of a cane to get around. At least he is getting around, she thought to herself thankfully. Amara took pictures of her newly arrived guest. When the doorbell rang again Amara excused herself and went to answer it.

She opened the door and let out a loud shriek. It was Brianna, Clayton, and Sam. Amara hugged them all and grabbed Brianna's ring finger. "Wow, that is a beautiful cut," she said, looking at Brianna and Clayton. Clayton smiled proudly. "Hey thanks for inviting us," he said and kissed her on the cheek. Brianna handed her a housewarming gift, which Amara knew to be a photo of them together.

Amara hugged Sam and asked about Franni. Sam frowned. "She's at a photo shoot in the Bahamas and couldn't make it," he said glumly. Amara patted Sam on the back and smiled. "Well, you all help yourself to some great food!" exclaimed Amara. Myra walked over and gave Brianna a big hug. Brianna introduced her fiancée to Myra and she congratulated them both on their engagement. She turned to Sam and gave him a hug and asked him where his beautiful fiancé was. Sam told her and Myra told him that he'd have to bring her another time.

Amara felt giddy surrounded by so many of her good friends. She waved across the room at Shirley who was engrossed in a conversation with a handsome reporter from the local paper. Her doorbell rang once more and she rushed to answer it. It was Tony. He had changed into a pair of loose fitting slacks and a sweater that showed off his muscular torso. Amara thought he looked really sexy.

She smiled widely, took his hand, and led him inside. She introduced him to some of her friends and walked with him to the buffet table. Brianna and Clayton were preparing their plates and Brianna gave Amara a knowing smile. Sam frowned at Tony. He knew he recognized him, but couldn't figure out where they had met.

Amara introduced them all and led Tony over to a table with some of her other friends. She went and prepared a plate for herself and walked over to join Tony. As she walked past Sam, he touched her arm lightly. "Hey, can we talk later?" he asked. Amara smiled warmly. "Sure," she said as she continued to walk toward Tony.

Tony and Amara became an item for the evening. After she had mingled with her friends and the crowd started to thin, Amara took Tony by the hand and walked out onto the patio. They were in deep conversation when Brianna and Clayton joined them. "Are we interrupting anything?" Brianna asked. Amara looked up at them both and motioned for them to sit down.

"Tony was just telling me the latest developments involving Michael, Shareese, and those police officers," she said in a serious tone.

Tony looked over at Sam. "Hey, I heard you saved the day," he said as he looked at Sam. Sam smiled, but said nothing.

"I am glad nothing happened to Amara. I had a chance to read the report and it seems things got a little hairy," he said. "I am glad you maintained a cool head and was able to stabilize the situation," he said admiringly. Tony scooted over by Sam and began to talk about the private investigation business.

Brianna began to tell Amara about the wedding plans. As usual she spoke quickly and with a lot of animation. Clayton joined in the conversation. "I just told her what I didn't want to see or have at our wedding and left the rest to her," he said in a joking manner. Brianna swatted his leg playfully. "This has really been a joint effort. A day as important as this should have the input of both involved, and in our case all four involved," she said giggling.

She took out a snapshot and passed it to Amara face down. Amara picked up the photo and admired the dress. "Wow, this dress is absolutely gorgeous!" she said. Clayton tilted his body to one side to steal a peak. Amara pressed the picture close to her chest, so he couldn't see it. "Now you see what I have been up against? He is so nosy," Brianna teased as she kissed him gently.

Clayton smiled. "I have a few surprises of my own," bragged Clayton. "I am in charge of the music," he said as he whispered something in Amara's ear. "Oh, my gosh!" was all she could say.

Brianna looked at her best friend with pleading eyes. "What?" she whined. "Mari, we have no secrets, tell me!" she squealed. Amara shook her head. "We have a secret now, sweetie, but only for a short while," she said assuredly. The wedding was to take place in about six months. It was already the end of June. December is right around the corner, thought Amara.

Amara looked at Sam. "So, Sam, what is your contribution to the upcoming wedding?" asked Amara. "I am picking out the groomsmen's cakes and Clayton and I will pick out the groomsmen's tuxes together. We have found a seamstress who is going to design and sew groomsmen cummerbunds that tie together the tribal colors originating from Franni's family's African tribe and our family crest." "Wow, that sounds really neat," said Amara. "This is going to be a wedding to remember," said Amara.

Tony leaned over and whispered in Amara's ear. Amara nodded and stood up. Tony joined her and took her hand. He told everyone he enjoyed meeting them but had to leave and get ready for work. Amara walked Tony to the door. The sensation from his touch sent tingles though her body. When she got to the door, he kissed her on the cheek and thanked her for the invitation. "I really enjoyed myself. And you have some really nice friends," he said softly. Amara looked into his eyes and felt mesmerized.

"I am so excited about your mother coming over to my place tomorrow," he said. "I have been so busy I haven't taken time to do anything with my house. I have lived in that house for almost one year and I still have boxes to unpack."

Amara chuckled. "Join the club. Before I moved here, I always had a ton of unpacked boxes, as if I was always expecting to move on a moment's notice," she said.

Tony shook his head. "Exactly!" he said.

Amara got nervous. Tony had a look in his eyes as if he wanted to kiss her. What was worse, she wanted him to kiss her. She felt foolish about the feelings she was having. "Amara, thanks for a lovely evening," he said and kissed her hand. Amara giggled softly as he kept hold of her hand. "Maybe we can get together sometime?" she suggested.

Tony smiled widely, "I'd like that a lot, Amara." He gently let go of her hand and walked outside. He looked back and waved as he crossed the lawn to his house. Amara let out a loud sigh.

When Amara turned to close the door, she noticed Brianna was standing next to her. "Girl, that man is fine," she said.

Amara hugged her friend. "I know," she mused, as she fanned her face.

Amara spotted Paul and his date sitting across the room and went over to talk to them. She quickly took another picture of them and smiled. Paul saw Amara and stood up slowly. He was still in therapy and working on regaining full motion of his legs. Amara motioned for him to sit down.

She sat down by them both and talked to him about the family business and she also talked to his date. Amara was surprised to find out that they worked together. Paul dabbed his mouth with his napkin and told how they started working together. "After Michael's arrest, I set out to find a partner." Paul grasped Michelle's hand. "Michelle is a graduate of Yale and came with some great ideas on how to streamline the business. She has only been with us one month and her ideas have already netted us a ten percent profit," Paul beamed. Michelle blushed and looked up at Paul with love and respect in her eyes.

Amara asked how they met and they both laughed. "She placed a complaint about one of my restaurants and provided a proposal on how to remedy the problem. I was so impressed with the proposal that I called her in for a job interview. Lucky for us, she had just left a large firm and was looking for a challenge. I think she's found it!" he said happily.

"And Pops is happy. He limits his visits to once every other week and I think in due time he won't come and visit at all," he said, as he beamed with pride.

Michelle shook her head. "I think he has a lot of confidence in this team," she said as she squeezed Paul's hand. Amara was so happy for Paul.

She looked at Paul and then at Michelle. "I am so glad you have found a great partner in business and love," she said earnestly. Both blushed.

Amara excused herself and mingled with some of her other guests. Sam watched Amara and felt himself getting jealous and didn't know why. He had made his choice and was in love with Franni. He couldn't understand why he was feeling so jealous about Amara's budding relationship. He ran his hand over his head as he attempted to push the thoughts out of his mind.

After helping her mother and aunt Sarah clean up the house, Amara plopped down by Sam on the patio. The sun had begun to set. "So, what did you want to talk to me about?" she asked.

"Huh?" he answered, as if he were pulling himself out of a daydream.

"Earlier this evening you said you wanted to talk to me about something?" she asked again.

"Oh, it was nothing. Tony seems very nice," he remarked as he changed the subject.

Amara smiled and crossed her arms over her chest. "Yes he is," she agreed.

Sam frowned. "How well do you know him?" asked Sam abruptly. Amara looked at Sam and shook her head. She gently patted his back and got up from the table. She walked over to Brianna and Clayton and joined in on their banter about the greatest slow jam artist of all time.

Sam remained on the patio and sulked. He felt foolish for pressing Amara about Tony. He did seem like a nice guy and Amara seemed to be very happy about the attention she was receiving from him. He rationalized it by saying he missed Franni and was taking it out on Amara.

Myra walked over and sat by Sam. She placed her arm around his shoulder and spoke gently. "When you are preparing to take a big step like marriage, you always have second thoughts. I know you love Franni very much, but are feeling a little sad without her. Why don't you give her a call tonight and say something positive about what she's doing and let her know you miss her."

Sam hugged Myra. "Myra, you are the greatest. Can I follow you home when you leave?" he asked.

Myra shook her head. "We are preparing to leave now. I have invited Bre, Clayton, and Mari for brunch tomorrow, so you will see them later," she said, and she got up to prepare to leave. Sam followed her and told his brother and Brianna he was leaving. He gave Amara a big hug and apologized. Amara shook her head and told him everything was fine between them and she'd see him in the morning.

Chapter 13

S hareese waited patiently for her turn to use the jail phone. She tried to smooth her hair into place, but it was to no avail. She looked around at her surroundings. Shareese had never been incarcerated. She was the one who usually went to visit others who were incarcerated. This was not how she planned to spend the rest of her life. Her orange jumper scratched her soft skin and her feet ached from the shoes she was forced to wear.

The person in front of her hung up the phone and Shareese walked up and picked up the phone. She wiped the greasy receiver on her jumper and dialed the number.

A drunken voice answered. "Hello?" slurred the person at the other end.

Shareese sucked her teeth. "Charlene, I thought you were clean?" she asked in an irritable voice.

There was silence on the other end. "This ain't Charlene, hold on," said the voice as the phone slammed down on the hard surface. Shareese quickly pulled the phone away from her ear and sighed loudly.

"Hello?" said the voice on the phone.

Shareese exhaled and began to speak. "Char, this is Reesey," she said.

"Hey, girl, heard you got locked up." Charlene began to laugh at her private joke. "It's usually me calling you, not the other way around," she teased.

Shareese ignored the ribbing. "Char, I need for you to do something for me," she said.

Charlene let out a shrewd laugh. "What do you need for me to do and how much can you pay me since you are in there and I'm out here?"

Shareese gave a sigh and adjusted the phone. "Do you remember the cop that helped get you off from that last bum rap?" she asked.

"Of course I do. Officer Riley, Tony Riley," she said excitedly.

"Well, rumor on the block is that Miss Thing has moved next door to him. I need you to blackmail him into letting me out on bail," she said.

"And how am I supposed to do that?" she asked.

"Remember that rape thing with Maurice?" she asked.

"Yeah, so what about it?" she asked irritably.

"Accuse him of it and say the baby is his," said Shareese.

"First of all, sister, there isn't any baby."

Shareese was shocked by her sister's clarity of speech. "Since when did you start talking all proper? You sound like you are clean."

Charlene smiled into the phone. "I am going to night school and I am clean. Been clean for close to six months now," she said proudly.

Shareese frowned. "So are you going to do this for me?" she asked brusquely.

"Reesey, Officer Riley has been pretty good to me and I am still on probation," she said wearily.

"All right, I've got a couple of thousand stashed in one of my accounts. It's yours if you do this," she said.

Charlene took a deep breath. She could really use the money, since she was no longer turning tricks for Maurice. Her part-time job barely made ends meet and she wouldn't be eligible for the office assistant job until she completed her training, which would take an additional three months. Charlene sighed. "All right. What do you want me to do?" she asked. Shareese smiled and began to explain the details.

Brianna, Clayton, and Amara ended up staying awake and drinking wine for most of the night into the wee hours. They laughed and joked about their love mistakes and funny experiences from college and their relationship with one another. Amara laughed so hard she cried when Clayton told a story about him and Sam dating twins and the twins had switched on them, and they found they liked the other twin better than the one they were actually dating. "And to top it off, we ended up with neither of them. They fell in love with twin brothers down the hall," he said laughing as he remembered the experience.

Amara looked at her watch and stood up. "Well, guys, see you tomorrow," she said and hugged Brianna before retiring to her new room. Brianna hugged her back and told her that she thought her new home was beautiful. Amara smiled brightly. "That means a lot coming from you, Bre," said Amara. Brianna took hold of Clayton's hand and they walked into the guest room together, talking quietly about the evening's events.

Amara slowly got dressed for bed and thought about Tony. She really liked him, but didn't want to rush into things. She felt he liked her also. She caressed her hand as she thought about the kiss he had planted on her hand earlier that evening. She wanted to kiss his lips so badly, but she knew that would not be appropriate. She sighed and got into her bed and hugged herself. "My own home," she said, as she sank into a deep dreamless sleep.

Once Sam got settled at the Glenton's home, he walked to the den and closed the door. He took a card and quickly dialed the number to Franni's hotel. The hotel desk attendant immediately connected him with her room.

Sam was shocked when a man picked up the phone and announced it was Franni's room. Without any pleasantries, he demanded to speak with Franni. "She can't come to the phone right now," the man said with a slight British lilt in his voice. "She is in the process of having honey licked out of her navel," he said as he guffawed out loud. Sam hung up the phone angrily. "Who was that?" asked Franni as she wiped the residue of honey from her navel. "Some guy named Sam," said the guy, as he moved her hand and licked the remainder of the honey from her navel.

The next morning, Brianna, Clayton, and Amara showed up for brunch at Myra's house. They all bustled in and spotted Sam alone on the patio. "He's been moping around all morning. I think he had a fight with Franni," whispered Myra. They all went out on the patio and tried to cheer him up. Sam looked at Clayton with watery eyes and asked to speak to him alone.

The women left and went to the kitchen to talk to Myra and help out with brunch. Sam looked at his brother. Clayton waited patiently for Sam to start. He was concerned, but he wanted Sam to talk about it in his own time. "I called Franni last night and some guy answered the phone and said she couldn't come to the phone because some other guy was licking honey out of her navel. Clayton, I was so angry. What's worse, Franni never called me back!" he said exasperated. His forehead was creased with worry lines. "What do I do?" he asked his brother.

Clayton took a deep breath. "Sam, first, don't jump to any conclusions. Try to call Franni again and talk to her. I am sure once you talk to her, you will see that it was all a big misunderstanding."

Just then Sam's cell phone rang. "Hello?" he answered dryly.

"Sam, honey, I know you are upset about last night. We were just having a little fun and things got out of hand. I am truly sorry that I did not phone you back, but I knew you'd be angry and I wanted to give you time to cool off," she rattled on.

Her French accent was very heavy. He knew that only happened when she was drunk or very upset. "Honey, I am so sorry. It will never happen again. Forgive me?" she asked timidly.

Sam frowned. "Franni, I am really glad you called. I have to admit, I am still a bit angry. Did you really let a guy lick honey from your navel?" he asked, as if he couldn't believe what he was told.

There was no quick response on the other end. "Yes, it's true," she said.

"Is there anything else I should know about?" he asked in a tone that seemed he was afraid of her response.

"No," she whispered.

Just then he heard a man's voice. It was the same British accent he had heard the previous night. "Franni, get your ass back to bed, I am getting cold!" he yelled.

154

Franni gasped and Sam was stunned. "Franni, what is going on?" he demanded.

Franni began to stutter. "Can we discuss this tomorrow?" she asked. "My flight is due in tomorrow morning at eight. We can have coffee and talk about all of this," she pleaded.

"Were you in bed with another man?" he demanded in a raised voice.

Franni pulled the phone from her ear. "Yes, but it's not what you think. There are several of us in the bed and no—."

Before she could finish her sentence, Sam hung up the phone. He looked over at Clayton with an anxious look in his eyes. "She was in bed with another man," he said quietly. "She said there were several of them in the bed. It was just too much for me to handle right now. I hung up on her," he said in a cowardly voice.

Clayton gripped his brother's shoulder. "Give her a chance to explain," he said assuredly. "Franni has always been honest with you. Isn't that what you said you loved most about her?" he asked.

Sam allowed himself to smile. "Yes, you're right Clayton. I will fly out of here tonight and meet her plane tomorrow morning," he said confidently.

"That's good. Give her a chance to tell her side of the story. I am sure you will see things differently once Franni has had a chance to explain fully," he said.

After a delicious brunch, Amara followed Clayton, Sam, and Brianna to the airport. They all had to be back to work bright and early the next day. Amara gave them big hugs and hugged Brianna twice. "I am so happy for you," she said with a big smile.

Brianna winked and said, "I am happy for you too. Tony seems really nice. What a great neighbor to have," she teased. "Hey, if you two are an item in six months, bring him to the wedding!" said Brianna.

Amara smiled. "You bet I will!" They all left to go to their gate.

Amara pulled her sunglasses over her eyes and headed out to her car. When she got home, she noticed a bouquet of flowers on her doorstep. They were tucked in the screen door and had a card attached. "Thank you for a wonderful evening. I am glad we are neighbors, your friend, Tony." Amara looked around and smiled. She picked up the beautiful glass vase and smelled the sweet scent of the yellow roses. She opened the door and placed the flowers on her coffee table in her den, which had become her favorite room. She eyed the gifts from her friends. They were great gifts and she could use them all. She was thankful she had so many good friends. As she sat down to write thank you notes, the phone rang. It was Tony.

"Hey, Tony," said Amara. "Thank you very much for the flowers. They are so beautiful! That was very thoughtful of you," she said.

Tony chuckled. "I am glad you liked them. I wanted to get you something more exotic than roses, but I didn't know your favorite flower, so I settled for the roses."

"Tulips and daisies," responded Amara.

"I will remember that," said Tony. "I was wondering if you were busy? I wanted to share some of the ideas your mom gave me. I gave her carte blanche to redecorate this whole house. She said it would take six weeks. She would decorate each room with its own special personality...whatever that means."

Amara laughed. "Don't worry. She is truly gifted at what she does, but I do suggest you set a price limit or you will be hooked up like the rich and famous," she joked.

Tony laughed. "So how about it? Want to come over for some pizza and a video?" he asked.

Amara was very tempted by the offer. "Sure," she said. "Give me about fifteen minutes to change and I will be right over."

Tony agreed. "I will order the pizza now. Any preferences on your half?" he asked. Amara liked it that he had considered her preference before he ordered. "Yes, ham and pineapple," she said.

Tony scrunched up his nose. "Well, all right. You sure don't have to worry about me eating any of that!" he teased.

After they hung up, Amara raced into the shower and changed into a pair of slacks, loafers, and a soft red cardigan. The sweater accentuated her full breasts, but she decided to wear it anyway. She had also put on the sexy lavender lingerie Brianna had purchased for her, just in case. She sprayed her favorite cologne in all the right places, quickly combed her hair, put on some lipstick, and headed over to Tony's house.

Tony opened the door and invited Amara inside. Amara looked around. His house was designed differently than hers and he was right, he hadn't done any decorating. His bare walls were basic white. His furniture was plain, but masculine. She liked the leather sofa and recliner in his den and he had a dining set that looked to be from Asia, with a pearl inlay and lacquered finish. Her mother was going to have a great time with Tony's house, she mused.

Tony gently took her hand. "Let me give you the grand tour," he said. After he had shown her the house, she walked over to the dining room table and sat down. He went over all the plans her mother had laid out for decorating his home. "I am especially excited about her plans for my family room. That is where I spend most of my time," he said excitedly.

Amara was impressed. "Like I said before, she is very good at what she does and she takes it seriously," she said. "I have to warn you, she can be quite a drill sergeant," she said.

Tony laughed. "I know, she has already started barking orders. She is going shopping for material tomorrow and will start decorating first thing Monday," he said happily. "But I'm totally sold. I even gave her a copy of my key, so she can work when I am at work," he said happily.

The doorbell rang, and Tony got up and grabbed his money and coupon. "It's the pizza!" he said excitedly. He brought the box in and set it on the table and went into the kitchen for plates and glasses. "May I help?" asked Amara. Tony told her he didn't need any help. He brought in some plain white ceramic plates and empty mugs. "I hope you like root beer because that and water is all I have," he said grinning.

"Water would be great, thanks," said Amara.

Tony brought everything they would need into the dining room and set it on the table. Amara placed mats under the plates and poured the water and root beer. They each took a slice of pizza and bit into the hot messy cheese. Tony scrunched up his nose in disgust. "How can you eat that stuff?" he asked as he pointed at the side with pineapple and ham. Amara took a big bite of her pizza and smiled. Tony took a sausage ball from his pizza and fed it to Amara. "Taste this," he said and he popped it into her mouth. "Not bad, but at least try this," she said as she fed him a piece of ham. They both giggled like children as they finished their own slice of pizza.

Amara had a piece of cheese on her chin and Tony took a napkin and gently wiped it off. He caressed her lips with his index finger. Tony tilted her chin upward and kissed her. Amara kissed him back and they wound up in a passionate embrace. Tony pushed her hair from her face and whispered, "The first time I saw you at your parents' house I thought you were the most beautiful woman, and now you live right next door." He kissed her again. He pulled her close and kissed her passionately. He asked her if they could go into the den. She nodded yes.

They went into the den, where he had started a fire, and sat down on the leather sofa. Tony began to slowly run his hand over the back of her soft sweater. He kissed her neck and ear lobes. Amara slipped her hand under his shirt and caressed his chest. He looked into her eyes and smiled. "I am so glad you are here," he said. Amara smiled. "I am glad that I am here too." Tony began to play with the soft curls of her hair. He brought his nose to her head and sniffed the fresh scent of her hair and cologne. He cupped her face in his hands and kissed her again. Amara felt herself getting excited.

She pulled back and looked at Tony. "What are we doing?" she asked as she looked into his eyes. She was afraid of going too far, since she really didn't know him well. Tony stopped and looked at her with deep passion in his eyes. "Mari, I won't do anything you don't want us to do," he said. "Do you want to stop?" he asked her gently.

Amara looked down at the sofa and answered softly, "I don't want to stop, but I think we should. I am really attracted to you and I would like to get to know you better," she said. She raised her head and looked into his eyes. He smiled and gently kissed her eyelids.

"We will move as fast or as slow as you like. I want this to be right. I don't want you to regret anything that happens between us, because I really like you and I want to spend time with you and get to know you too," he said sincerely. He looked her in the eye and said sternly, "But I don't want to play games, Mari. I am too busy for that. I want to share myself with you, but only when you are comfortable with that," he said. He propped himself on one elbow as he waited for her response.

This was all happening so quickly, but Amara really did want to get to know him and spend time with him. She kissed him gently. "Let's take our time and get to know one another," she said. Tony smiled. He went to his bedroom and brought out a blanket. He also brought over their drinks. He placed the blanket on the floor and placed the drinks on the nearby table.

He pulled Amara down on the blanket and propped her head up with one of his pillows. He pulled the other pillow down and placed it under his arm and propped himself up on one elbow. "So, Miss Glenton, tell me all about yourself." The tension rushed away. Amara laughed and relaxed beside him. She began to tell him all about herself. They laughed, kissed, and joked until dawn.

Amara looked at the clock and yawned. "Tony, my goodness, it is almost five in the morning! We stayed up all night talking."

Tony smiled and kissed her. "Don't forget the kissing part," he joked.

Amara laughed and kissed him back. "How could I forget that part?"

Tony got up and pulled Amara to her feet. Amara straightened her clothes. He ran his hand over her face and clutched her hair. He kissed her passionately. She moaned softly as she placed her hands around his neck.

"That was nice," he said as he took her hand and walked her to the door.

"Very nice," murmured Amara.

He tilted her chin upward and kissed her once more. "You taste so good." He looked at her and paused. "I want to see you again," he said with lust in his voice.

"I want to see you again too," she said.

"Can I call you later?" he asked.

"I'd be disappointed if you didn't," she said with her lids half closed. He took his cue and kissed her once more.

Amara sighed. "Well, I'd better leave. The drill sergeant will be over early." Tony laughed and opened the door. "I'll give you a call later, okay?" he whispered in her ear. She closed her eyes and pictured them together. "Sure," she answered, nearly out of breath.

Amara walked slowly out of the door and regained her bearings. She quickly headed over to her house. She turned to wave. Tony waved back. He watched until she was safely inside her house. He closed the door and groaned. He was rock hard with excitement.

He walked quickly to his room and changed into his workout clothes and placed a reflective belt around his waist. He walked out of his front door and stretched his muscles. He set his watch and took off, running hard. He had to get his mind together. But all he could think of was Amara. He fell for her the first time he saw her. Sweat poured down his face as he tried to focus on his workout. He ran harder, until he was miles down the road.

"Ugh!" Amara groaned. He drove her wild with desire. She had wanted so badly to take her clothes off and make love to Tony on that blanket. But, she heeded the warnings her mother had given long ago. "Take your time. Get to know the one you are with before you are 'with' him." She hugged herself and moaned again when she thought about his lips on hers and his body touching hers. She stomped to the bathroom and took a long shower.

Sam stood at the gate, blurry eyed. He had not slept at all. He kept thinking about the recent incidents with Franni. He questioned if this was the type of life he wanted to lead? He wasn't sure. He questioned the fact that he was jealous about Amara's new friend, though he had had his chance and had chosen Franni. His feelings were so mixed up that he wasn't sure about what he felt.

As he continued his deep thought, Franni walked up to him and kissed him gently on the lips. Startled, Sam jumped. He then put his arms around Franni and kissed her deeply. Somehow, he knew they'd get through this. Sam walked with Franni to the baggage claim and collected the rest of her luggage. They rode home in silence. Once inside, Franni began to cry.

Sam looked at her, but did not comfort her. He calmly waited for her to speak. "Sam, I had sex with another man last night," she said. Sam just stared at her and said nothing. Franni continued. "After you hung up on me I got angry and acted irresponsibly. I felt that if you thought I was having sex with another man, I might as well go ahead and do it," she said, between sobs.

Sam was surprised how calm he remained. Without saying a word, he walked into the bedroom and packed a small bag. "I can't be with you right now," he said. He zipped up the bag. "I am going to Clay's. I will be back tomorrow to get the rest of my clothes at noon. Please be gone," he said harshly. Franni continued to sob as Sam walked out and slammed the door.

Sam got into his car and drove off. He wiped a lone tear from his eye. He felt numb and betrayed. When he reached his brother's house, he pulled into the drive and grabbed his duffel bag. He got out of the car and slowly walked up the sidewalk. He found the hidden key and went inside. He knew that Clayton was at Brianna's, which is where he spent most of his spare time. He was glad. He needed some time alone to think about all that had transpired between him and Franni.

Sam prepared himself a snack and turned on the television. Clayton walked in shortly afterwards and placed his keys on the hook. He walked into the den and sat down by his brother. "Want to talk about it?" he asked.

Sam looked at his brother and clenched his jaw. "Clay, she slept with another man last night," he said angrily. "She said since I hung up on her when she was trying to explain, that she just went and did what I thought she was doing in the first place," he said.

Clayton shook his head. "Sam, that doesn't sound like Franni at all. Did you two discuss it any further?" asked Clayton calmly.

Sam slammed his fist on the table in anger. "Discuss what?" he yelled. Sam got up and began to pace. Clayton asked Sam to sit down and try to calm himself.

"Sam, I never told you this, but Vida cheated on me once. She told me about it and I felt the same as you do now," he said.

Sam looked at his brother in disbelief. "Why did you stay with her? Is that when your relationship changed?" he asked.

"I stayed with her because I loved her, and thought she was the one for me. But the truth of the matter is, I never got over it and our relationship was really over after that," he said as he drew in a deep breath. "Fidelity is important. If you can't get over it, don't hang on a dying vine," said Clayton.

Sam shook his head. "I still love her, but I really feel betrayed. What if I jump to conclusions again? Is she going to do it to prove me right?" he asked sarcastically.

Clayton shook his head. "I don't know the answer to that," he said. "I just share my experience with you. I can tell you it damaged my trust and self-esteem," he said truthfully. "It happened right around the time I met Brianna. That was one of the reasons it was so easy to be friends with Bre. There was no pressure and she gave me what I was lacking with Vida, trust," he said.

Sam rubbed his head in frustration. Sam looked at Clayton wearily. "Bro, what have I done? Did I give up the wrong woman?" he asked.

Clayton shook his head no. "You weren't in love with Amara. You were, and I believe still are, in love with Franni," he said.

Sam shook his head in agreement. "What do I do?" he asked.

"Just give it time, bro, it will work itself out," he said, as he gently patted Sam on the shoulder.

Sam got up and grabbed his cell phone. "I'm going for a walk, be back later," he said abruptly. "Don't turn to someone else out of scorn or pain," Clayton warned.

Amara was in the darkroom developing pictures from her housewarming party when the phone rang. She smiled and assumed it was Tony calling after his first day with her mom. She hung up her last photo and walked behind a partition. She turned on a dim light. She was glad she had had a phone put in the dark room.

"So how did it go with Mom?" she said sweetly. There was silence on the other end. "Hello?" she asked.

"Amara, this is Sam," he said in a serious tone. Amara rolled her eyes. She did not need any more of his antics. "What's up, Sam?" she asked nonchalantly. Sam could tell the change in her attitude and quickly regretted calling her. "Hey, I just called to let you know I had a really nice time and to apologize for being such a stick-in-the-mud," he said.

Amara looked at the phone and frowned. "Great, glad you had a nice time. Did Franni get in okay?" she asked, as she shifted her weight to the

160

other foot. "Yes, she did and we had a terrible fight," he said miserably. Why does this guy keep calling me every time he and Franni have a fight? Amara thought to herself. There was a long silence between them.

Sam sighed heavily. "Look, Amara, I shouldn't have called. Let me get myself together and call you another time," he said in a depressed tone.

"Are you sure?" asked Amara, genuinely concerned. "I am here to listen if you want to talk," she said, as she grabbed a torn chair she had hidden in the room before the party.

Sam let out a heavy sigh. "I will talk to you some other time. Thanks for listening," said Sam.

"You really haven't said anything for me to listen to," said Amara. "But I will tell you something. Instead of calling me, why don't you try to talk to the person who really matters, Franni," she said gently. Sam shook his head in agreement, said goodbye, and quickly hung up. Amara shrugged, hung up the phone, and went back into the darkroom to work on her photographs.

Five minutes later Brianna called. Amara was happy to be receiving so many calls in her new home. She answered the phone, full of pep and excitement. "Girl, you won't believe what has just happened with Sam and Franni," said Brianna rapidly. Before Amara could respond, she said, "He found out Franni slept with another guy while on her last shoot, and he moved out and moved in with Clayton," she said, barely pausing to take a deep breath.

"Well, that explains the phone call I just received from him," said Amara. "Sam just called and I told him he should talk to Franni instead of me. I guess he was a bit embarrassed and got off the phone right away. I like Sam, but he needs to work out his problems with Franni on his own," said Amara in an irritated tone of voice.

"You are right there," agreed Brianna.

Amara changed the subject. "Bre, I did something last night that was totally wonderful!"

"You slept with Tony and it was fantastic!" exclaimed Brianna.

"No, but we stayed together all night. It was so romantic and nice. We just connected."

Brianna laughed. "Girl, it was written over both of your faces! You two could barely keep your hands off one another at the party," joked Brianna.

"Bre, was it that obvious?" asked Amara a bit embarrassed.

"Only to me, Clay and Sam," she said.

Amara smiled. "Bre, it was truly a great experience. We plan to see each other again," she said excitedly. "I really like him a lot. Bre, I am in love with him, though I know how juvenile that might sound, since I've only known him a short while," she said.

Bre laughed aloud. "I felt the same about Clayton the first time we met. Imagine how many cold showers I took? He was still with Vida and I was hanging on to that sinking relationship I had with Charles," she said bitterly.

"How did you keep your self-control?" asked Amara. "That's a good question. If we had not gotten together when we did, I don't know how much longer my restraint would have lasted. It was like fireworks between us each time we got together!" she said.

"Well, then you know exactly how I am feeling," she said.

Brianna laughed a hearty laugh. "I know, because it was the same for Clay and me," she said. "I am so happy you have found someone special," said Brianna.

"Me too," said Amara. "I hope Sam and Franni can pull it together," said Amara.

Brianna shrugged her shoulders. "Who knows, our double wedding might just be a wedding just for two," she said sadly.

Amara heard a knock on her door. "I have to get off the phone. There's someone at the door," she said. Each said goodbye and Amara hung up. When she opened the door, she found her mother and Tony laughing hysterically about a piece of shredded fabric Myra was holding. Tony walked over and kissed Amara gently on the cheek. "Your mother nearly knocked a woman out for a piece of fabric!" he said, still laughing.

"That woman pulled the bolt of fabric out of my basket. I tried to be courteous and told her it was my fabric," said Myra.

"The woman ignored her," interjected Tony. "So your mom grabbed the fabric and gave it a hard tug. The bolt of fabric went flying through the air and landed in an open can of paint someone was looking at. What a mess," he said chuckling.

"So I walked away with this little piece of fabric in my hand and left the woman, who was covered in paint, and the ruined bolt of fabric in the store." They both began to laugh again as they described how the woman covered in paint looked. Amara laughed with them.

"So what fabric did you get instead?" asked Amara.

"This!" said Myra proudly, as she held up a piece of very expensive cloth.

"Mom, that is beautiful!" exclaimed Amara.

"I love it," said Tony as he kissed Myra on the cheek. "Myra said she'd make me a quilt for one of my guest bedrooms and use this piece of fabric. Won't that be great?" asked Tony, as he looked into Amara's eyes. Amara smiled and said that it would. Myra looked at the interaction between Amara and Tony and smiled. My baby is in love, she thought to herself.

Amara offered them each something cool to drink and Myra declined. "Jackson is taking me on a date tonight, so I have to get home and get ready," said Myra, as she checked her watch.

Amara smiled. "They've been married over thirty years and they still have a date night," joked Amara.

Myra nodded. "It keeps the excitement in the relationship," she said and winked.

Tony and Amara laughed. "Thank you, Myra. I love the fabrics you chose," said Tony.

Myra smiled. "Oh, before I forget, you said I could strip your bedroom furniture, right?" she asked.

Tony nodded his head. "Anything you want to do with the interior of that house is fine." Myra picked up her keys and placed Tony's spare key on her key ring and prepared to leave. Both Tony and Amara walked her to the door. They waved as she drove away.

When Amara closed the door, Tony grabbed her and kissed her passionately. "I missed you," he said tenderly.

Amara laid her head on his chest. "I thought about you and our experience last night all day," said Amara sensuously.

Tony kissed her forehead. "How about a date night for us?" he asked. "Would you like to go to dinner and a play?" he asked.

Amara's eyes perked up. "Are you referring to the sold-out play everyone, particularly me, has been dying to see?" she asked anxiously.

"That's the one," he said. Full of excitement, Amara yelled happily as she danced around the room. "I have been trying to get tickets for over two months!" she exclaimed. "How did you do it?" she asked.

"I saved a girl in the park last week and her mother gave me two tickets as a form of gratitude. Turns out she is one of the stylists in the show and gets complimentary tickets for each show," he said.

"Wow, that's fantastic! What time do we leave?" she asked.

Tony checked his watch. "I will be back over in about three hours. Is that all right with you?" he asked. "That way we can have a leisurely dinner at my favorite restaurant and then go to the play," he suggested.

"Where is your favorite restaurant?" she asked.

He looked down at the ground before responding. "Mari, it's nothing fancy. But the food and atmosphere are out of this world. I haven't met the owner yet, but I sure love her food," he said.

"So what's the name of this place?" she asked.

"Sarah's," he said. Amara broke out in a wide grin.

"That's my auntie and she catered the food at the party last night," she said excitedly.

"That was Sarah?" he asked. "She looked nothing like I thought," he said. "The heavyset woman with the reddish-blonde locks down her back? Is that her true hair color?" he asked.

"It sure is," she said.

"Wow, so that was Sarah," he said as he rubbed his chin. "Small world is all I can say," he said. "See you around five," he said as walked toward the door. Amara said that was fine as she opened the door. He kissed her once more and walked back to his house.

A woman with binoculars watched as Tony walked back to his house.

Her sister had been right about one thing. That woman had wasted no time getting her hooks into Officer Riley. She took a deep breath and rehearsed what she would say. Charlene got out of the rented car and walked up to Amara's house and knocked on the door. Amara answered the door. "Yes," she asked.

Suddenly Amara recognized the woman. "Charlene, what are you doing here?" she asked, stunned.

Charlene's mouth dropped open. She quickly regained her composure. "How you know me?" she asked in broken English, as she rocked her head from side to side.

"You're Shareese's sister, right?" asked Amara, as she crossed her arms in front of her chest.

"How you know so much 'bout my 'bidness'?" asked Charlene as she popped her chewing gum for special effect.

"What may I do for you today?" asked Amara as she leaned against the door jamb. Charlene shifted her weight and placed her hands on her hips. "You best stay away from my man, Tone," she said.

Amara bit her lip to keep from laughing. "Why would Tony go out with a convicted felon when he's on the police force?" asked Amara. Charlene backed away and narrowed her eyes. "I don't know how you know so much about me, but you ain't heard the last of me. I am going over to Tone's and get this mess straight right now!" she screamed. "I'm gonna have his baby and he'd better be ready to pay!" she said bitterly and stomped away.

Amara closed her door and shook her head. She returned to her task of framing her new photos. She had planned to give all her guests a framed black and white photo of themselves from the party, along with their thank you note. She wrapped the last one and checked her watch. It was nearly four in the afternoon. She decorated the last frame with a brightly colored satin ribbon. Amara gently placed the gifts in a large shopping bag and put the bag in her storage closet. She walked into her master bathroom to take a shower and got ready for her date with Tony.

Charlene was stunned that Amara knew who she was. That threw her off balance. She would try to do what her sister wanted, but she didn't think it would work. On top of that, her heart wasn't in doing anything mean or deceitful to Officer Riley. He had been really good to her. She didn't want to do anything to jeopardize her parole and upcoming full-time job.

She knocked hard on Tony Riley's door. Tony answered the door, looked at Charlene, and smiled. "Charlene, you look great! I heard you got into the training program, congratulations! I also wrote a letter of recommendation, so I hope that will help your cause," he said. Charlene said nothing. She looked down at the ground and shuffled her feet.

"Look, Officer Riley, my sister, Shareese Miller, is in jail. She's somehow mixed up with that ransom scandal. You know, the stolen million dollars?

Anyway, she asked me to come to your house and try to blackmail you into helping her get bail. You have been very good to me and I am trying hard to turn my life around," she said earnestly.

Officer Riley placed a hand on Charlene's shoulder. "Charlene, you've got your whole life ahead of you. Don't blow it. Your sister made her choices, just as you've made yours. You are doing something good for yourself. Something that you alone can be proud of. I will forget this ever took place. Go home and continue to study and stay clean. I can tell you that you look and sound great!" he said to encourage her. Charlene broke into a huge smile. "Thanks Officer Riley," she said. "And take care of your new girlfriend," she said laughing.

Officer Riley frowned at the last remark and waved as she drove away. As Charlene drove away she smiled, and thought to herself that Shareese would have to get out of this jam on her own. She had already hidden the money that she had taken from her sister's account in a safe place. She would keep it tucked away and do as her mother had taught both her and Shareese to do, save it for a rainy day.

Tony showed up promptly at five and rang Amara's doorbell. When she opened the door, he let out a low whistle. "Wow, you clean up nicely," he joked. Amara was wearing a black silk dress with a brightly colored shawl. Her hair was down and straight. She had placed one of his roses in her hair. She looked very exotic.

Amara smiled. "You clean up pretty good yourself," she said, admiring his outfit. Tony was wearing black slacks and a matching black silk shirt. He had on a colorful vest that pulled the whole ensemble together. "Did my mom pick that vest out for you?" she asked.

Tony blushed. "Yes she did, do you like it?" he asked.

"I love it. But did you happen to notice we nearly match tonight?" she asked jokingly. Tony laughed and took her hand. Amara grabbed her small clutch bag and they headed off on their date.

When they got into the car, they discussed the incident with Charlene. "She's a good kid," said Tony. "She's really had a hard life. Her real father abused her and I think that somehow affected her," he said. "Her mother threw him out once she found out about it, but I think the damage was done. Shareese was already out of the house by that time so she was unaffected by his abuse. Since that time, Charlene has been in and out of trouble with the law. But I am proud to say that she is clean and doing really well in one of the community rehab programs. She will get her first real job with a salary in four months. It has already been arranged, as long as she keeps her nose clean," he said with a sly grin.

Amara smiled and squeezed Tony's hand. "You are such a kind, giving person. That's probably why she couldn't go through with Shareese's scheme," said Amara.

"Shareese is where she needs to be," said Tony grimly. Amara nodded and dropped the subject.

Shareese paced back and forth in the small cell. She was nervous because her sister had not come to see her during visiting hours as they had planned. She couldn't figure out a way to get out of jail and it pained her to have to rely on her drug-addicted sister to get her free. Shareese blew out her breath and twirled her matted hair with her index finger. She had to find a way. She always landed on her feet and she wasn't about to give up now.

Sam was sitting alone in Clay's den clicking the television remote from one channel to the next when Franni quietly walked in. "Sam," she said with a slight French accent, "can we talk?" Startled, Sam sat straight up and gently patted the seat next to him. Franni walked over to the sofa and sat down. She explained everything that had happened and asked Sam to forgive her. Sam took her in his arms and hugged her. He then pulled away and told her he had lost his trust in her and it would take awhile to get it back. He suggested they postpone the wedding and work on their relationship. Franni readily agreed.

They hugged again and talked for hours. Sam realized it had gotten late. He followed Franni home and walked her to the door. "I don't think it's a good idea that we live together," he announced. "I will find my own place next week." Franni acknowledged what he had said and tried to give him a kiss. He instantly backed away as if she repulsed him and then caught himself. He walked toward her and gave her a hug. Without saying another word, he walked to his car and drove back to Clayton's house.

Tony and Amara were enjoying a lovely dinner when they spotted Amara's parents feeding each other dessert a few tables away. Amara smiled. "That's how I want to be with my husband," she said dreamily. Tony mixed a chunk of bread in the olive oil mixture and fed it to Amara. Amara closed her eyes and savored the wonderful mixture of spices and tangy vinegar and sweet oil. "I hope to be that husband some day," said Tony, as he placed the remainder of the bread in his mouth. Amara's eyes popped open and she stared at Tony, but he carried on as if nothing had been said.

Amara felt warm and scared at the same time. She was really falling for this guy and the feeling seemed to be mutual. Tony broke into her thoughts. "We'd better get ready to leave so we can make the play," he said. Tony pulled Amara's chair back and helped her with her shawl. "I can hardly wait!" said Amara.

The following week Sam moved the last of his personal belongings into his new loft. He really liked the high ceiling and the view of the ocean. He had many large picture windows, but would not need any curtains because it overlooked the water. He had met his neighbors on either side and they both seemed very nice. This place was airy and open. The openness gave him a good feeling.

"Knock, knock," said Franni as she carried in a large plant. "I thought you could use a bit of greenery with all this beautiful blue sea," she said, smiling. Sam wiped the sweat from his forehead and walked over to Franni. He took the plant and sat it by one of the expansive windows. "What do you think?" he asked pointing at the plant. "I think that's the perfect spot," she said cheerfully.

Franni rolled up her sleeves and walked into his kitchen and began unpacking his dishes. Sam smiled at her and walked into the bedroom to set up his bed and put away his clothes. It was well after ten in the evening before he had everything in place. Franni plopped on his sofa, exhausted. Sam snapped his finger and said he had forgotten the final touch.

He went into his bedroom and pulled out a large photo of himself and Franni together, taken during the early summer. He sat it on the end table in the living room. Franni giggled and gave him the thumbs up. "Does that mean we are all right?" she asked cautiously. "It means I am willing to work at it until we are all right," he said sincerely. Franni walked over and hugged him tightly and kissed him on the lips. He continued to hold her as he fought back his feelings of insecurity and distrust.

Tony walked Amara to her front door. He gave her a long kiss on the lips. He pulled the wilted rose from her hair and caressed her face with the soft petals. Amara inhaled the sweet smell of the rose and smiled. "Would you like to come in?" she asked. Tony smiled. "I'd better not. Mari, I am really attracted to you and my willpower is only so strong," he said as he ran his hand through his close-cut hair. He sighed nervously.

Amara looked up at him. "I feel the same way," she said and kissed him. "I know this is only our third time together, but I have very strong feelings for you. It is scary."

He shook his head. "I am just relieved that we both feel the same way," he said and smiled.

"Thank you for a wonderful evening," she said as she leaned against the door.

He backed up and wiped the sweat from his brow. "Don't lean into the door like that. You are driving me crazy tonight in that sexy dress," he said.

Amara smiled a wicked smile. "Glad it had its intended effect." Tony laughed and walked away.

"Brunch tomorrow?" he asked. "My treat. I know just the place." She smiled. Tony had a puzzled look on his face.

"I look forward to it!" Amara looked at her watch. "Come over around ten, okay?" she asked.

"Ten it is," he said. "Goodbye, Mari," he said as he cut across the lawn.

Amara smiled. "Bye, Tony," she said, as she walked into the house.

Tony showed up at ten sharp. Amana was dressed casually in a pair of cotton drawstring pants and a brightly colored t-shirt she had purchased from the play last night. Her hair dangled in a high ponytail at the top of her head. Tony smiled. "Nice shirt." Amara laughed hard as she looked and saw Tony was wearing the same shirt in a different color. She felt her face flush as she checked out the fit of his snug jeans. Tony tilted his head to the side. "Like what you see?" he asked. Amara blushed even more.

Without answering, Amara took him by the hand and led him to the car. "Hop in," she said. "I'm driving."

Tony laughed. "I love a woman who takes control and knows how to avoid answering embarrassing questions.

Amara threw her head back in laughter. "You'd better believe I like what I saw," she said. "Buckle up. I don't want that sexy body getting damaged," she joked. It was Tony's turn to blush. Amara laughed hard as she drove out of the driveway.

Myra met them at the steps and gave both of them a big hug and kiss. Jackson was in the kitchen putting the final touches on his world famous brunch. Tony's eyes bugged out at all the food. "Who all is coming over?" he asked.

Jackson's body shook with laughter. "Hope you brought your appetite," he joked.

Tony pulled at the neckline of his t-shirt. "This is scary."

Amara and Jackson roared with laughter. Amara rubbed his back. "Don't worry, my aunt and uncle are joining us," she said. "Great," said Tony, relieved.

Everyone sat at the table, with full bellies. They were laughing at a story Tony was telling about one woman who got locked out of her house naked. "I saw this pale arm wave at me from the bush in front of this house and the poor woman was naked. She had run out the back to retrieve something, I forget what, and her dog shut the door and it automatically locked." Everyone was laughing. "I finally got in touch with her husband. I had gotten her a blanket from the trunk of the car, but she was so embarrassed. Her husband rushed home to let her back in the house and he ripped his pants getting out the car. He was wearing red heart boxer shorts. I almost lost it there," he said. Myra and Sarah were in tears from their laughter. "Then the key broke in the lock." Everyone started to laugh all over again.

When the brunch was over, Tony sat and talked with Raymond, better known as Raymey, and Jackson while the women went to the screened porch to catch up on the gossip. Hours later Amara and Tony got ready to leave. Tony thanked Jackson and Myra for their hospitality and he told Sarah and Raymond it was good to meet them.

Jackson stuck his hand out to Tony. "Son, you have an open invitation to our weekly brunch anytime," he said. Tony got choked up by the gesture and quietly thanked him. Jackson smiled and slapped him hard on the back. Myra gave him a kiss and a hug. "See you tomorrow!" she said. "I want to finish that guest room." Tony smiled and gave her the thumbs up sign. "It's a date."

When they got into the car. Tony's eyes became glassy. He looked out the window as Amara drove away and chatted about the afternoon. Suddenly she stopped. "Tony, what's the matter?" she asked. Tony let out a shaky sigh. "You have a wonderful family, Mari. You are so blessed. I lost my parents when I was a teenager, and I missed all that," he said as he waved in the air. "They treated me like part of the family," he said quietly. Maybe someday you will be, thought Amara to herself. Instead she squeezed his hand and told him she was glad he felt so welcome

Chapter 14

$\mathcal{S}$ everal weeks later, Myra was adding the finishing touch on Tony's master bedroom. She had saved that project for last because it was so extensive and the bedroom is a very personal living space. She wanted to make sure she got it perfect. Amara and Tony had made her a business portfolio of this job. Amara took before and after pictures of each room she had decorated. Tony placed the photos and details of the redecoration in chronological order. Myra would flip through her book every night and check the progress and make notes on changes she made to the original redesign idea. She was very proud of her work.

Soon Myra realized Tony and Amara had become inseparable. Myra had never seen Amara so happy or fulfilled. Tony had brunch with them every Sunday when he was not on duty. He had become part of the family.

Myra was stapling the last piece of cloth on the overstuffed chair she had reupholstered. She smiled when she thought about seeing the large chair put out on the curb for garbage and stopping a young man who happened to be walking by to help load it in the trunk of her car. Tony loved the chair even before she had reupholstered it. He was so easy to please that Myra made an extra effort to make sure everything was to the specifications they had agreed upon.

She stood back to appraise her handiwork. She was very pleased. The chair looked brand new and the colors of the fabric really picked up the color of the re-stained wood, drapes, and bedding she had purchased or made herself. This room was truly a labor of love. Myra thought Tony was a special man, and more important, he was in love with her daughter.

Myra's thoughts were interrupted when she heard the tinkling of ice in a glass. Tony walked in holding a tall glass of ice-cold lemonade. Myra smiled and removed the pins from her mouth. "Wow, this looks fantastic," he said as he handed her the glass of lemonade and kissed her lightly on the cheek. Myra smiled at the compliment and sat on the chest that had once belonged to his mother. She had added a cushion to the top, so that one could sit on it, but she had left the outside wooden casing in its original state.

Myra took a long sip of her lemonade as Tony sat next to her. He had a serious look on his face. Myra set her drink on the floor. "What is it, Tony?" asked Myra, clearly concerned.

Tony took her hands into his. "Myra, I want to ask Amara to marry me, but I am afraid. We've only been dating a couple of months, but I know she's the one for me," he said earnestly.

Myra smiled and squeezed his hands in hers. "Let me tell you a secret. Jackson proposed to me on our second date, and we have never looked back. We both knew we were meant for one another. I know my daughter is in love with you. I have never seen her as happy or as fulfilled as she is right now," said Myra.

Tony smiled and kissed Myra again on the cheek. "Thanks, Mom," he said and winked.

Myra let out a slight chuckle. "You're welcome, son," she said as she drank the last of her lemonade and returned to her work.

Amara sat in the back of the courtroom as Michael Whitman was escorted to his seat for his bail hearing. She quickly drew a sketch of him as he stood and looked around the courtroom. Amara noticed he was dressed in an expensive Armani suit and his hair had been cut and he was clean-shaven. Amara began to write in her notebook about his appearance and the courtroom.

As Michael looked around the courtroom he spotted his brother Paul, a woman sitting beside him he didn't recognize, and his father. They were sitting in the seats directly behind his and his lawyer's seats. Michael turned to face them. Amara could see his eyes were filled with shame. Amara wondered if it was shame for what he had done or for getting caught. She smirked as she wrote more notes. Before he sat down, he looked at her with a scowl on his face.

Amara stared back at him. She wanted him to know that she had already been through hell because of him and would see justice done. She gave him the meanest look she could conjure up. She then stared at his handcuffed wrists and lifted an eyebrow. Michael immediately looked down at the ground sheepishly and quickly took his seat. His lawyer whispered something in his ear and he nodded.

Everyone rose as the judge was announced. Amara smiled when she saw the judge. She sketched a drawing of Judge Marion's face. She seemed to wear a permanent scowl. Everyone called her Judge Hatchet. She was known for giving heavy sentences to criminals, especially repeat offenders.

Michael's lawyer stood up and stated his case. He spoke about how Michael and his family were pillars of society, how much he had done for the community, that he was an upstanding citizen, and should be released on bail because he was not a flight risk. The prosecution argued that he had tried to have someone killed to hide his own guilt in another offense he had committed, and that he had been unsuccessful in the attempted murder but might try to finish the task if he were released.

The judge read over the paperwork in front of her and began to speak. She placed her half reading glasses on the top of her head as she spoke. "In view of the evidence I have in front of me, bail is not granted. The defendant will be held in jail until his trial." Michael slammed his fist on the table and the judge slammed her gavel down and then pointed it in the direction of Michael. "You try another stunt like that and you won't be able to raise your hands to do anything!" she admonished. The court was adjourned and Michael was escorted back to his jail cell.

After the courtroom was nearly empty, Amara sat down on the long bench and gathered her thoughts in the quiet courtroom. She wrote up her remaining comments and began to put everything inside her briefcase.

She was startled by a man's voice. She quickly placed her hand over her heart as if to steady herself. "Try not to judge him too harshly," said Paul, with a crooked smile on his face.

Amara closed her briefcase and stood up. "Paul!" she gasped. "You scared me."

Paul apologized. "I know my brother has a lot of issues and he is responsible for me walking around with a cane, and for you being shot."

Amara held up her hand to stop him. "Paul, you know what's really scary. I don't think he feels remorse for anything he has done to you or me. I believe he only feels remorse because he got caught," she said sternly. Paul hung his head and left without saying another word. He knew what Amara had said was probably true. Throughout their childhood Michael had never seemed to be sorry for the mean things he had done to him or to others. He had only showed sorrow when he had been caught doing those things.

Amara checked her watch and rushed out of the courtroom. She nearly collided with Tony as she headed for the courthouse doors. Amara mumbled, "Excuse me," but never looked up from her paperwork. She was so engrossed in her thoughts about the article she was writing, she had not paid attention where she was walking. Tony called her name quickly to keep her from running into someone else.

She looked up at Tony and smiled. "What a pleasant surprise!" she said. "You got off from work early today!" she said. "Are we still on for tonight?" she asked.

Tony hung his head. "No, I am glad we ran into each other. I won't be able to make it. Can we have an early dinner and then go to our favorite place in the park?" he asked.

Amara looked at him and frowned. He would not make eye contact with her. "Tony, what's wrong?" she asked.

Tony smiled and held up his hand. "Nothing, nothing, I just have something on my mind I want to share with you and I want to do it in the park, okay?" he asked. "All right," said Amara suspiciously.

Later that evening they arrived at the restaurant and were seated. A tall, elderly waiter came and took their order. The fun and banter that usually took place between Amara and Tony was missing. Once their dinner was served, they ate in silence. Amara moped. He didn't even try to feed me my favorite bread and sauce, she thought. This must be something really awful. Tony kept looking at Amara when he thought she was not looking at him. His stomach was in knots. He could not eat his dinner, even though he had ordered his favorite dish. Instead, he shifted his food from one side of the plate to the other. What if she says no? he thought to himself. Their eyes connected and they both smiled a half smile and continued to eat their dinner.

Tony paid the bill and they walked to the park in silence. They walked side by side without touching. Amara was concerned that he wanted to break off their relationship. Tony walked over to the bench where they usually sat and waited for Amara to take a seat. Amara sat down slowly.

To Amara's surprise, Tony knelt beside her on the grass and produced a delicate black velvet box. He opened the box and exposed the most beautiful ring Amara had ever seen. Tony took Amara's hand. "Mari, this ring belonged to my great-great-grandmother. Her mistress gave it to her, so she could buy her freedom. Instead she fled on her own and kept the ring. She passed it on to her daughter, and so on until it got to my mother. Before my mother died of cancer, fifteen years ago, she gave this ring to me to give to the woman I planned to spend the rest of my life with. Amara, that woman is you. Will you marry me?" he asked. Amara burst into tears and could only nod her head yes. Her outstretched hand trembled as he held it and placed the delicate ring, which had four diamonds in a shape of a beautiful flower, on her ring finger. The ring glistened in the moonlight.

Amara admired the ring and threw her arms around Tony. By then they were both laughing and crying at the same time. "You have made me the most happiest woman in the world!" she said, between her tears. "I thought you wanted to break off the relationship," she cried. "I was so afraid that I had done something to lose you."

Tony gave her his handkerchief and she blew her nose and wiped her eyes. She stared at him and cupped his face into her hands. She kissed him passionately for what seemed like several minutes. Tony looked at her and smiled. He took her hands into his. "Amara, you have made me the happiest man on earth. I promise I will never stop trying to make you smile as you did tonight. "He traced her deep dimples with his finger. I love you baby," he said as he held her tightly.

"Can we share this with my mom and dad?" she asked. "And your aunt?" he asked. Amara smiled. She had told him the whole story about her aunt and her parents. "Yes," she said happily.

"You know, since both my parents are no longer living, your parents have become like my parents too," he said. Amara kissed him again and took him by the hand. She couldn't wait to break the good news to her parents.

Sam and Franni were enjoying a quiet dinner together in an upscale restaurant. Franni had not been on a photo shoot for nearly three weeks because of a virus she had picked up a couple of weeks ago. Tonight was the first night she had felt well enough to share a meal with Sam since she had helped him move into his new loft. Their relationship was strained, but it seemed to improve each day. They had agreed to go to counseling, starting the following week.

Sam looked over at her with worry in his eyes. "Franni, you don't look so well," he said. "Have you been to see a doctor?" he asked.

Franni shook her head and tears formed in her eyes. "Sam, I'm pregnant," she said sadly.

Sam felt as if a dagger had slashed through his heart. He and Franni had not had sex since she returned from her last shoot. She had complained of feeling ill for some time.

Sam looked at her with deep pain in his eyes. This was insurmountable. He didn't feel he could raise another man's child. Sam became angry. How could she have unprotected sex? We never had unprotected sex. She was always so worried about getting pregnant.

As if she read his mind, she said, "I don't know why I had unprotected sex. I have never been so careless in my life. I am truly sorry, Sam. But I thought you should know."

Sam glared at her. "Does the father know?" he asked bitterly.

Franni shook her head. "Yes, he has agreed to pay for the abortion," she said quietly.

This was more than Sam could take. He excused himself, placed his napkin on the table, and walked out of the restaurant. Franni sobbed quietly into her napkin. A few moments later, the maitre d' came over and announced her guest had paid the bill and a taxi was waiting to take her home.

Amara and Tony raced up the stairs to her parent's home. They were both out of breath when Myra answered the door. She tried not to smile and to act as if she knew nothing about their evening. Amara burst in and showed her mother her new engagement ring. "Tony, this is so beautiful. The diamonds are spectacular," Myra said in awe. She held her daughter's hand up toward the light. Tony blushed.

"Jack, come out here," yelled Myra. Jackson walked quickly into the hallway and Amara shook her ring finger in the direction of her father. He hugged her tightly and whispered in her ear. "I am glad you finally found someone who deserves you," he said. Amara began to cry once more. Jackson hugged Tony and welcomed him to the family. "Dad, I already feel like I am part of the family," he said happily. "I promise to do my best to make Amara happy," he said. Both Jackson and Myra were on the verge of tears. They knew that Amara and Tony really loved each other, and they really liked Tony.

Jackson ran down to his cellar and brought up a bottle of vintage wine. "I would have gotten champagne, but I know how much Mari likes wine," he said in an unsteady voice.

"Honey, we bought this a while back for this very occasion," sniffed Myra as she wiped a tear of joy from her eye. Tony and Amara held hands. Myra ran to get the glasses and Jackson opened the bottle. He poured the rich liquid in the glasses and toasted his daughter and soon-to-be son-in-law. They each took a sip of wine and went into the den.

Tony and Amara took turns talking about the proposal. Jackson and Myra smiled while Jackson placed his arm around his wife. "Have you two decided on a date?"

Tony and Amara both looked at each other and said, "Christmas!"

Myra laughed. "My goodness, there will be three weddings in December," she said as she took another sip of wine.

Amara frowned. "Perhaps only two, Mom," she said. Myra looked surprised. "I'll tell you later," she said.

After the happy couple finished their wine, they went and sat out in the screened patio. Amara looked at Tony and took his hands. "Tony, I am so happy! I can't ever remember being more happy than I am right now." Tony kissed her tenderly. "And I plan to keep it that way," he said.

Amara cleared her throat. "Tony, I know we haven't really talked about what type of wedding we'd like to have. Do you have any thoughts on this?" she asked.

"You might think this is really corny, but I don't want a big wedding. I'd like to have a small ceremony at our church and a small reception in your backyard, since it's much prettier than mine," he said smiling. "And what would you think about a cruise?" he asked.

Amara's eyes lit up. "Tony, that is exactly what I'd like," she said. "Brianna's wedding is going to be huge and very glamorous. I really want a small wedding with the people who mean the most to us and then to go away together," she said.

This time Tony cleared his throat. Amara looked at him. "Tony, what's wrong?" she asked.

Tony cleared his throat again. "What would you think about inviting your parents to go on the cruise with us?" he asked timidly. "You've told me they've never really had a honeymoon, and they got married in January, so it's pretty close," he said.

Amara covered her mouth and began to cry. "Tony, that is the most thoughtful thing anyone has ever said to me. I would love that! Could that be our wedding present to them?" she asked.

Tony smiled. "I have a lot of money saved up, and I would love to spend some of it on Mom and Dad," he said.

Amara laid her head on his chest and he held her close. Soon her tears permeated his shirt. "Honey, you are making my shirt into a hanky," he teased.

Amara wiped her eyes and looked at him. "Tony, you have made me the happiest woman in the world, I love you," she said dreamily. Before Amara left, she and Tony called her Aunt Sarah and her husband Raymond. They whooped and hollered for nearly five minutes at the news. She had already volunteered to cater the affair. Amara and Tony told them that they loved them both and hung up the phone.

When Amara and Tony arrived at Amara's house, she ran to the phone to call her best friend. Tony smiled and shook his head. Amara looked at Tony, and grinned ear to ear as she picked up the telephone. She dialed the number quickly. "Hello?" answered a sleepy voice. "Bre, wake up! I've got something important to tell you!" she exclaimed.

Brianna looked at the clock and saw that it was nearly midnight. Brianna wiped the sleep from her eyes and yawned into the phone. "What is it, Mari?" she asked sleepily.

"I'm getting married!" she screamed into the phone.

Brianna sat up in bed. She was wide awake now. "What? Tell me everything? When is the wedding?" she asked in her usual rapid fire.

Amara laughed and told her all about the proposal, the wine at her parent's house, the proposed wedding date, and the cruise for them and her parents. "Wow, Mari, that sounds beautiful!" she said excitedly. "Well I know I am your choice for maid of honor!" she said.

Amara laughed. "You know it! The problem is our wedding is so close to yours and I didn't know about your honeymoon plans," she said.

Brianna laughed. "Worry your pretty head no more. We aren't taking our honeymoon right away because of the release date of the movie. We will take it in April or May, so your plans are fine!" she said excitedly. "Mari, I am so happy for you. Call me tomorrow when I am awake, and tell me what help you'll need. Trust me, a wedding takes a lot of planning," she said. They ended their conversation and hung up the phone. Clayton stirred in the bed. "That was Mari, I gather?" he said half-asleep.

Brianna kissed Clayton softly on his lips. "Yes, and she's getting married in December also," she said happily.

"Good for her," said Clayton before falling back asleep.

Amara went into the bedroom and saw Tony lying on the bed. She smiled and walked over to him. She looked into his eyes. "Are you ready to make love to me?" he asked her softly. Amara nodded her head and kissed him tenderly and began to remove her clothing. Tony began to remove his as he watched her undress. He loved her body and liked to watch her slowly disrobe. They began to kiss and fondle one another as they usually did. But this time he reached in his pants pocket and pulled out a condom. Amara helped him put it on.

As he entered her, he could feel the tightness all around him, she seemed to fit like a glove. He was gentle and continued to ask what she liked and what pleased, her all the while moving slowly inside of her. Sensations and emotions spilled out of her as he continued to caress and kiss her all over. She had never felt this way with anyone else. They moaned and yelled together as they climaxed in unison. Amara and Tony held one another for several minutes, each enjoying the experience they had just shared.

"Wow," said Amara. "You, you are fantastic," she said out of breath.

"It takes two, baby," he said as he kissed her gently and held her tight. They talked into the early morning hours about their future together and about their first time making love. They both agreed it was explosive and well worth the wait. Finally they closed their eyes and fell asleep in each other's arms.

The following week, Amara spent most of her time in the courtroom. Today she was going to sit in on Shareese's bail hearing. As Shareese strode past in handcuffs, Amara noticed that she didn't have the same polished look as before and she seemed a bit more humbled. Perhaps her stay in jail has been beneficial, thought Amara. Shareese did not make eye contact with anyone as she walked to her seat in the courtroom.

Once seated, she spoke quietly to her lawyer, a sharp, smartly dressed African American woman who had a good reputation in the community as a defense lawyer. Amara remembered reading an article about her in her favorite African American magazine, Jet. Shareese must have had a lot of money tucked away, because Deirdre Young's fee was very expensive, though she usually produced positive results.

Deirdre explained to the judge that Shareese had never been in any trouble, was an upstanding citizen, and would not be a flight risk if released on bail. The prosecution argued that she was a definite flight risk. He pointed out that she had been apprehended with close to one million dollars of marked ransom money in her suitcase, and that she had planned to leave the country within hours if she had not been captured. Deirdre tried to argue that the money did not belong to Shareese, but was Michael's. She surmised that Michael had unknowingly hidden the money in one of her suitcases and that she was just taking a vacation overseas. The judge rapped his gavel and reminded Deirdre that this was merely a bail hearing and that she would have the opportunity to try her case at a later date. Deirdre sat down quietly. The judge ordered Shareese Miller held without bail until her trial.

Amara noticed a Latino woman sitting in the back, to her right. She wiped a tear away from her face with a lace handkerchief. Amara tried to think who the woman was, and then she suddenly recognized her. It was Mrs. Cooper, the poor woman who had had her first child kidnapped from the hospital, only to find out it was not her child. Amara also saw Charlene, Shareese's sister.

At the end of the hearing, the bailiff escorted Shareese out of the courtroom. Shareese looked at her sister and mouthed something, but Charlene shook her head no and looked the other way. Later, Shareese's lawyer walked over and handed Charlene a note. Charlene frowned as she read her sister's rushed handwriting.

The note read, "Bring Charity to visit me next visiting day, please!" Charlene folded the note and placed it into her pocket. She would bring Charity to visit, but if she sensed that there was trouble, she would take Charity away. Shareese had always been able to control Charity. Except this time it would be for keeps. Shareese was desperate and Charlene knew that she was capable of doing anything in her current state of mind.

On the way out of the courtroom, Shareese spotted the diamond ring on Amara's finger and grinned like a cat prepared to eat a mouse. Amara never looked up. She continued to write notes on the hearing. When the courtroom was empty, Amara got up and walked through the hallway. She checked her watch to see how long she had before the next hearings began. The two police officers' hearings were scheduled later in the afternoon. She felt sad for Maria, especially since she was pregnant. Amara headed to a nearby sandwich shop at the corner to grab a quick lunch before the hearings began, later that day.

Amara took her seat in the back of the courtroom and waited for Maria to enter the courtroom. While she waited, she was surprised to see Michael's father, Ryan, in the courtroom. Perhaps he felt some affection for her since she was once Michael's wife, she thought to herself.

Maria was escorted into court with handcuffs around her wrists. They were removed after she took her seat with her lawyer. Amara was also surprised to see Maria had one of the best lawyers in the state defending her.

When it was her lawyer's turn to speak, he talked about her hardships and also talked about her not being a flight risk. "In fact, Mr. Ryan Whitman has volunteered to post bail and to be responsible for her until the trial," he said. The prosecution agreed that she was not a flight risk and had no concerns with her being released on bail. "Beside the fact she nearly kicked all the teeth out of Michael's mouth," said Amara under her breath. She sketched Maria and noticed that she was beginning to show, just a little since her frame was so small.

Macey was not as lucky. Although he was not considered a flight risk, he was considered dangerous. He was denied bail and moved to a different facility for his own protection since he was an ex-police officer. Amara saw no remorse on the face of either officer.

She shook her head sadly and completed the notes for the article she was working on. She closed her notebook and quietly placed her things in her briefcase. She left her seat, eased open the doors, and slipped out into the hall.

Amara's thoughts were completely jumbled in her mind. Her editor feared that she was too close to the issues to write an objective article for the magazine. She wanted this article to show both sides. For that, she would need to talk to the Coopers.

Amara quickly dialed the Cooper's answering service and left a message. Her call was returned immediately. It was Mrs. Cooper. She told Amara that she had seen her in the courtroom when she sat through Michael and Shareese's hearings. She wanted to tell her side of the story. Amara sighed with relief. This will be easier than I thought, she said to herself as she jotted down the Cooper's address.

Amara walked up the stone walkway and rang the bell to the Coopers' mansion at the appointed time. The maid opened the door and led her to the formal living room where Mr. and Mrs. Cooper were sitting. Mrs. Cooper was holding a plump infant boy, who was sucking on a bottle. She called for the nanny, who immediately retrieved the baby and quietly left the room. Amara introduced herself and shook hands with Robert and Sonya Cooper. Amara asked their permission to tape the interview. They both said yes.

Sonya Cooper began. "No one has ever asked us our side of the story or about the pain we endured when we thought our newborn son was kidnapped, only to find out he had died at birth. It was a tremendous tragedy, not to mention the pain we went through when we found out the child we thought was ours was not and we had to give him back to his mother, who happened to be one of my closest friends." Sonya wiped a tear from her eye with one long manicured finger.

Robert consoled her and began where she left off. "We feel so betrayed by people we thought were our friends. We understand all this came to light because of photos you had of the ransom delivery?" he asked. Amara turned off the tape and jotted a couple of notes before responding.

She set down her pen and notebook and looked at the Coopers. "That is correct. I had forgotten all about the photos until Duke Ellington tried to kill me one night. The truth began to slowly unfold as the news of the photos surfaced at the police department," said Amara.

Robert smiled a crooked smile and chuckled. "I am just glad to see those crooked cops and Mike, who I thought was a good friend, get what they deserve. All because you caught their betrayal in a series of photos," he said deliberately. He clamped down on his jaw to keep from getting emotional.

Amara could see that this was very difficult for both of them. She offered to give them a few minutes before starting again. Sonya thanked her and rang a bell for some refreshments. Cold beverages and fresh fruit were brought into the room on a silver service tray. The maid quickly set the tray on the large cart and slowly pushed it toward them. She stopped when it was in a central location and quietly left the room.

Sonya offered her a beverage and some fruit. Amara took a bottle of chilled mineral water and a glass. She poured the mineral water into the glass and took a sip. It was tasted so good and cool she took a longer drink. She picked up some strawberries and placed a dollop of whipped cream on top. She took a bite of her strawberry and went back to the interview. She looked at the Coopers and asked them if they were ready to continue. They said they were prepared to continue.

Amara turned the tape recorder back on and picked up her notebook and pen. Robert Cooper continued. He smiled ruefully. "Just for the record, only one hundred thousand of the million was real. The rest was counterfeit." Amara's mouth dropped open in surprise. "Weren't you concerned that they would find out and hurt your child?" she asked. Mr. Cooper shook his head. "We had a suspicion that the kidnapped infant was not ours. You see, in my wife's family all the children are born with a special birthmark on their thigh. Although I did not know our child was dead at birth, I saw the birthmark on his thigh when he was delivered by the doctor," he said reluctantly.

Amara tried to remain calm. She could not believe what she was being told. "Days later, I saw photos of the dead infant and I spotted the birthmark on the thigh. I was sick to my stomach to learn our baby was dead in the hospital morgue," he said sadly.

Amara looked shocked. "You mean to say you knew the kidnapped infant was not your child the whole time?" she asked. Mrs. Cooper smiled wearily. "Of course not," she said. "When the little baby was returned to us, we noticed immediately that the facial features did not match ours and the birthmark my husband said he saw on our baby was not there," she said. "Then why didn't you tell the authorities that the infant was not yours?" she asked.

"We had already hired a private detective. He told us that the hospital had delivered a stillborn child the day I gave birth. Our detective informed us the documents read it was Amelia's child. Well, the child we were given looked just like a miniature Amelia," she said. "We called Amelia right away and told her what we knew. She asked if she could come get her baby. I said yes of course," responded Sonya.

"Then Michael got on the phone and said he was going to sue us for mental damages because we had kept a baby we knew was not ours. He said he was suing for one million dollars," Robert Cooper bitterly interjected. "I was so angry that I called his bluff and told him we'd see him in court. He quickly backed off, but we did not. We took it to court and made him pay the court costs.

"One month later, we gave the baby back to Amelia. As you know, the baby died shortly after we returned him," he said sadly. "I wish I had not been so stubborn. That case dragged on for a whole month. That would have been one month she could have spent with her baby," he lamented.

Sonya smiled and said, "She came over every day after Michael went to work and spent most of the day with her son." Robert looked at her with surprise. "A mother could never keep another mother from seeing her child, no matter how silly the husbands act," she said matter-of-factly.

Robert smiled and took Sonya's hand and gently kissed it. "That makes me feel better that you showed such an act of kindness," he said softly.

"It is a shame he died so quickly after she got him home," said Sonya. "That just proves how fragile life is and how important it is to live it to the fullest," she said as she excused herself.

"I am going to spend some time with little Robert," she sniffed. Sonya Cooper extended her hand. "Thank you for coming and listening to our side of the story," she said. Amara shook her hand and looked at Robert Cooper. He directed his attention back to Amara. "When do you plan to release this story?" he asked.

"In a couple of weeks, then I will do a follow up after their trials are completed," she said. "Is it possible to leave out the part about the money being counterfeit?" he asked. Amara smiled and assured him she would leave that information out.

Robert smiled. He stood up and walked Amara to the door. He shook her hand and thanked her for her time. Amara smiled and thanked him for providing their side of the story. Amara turned to leave. Robert Cooper quietly closed the door and walked up the stairs to join his wife in the nursery.

Amara was totally focused on her work when she heard a knock on the door. She checked her watch and was surprised it was ten o'clock. She had been working nonstop since three. She typed the last sentence and saved her document. She felt she had produced a great article. She decided she'd let it sit and come back and proofread the whole article later.

The knock on the door became harder. "Coming," she said and went to the door. When she opened the door she smiled. It was Tony, with two large containers of Chinese food in each hand. He also had a bag with beverages. "How did you know I hadn't eaten?" she asked. Tony grinned. "I know my woman," he said authoritatively.

Amara laughed and opened the door wider, so he could come in. She took the bag of beverages and set them on the table and went into the kitchen to get plates, napkins, glasses, and flatware. Tony began to open the containers. Amara's stomach growled loudly as she smelled the sweet aroma wafting through the air. "Mmm," she said. "Tony, that smells wonderful and your timing is excellent. I just completed my article!" she said excitedly.

Tony sat down and served himself. Amara joined him and placed the different delicacies on her plate. Tony blessed the food and they both started to eat. Tony took a bite of his chicken and broccoli and looked at Amara. She was busy eating her moo goo gai pan when she saw Tony staring at her.

She wiped her mouth with a napkin and looked at him. "What?" she asked, as she took another bite.

"Are you going to let me read your article?" he asked.

Amara smiled. "Tony that would be great!" she said beaming. She couldn't believe how fortunate she was to have someone who really cared about what she was doing.

She looked at him, and it was his turn to ask what she was thinking. "You are just so supportive of my career. It feels really good to know that you care about what I'm doing," she said happily.

Tony laughed. "I think you are just giddy because I bought you some food," he joked.

Amara got up and kissed him on the forehead. She picked up his fork and fed him another bite of his chicken and broccoli. "No, Tony, I am serious. That really means a lot to me," she said.

Tony blushed and looked her in the eyes. "We are a team now. Don't ever forget that. Believe me, there will be days when I am really going to need your patience and understanding."

Tony gave Amara a quick kiss and shooed her away, so he could finish his favorite Chinese dish. Amara finished her meal and cleared the table. She took the dirty dishes in the kitchen and put them in the dishwasher. When Tony had finished his dinner, he walked over to the computer and printed a copy of Amara's article. He sat in her recliner and began to read. Amara leaned over and watched as she stacked the last of the dishes in the dishwasher.

Tony pulled a pen from his pocket and began to write notes in the margins of the paper. Amara frowned as she saw him rereading several pages and writing notes. She turned on the dishwasher and cleared the empty boxes from the table. Once she was finished in the kitchen she walked over to the recliner and sat on the arm of the chair and peeked over his shoulder.

Tony finished the last page and stuck the pen behind his ear. "Sweetheart, you are too close to this, in some places you've lost your objectivity entirely," he said pointing at two separate pages. Amara smirked. Tony saw the change in her expression and held up his hand. "Now, before you take offense, read my notes and reread the portions I indicated and then make a decision," he said.

Amara took the pages back without comment. She went over to the sofa and began to read. She stopped after the third page and looked at Tony. "You're right," she said quietly. "Thanks. I just need to let it sit a bit more and come back to it. Most of your comments were dead on," she said.

Tony smiled and got up from the recliner. "Glad I could help," he said. He walked over and gave her a hug and a kiss. "It's well after eleven and we both have to go to work tomorrow," he said. Amara yawned and agreed. She walked him to the door and closed it gently behind him. She turned off her computer and lights and went to her bedroom.

Early the next morning, Amara fixed herself a big mug of cocoa with lots of marshmallows. She went over her article once more and smiled. She knew the angle she would use for her article. She kissed the papers, quickly turned on her computer, and began to type. Tony was scheduled to work the swing shift, and Amara gave him a call.

Tony answered the phone on the first ring. "Good morning, Amara," he said cheerfully. Amara looked at the phone. Tony laughed at the pregnant pause. "Caller ID," he said, as if to read her thoughts.

Amara giggled. "You got me on that one," she said playfully. "Hey, would you mind coming over and reading through my article once more?" she asked.

"Sure," said Tony. "Just give me a few minutes. I just finished my workout, and I need to take a shower and change clothes," he said.

Amara nodded. "Okay, see you in about half an hour?" she asked.

"As long as you have my favorite muffin and a hot cup of coffee," he said.

"You mean a nice cup of hot cocoa, right?" she teased.

"I am not putting a cup of sugar into my fit body," he bragged.

"And coffee is so much better for you, with all that caffeine," she teased.

"Well, I have to have some vices," he retorted lamely. Amara laughed. "All right, apple cinnamon muffin with a cup of home brewed java," she said as if she were taking his order.

"And, if you're nice to me, I may leave a tip," he teased.

Amara laughed and said goodbye. They both hung up. Thirty minutes later, Tony knocked on the door. Amara opened the door and let him in. Once she had closed the door, she gave him a big kiss. "Wow," he said as he held her close. "I need to come over for muffins and coffee more often," he said in a sensuous voice. Amara kissed him again and went to get his coffee and muffin. Tony sat down at the dining room table and Amara set the food and beverage in front of him. She also handed him a copy of her revised article.

He took a big bite of his muffin and a sip of coffee. He set the cup down and began to read the article. Tony didn't eat or drink anything else until he completed the article. When he got to the end, he sat the article down on the table and smiled. "Amara, this is brilliant! I really like it. I love the way you totally removed your personal feelings and wrote it as if you were watching a show on the television. Truly a remarkable job!" he said proudly.

Amara smiled widely. "It was your advice that gave me the idea. Your observations about my article were right on target last night," she said. "I was too wrapped up in what had happened to me fully to tell the story that has affected so many lives in so many ways," she said emotionally.

Tony got up and hugged her. "Truly a labor of love, but I also think a bit therapeutic?" he asked.

Amara laughed and agreed. "Definitely therapeutic," she said crying and laughing at the same time. "Tony, I didn't know I had so much anger and animosity pent up inside me," she said in a serious tone. "I mean, here is a man, who was my biological father, trying to kill me because my ex-boyfriend's brother doesn't want to be exposed for the wrong he had done. I guess that's what you read in the first edition of this article," she said quietly. Tony held her close and nibbled on her ear.

He pulled her away and looked at her. "Now this is the type of story from which legends are made," he teased.

She took her article and placed it inside her briefcase. "I will deliver this one to my editor today," she said, relieved and happy she had completed the article. Tony popped his muffin into the microwave and poured himself a fresh cup of coffee. He grabbed the daily newspaper and read while he ate his breakfast. Amara watched him read and smiled. I am one lucky lady, she thought as she went to change into her office attire.

Chapter 15

S hareese sat in the visitor area of the jail with her two sisters. She held Charity's hand and asked her how things were going. "You've been a bad girl," Charity said as she rocked back and forth. "Bad girl, Shareese," she said as she continued to rock. Charlene casually mentioned that she was invited to attend Tony and Amara's wedding in December. Shareese acted unaffected by the news.

Charlene told her she was going to take her new boyfriend to the wedding. Shareese perked up. "What does he do? How much money does he make?" she asked excitedly. Charlene rolled her eyes. Her sister would never change. Charlene was getting bored with this visit. Although she loved Shareese dearly, she had come to terms with the knowledge that Shareese was selfish and if it didn't involve her in some way, she wasn't interested.

Charlene checked her watch. "Five more minutes, okay, Charity?" she asked as she stood up. Charity shook her head like a small girl. Charlene smiled. She got up and walked to the fenced and barred window. She crossed her arms across her chest as if she felt a sudden chill. She had been where Shareese was so many times that she dared not count. But now she had a new lease on life and she had to study for her upcoming exam, so she couldn't stay out too late tonight.

Shareese smiled and put her head to Charity's and began to whisper names and addresses. Charity had a photographic memory when it came to numbers and names. Shareese told her what she wanted done and when. She told Charity she would call her to confirm all the details. Charity continued to rock. "I like playing cowboys and Indians," she said without any intonation.

Charlene walked back and told Shareese she needed to leave. Shareese gave Charity and Charlene a big hug. She then reminded Charity not to forget their game. Charity stuck her thumb up. "I won't," she said. "Call me soon, sister," she said as she walked away. Charlene looped her arm through Charity's.

When they got outside, Charlene asked Charity what she and Shareese talked about. Charity smiled. "We are going to play cowboys and Indians!"

she yelled. Charlene calmed her down and they went out to Charity's favorite restaurant, Sarah's Café. In fact it was the only place she would eat outside of the home.

The cold winter air seemed to come early as both Amara and Brianna busily prepared for their own wedding and helped the other as maid of honor. They were both giddy as their wedding dates neared. They agreed it was fun having the other to lean on for their wedding preparations. Amara flew to San Francisco twice to throw Brianna a bridal shower and be fitted for her maid of honor dress. In turn, Brianna flew to Seattle to throw Amara's bridal shower and get fitted for her maid of honor dress.

On Friday, Amara drove Brianna to the airport. They giggled like two young schoolgirls the whole way. "Can you believe your wedding is only six weeks away?" exclaimed Amara.

Brianna nodded her head. "I am ready to marry that man, Mari," she said confidently. Amara gently squeezed her hand and released it. "We are the most luckiest women on earth," said Brianna as she slapped her leg.

Amara smiled. "Who would have thought," she joked.

"Don't get me started on that!" said Brianna, joining in the joke. They laughed. In college they had pledged to meet the right man and have a double wedding. "Not quite a double wedding, but pretty close," said Amara smiling.

Amara walked Brianna to the ticket counter and gave her a big hug. "Security is so tight, I can't go any further," she said.

"I'll call you when I arrive," Brianna told Amara.

"If you don't I'll be waiting by the phone like an old mother hen," she joked. They waved at one another and Amara walked out of the airport terminal.

Amara smiled as she pulled on her jacket lapels together and got into her car. Feels like snow, she thought, as she started the car and drove away. As Amara drove home, she thought about Brianna's wedding. Brianna had hired one of the top wedding planners in the area. Even though she had the wedding planner, she had begged Amara to come down early and help her organize some personal things.

Amara was flattered and more than happy to help out her best friend on her most special day. In fact she submitted a request for five day's leave, so she could use the extra days off to be there and assist Brianna with any loose ends. "Brianna's wedding is going to be the wedding of the decade," she said aloud as she drove toward home.

Early Saturday morning Amara jogged to the newsstand and picked up the new monthly edition of her magazine. Her article was to appear in this month's edition. She tore open the plastic and removed the magazine. She opened it up and went directly to the page.

"For the Love of Money, by Amara Glenton," she read aloud. She looked at the sketches and the collage of actual pictures of everyone involved. She smiled widely with pride and satisfaction. She let out a big breath. The man at the stand stared at her as he rang up the magazine. "My article!" she said excitedly as she pointed to the article in the magazine and grabbed another copy. The man nodded and smiled as he rang up the extra copy. She handed him the money and tucked the magazines under her arm and jogged home.

She let herself in and checked her watch. Tony was still at work. She carefully laid the magazines on the kitchen table and reread her article. It was really good. She re-read the portion about Shareese. Shareese had been portrayed as a selfish, money-grubbing, conniving woman who used everyone to get what she wanted, which was money. She shook her head sadly. Amara pictured Shareese in her little jail cell. "What a waste," she said aloud.

She read the portion about Duke and Michael. She was glad she no longer felt the rush of anger toward them. Duke was dead and Michael would get his just desserts in the courtroom. She had no doubt about that, especially with Judge Marion presiding.

She looked out the window and thought about Maria. She was now living with Ryan, Michael's father. It was rumored they were getting married after the trial. Now that's a twist of fate, thought Amara. Amara didn't begrudge Maria's happiness and future security if that rumor was true. She had found out that Ryan had continually sent Maria money throughout the time she was away, even after the baby died and he had withdrawn the trust fund. Seems as if he has always had a soft spot for her. Only time will tell on that one, she mused.

Excitement filled Amara's eyes as an idea hit her. She went into her closet and pulled down a big tan wicker basket. She lined it with one of the towels her mother had designed for the kitchen and placed Tony's favorite muffins, a new coffee cup with his name on it that she had purchased at a sale for Christmas, his favorite brand of coffee, napkins, plastic spoon, and a copy of her magazine. She pulled out one of her favorite scented stationery cards and matching envelopes and jotted a note. She tucked the card into the envelope and stuck that inside the basket as well. She strolled over to Tony's house and set the basket of goodies inside his screen door. She giggled softly as she cut across the lawn and returned to her house.

When Tony arrived home, he saw that his screen door was ajar. He parked the car in the garage and slowly approached his screen door. He smiled when he recognized the towel in the basket. It was from Amara. He picked up the basket and took it inside. Once inside, he looked at the basket and laughed aloud. He pulled out the magazine and turned to the tabbed page. He set the magazine down and went to change his clothes.

Once he was comfortable, he sat down in his recliner and read her article. He shook his head in satisfaction. The editor had made very few changes from the initial draft he had read. He looked at the several sketches and photos of everyone involved. He chuckled and said aloud, "My girl has got it going on!" He then read the card and smiled. It read, "I could have never written such a great article without your help. Thanks for your support and love. Love, Mari."

He looked at his watch. It was already close to eleven o'clock. He would try to reach her first thing in the morning. He reread the article and tore it from the magazine. He went to his desk and pulled out a large scrapbook. He removed a glue stick from his desk drawer and glued the article onto the second page of the scrapbook. He glued the card next to the article. He placed a date at the top, closed the book, and placed it back inside the desk drawer.

The next morning, Tony showed up at Amara's door with fresh muffins and two cups of coffee. Amara laughed and let him inside.

The following day, Myra called Tony on the phone. She was in the middle of decorating a room and needed some advice. Tony described how he wanted the room to look and Myra immediately knew what she needed to achieve the right effect. She thanked Tony and hung up the phone. Tony quickly got dressed in his starched police uniform and departed to work the swing shift.

Amara was in her office when she got a message that something big had occurred at the jail with one of the people being held in the big kidnapping, ransom, and attempted murder case. She shoved her feet into her shoes under the desk, grabbed her bag and camera, and headed for the door. She was only a few blocks away from the station, so she walked at a brisk pace. When she arrived, one of Tony's friends recognized her and waved her through. She stopped and asked what happened. Officer Randall Bennyberry shrugged and just said one of the people involved in the big court case she was covering had been seriously injured by another inmate last night. Amara assumed it was Shareese and thanked him and walked inside the station.

Amara placed her camera inside her bag. She knew any type of photography would be forbidden. She searched the halls and spotted Tony going through an entryway in the direction of his office. She walked swiftly past several detectives talking and caught up with Tony. Tony frowned when he saw her. "Mari, what are you doing here?" he asked. Amara was taken aback by the terseness with which he asked the question.

"I, I heard that one of the defendants in the upcoming court case was seriously injured. Was it Shareese?" she stammered.

"Honey, it wasn't Shareese, it was Macey," he said quietly. "He was stabbed last night in the cafeteria. We aren't sure if he's going to make it," he said. Amara stood and looked at him. "Hey, sorry for snapping at you. It has been one hellacious day," he said with a small grin. Amara smiled back and said she understood. He told her he'd call her when he got off shift. "That sounds great. I will wait up," she said. Amara headed for the door while Tony prepared to leave with his partner to investigate a case they had been working on.

When Tony arrived home after his shift, he walked right over to Amara's and softly knocked on her door. She looked out of the peephole and saw it was Tony. She smiled and opened the door. "I look a mess," she said. He looked at her fuzzy pink slippers thick pink terry robe, and hair piled recklessly upon her head and chuckled. She hit his arm as she pulled him inside. "Want some cocoa?" she teased. Tony wrinkled his nose. "Nope, but I will take some coffee," he said as he caught the belt on her robe and pulled her close to him.

He kissed her tenderly as his hands roamed inside her robe. Amara moaned softly as he opened her robe and pulled her body to his. His badge felt cold to her breast and she stood back and began to unbutton his shirt. His shirt landed on the floor along with her robe. He then picked her up and carried her to her bedroom.

Amara giggled. "Mr. Riley, what strong arms you have," she mocked.

"The better to hold you with, my dear," he responded. Amara laughed at their corny jokes and became serious when he laid her on the bed. She grabbed his t-shirt and pulled him toward her. She then lifted his shirt over his head and looked at his wide chest. She played with the small patch of curly hair while he removed her gown.

They looked at each other and he kissed her passionately. She moaned softly as she felt him harden against her. She unbuckled his large belt and allowed his pants to fall to the ground with a loud thud from the handcuffs that were attached to his belt. The loud sound startled her. Tony pulled her close and held her tightly.

Tony took his time and fondled her until she was ready for him. Slowly he entered her and continued to take his time while they touched and found different ways to please each one another. She raised her hips to meet his thrusts as the momentum began to build. Her breathing became erratic as she felt the wonderful sensations travel through her body. She yelled out his name as she felt the warmth of her climax flow through her. Amara grabbed him close as he continued to move inside her. He kissed her lips and began to move rapidly until he exploded his juices inside her. She clutched him tightly as he called her name and told her not to let go of him. She held on until his body relaxed and lay limp beside hers.

She covered his face with tiny soft kisses, as she whispered how much his love meant to her. He smiled, exhausted and fully satisfied. He took her hand in his and kissed it gently. "I can't wait for you to lie beside me every night as my wife," he whispered in her ear.

She turned and supported herself on her elbow. She looked at his face, as if she were memorizing every detail. He laughed uncomfortably. "Mari, why are you staring at me?"

She smiled a crooked grin. "I can't describe how happy you make me and how much passion you bring out in me. You bring about feelings that I was always too scared to express and some I didn't even know I had."

Tony looked at her and was speechless. "I have never met anyone who is so forthright. You amaze me each time we are together. I said I didn't want to play games. You have kept me honest. I love our relationship and I love being able to talk about the most mundane to the most intimate things with you," he said.

Amara traced the hairs on his chest and snuggled close to his body. "That's 'cause we're a team," she yawned.

"Yeah," Tony responded as he yawned. Minutes later, the room fell silent to soft snores.

Amara was putting clothes in her suitcase for the trip to San Francisco when the phone rang. She picked up the phone and it was Brianna, in a panicked state. "The wedding planner has the measles!" she cried. "In fact, her back-up planner and half her staff also have the measles!" she wailed. Amara got her to stop crying and tell her what had happened.

Brianna sniffed, and began to tell Amara the story. "The last wedding was a second marriage for the bride and groom. The ceremony involved the children from their previous marriages. The ring bearer, who was the groom's youngest son, had the measles and the wedding planner didn't know until it was too late. Now, her entire staff that had worked the wedding had caught the measles, except for one, who had already had them as a child." Brianna started to cry again. "Mari, what should I do?" she asked. "Everything is a mess!" Amara could hear Brianna's mother in the background trying to soothe her. Amara told her she would fly down on the next flight available.

Amara hung up the phone and quickly finished her packing. She left a quick message on the answering machine for Tony and her parents. She called a cab to take her to the airport and flew down to be with Brianna. Amara arrived at the airport in San Francisco and took a cab to Brianna's house. After comforting and reassuring Brianna, she sprang into action. Organization was her forte, and she had everything under control in a matter of minutes. Brianna had already had everything organized, and that made Amara's job easy. Amara split the list in half and gave part of it to Brianna's mother. Kuyono was relieved to have something to do and immediately began making calls to ensure all the arrangements were still in place. Amara did the same.

In less than one hour they had confirmed all of the arrangements on Brianna's spreadsheet. Luckily, everything already had been coordinated, ordered, and it was just a matter of assisting with the set-up and deliveries. Clayton had volunteered his brother's assistance to help Sam keep his mind from his own failed wedding plans. Brianna had made many changes in their original wedding plan and that had kept Sam from taking time to feel sorry for himself.

Everything was ready. All appropriate coordination had been done. Amara thanked Brianna's mother for her help. Brianna smiled and hugged both her mother and Amara. Amara went into the bathroom and began to run a hot bath for Brianna. She added soothing bath salts that she knew Brianna loved and ushered her inside. Amara placed a gossip magazine on the edge of the tub and left Brianna to soak in peace and quiet.

Amara continued to study the sheet and got together with Kuyono and Sam. They discussed their plan of action for the following day. Each of them had specific duties. After they were finished, Amara made a mental note that Tony and her parents were going to fly in together in two days. She smiled when she thought about the fun weekend she and Tony were going to have during their extended stay. She had gotten them a really nice room at a nearby bed and breakfast and had planned several events that involved just the two of them.

Amara's smile faded when she saw Sam sitting in the corner staring out of the window at the Japanese garden. She walked up behind him and tapped him on the shoulder. "Want to talk about it?" she asked gently. Sam smiled but said nothing. Amara had heard about Franni's pregnancy and the cancellation of their wedding, but she had hesitated to bring the subject up. She stood by him in silence for a moment more, and began to walk away.

He touched her hand lightly and she stopped. He looked into her eyes. She could see the tears well in his eyes. "I guess congratulations are in order?" he asked with fake enthusiasm.

Amara's deep dimples appeared. "Yes they are. He's the one Sam," she said sincerely. "I have never been so happy in my life," she said.

Sam looked at the ground. Amara gently took his hand. "How are you taking all of this?" she asked.

Sam took a deep breath. "Franni had the abortion last week. Her friend, the one she had the affair with, flew in from London and took her. We've called it quits for good. She goes on her next photo shoot next week and is moving to New York," he said bitterly.

"I am really sorry Sam. I know how much you love her."

Sam looked into her eyes and moved closer. "Amara, I should have kept you when I had you," he said earnestly.

Amara frowned and stepped back in order to provide a little distance between them. "Sam, I am not some booby prize or faithful lapdog. You didn't love me, and you were right to pursue the woman you were in love with. And I know now that I wasn't in love with you, because Tony is the most wonderful man I have ever met. Sam, he is truly my soul mate," she said emotionally. "If you hadn't been truthful with me, I would have never found him. I owe you a debt of gratitude," she said, smiling.

Sam was speechless. He was happy for her and jealous at the same time. He took her hand in his. "I wish you and Tony much happiness," he said softly. He released her hand, grabbed his keys, and quietly walked out of the door. Amara sighed and hoped his broken heart would mend. Kuyono was waiting for Brianna to come out of the bathroom. Amara gave Kuyono a hug and went to the guestroom to sleep.

Bright and early the next morning, everything began to arrive and the trio launched into action. Amara walked around to the reception area and checked the delivery of tables and chairs. A representative from the florist came and began delivering some of the flowers that required overnight set up. Amara ensured they were the correct type of flowers and reviewed the diagram Brianna's wedding planner had drawn and discussed the locations with the florist's representative.

As they worked their way to the final location of the flowers, she saw Sam. He was walking toward her carrying his diagram and list. She shook hands with the florist's representative and spoke to Sam as he came near. "Hey, Sam," said Amara casually. Sam smiled and waved hello. He continued about his tasks as Kuyono met with the caterers.

It was to be a full and productive day. At the end of the day, Amara met with Kuyono and Sam to make sure all the tasks for the day had been completed. She smiled and asked Kuyono to call Brianna and give her the thumbs up for the day. Later that evening, after they had all returned to Brianna's home, she and Brianna sat down and shared some wine. Sam sat alone in the corner staring out of the window. Brianna stood up and walked over to her stereo and put several CDs in the CD changer. Some were oldies and others were the latest hip-hop grooves.

Brianna selected a musical group that had been popular while she and Amara were in college. She began to dance to the beat. "Hey, Amara, remember this dance?" she asked as she made a funny face and executed the steps of a dance long forgotten. Amara shook her head and laughed. She got up started to dance. "Bre, remember this one?" she asked. Brianna laughed at the out-of-date moves. "Girl, I cannot believe we did a dance that looked that stupid," she said, laughing.

Just then, Clayton snuck in and placed an old Barry White CD in the player and started to pantomime to the song. Amara and Brianna fell down on the sofa as they laughed and pointed at Clayton. He then picked them up and twirled them around to be his back-up singers. Just then, Brianna's dad, Brian, walked in with a bottle of root beer pop and chips and pretended to be Barry White.

They all fell over with laughter until Brianna's mom changed the CD to Diana Ross and began to mimic her. The girls quickly stood up and became the Supremes, while Clayton and Brian pulled Sam out of the corner and the three of them pretended to do the moves of the Temptations. When the song was over, everyone fell to the ground and laughed heartily. Kuyono began to fan herself and went to get cold beverages for everyone.

"We used to do that all the time when Brianna was a child," said Kuyono as she set the tray of beverages on the table. Brian walked over and spun his wife around and danced cheek to cheek to the next Diana Ross song. "She is my favorite!" said Kuyono as she danced slow with her husband.

Brianna and Amara sighed. Clayton grabbed both women by the hand and began dancing with them. Amara laughed and handed Clayton Brianna's other hand and they too danced cheek to cheek. Sam quietly got his keys and tiptoed out of the front door. Amara grabbed a bottle of mineral water from the tray and quietly tiptoed out of the room to call Tony and catch up on events back home.

Early the next morning, Tony, Jackson, and Myra arrived at the airport. Amara made sure she was there early in order to give herself plenty of time. She was finishing her morning cup of cocoa when she spotted them coming down the escalator. Tony saw Amara first and rushed toward her. He grabbed her by the waist and swung her around and gave her a big kiss. "I missed you," he said. Amara blushed and Tony released her so she could greet her parents. Amara walked over and hugged her mother and father. Amara followed them to the baggage claim to gather their luggage. They walked a short distance to the rented car.

Once they arrived at the hotel and Amara ensured everyone had checked in, she raced back to her car to return to the church and the reception area. Tony called after her. "Mari, can I help you with anything?" he asked. "Sure, hop in," she said. Amara explained about the illness involving the wedding planner and how the scope of her responsibilities had suddenly grown. Tony smiled and clutched her hand, "That's my girl, taking care of business," he said proudly. Tony and Amara laughed and joked all the way to the location where the wedding and reception would take place.

Tony got out and removed his sunglasses. "Mari, this is definitely a set up for the rich and famous," he said, thoroughly impressed. Amara pulled out two sheets of paper from her pocket. "We've got to double-check the seating, check the flowers in the church, rope off the area for the wedding gifts, and pick up the rings from the jeweler," she said in a businesslike tone.

Tony playfully saluted her, and took one of the lists. "I can check the seating, since I am a fresh set of eyes. Why don't you check the flowers and rope off the gift area? I will meet you in the foyer and we can go get the rings." Amara agreed, as she walked quickly to the destinations on her diagram. Tony checked his diagram and headed for the area where tables and chairs were set up.

The hired staff had just finished placing the chairs around the last maroon topped circular table. The nameplates were neatly arranged at each table. Tony immediately set about the task of verifying the names and ensuring they were set in the correct spot.

As he completed the task Brianna ran over to him, close to tears. "Tony, I forgot to seat my auntie from Japan. She doesn't speak much English and she needs to sit by my uncle who is coming from Hawaii, and there's not enough room at their table," she said as she tried to contain her emotions.

Tony scanned the seating diagram once more and smiled. He pointed at the diagram as he spoke to Brianna. "Bre, how about we move this guy, Mr.

Norris, to the spare chair at table six, which will free up space for your aunt at table three and we can place her right beside your uncle, Mr. Nakamura?" he suggested.

Brianna looked at the change and smiled. "That's perfect. Mike has a crush on Seretta and now they will be sitting by each other! Tony, you are a genius!" she squealed, as she gave him a big hug.

"Hey, hey, who is that hugging my wife-to-be?" asked Clayton, jokingly. Tony laughed. "Hey man, how are you?" he said, as he extended his hand to Clayton. "This place is absolutely fabulous," he said looking around. Clayton placed his glasses on top of his head and shook Tony's hand. "Getting any ideas?" he joked.

Tony smiled. "Mari and I are going to keep it small and simple. We plan to plunk all of our money into the honeymoon," he said proudly.

Clayton smiled. "Hey, I think that's really cool of you guys to include her parents. They seem like really sweet people," he said.

"They are," said Tony. "They are like my parents," he said. "My own parents died a long time ago, and they have been really supportive of our wedding plans and of me. We haven't told them about the cruise, so don't let the cat out of the bag," he said.

Clayton made a motion as if he were zipping his lips. "Your secret is safe with me," he said.

"What secret?" asked Sam. "Hey, Tony, good to see you again and congratulations on your upcoming wedding. It's just a few weeks away right?" asked Sam.

Tony went over and shook Sam's hand. "That's right! I can't wait to make Amara my wife. She is some kind of special," said Tony. Sam and Clayton looked at each other and said in unison, "He's got it bad." Tony began to laugh with them and went to meet Amara in the foyer, so they could go and pick up the rings.

The rehearsal dinner went off without a hitch. Everyone was shocked to see Franni with Sam at the dinner party, but they were laughing and seemed to be having a good time. Brianna and Clayton were really hamming it up, and having a wonderful time. The stories and jokes kept everyone at the reception hall until late in the evening. Finally Clayton announced everyone should leave, so he could get ready for his bachelor party.

All the men began to yell and shout. Sam had really gone to a lot of trouble to reserve one of the most classy strip joints in town. Amara had booked a spa for the women's bachelorette party. The women were excited because Amara had arranged for the masseurs to be built like the Chippendale strippers.

Both Amara and Sam went about their task to made sure everyone was in the proper vehicle, and each car had a designated driver. Amara walked over and gave Tony a quick peck on the lips. She began to laugh when she saw her father jump into the car driven by Tony. "Dad!" she exclaimed. Her father grinned and gave her the thumbs up sign. Meanwhile, the last few women were piling into their appropriate cars and engines were revved and ready to go. Amara got into the car with Brianna and their caravan headed to the local spa while the men headed in the opposite direction, to the strip club.

Sam smiled as the men gawked at the beautiful women when they entered the tastefully decorated building. Three scantily clad women with perfect figures came to greet them. The men groaned as they swarmed around Clayton. Shortly, several other women came out and led the rest of the party their private room, where the fun would take place. As the show began, several men removed their ties and got their dollar bills ready. All the women were gorgeous and each man in the group was treated as if he were the most important man in the room. Drinks were brought out steadily and everyone seemed to be having a great time. Except for Sam. He sat quietly in a corner and nursed his beer. He thought about Franni and the ending of their relationship. He thought that he should be celebrating like Clay, but that wasn't in the cards for him. He sighed and chalked it up to the reality of life.

As he took another sip of his beer, a beautiful woman walked up to him. "You look like you could use some company," she said in a sensuous voice. Sam looked at the beautiful woman and smiled. "Ordinarily I'd say yes, but tonight, you are the last thing I need," he said sadly.

Acting offended, the woman walked away and joined her other friends who were standing in a corner. She spoke to them in a low voice. When she finished, the women laughed and raced over to Sam. She pointed at the DJ, and the music changed. The women grabbed Sam and pulled him on stage. They surrounded Sam on stage and began to take his clothes off. The other guys sitting in the audience began to encourage him. "Take it all off!" they yelled. Sam began to laugh and take off more clothes. The women formed a circle around him and started to take off their clothes. They rubbed their tasseled breasts against him in a teasing manner. He began to howl and stripped to his underwear. The other men roared with laughter and gave shrill whistles. Sam was wearing a pair of black thong underwear. Clayton threw his head back and laughed the hardest. "Take 'em off!" he yelled. In response Sam turned and shook his butt at his brother, while the women took turns lightly tapping his butt. The music suddenly changed and Sam was escorted off the stage so the next act could begin.

Sam gathered his clothes and ran over to his brother's table. As he put his slacks back on, he smiled. "Thanks, brother, I know you had something to do with all that. I needed the diversion," he said, somewhat out of breath. Sam mopped the sweat from his head with his handkerchief. "I don't know how they do that up there," he said, pointing to the women on the stage. "It is really exhausting!"

Clayton smiled. "That's probably why they look as fit as they do. They work out to get to that level," he said, laughing.

The night was quickly coming to an end, the men finished their drinks and began heading for the door. As Sam walked to the exit, the beautiful woman who had approached him while he was sitting in the corner walked past and placed her number in his pocket. He looked at her and grinned. She smiled seductively and kept walking.

The women were all chatting at once when they arrived at the spa. A tall handsome man who must have been a pro wrestler in his previous career came out and introduced himself as Walt and welcomed them to his spa. A hush fell over the crowd as he told them what was in store for them. He broke them into four large groups. "This group here will go to the Pedicure Palace with Ryan," he said, as he pointed at a well-endowed man dressed in spandex shorts and a tank top standing at the far wall. The women raced over to Ryan and grabbed a hold of the two muscular arms he offered them. They walked through an opening and disappeared.

Walt then pointed at the second group and told them they were going to the Manicure Mansion with Mike. The women spotted a tanned muscular man with dark curly hair and ran over toward him. He smiled graciously and led them through a door and disappeared.

The third group was directed to go to the Massage Villa with Doug. The women let out a groan and quickly walked over to a man dressed in a white robe. His smooth muscular chest was partially exposed and it drove the women wild. His robe was short so the women also got to view his dark muscular thighs and well-defined calves. He too stuck out both muscular arms for the women to hold and led them through a designated door.

"The last group," he said, pointing at Brianna, her mother, Amara, and her mother, "will go to the Seaweed and Mud Hut." They clapped as they walked quickly toward their designated door. Brianna stopped and looked at Walt. "Hey, Walt, where's our special guy?" she asked. Walt placed his fingers in his mouth and made a loud whistling sound. "You mean your four men?" he asked, smiling.

The women shrieked and ran over to the four men. Each man rippled with muscles. Each smiled, stuck out his arm, and led the ladies through their designated door. The rest of the evening was spent rotating to the four different areas and being treated like queens. The men served them champagne, fresh fruit, and sparkling water at each station. At the Manicure Mansion, the men fed them because their fingernails were wet with polish. "Mari, I am in heaven," said Brianna with a mouth full of strawberries.

"Me too!" said her mother.

Myra and Amara just smiled and allowed themselves to be pampered. "I could get used to this," said Myra.

"Me too!" said Amara, as the man wiped her mouth with a soft cloth napkin.

Their evening ended much too quickly. The women left rested, polished, and totally pampered. Amara gave Walt a very large tip and thanked him for everything. Walt smiled and told her to come back again. Once the women were outside, the owner placed the closed sign in the window and turned out the lights in the waiting room.

"What a night," sighed Brianna. "Mari, that was one heck of a party! I loved it!" she said as she gave her a big kiss and hug. Everyone loaded into their respective vehicles and headed to the hotel.

When Amara got back, Tony was also arriving at his door. He had a silly grin on his face as he placed his key into the door lock. "Have a good time?" Amara asked quietly. Tony shook his head, yes. "Want some company or are you too tired?" he asked. Amara smiled and motioned him over her with her finger. Tony smiled and removed his key from the door. He walked to her and took her key and opened her door. "Mm, you smell wonderful and feel so soft," he said admiringly. "What would you think about donning a pair of tassels?" he asked innocently. Amara threw her head back in laughter as they both went into the room. Tony placed the 'Do Not Disturb' sign on the outer door and shut it quietly.

When Brianna and Kuyono returned home, Brianna went into her room and changed into her pajamas. Her mother knocked softly on the door and came in. Brianna was sitting at the dressing table preparing to brush her hair for the night. Her mother took the brush out of her hand and began brushing her hair. It had been years since her mother had done that for her. When she was growing up, her mother would come in and brush her hair and they would have their most serious and intimate conversations during that time.

"So, are you ready for your big day?" Kuyono asked, in Japanese.

"Yes, mother," she responded in Japanese.

"You are marrying a good man. I am proud of all that you have done. I think you will be happy with him," she said. Brianna closed her eyes and enjoyed the soft strokes of the brush. Her mother brushed with a rhythm that usually put her right to sleep.

Brianna opened her eyes and looked at her mother in the reflection of the mirror. "Mother, how did you know father was the one for you?" she asked. Kuyono stopped brushing her daughter's hair and smiled. "He was in the Army at the time. He was stationed in Okinawa. He was such a good man, such a proud man. We had met at one of those service dances in town. I told him I could not date an American. So, he went to my father and asked if he could take me out on a date. Well, father chased him away because he was not Japanese," she said laughing softly. "But, he kept coming over to talk to my father. He even learned some Japanese!" she said. "After nearly six months of his persistence, my father relented and told him we could date. Shortly afterward, he asked my father for my hand in marriage," she said. "My father told him yes. I was never so happy.

"It was very hard for my father. You see, he was sick and dying. I was the only one left in the family. He was afraid if he died I would have no one to take care of me. He knew Brian would take good care of me. Father told me that I would have to go away to the United States because it would be too hard to stay in Japan and be married to a black man," she said wistfully. "Father died a few days after that. So when we married and his orders took him back to the United States, I went with him. That was over thirty years ago and I never returned to my home in Japan after that," she said sadly.

She kissed Brianna. "But my life has been full with taking care of you, Alexis, and Brian," she said. "You know I have always taught both of you girls to embrace and love both of your worlds. That is why I insisted you learn Japanese and attend those classes on how to write calligraphy and to learn some of the dances from my country. I also encouraged you to learn about your father's culture, meet his people, and learn to cook the food from their culture. You even attended gospel service on Sunday with Brian and me, remember?"

Brianna nodded her head. "Because of you, I never felt like a misfit, except for being skinny and tall, but never because of my two heritages. You taught me always to be proud of both, because they are both special." Kuyono shook her head. "When you have children, you make sure they know about both too, understand?" she said in Japanese shaking the brush for emphasis.

Brianna smiled and bowed to her mother. "I understand, Mother," she answered in proper Japanese. Kuyono smiled with satisfaction and continued to brush Brianna's and hum one of her favorite gospel hymns. Brianna smiled at her mother. "I am lucky to have such a smart mother," she said in English. "And I such a beautiful and gifted daughter," answered her mother, in English.

Chapter 16

On the morning of Brianna's wedding day, the December sky was clear and the air was crisp. Guest began to arrive and slowly enter the church. Brianna looked beautiful in her Tanaka gown. It flowed gracefully to the floor, with a soft flowing train. The color was antique white and the gown had a plunging back-line that resembled the back of a halter-top.

The gown itself was sleeveless with detached satin sleeves that hugged her small arms and fit like a pair of long gloves. Small pearl buttons kept the sleeves in place at the wrist. The neckline in the front resembled a mock turtleneck collar. It too had a small pearl button in the back. Her dress was formfitting from her breasts to the top of her knees, and flowed freely from her knees to the floor, flared in back with a short train.

She wore a short veil with a pillbox satin hat. Her hair was gracefully styled in a chignon. She looked absolutely gorgeous. Amara came in and helped her with her shoes and veil. "Bre, you are breathtaking," she told her friend.

Brianna was close to tears. "Mari, I had the most wonderful talk with my mom last night. I got her blessing," she said, fighting back the tears. Brianna reached for Amara's hand and held it tightly. "I am so happy you are here to share this perfect day with me," she said.

Amara had to look up at the ceiling to prevent herself from crying. "Let's get going," she said, as her voice quivered. Brianna joined her father at the end of the staircase. He gently kissed her hand and asked if she was ready. She nodded her head, yes. The wedding march began and Brianna and her father entered the church. The church suddenly fell silent and then exploded with oohs and ahs above the music. Brianna looked at the quartet that was playing. It was her favorite quartet from college. Brianna couldn't believe Clayton had found them after all this time! Brianna flashed a brilliant smile as she walked down the aisle to meet Clayton.

Clayton looked at his beautiful bride and quietly thanked God for his wonderful gift, his new wife. Brianna thought he looked dapper in his tux. He had decided not to wear the cummerbund he and Sam had designed.

Instead, Myra had whipped up several burgundy paisley cummerbunds that matched the bridesmaids' dresses perfectly. Clayton smiled from ear to ear as Brianna's father released her hand and placed her beside him.

The wedding ceremony went off without a hitch. Everyone blew bubbles instead of throwing rice because of the harm to nature's little birds and the waste of an important Asian staple, as Kuyono would say. The couple returned to be photographed and then joined everyone at the reception. Sam drank heavily at the reception, and walked unsteadily toward Amara. Tony intercepted him and quietly walked him back to his seat.

Embarrassed, Amara left her seat and walked over to the punch bowl. She picked up one of the small glass cups and poured a ladleful of the cool liquid into her cup. As she took a sip, she turned to look at Brianna and Clayton on the dance floor. Amara was glad all the attention was directed toward the dance floor where Clayton and Brianna were sharing their first dance.

Tony joined her at the punch bowl and poured himself a drink. He drank it in one gulp. He took Amara's cup and sat it down on the table with his. He then pulled her to the dance floor as the beat of the music became lively, inviting everyone to dance. They danced and laughed while Brianna and Clayton mingled with their guests.

Shortly after midnight, the couple ran to the limo and drove away to a small villa by the ocean where they planned to spend the entire weekend uninterrupted. Tony hugged Amara and handed her the small clutch bag from her seat. They held hands as they exited the reception. Amara and Tony spotted her parents and walked over to meet them.

Myra wore a pinched expression as she loosely held an envelope. "Mari, Sam asked me to give you this," she said, handing her the envelope. Amara frowned as she took the envelope. She looked over at Tony. He shrugged and suggested she read it later. She folded the envelope and placed it in her purse and they all headed back to the hotel together.

When they arrived at the hotel, Tony looked at Amara and could tell she was very tired. She walked slowly to her room. "Can I join you tonight?" she asked wearily. Tony smiled and took her hand. He asked for her key so he could get her toiletries and something to sleep in.

Amara sat on Tony's king-sized bed and waited for him to return. She removed her shoes and rubbed her aching feet. She stumbled off the bed and walked to the bathroom and noticed the complimentary toothbrush and face soap on the counter. She washed her face and brushed her teeth and got into the shower and took a quick shower.

When Tony returned with her things, he found her asleep on his bed, draped in a towel. He chuckled and gently removed the damp towel and placed her nightgown on her body. He tucked her into bed and left to take a shower. When he returned, he found Amara lying on her back, snoring loudly. He repositioned her, put on his pajama bottoms, and got into bed also. He too fell asleep immediately.

Meanwhile, Sam waited down in the lobby and checked his watch every fifteen minutes. He had left a note for Amara, asking her to meet him and talk. He just needed to talk to someone about Franni. He still loved her and didn't know what to do about it. Tonight was supposed to have been his wedding night also.

He checked his watch one last time. It was close to one A.M., so he called a cab. He gave the cab driver his address, and got into the back seat. He leaned his head against the vinyl headrest and sighed loudly. What a mess I have made of my life, he thought to himself. When the driver stopped in front of his house, he got out, paid the driver, and forced himself to walk the few paces to the front door.

As he neared the front door, he slowed even more. He scratched his head, as he tried to think. All of the lights were on in his house, and he didn't remember leaving them on. As he pulled out his key, the door opened. It was Franni. She was dressed in a beautiful formfitting short satin white dress and was holding a single white lily. "If you will have me, I want to be your wife," she said emotionally.

The ringing of the telephone awakened Amara and Tony. Tony stirred first and looked at the digital clock. He looked at it again, in disbelief. "Mari, wake up, it's nearly noon," he said. The phone continued to ring and Tony picked it up.

"Hello, sleepy heads!" said Brianna cheerfully.

Tony smiled into the phone and responded with a grunt. "I can't believe you guys are awake," he said joking. "We had to bring the morning in right," said Brianna gaily. Tony laughed at her joke.

"Hey, just tell Amara that Sam and Franni got married this morning by the justice of the peace, and he is moving to New York with Franni," she said. Tony chuckled. "I can't believe you interrupted our great sleep for that. We all knew he was going after her."

Amara woke up fully and asked what was going on. Tony placed his hand over the receiver and told her the news. She smiled and clapped her hands. "Good for them," she yelled into the phone. Brianna wished them a great day and hung up the phone. Tony smiled and kissed Amara. "Wonders never cease," he said.

Amara got up and pulled the folded envelope out of her purse. She opened the envelope and read the letter that Sam had given her the previous night aloud, and laughed. "He wanted to talk to me last night about Franni. He said he still loved her, but he didn't know how to get her back," she said giggling.

"Well, I guess he found a way," joked Tony.

Amara rolled on top of Tony and spoke sensuously. "When it's meant to be, it's meant to be," she said, as she kissed him.

He pulled her gown off over her head. "Why don't you show me what's meant to be right now," he teased.

Amara began kissing him all over his body. "Well," she said, "Let's see what I can do about that last request." Tony moaned softly and pulled the sheet over their heads. Amara began to giggle and moan as they played and made love together.

The following weeks were hectic and flew by in a blur for Amara. She had finished her big article for the magazine and made final preparations for her wedding. It was going to be just as she and Tony had planned, small and intimate. Amara and Tony decided not to have bachelor and bachelorette parties. Instead they invited their closest friends and relatives and had a short prayer session at their church where people prayed for them and shared their good wishes. There was not a dry eye in the house when Myra completed her prayer of thanks and prayer for their future happiness.

Afterwards, they had a small reception dinner at Sarah's restaurant. She closed the restaurant for the evening and reserved it just for the invited guests. Sarah made Amara's and Tony's favorite dishes and had the lavish desserts catered by a close friend of hers who owned a bakery at the end of the block.

Myra had transformed the restaurant into a Christmas hideaway. There was fake snow, gifts under the tree that bore the names of the wedding party members, mistletoe hung from the doorways, and gay Christmas music played as everyone entered. She had rented a fountain, where a nonalcoholic beverage flowed through what looked like a frozen waterfall. The place cards were delicate crystal ornaments that had the guest's name on one side and a beautiful picture of Sarah's restaurant blanketed under two feet of snow on the other. Amara had taken the picture a few years ago, and had had it miniaturized as a keepsake for all the guests. Myra had stumbled on the glass ornaments during last year's after Christmas sale at The Bon department store. Brianna had come up with the idea of using them for the wedding. The three women had put their heads together and come up with the idea of making them a keepsake, as well as a seating place card for the guests. Brianna had volunteered to write each attendee's name and the date on one side in calligraphy. Myra had enlisted Shirley's help to transfer the picture onto the ornament from a card Amara had sent a couple years back. Amara had provided the negative and Shirley had provided the technical skill, and they had made adhesive photos and had neatly placed the photo on each side.

There were plenty of oohs and aahhs when everyone walked into the transformed restaurant. The food was laid out buffet style on a beautiful shimmering cloth, whose flowing skirt reflected lights in the restaurant. There was lots of laughter and full stomachs at the end of the night.

Amara looked into Tony's eyes as she fed him her last piece of bread that she had dipped in their favorite vinaigrette. He took it and smiled as he savored the great taste. "This was so perfect," she whispered in his ear. Tony licked his fingers and nodded in agreement. As the guests began to leave, Amara snapped pictures of her close friends and relatives who had come to share her special evening before their wedding night.

The following evening about fifty of Tony and Amara's closest friends and family filed into the church that Amara had attended her whole life. Amara was surprised at the number of guests from the police department. Even Chief Chaddam and his wife were in attendance.

The two bridesmaids and matron of honor wore off-the-shoulder navy velvet floor-length dresses that hugged their bodies and had a long slit in the back, so they could walk. Brianna's dress was topped off with navy satin that allowed the soft folds of material to fall off her shoulders gracefully. Each of the women wore their hair in a neat chignon with baby's breath snugly tucked in the folds of her hair.

As wedding gifts to her bridesmaids Amara presented each of them with real pearl post earrings and faux pearl necklaces. Their short navy heels were made of soft leather and very comfortable. Amara believed this was sensible, since she herself hated any sort of high heel and they could wear these shoes with other outfits.

Hundreds of candles flickered throughout the church and provided a cozy and intimate atmosphere for all of the attendees. Amara's mother had surprised her and made her wedding gown. Nearly five months ago, Amara had shown her mother a picture of the gown she wanted, but it was much too expensive for her to purchase. Within one week after showing her the photo from the magazine, Myra had already sewn the shell. It looked exactly like the picture when she was finished.

Tony wore a white tux jacket with black trousers and a navy velvet vest and tie. His three groomsmen wore black tuxes with navy velvet cummerbunds. Tony added a twist to the ceremony. He asked Amara's dad, Jackson, to be his best man. He told him he was the father he never had, since his father had died when he was a young boy. After Jackson walked his daughter down the isle, he would take his place as the best man.

Jackson stood in the back of the church and checked to make sure he had the rings. He was so happy for both his daughter and his new son. Myra was already crying and the ceremony had not even begun.

Brianna was in the dressing room with Amara. She placed the finishing touches on Amara's makeup. "You look so beautiful," she said, admiring Amara.

Amara clutched her hand. "Did you feel this nervous?" she asked. Her stomach felt queasy.

"Yep," said Brianna. "Until I saw Clayton standing there," she said dreamily.

Brianna placed Amara's formal veil over her cascading curls. "Guess what," she said. "I'm going to have a baby!" she squealed.

Amara covered her mouth. She was so full of excitement and emotion. "When did you find out?" she asked.

"Today. And you are the first to know, so don't say a word," she warned.

Amara hugged her tightly. "I am so happy for you," she said excitedly. "Don't twins run in Clayton's family?" she asked. Brianna nodded her head.

"Let's get you down the aisle, girl," said Brianna softly. She then handed her a blue lace handkerchief. "You probably don't remember this, but you gave me this handkerchief when we first met. I was crying about that terrible grade I had received, and you comforted me and gave me your blue hanky," she said. "So something borrowed and blue," she said sincerely. "You are my best friend and I love you," said Brianna.

Amara bit down on her lip. "Are you trying to make me cry or something?" asked Amara. Brianna laughed.

There was a light tap on the door. "They are ready for you, "the attendant whispered. Brianna left Amara alone and Amara took the time to say a prayer of thanks. She felt so blessed and lucky to have met such a wonderful man.

Amara opened the door, walked into the hall, and saw her father. He looked so handsome in his tux and so proud. "Baby, you look beautiful," he said. Amara fingered the pearls she was wearing. Her aunt had given them to her the night before. She said they had been in the family for years and she wanted her to have them.

Amara smiled at her father. "You ready for this?" he asked.

"I sure am, Dad," she said. Jackson smiled and put his arm out for her to take.

Jackson and Amara began their walk down the aisle to a sweet melody sung in person by one of her favorite artists, M'ya. Amara nearly died with delight. That was a gift from Sam and Franni. He and Franni were in Africa on their honeymoon. The candles flickered in the breeze as the bride and father of the bride strode down the aisle.

Amara looked angelic in her high-necked gown that had a row of pearl buttons running down the side of the neckline. The delicate, long, lace sleeves gently molded over her arms. The gown was formfitting to the waist and flowed out into a large bell from her cinched waist to the floor.

Amara looked down the isle at her bridesmaids, Tammy and Shirley. She was glad that both of them had the figure to pull off such a daring dress. She then saw Brianna, who winked at her as she continued to walk, carefully avoiding the hem of her gown. As she neared the end she saw the preacher gently turn the page and perch his reading glasses on the tip of his nose.

Tony looked at her with eyes full of admiration and love. She smiled nervously to keep herself from crying. She squeezed her father's arm as he released her and walked over to stand beside the groom as best man. They had written their own vows, which were actually their pledge to one another. There wasn't a dry eye left in the church when they were finished.

M'ya sang another song as they lit the union candle. At the completion of the ceremony the preacher pronounced them husband and wife and Tony pulled her close and gave her a passionate kiss. Everyone in the church cheered as they faced them as husband and wife.

"Help!" cried Shareese. "Somebody help! I have been stabbed!" she screamed. The police officer ran to her jail cell and opened the cell door. She saw Shareese lying on the ground in what looked like blood. She holstered her weapon and told everyone else in the cell to move back. They all did as instructed. One of the inmates chuckled. Another poked her in the ribs sharply and she stopped.

The police officer looked around cautiously. As she looked back at Shareese's body, she was splashed in the face with a wet, oily substance. She yelled for help because she couldn't see. Shareese got up and ran out of the jail cell.

She pulled a key from the lining of her jumper that was aligned with the zipper and used it on the high security door at the other end. She ran past the unsuspecting police officers down to another floor. She gained access to another room and ran inside. There were no bars on the window. She opened the window and climbed out on the ledge. She shimmied down a long pole to the next floor. She heard voices and dogs barking below. She took off her jumper and threw it down. It landed in some bushes approximately fifty feet from the waiting police officers. The dogs immediately lit on the suit and began a barking frenzy.

Shareese took advantage of the distraction and went back inside the office. Luckily for her, someone had left their sweater and a pair of sweat pants. She quickly put on the mismatched outfit. She rummaged through the drawer and found an employee's expired badge. The photo on the badge was of a black woman. She pinned the badge on her sweats and calmly walked out of the office.

Since she had worked in the chief's office, she had made it her business to get to know the adjoining building well. She smiled. Good old Mr. Jenkins, she thought as she wove her way through the back doors and back steps of the building. That flirting and hanging around the night janitor had really paid off.

She ran down the back steps down to the maintenance room and out of a side door that was rarely used. It opened up outside, next to several large trash bins. She calmly walked past the trash bins to the back of the station and out into the street. She was free and had made it undetected.

She waved a cab down and gave the driver the address to Michael's house. She had clothes and money stashed there. She was hoping the house had not been sold or repossessed. When she arrived at Michael's house, she was surprised to see the lights on. She slowly crept up to the large bay window and peeked inside. She saw Maria and Ryan, Michael's father packing up

Michael's belongings. Maria had grown large. Ryan rubbed her stomach and kissed her tenderly on the lips.

Shareese frowned. Now she would have to wait until they departed before she could go into the house. She shivered as she crept to the back of the house. She found the spare key and clutched it tightly.

A half-hour later the house darkened. Shareese climbed out of the shrubbery, used the spare key to open the door, and quickly ran into the dark house. She knew his house even in the dark. She padded quietly into Michael's bedroom. She got on her hands and knees and felt under his bed. She felt for the hidden storage area installed beneath the floor. She punched in the combination and pulled out her suitcase that was already packed. She moved quickly.

She took a quick shower and pulled out a brochure she had hidden in the storage area. She laughed and folded it neatly in half. She tucked it into the side of her suitcase. She also pulled out the airline tickets. "Charity, you are the best, "she said as she kissed it. She then looked at the tickets for the cruise line.

"Damn!" She opened the nightstand drawer and pulled out a penlight. It was the wrong cruise line and she didn't have time to make an adjustment. Shareese smiled confidently. "I always land on my feet!" She got dressed and called a cab and walked outside under the cloak of darkness with her suitcase. She set her suitcase down and waited next to the large evergreen tree until the cab showed up.

The party was in full swing when Tony and Amara arrived at the reception party, held in the festive tent in the back yard at Amara's new home. Myra and Sarah had done a wonderful job setting up all the white lights and beautiful table settings. Myra had strung hundreds of small white Christmas lights inside the tent, outside in the trees, and along the path leading to the back yard. The tables inside the large heated feast tent were adorned with white and navy linen cloths with small poinsettia plants. The guests felt as though they were in a Christmas wonderland.

Everyone danced and celebrated as they enjoyed the great food and socializing. As the couple mingled with their guests, Amara nearly choked when she saw Tammy with the mechanic lawyer she had met at the club that fateful night. Amara later learned that he was a lawyer who had a passion for racecars. He raced and worked on cars almost every weekend, thus explaining the oil under the nails.

Tammy seemed so happy. She had already received a raise and a promotion at her new job. Amara was delighted to learn she had transferred back to Seattle. She guessed it was to be closer to her beau, John.

Amara saw a familiar face and walked over to say hello. It was Charlene. "I am so glad you made it, Charlene!" she said sincerely. Charlene smiled shyly. A handsome man sat next to her with his hand covering hers. Amara had noticed he had not let her out of his sight all night. Charlene smiled.

"Thank you for inviting us!" she said happily. "Oh, this is my boyfriend, Donald, he works in construction," she said proudly. Amara shook his hand and smiled. Charlene had come a long way.

"How's your job?" she asked. Charlene smiled. "It is wonderful. In fact, I am still attending school at night and they tell me when I get my degree next year, I will be promoted to an administrative manager."

Amara smiled widely and gave her a high five. "Handle your business, girl!" she joked. Charlene laughed and told her she would. Tony came and nuzzled her neck and whispered in her ear. She shook her head and started to walk away. Tony thanked Charlene and her date for coming as he joined Amara.

At the close of the reception, Tony clinked his glass and said he had an announcement to make. He asked his new mom and dad to come forward. "Mom and Dad have never really had a honeymoon," announced Tony.

"So we decided to do something about it," interjected Amara. Jackson and Myra looked at each other and wondered what was going on. Tony pulled a large gift-wrapped envelope out of his coat and handed it to Myra.

"Mom and Dad, this is our gift to you. You have treated me like a son and as part of this family from the first day you met me," he said emotionally.

"We love you both and wanted to give you a special gift on our special day," said Amara. Jackson and Myra started to whisper to one another. "As most of you know, we head off on our cruise next week," said Tony. "And before we leave, we want to give you this," said Amara, as Tony handed the envelope to Myra and Jackson.

Myra's hands shook as she opened the envelope. They didn't know what to expect. When Myra read what it was, she screamed and jumped up and down. Jackson gave a thumbs up and wiped a tear from his eye. "They gave us a seven-day cruise," said Jackson all choked up.

"On the same cruise they are taking!" said Myra, ecstatic.

"I guess we are going on our honeymoon too!" said Jackson, happily.

They both ran over to Amara and Tony and gave them a big hug and a kiss. Myra wiped Amara's tears away with the back of her hand. "This was Tony's idea," said Amara. "He wanted to share our honeymoon with his new parents," she said tearfully. Myra began to cry once more and hugged Tony and kissed him twice on the cheek. Jackson hugged them both. Everyone at the reception cheered and clapped. Myra placed her hands on her hips and looked at her daughter. "That's why you dragged Jackson and me to that horrible summer sale in the middle of winter," she shouted. Everyone laughed.

The music started to play and everyone ran to the dance floor for the final dance. Brianna and Clayton came over and hugged the new bride and groom. "This was really classy," said Clayton. "We hope you guys have a great time on your honeymoon," said Clayton and Brianna. Amara looked at Brianna and she shook her head, no. "We have to leave, Brianna isn't feeling well," said Clayton as her grabbed her coat. Brianna smiled.

Amara made sure Brianna had the key to Tony's house, where they'd be staying for the night. "I'll call you 'late' tomorrow," teased Brianna.

Tony and Amara laughed. Tony looked at Amara. "What was that all about?" he asked. "Brianna is pregnant," she whispered happily. Tony hugged Amara and whispered in her ear. "Would you be upset if you came back from our honeymoon that way?" he asked. Amara looked at him and smiled. "Not in the least," she said.

"Well we will see what we can do about that," he said excitedly. "I've always wanted to be a father. I want tons of kids," he smiled.

"So do I," she said. "We'd definitely have to get a bigger house," she said smiling. Tony didn't respond and Amara looked at him and wondered why he was so quiet.

Police Chief Chaddam was coming around the corner of the house when he bumped into a lady who seemed to be hiding. She turned to look at him. Chief Chaddam's eyes grew wide. "Shareese—uh I mean, Charlene, how are you?" he asked.

The woman smiled. "Just fine," she replied in a childlike manner. "Do you like to play cowboys and Indians?" she asked.

Chaddam laughed. "Well yes I do. I play that game with my grandson all the time," he responded.

"I like it too, I play with my sister. Gotta go," she said as she backed around the corner and headed to the front of the house.

Chaddam scratched his head and shrugged his shoulders. "Very strange," he remarked. "Very strange indeed." Suddenly Chief Chaddam was paged with a 911 call and immediately returned to his car to use the cell phone.

Upon hearing the news that Shareese had escaped he placed a patrol to watch both Tony and Amara's home. He looked for Tony so he could tell him about Shareese. He spotted Tony and waited while he talked to well-wishers. While he waited, he turned to talk to a fellow police officer. When he turned back to check if Tony was free, he and Amara were gone. He slapped his forehead and called the station to get a phone number for Tony.

As the reception came to an end, Tony maneuvered around the cleaning crew and grabbed his car keys and told Amara to get her coat and join him in the car. Amara stared at him again. "What is this about?" she asked. Tony didn't answer. He started up the car and headed down the road. "Are we going to my parent's house?" she asked. Tony turned down a road about three miles from her parent's house. "I guess not," she said aloud.

He turned up a well-lit driveway. "Who lives here?" she asked. Tony still didn't answer. "I just need to pick up something very important," he said. "Come with me, it's too dark for you to stay out in the car." Amara got out of the car and walked up the drive. Tony opened the door and walked in. Amara remained outside. Tony pulled her in. "Hello?" said Amara. Tony smiled. He led her into the family room where a fire was blazing. "Tony?" she said as she looked at him for an answer to the riddle.

Tony took her coat and led her closer to the fire. She stuck her hands toward the heat. "This feels wonderful," she said blissfully. Tony stood beside her and stared, offering no response. "Is this a friend's house for us to use for tonight?" she asked. "You would never tell me where we were spending our wedding night," she said exasperated.

He smiled and placed the key in her hand. "This is our new home," he said quietly. The fire crackled, as she allowed what he had said to sink in. Her mouth gaped open.

The house was a beautiful two-story traditional home, with a wooden banister that wrapped its way to the second floor. It was already furnished with beautiful antique furniture. The whole house felt warm and cozy. It was perfect. "Tony, we can't afford this house!" she exclaimed. Tony smiled. "My father left me this house and some other property when he died. I have spent the past five years refurbishing this home. The interior is compliments of none other than...." Amara didn't even allow him to finish before she blurted out her mother's name.

She looked at Tony and placed her hands over her mouth as tears sprang to her eyes. She slapped Tony on his shoulder. "You! How could you keep this from me," she said smiling widely.

Tony smiled. "Do you like it?" he asked.

She just stared at him in disbelief. "Do I like it? Are you kidding?" she yelled. She grabbed him around his neck and hugged him tight. "This is my dream home. I love it!" she said, crying.

Tony gave her a full tour of the house. There was a small room that adjoined theirs. "What is that room for?" she asked. He smiled and patted her tummy. She laughed and grabbed his hand. He took her to the master bedroom. Amara stopped at the threshold and admired her mother's beautiful work.

"Do you like it?" he asked timidly. Amara smiled. "This is the most beautiful room I have ever seen. It is a mixture of both of us, both feminine and masculine. Mom has created the perfect room," she lamented. She walked over the sitting area and saw the matching chairs. She laughed when she saw the quilt with the piece of fabric her mother had torn away from the woman at the store. Tony wrapped his arm around her and picked her up and carried her over the threshold. "Welcome home, Mrs. Riley," he said as he kicked the door shut.

The phone rang and scared both Tony and Amara. Amara didn't know they had a phone and Tony had only given the number out to Amara's parents and to the police station. He picked up the phone. His voice was thick with sleep. Once hearing his captain's voice he immediately became alert. "Yes, sir!" he responded. "Right away, sir," he said and quickly hung up the phone. Tony leaped out of bed and ran to the closet where his uniform and other clothes hung.

Amara sat up in the bed and rubbed the sleep from her eyes. "Honey, what's the matter?" she asked.

"Honey, someone broke into my house," he said.

Amara sprang out of bed, panicked. "Honey, Brianna and Clayton are staying there!" she shouted, close to hysterics. "She's pregnant. Oh God, oh God," she said crying.

Tony didn't have time to calm her. He rushed out of the house and jumped into his car and quickly drove away. On the way, he called Myra on his cell phone and asked her to go to Amara.

As Tony approached their street, he saw the reflection of red and blue lights flashing in the winter night's darkness against the smooth pavement. The neighbors had come out of their house to see what was going on. An ambulance was parked on his lawn and he watched medics rush out of the door, pushing a gurney. Tony stopped the car and rushed over to the lead officer.

Officer Tom Brandon recognized Tony immediately and gave him a quick run-down on the situation. "We had a patrol out on the street and we received a 911 call of an intruder in your house," he said. The police officers had rushed to the front door when they heard shots fired. They entered and found a deceased female lying on the floor. The officer flipped open his small notebook and read the personal information he had written. "The identification we found on the perp leads us to believe she was Shareese Collins, AKA Shareese Miller, who was incarcerated at the city jail awaiting her trial.

"We received word that she escaped tonight. Apparently she persuaded Scott Henderson, a young police trainee who used to work as a security guard on the executive floor, to bring her some ointment for her hair and some other toiletries. Well, she mixed the ointment with water and threw it into the guard's face and managed to escape through a door that she had the key to.

"Once Scott heard about the 911 call he immediately went to the chief and told him what he had done and that he had been seeing Shareese for the past few weeks. It is my guess that she somehow got his keys and made copies.

"She was already well acquainted with the layout of the entire building, including the jail portion, because she escaped out of a door that is known by only a few. Scott swears he never showed her the layout of the building. They are bringing in the night janitors, and others who associated with Shareese and had a thorough knowledge of the layout of the buildings, for questioning.

"Apparently, she thought you and Amara would be here. The victims inside said she broke in and was wearing a cowboy hat. They called 911. She got trapped in the kitchen by Mr. Clayton Peters and brandished a gun. That's when," he looked at his pad once more, "that's when Mr. Peters drew his pistol and shot her several times in the chest," he said as he read from his notebook.

Tony shook his head and went inside the house. Brianna's eyes were swollen from crying, but otherwise she looked unharmed. Clayton was talking with one of the officers at the dining room table. He looked up and gave Tony a curt nod and continued answering the officer's questions.

Tony waited patiently until the officers had completed their work on the crime scene and had questioned both Brianna and Clayton. Satisfied with the information they had, they packed their equipment and left. Officer Tom Brandon left his card with Clayton and patted Tony on the back. "Rough way to spend your wedding night," he said, sincerely. "Congratulations by the way," he said as he walked out the door.

Tony thanked him and walked over to Clayton and Brianna. "Are you two all right?" he asked. Brianna hugged herself. "Clay, honey, I can't stay here, I want to go to a hotel or Mari's mom's," she said as her voice quivered. Clayton put his arm around Brianna as she quietly sobbed.

"Hey, why don't you come with me to our place. We have plenty of room," said Tony.

Clayton looked at Brianna and she nodded her head in agreement. "Let me go and get our things and we'll follow you to where you are staying," Clayton said calmly. He said something softly in Brianna's ear and quickly went into the bedroom and returned with two small bags.

Tony looked at the large bloodstain on the kitchen floor and made a mental note to call a cleaning team and get the mess cleaned up quickly. Luckily the bloodstain was on the tile and not the carpet. Clayton checked the back door to ensure it was locked and walked to the front door. Tony got a small sheet of plywood he had stored in his pantry and quickly nailed it over the broken windowpane in the back door. They all left together and drove to Tony and Amara's new home.

When the cars drove up to the driveway, Jackson opened the door. He had a serious look on his face. Myra joined him. "Everybody okay?" he bellowed. Tony assured him everyone was. "Brianna, honey, how are you doing?" asked Myra. Upon hearing Brianna's name, Amara burst through the door and ran toward Brianna. She gave her a big hug and a kiss. They both laughed and cried and began talking at once. Tony and Clayton led them into the house. Jackson had already started preparing hot cocoa, coffee, and tea for everyone.

Brianna entered the large foyer of the house and looked around. "Wow Mari, this place is gorgeous! Look at all the fancy decorating. Who lives here?" she asked. Amara smiled and hugged her friend once more. "We do. Tony inherited it from his father and refurbished it. Momma decorated it. I swear I feel like Town and Country up in here!" she said jokingly.

Brianna shook her head. "Mom, this place is fabulous. Would you consider doing a little something for our place?" she asked.

"I'm not cheap, baby, but for you, I will give a discount," she joked. Everyone laughed. It felt good to break some of the tension.

Jackson placed the mugs on the table along with the coffee and hot milk and hot water. He poured hot cocoa for himself and Amara, and everyone else helped themselves to coffee or tea. Once everyone was seated, Clayton and Brianna retold what had happened at Amara's house. "She was really acting crazy, Mari," said Brianna as she sipped some hot tea. "She kept calling me by your name. Her eyes were glazed over and she kept waving her pistol all over the room. Her speech was slurred and she kept zoning out. I am not sure if she was on drugs or drunk," she said nervously as she shredded her napkin.

Clayton rubbed her back to calm her and told the rest of the story. "Well, initially we heard a loud crashing sound come from the kitchen. I immediately got my pistol and tiptoed out of the room and positioned myself, so I could see the intruder. By the time I had gotten into position she was already in the house. I got up and took another position and told her not to move and that she was trespassing.

"I think she was shocked to hear my voice. She demanded to see Amara. I told her she wasn't there. She told me I was lying and pulled out her revolver. I wasted no time. I shot her until she fell to the ground," he said without emotion or inflection in his voice.

Everyone was quiet. Brianna took a deep breath. Amara looked at Brianna. "Bre, why did you come out of the bedroom?" she asked. Brianna shrugged. "Clayton asked me the same question. I don't know. I mean I know Clayton can protect himself, and I didn't have a gun. I just wanted to be near him. It was dumb, I know," she said sadly.

Clayton kissed her head and rumpled her hair. "You are okay, and that is what is important," he said sincerely. Brianna folded her hands on the table and smiled. "I would like to end this evening on a positive note and say that Clayton and I are expecting our first child!" she said. Myra clapped her hands and shouted for joy. Tony and Jackson slapped Clayton on the back and congratulated him. Amara hugged Brianna tight and rubbed her tummy. "Now you have another person to worry about," she said. Brianna looked at her stomach and smiled.

Clayton gave her a hug. "She is going to make the most beautiful pregnant woman...fat chubby cheeks, swollen ankles, and...."

Brianna cut him off before he could finish. "Hey, you'd better be careful, sometimes the dad gets sympathy pains and fat chubby cheeks and swollen ankles," she mimicked. Everyone laughed as Clayton blushed and fell silent. "Touché," he said quietly. Everyone laughed once more.

"Well, Jackson, let's get going. We have a plane to catch early tomorrow morning!" said Myra, excitedly. Jackson smiled widely. "Yes, indeed!" he said. He looked at Tony and Amara with love in his eyes. "This is truly the most special gift that Myra and I have ever received. Thank you, from the bottom of our hearts," he said, trying to control his emotions.

Amara brushed a tear from her eye and Tony hugged them both. "We were so happy to do it," he said. "And we both love you very much!" Amara said, finishing Tony's sentence. They looked at each other and smiled. "My mom and dad do that all the time," she whispered.

Jackson helped Myra with her coat and they walked to the door. "See you guys tomorrow," said Tony and Amara in unison. Clayton and Brianna waved goodbye as well. Tony shut the door once Jackson and Myra were safely in their car and were headed down the driveway.

"Let me show you the rest of the house!" said Amara excitedly as she pulled her toward the stairs. Brianna looked at Clayton and he shrugged. Brianna stopped. "We've already taken up enough of your wedding night," she said solemnly. Amara smiled. "We've got the whole cruise to make up for tonight," she said wickedly. Tony agreed. "Let her show you the house before she bursts," he joked. "I've got a few things I want to show off to Clayton too," he said as he guided Clayton toward the entertainment and workout rooms.

After Brianna had seen the whole house she was overwhelmed by it all. "Mari, this house is so gorgeous. I am so happy for you. Tony is a wonderful man and I can see how much he loves you and how happy he's made you," she said. Amara hugged Brianna and looped her arm through hers like they used to do in college.

Amara stopped and looked at Brianna. "Are you okay?" she asked.

Brianna nodded her head yes. "It was scary, but it was over so fast!" she said. "I am doing fine and I am thankful Clayton or I were not hurt in all of that," she said quietly. They hugged one another tightly.

"Let's go find the guys!" said Amara. They heard voices and men's laughter at the end of the hall. Brianna giggled as they walked toward the entertainment room.

Clayton and Tony were playing pool while three different sports games were showing on the big screen TV simultaneously. Both were holding a beer and in deep conversation. They looked up at the women and smiled. "Time to go to bed," sang Amara. Tony immediately placed his pool cue in the rack and told Brianna and Clayton goodnight. Amara had already shown Brianna where they were staying, and Brianna guided Clayton upstairs toward their room at the opposite end of the hall.

Clayton smiled at Tony and teased, "I know why we are at the other end of the hall. Just don't swing from the chandelier," he said laughing. Tony and Amara laughed.

"All bets are off tonight, man, I am not guaranteeing anything," he said as he looked at Amara amorously. Amara blushed and took his hand. Everyone said good night, went to their rooms, and softly closed their doors.

Chapter 17

The following day, Amara left a note for Brianna and Clayton and told them to stay the rest of the weekend as they had planned. She left a key and told them there was plenty of food in the freezer. They departed before daylight and headed to the airport. Amara and Tony met Jackson and Myra at the terminal gate. Myra was giddy with excitement. Jackson tried to remain calm, but when he thought no one was looking, his face cracked into a huge smile.

They went into the terminal and sat in the first class lounge. They talked excitedly about the upcoming cruise. Myra had already looked at several of the cruise brochures that offered different tours and had planned almost all of their activities while on the cruise. Jackson laughed and told her to slow down. Amara and Tony cuddled with one another and talked quietly about the cruise. Their flight was called and they lined up with the first class passengers to board.

Shareese bit her nails in desperation. How was she going to get on the ship? She paced the floor. Her flight was being called. It was then it hit her. She saw a man sitting alone, reading a newspaper. Although he had gained several pounds, she could never forget that face. It was her late husband's best friend. Shareese smiled as she walked toward him. She knew he was going on the cruise she wanted to be on. She'd have to talk fast. Once she reached his seat she gave him the biggest smile she could muster. She removed her dark sunglasses. "Michael!" she said as she bent down to kiss his cheek.

The Rileys and Glentons were ecstatic! None of them had ever been on a cruise and were looking forward to the new adventure. The flight attendant passed out complimentary champagne to the wedding couples in the first class. There were three other couples. Amara whispered to the flight attendant and she smiled and left. She returned with two more glasses of champagne for Jackson and Myra. "Happy anniversary!" she said as she handed the glasses to Myra and Jackson. Myra giggled and clinked her glass gently against Jackson's. He gave her a quick kiss and took a sip. Amara and Tony laughed at their parents' giddy behavior.

The flight attendant for the coach class walked through the aisle and closed all overhead compartments. "Miss," she said, tapping the shoulder of a well-dressed woman, who wore sunglasses and a scarf wrapped stylishly around her head and neck. "Yes?" responded the woman. She lifted her sunglasses from her eyes and looked at the flight attendant. "Please buckle your seat belt," she said. The woman smiled and buckled her seat belt and the flight attendant continued down the aisle.

The plump man next to the stylishly dressed woman rested his hand on her well-shaped thigh. "I can't believe how lucky I was to bump into you. It has been years!" he said with a chuckle. "Your husband was a fine man," he drawled in a deep Texas accent. "I always wondered what in the world he was doing with you?" She looked at him with distain as he guffawed at his own joke.

He gave her thigh a hard slap and looked out of the window of the plane. "Yep," he said, sucking in his breath. "I'm so sorry to hear about the mix-up over your suite on the cruise. I am glad you agreed to share my room. I would have never thought to ask if you hadn't brought it up," he said cheerily. The woman forced a smile on her lips. "I am so appreciative for your hospitality."

She held her hand up. "This is only temporary until I get the matter straightened out with the cruise director," she said. The man looked at her but said nothing. He turned and looked out of the window as they taxied down the runway. "This is going to be a very good cruise indeed," he said under his breath as he continued to look out of the window with anger in his eyes.

After the plane landed in Florida, Amara, Tony, Myra, and Jackson rushed to the baggage claim to retrieve their luggage. They followed the horde of people and boarded the shuttle that took them to their cruise ship. Jackson kissed Myra and squeezed her hand. "Happy anniversary, baby," he said. "Is it ever," she exclaimed as they walked across the long covered ramp that led to the ship. They showed their identification and passports and entered the ship.

On the next shuttle a slight woman and a rotund man with a gallon sized cowboy hat exited out of the back door. The woman was weighted down with several bags, while the man carried a small briefcase. "Come on, honey, don't want to get left behind!" he chuckled as he walked several paces ahead of her. She tried to keep up and finally signaled a porter to help her with all the bags. When they reached the ship the large man tipped him. "That's gonna come out of your allowance, missy," he laughed again at his private joke. She rolled her eyes and sashayed toward their room.

Amara and Tony settled into their honeymoon suite. The room was spacious and elegantly decorated. They had every amenity imaginable. Amara plopped on the bed spread-eagled. "This cruise is going to be so much fun! I can feel it!" she said excitedly.

Tony lay next to her. "Let's go see how Mom and Dad like their suite!" he exclaimed. Amara held his hand and kissed him passionately. "Thank you for all of this," she said earnestly.

"They are my family now too," he said happily. "You just don't know how much that means to me," he said. He swatted Amara gently on the thigh and told her to get up. She straightened her clothes and they left to check out the suite down the hall.

When Myra and Jackson arrived at their suite Myra placed her hand over her mouth and gasped. It was simply beautiful. "Jackson, look at this room," she whispered. Jackson was in awe as well. "This is some kind of beautiful," he said quietly. Their thoughts were interrupted by a loud knock on the door. They opened the door and Amara and Tony burst in, full of energy. "So, do you like it Mom and Dad?" asked Tony.

They both gave him a big hug. "Son, we love it," they said in unison.

Tony and Jackson walked over to the table and looked over the itinerary for the night. As the women joined them, there was a knock on the door. A small man with a deep tan and black straight hair stood at the door smiling. He introduced himself, and told them he would take care of them throughout the cruise. Anything they needed during the cruise he would get for them. He gave them his card and told them his name. "My name is Akeem, but please call me AJ. Everybody does," he said with a wide grin. They all smiled and thanked him. He explained the night's events to them and told them how to find their table for dining and the location of the large ballroom where everyone would meet for the mixer in the next half hour, once the ship had begun its voyage. He also gave them the itinerary for the next day.

"Please come to the mixer. You will meet the captain, and he and his staff will explain everything to you. I will make sure your room is ready for the evening. If you like, I can unpack your things."

Myra shook her head. "No thank you, AJ. You are so kind. I know you are going to be a wonderful asset on this cruise."

The large man opened the door of the modest cabin and walked in. The woman wrinkled her nose in distaste as she walked in. The porter brought up the trail with the luggage. He unloaded the luggage and waited patiently for his tip. The large man waved his hand carelessly in the air. "Honey, pay the man," he said. The woman sucked in her breath and dug in her purse to pay the porter. He smiled politely and left.

The woman took off her scarf and glasses, and sat down to catch her breath. "Since you aren't doing anything, would you unpack my things and put them away?" he asked. She sucked in her breath again and formed her mouth to say something nasty and then thought better of it. She needed to be kind until they got out to sea. Then she could maneuver her way around and find better accommodations.

He took out a large cigar and bit off the tip. He spat the tip onto the floor next to the garbage. "Oops, get that for me, honey, will ya?" he said. She bit her tongue once again, bent down, picked up the damp cigar tip, and threw it away.

As she put his clothes away, he sat smoking his cigar and reading a newspaper. Every once in a while he would lower the newspaper and admire her figure. "You haven't changed one bit, Sherry," he said. "Well, maybe a little more heft in the butt," he joked. She glared at him and gagged from the stench of the cigar. She hated cigar smoke. It reminded her of her father, and she hated him more than any other man.

She placed the last of his things in the drawer and closed it. She looked around and discovered there was no place for her clothes. She shrugged. She hadn't planned on staying anyway. She left her clothes neatly folded in the suitcase and hung up a few of her more expensive outfits and gowns. She had several wigs in her bag and she set them inside the small closet on the floor.

She glanced over at Mike McGowan. He had gained considerable weight since she had seen him last. She remembered that he had never really cared for her. She was surprised he had agreed to allow her to stay in his room temporarily. He and her husband had been inseparable. She knew she could not afford to make him angry. He had talked the boarding agent into allowing her on the ship even though her name did not appear on the passenger list. She was also living in his small cabin for free. She dusted her hands and grabbed her scarf and sunglasses. When she placed her hand on the door Mike lowered his newspaper. "Where do you think you are going, Sherry?"

Myra changed into one of her colorful short outfits and matching sandals. Jackson replaced his conservative slacks with a pair of khaki shorts, a comfortable cotton polo shirt, and sandals. He smiled. He couldn't remember the last time he had worn sandals anywhere. They were both bubbling with excitement. Myra grabbed her purse and the itinerary. "Colonial deck!" they said as they headed out the door.

As Jackson and Myra entered the Colonial deck ballroom, Amara and Tony waved from their seats. The room was nearly filled with excited, loud, chattering passengers. Myra spotted them and waved back. She and Jackson headed in that direction and joined them.

Charlene walked into the morgue. Her eyes were swollen from crying. She couldn't believe Shareese would do such a thing. How could she break into Amara and Tony's house? They had never done anything to her. She wept quietly as the coroner opened the door and pulled out the heavy metal drawer. The coroner unceremoniously uncovered the body and exposed her face and torso. Charlene gasped and screamed, "Charity!"

"I asked, where are you going?" Shareese froze. Without answering, she quickly opened the door and ran down the hallway. Mike stubbed out his cigar and sprayed air freshener. "So much for a fun cruise," he said as he moved his bulky body toward the door.

Shareese arrived at the Colonial deck and went into the large ballroom. It was simply gorgeous. She smiled as she spotted an empty seat in the back. As she moved into the room, a hand touched her shoulder. "I am glad you waited for me, Sherry," said Mike, smiling. Shareese sighed and allowed him to guide her to the back of the room where two spare seats were available.

As they passed several seats, Mike bumped against Amara's chair. She looked up and took in a large breath. She tapped Tony on the shoulder. "Tony, that woman looks like Shareese!" she said in a low tone of voice. Tony craned his neck to look at the woman. He had never actually seen Shareese, but he had seen her twin Charlene on a number of occasions.

The woman sat down and took off her glasses. "You're right. I know that's not Charlene," he whispered. "Look at that scar," he said.

"What are you two whispering about?" asked Myra.

Amara gulped. "We think we just saw Shareese," said Amara nervously.

Just then an announcement was made over the loudspeaker, summoning Tony to the front desk. "I am going with you," said Amara. Tony patted her hand. "Stay here, so we don't draw a lot of attention," he said. He walked casually out of the room and headed to the front desk.

There was a cable from Chief Chaddam warning him that Shareese had in fact, not been killed and might possibly be on the cruise ship. The corpse was her younger sister, Charity.

Charlene had identified the corpse that was once her vibrant baby sister. Charlene was angry. She knew Shareese had talked Charity into breaking into Officer Riley's home. She had talked her into shooting them under the guise of playing cowboys and Indians, Charity's favorite game.

Chaddam directed Tony to make sure the head of security was aware that Shareese might have gotten on the ship.

He took the message and went directly to the security office. He requested to speak to the head of security. A tall dark-skinned man of about six feet came out of one of the offices. He extended his hand and introduced himself. "Hi, I am Chad Williams, head of security."

Tony shook his hand and identified himself as a Seattle police officer and showed him the note he had received from the Seattle chief of police. He also told him he believed the woman was in the Colonial ballroom on the Colonial deck. She was sitting with another man. He gave a full description of her.

Chad immediately got on his radio and communicated with all of his staff. Each went to their designated station. He then told one of the security agents to go and remove her from the ballroom. He directed Tony to return to the ballroom and act as normally as possible so as to not alarm her.

Moments later Tony went back to his seat. Shareese placed her dark sunglasses back on. Mike asked to take her sunglasses off. As he removed them from her face, he dropped the sunglasses and stepped on them. "Oops, sorry," he said, as he picked up the broken pieces.

Shareese snarled. "You did that on purpose," she sneered. "I don't care how good a friend you were to my late husband and what you think you have on me, but the charade is over. I am out of here," she said and stood up. Mike tried to grab her arm without making a scene. She jerked her arm away and turned to leave.

As she turned, she bumped into the man who stood in front of her. "Excuse me," she said, careful not to make direct eye contact. He gently took her arm. "Ma'am, I am security. There seems to be a problem with your room. Please come with me," he requested in an official tone.

She looked at Mike with pleading eyes. He smiled and waved goodbye. He took out a cigar and put it in his mouth. "No smoking please!" said an elderly lady sitting beside him. He smiled and tucked it back in his shirt pocket. "Goodbye, Sherry," said Mike, as he relaxed in his chair.

The security agent handed Shareese over to Chad. He took Shareese into a small room and asked her to sit down. "We have checked our passenger list and you are not on it," he said authoritatively. Shareese looked at him and licked her lips invitingly. Chad frowned. "Ms Miller, Collins, whatever your name is? Why are you on this ship illegally?" he asked sternly.

She crossed her legs suggestively before answering. Chad rolled his eyes. This woman is a piece of work, he thought to himself. He crossed his muscular arms across his chest and glared at her. His jaw tightened. He was not smiling. Shareese kept quiet.

Finally she broke the silence. "My friend Mike McGowan...."

Chad cut her off. "Mike McGowan is a paid bounty hunter. He was going to turn you in at the next port. We had already talked with him when he registered. Though he said you were his personal guest, we did not know your fare was not paid," he said.

Chad spoke into his radio and summoned two security guards. "You will be a guest in our small holding cell for the night until we dock tomorrow. The accommodations are comfortable and you are away from all the other passengers, so there will be no embarrassment for anyone. When we reach our first port tomorrow, you will be handed over to the authorities and extradited back to Seattle for your crimes. Also, you are wanted for questioning in Texas for the possible murder of your late husband," he said lifting an eyebrow. "You have been quite busy, Shareese Collins," he said.

She glared at him as they placed handcuffs on her wrists and escorted through the back door and down the stairs to the holding cell. Shareese flirted, begged, and cried, but Chad paid her no attention.

Chad removed her cuffs and placed her in the cell. He locked the door and handed the key to Chris, the young security agent. Chris sat down in the chair and watched her, but said nothing. She lay on the cot and tried to get some rest, so she could think about her next move. "It ain't over, until it is over," she whispered, and smiled as she tucked her arms under her head and looked up at the ceiling.

The captain and his crew had handed out all the necessary administrative information and had encouraged the passengers to mingle and get to know one another. A live band softly played reggae music. Myra was busy chatting with two new friends she had met, when Jackson tapped her on the shoulder. He whispered into her ear and she giggled. She excused herself and Jackson took her hand and led her out of the ballroom.

Amara looked at her parents and smiled. Tony pulled her close and nuzzled her neck. "Our parents look so happy, don't they?" he asked. Amara smiled and responded with a kiss. Amara stood up and told Tony she wanted to look around and explore the rest of the ship. Tony stood up and took her hand. He grabbed his diagram of the ship and they left the ballroom.

As Tony and Amara stood on deck, the cool breeze from the sea met them. Amara turned her face toward it and her long hair billowed in the wind. Tony turned and looked at her. "You look so sexy right now, Mrs. Riley." Amara smiled at the compliment. "I haven't gotten used to being called Mrs. Riley, but it sure feels good," she said smiling widely. Tony laughed, and became serious. "Shareese should be off this ship when we dock in the morning. I won't really feel relaxed until that woman is off this ship and behind bars," he said angrily.

"What does she want from us?" asked Amara.

"The photos have been turned in to the authorities and Michael is in jail. Heck, even Maria has gone on with her life," said Amara, exasperated.

Tony shook his head. "I don't know, but I will rest a lot easier after tomorrow morning when we dock," he said with a frown.

Amara ran her hand along the side of his face and kissed him. "Don't let her ruin this time for us," she said.

Tony shook his head. "You're right. Want to go down to the next deck and get something to eat?" he asked. Amara nodded her head and they walked down to the next deck.

Myra walked into the room and Jackson followed. He closed the door softly and looked at his wife adoringly. "What are you looking at?" she said, a bit self-consciously. Jackson smiled. Myra was in good shape for her age. She was glad she had forced herself to exercise daily and watch her diet during the past two years. She was average height and had a medium build. Her full breasts still held their shape. Her hips were slim and she had very shapely legs from walking and exercising.

Jackson interrupted her thoughts. "I am looking at the most beautiful woman on the ship," he said adoringly. "My love for you has not changed from the day we met. In fact it has grown even more in the last thirty three years we have been together." He walked up to her and held her tight. He began to unbutton her blouse.

"And what do you think you're doing?" she asked seductively.

"Give me a few more minutes and you will find out," he growled. Myra laughed deeply as they both fell back onto the oversized bed.

Shareese walked over to the bars. She grabbed them and leaned over, exposing her full, voluptuous breasts. The young security guard's eyes widened as he stared at her. Outside of the room, Chad was watching on a closed circuit television set. "Damn, that is what I was afraid of." He looked at his female security guard. "Dominique, go in and relieve Chris," he said with a sigh.

Dominique snorted and stood up with her hands on her hips. "Can't Chris handle her?" she asked, annoyed. "I hate broads like her. Using her sexuality to get what she wants," she said, haltingly.

Chad looked at her. "Dom, what is it? You have never acted like this before," he asked.

"I just don't like her. She is dangerous and conniving. It makes me sick to think of all the things she has gotten away with by spreading open those legs of hers," she spat.

Chad lifted his brow. "Dom, what do you have against this woman? It sounds personal." Dominique turned deep red, but did not answer.

Chad didn't press it any further. He had his back to the screen as he called another security agent on the radio. "Shit!" Dominique yelled, as she grabbed her pistol out of its holster. She ran into the room, but it was too late. Shareese had fled through the opposite door. Chris lay unconscious on the ground in front of the bars. His pistol was missing from its holster. "Shit!" she yelled again as she radioed the other agents throughout the ship.

Once Shareese got on deck, she began to walk normally and blend in with the other passengers. She tucked the gun into the back of her waistband and tied her scarf around her waist to hide the bulge of the weapon. She had to get back to the room to change her clothes and get a wig to alter her appearance. She didn't know how she was going to do it with Mike around. I do have the pistol, she thought.

Instantly, a hand clutched her shoulder tightly. "Sherry, where do you think…" Before he could finish the sentence, she turned, pulled the gun out of her waistband, and shot Mike in his torso. In total shock, he fell to the ground and grabbed his heart. Shareese ran away and a crowd gathered around Mike.

Dominique was gaining fast. She quickly glanced at Mike's limp body but kept running after Shareese.

A passenger from the ship broke through the crowd and knelt beside him and took his pulse. "I think this man is having a heart attack, and he's been shot," he yelled. "Call the infirmary!" People began to move and take appropriate action. Security guards appeared and dispersed the crowd. In seconds, the ship's doctor was by Mike's side, taking his vital signs and barking out orders.

Shareese ran to the next deck. She slowed when she saw Amara and Tony standing close together, facing one another talking and laughing. As she approached they stopped laughing and Tony whispered something in Amara's ear. Amara laughed again and swatted his arm playfully. Shareese pulled out her pistol and aimed at Amara.

As she prepared to pull the trigger, Tony yelled, "Now!" Amara quickly fell to the ground and Tony ran toward Shareese while Dominique hit her from behind. The force of Dominique's body ramming into hers caused Shareese to go airborne. Tony saw Dominique and hit the deck. Shareese flew through the air and Tony stood up and helped propel her body forward. The momentum caused her body to sail over the railing into the sea.

She screamed and hit the water with a loud splash. Dominique immediately threw over a life preserver for her. Shareese grabbed it and was pulled up. Soaking wet, she was handcuffed and led back to the holding cell.

Chris glared at her as he held a pack of ice to the huge bump on his forehead. Dominique removed the cuffs that pinned her hands behind her and switched the cuffs to the front. She clamped down the metal bracelets and pushed her roughly into the cell with the cuffs on. Shareese slid across the floor and landed next to her bed.

"Can't I at least have a towel to dry off?" she pleaded. Dominique threw a plain white hand towel in between the bars. The towel sailed in the air and landed on the floor. Shareese picked up the towel and attempted to daintily pat herself dry.

Dominique rolled her eyes in disgust. "Little prissy," she hissed under her breath. Shareese glared at Dominique and started to say something nasty. Dominique pulled out her gun. "You try anything, and you are a dead woman." Dominique glared at her once more.

Shareese patted her face dry and tried to strike up a conversation. "You look familiar, where are you from?" she asked.

"Spain," answered Dominique bluntly. "I guess I look so familiar because you know my sister, Amelia Hernandez," she said bitterly. "You used her and tried to get all of her money. She used you to get Michael's sperm and his money. I don't know which of you paid the greatest price," she spat. "At least Amelia is with someone who loves her now," she said gently.

Shareese rolled her eyes. "Save the sob story. Amelia, or rather Maria, did get pregnant by Michael because of me and she did get her money, some of which should belong to me. She would have never gotten pregnant by Michael if it hadn't been for me," she yelled, slapping her chest with her cuffed hands.

Dominique rolled her eyes and said nothing. She just glared at Shareese's wet body. Shareese was shivering now. Dominique watched but did not move from her seat. Finally Shareese lay on the cot and tried to get herself warm.

Chad stopped watching the surveillance camera and sighed. "Turn up the heat in the cell, but no one goes near Ms. Collins. Understand?" he asked all of his agents.

One of his agents snickered. "Hey boss, what the hell has she got that makes guys and some women, lose their mind?" he asked.

Chad smiled. "A great body and a lot of sex appeal," he said. "Now get back to work, all of you."

Chad walked back to the video camera. He wanted to keep an eye on Dominique. He was shocked to hear that Shareese was somehow connected to her sister. "That woman has done it to everyone she meets," he said, with sorrow in his voice. He looked at her wet hair that was stuck to her head. He shook his head. "Too bad she doesn't use that energy for something good," he said. He let out a heavy sigh.

Dominique came out as he stared at the screen. "Not you too?" she asked with disgust.

Chad walked over to her and patted her on her shoulder. "I overheard your conversation. I am sorry about your sister. I know she has been through a lot with the loss of her first child," he said.

Dominique's eyes filled with tears. "She always wanted children, lots of them."

Chad smiled. "Sounds like she is in good hands now. She will be fine."

Dominique smiled and poured herself a cup of coffee. She ensured all the exit doors were locked and the jail cell was locked. She didn't want to be in the same room as Shareese, so she watched her through the monitor. Chad received a call on his radio and quickly headed out of the door. Dominique sat down in the chair the chief had vacated, and slowly sipped her coffee as she watched the monitor.

Amara sat in the bed in their suite. She couldn't stop shaking. Tony held her tightly and talked to her in a soothing voice. "It's over, Amara. She is locked up and it is over," he said, as he stroked her hair.

"She has ruined our honeymoon," she wept.

Tony smiled. "No she hasn't. This is only the first day!" he said excitedly. "Why don't we go get your parents and join in the newlywed game that is going on in one hour?" he suggested.

Amara sniffed and shook her head. "You're right. Let's get out and mingle and have some fun!"

Amara knocked on her parents' door but there was no answer. She shrugged and took Tony's hand. "Maybe they are already out and about?" she surmised.

"Knowing Mom, they are out doing something," Tony joked. They walked to the deck and into the ballroom where they were taking volunteers as contestants for the newlywed game. Tony and Amara immediately volunteered.

Jackson dried Myra's hair as he kissed her on her shoulder. "That was simply wonderful," he said.

Myra turned and placed her damp, naked body against his. "That was better than wonderful...we should do that more often," she purred.

Jackson smiled. "I can't usually get you to stand still long enough let alone lay still," he joked.

Myra pushed him playfully on the shoulder. "Jackson, you are awful. I will start making time for this," she said as she turned to get her clothes. Jackson playfully swatted her butt. "Jackson! You are so fresh," she teased.

Jackson smiled and hummed a catchy tune, as pulled out the clothes he intended to wear. "Hungry?" he asked.

Myra smiled. "After all that activity, I am ravenous!"

Jackson laughed. "Well get a move on and I will get you some food," he joked.

Myra looked appreciatively at her husband's tall firm body as he removed the towel from his waist. Myra smiled. My man has still got it, she thought to herself as she turned to the closet to get her clothes. She, too, hummed a catchy tune as she finished dressing.

Tony and Amara were in stitches as they sat in their mock contestants' booth. They had gotten all of their questions correct while playing the new-lywed game, but the couple beside them was not doing as well. The new wife was getting upset. She had hit her husband over the head twice with the sign because he gave the wrong answer. He frowned. Finally they got a question right. They kissed for at least one minute. When it was all over, Tony and Amara were the winners and got a nice gift. The other contestants congrat-ulated them as they left the stage.

Amara and Tony were still laughing about the other couples when they left the ballroom to get something to drink. They spotted Myra and Jackson. They were feeding each other fresh fruit. Tony ran up and held his mouth open and Myra popped in a piece of pineapple. "Wow, that was sweet," he said, kissing Amara. "Very sweet," responded Amara. Myra and Jackson laughed.

They told them all about the newlywed game and about the incident with Shareese. Myra clutched her heart. "Will it ever end?" she asked.

Jackson frowned. "Is she locked up now?" Tony nodded his head. "Did you send your boss a telegram?" asked Jackson. Tony shook his head, no.

"The head of security, Chad Williams placed the telegram. He also con-tacted the port authorities, and they will be ready for her tomorrow morn-ing." Tony looked at his watch. "In twelve hours she will be off this ship and out of our lives!" he said happily.

"Thank God," said Myra. Amara shook her head in agreement.

Amara picked a piece of fruit from her father's plate. "So, what have you two been doing?" she asked. She noticed her mother and father had changed clothes. She squinted at her mother and smiled. "Nice outfit," she said laugh-ing. Myra turned red with embarrassment. Jackson put his arm around Myra. "Yes it is nice, but it won't be on for long," he said jokingly. Myra swatted his arm and continued to blush.

Tony gave Jackson a high five. "That's what I am talking about, Dad!" he said. Tony could hear music from the upper deck. "Hey, you guys want to dance?" he asked. Myra and Jackson finished the last of their fruit and they all headed upstairs to dance to the funky beat of the live band playing in the center of the deck by one of the large pools.

Mike lay in the hospital bed. He was pale, but the doctors said he'd be okay. The nurse took his vital signs and motioned Dominique toward his bed. "How are you doing?" she asked with a heavy Spanish accent.

He smiled thinly. "I am alive," he wheezed.

"Yes, you are. And lucky," she said. "We have some great docs and they patched you right up. Uh, you know you are going to have to lose some of that weight, right?"

He smiled. "It was a fat suit," he said. "It was makeup and a fat suit. I am a bounty hunter and I was after this crook that was supposed to be on this ship, but as it turned out, I met Shareese on the way to the ship. She is some piece of work. She was married to my best friend. She sucked him dry and I believe she killed him. Unfortunately, I could never prove it.

"I was trying to get her to admit she killed him, but she was much too clever for that. She thought I wanted to have sex with her. If she only knew how much she made my stomach turn. I just wanted her to go to jail to pay for killing my best friend," he said sorrowfully. "He deserved so much better."

Dominique rubbed his hand. She could now see how thin his hand was. Also, she could see his face was thinner. The sorrow in his eyes made her feel sad. She gently kissed him on the forehead and looked at her watch. "I must go now, but I will stop by and see how you are doing tomorrow, okay?" Mike smiled. "Thanks, I'd like that," he said earnestly.

The ship docked early the next morning. Chad took extra precautions and got Shareese off the ship before the passengers began to stir. She was immediately handed over to the authorities at the port. There were plans in place to extradite her. A team of FBI agents had arrived early that morning to take her back to Seattle. The authorities immediately released her to the FBI and they all got into their cars and sped to the airport to board a private charter plane. Chad remained until he saw the charter plane take off from the nearby airport.

It was nearly five in the morning and the first thing Amara did was quietly put on her jogging clothes and swiftly place her long hair in a ponytail. She quietly opened the door and headed to the office of the head of security. She wanted to make sure Shareese was off the ship and in custody.

Chad was returning to the ship when he spotted Amara walking toward his office. Her long ponytail swung from side to side as she walked toward his office. "Mrs. Riley?" he called. Amara turned around and smiled. "Mr. Williams, I was just coming to see you." Chad took her hand and patted it. "No more worries, Mrs. Riley. Ms. Collins is off the ship and is in the custody of the FBI. They boarded a private plane a few minutes ago," he said calmly. He looked into her eyes.

Amara released her breath. She had not realized she was holding her breath. Chad let go of her hand. Amara smiled again. She was overwhelmed with relief. "Thank you, Mr. Williams!" she said gaily.

225

"Call me Chad," he said as he admired her.

Amara acknowledged it with a friendly wave, but did not turn back as she headed to her suite. Tony was sitting up in bed with a worried look in his eyes. "Amara, where did you go? Why didn't you wake me?"

She looked at him and smiled. "I went to see Mr. Williams, head of security. He confirmed that the FBI took Shareese away, and that they boarded a charter plane back to the United States," she said happily.

He looked at her, worriedly. "Please don't run off like that. I was really worried," he said, in a serious tone.

Amara kissed him gently. "I am sorry. I just had to know. I could barely sleep last night," she said.

"I know. You were distracted all night and you kept me awake," he complained.

She took off her workout tank top and her black leggings and climbed back into bed. "Is there any way I can make it up to you?" she asked kissing him all over his chest. He smiled and lay back against the pillows. "I will leave that up to you," he said smiling.

"Well, in that case," said Amara, as she got out of the bed. Tony watched her take off the rest of her clothes and return to bed naked. "Let's see what I can do to make it up to you," she said as she continued to kiss where she had left off.

Tony moaned. "You are doing great so far," he said breathlessly.

"You ain't seen nothing yet," she said as she pulled the covers over her head.

The remainder of their cruise was filled with fun, excitement, and lots of activities. They went snorkeling, horseback riding, and swimming. Jackson and Myra went on a couple of tours by themselves while Tony and Amara sunned themselves and swam. Myra picked up bolts of beautiful fabric as they docked in the different Caribbean islands.

All of their movements were monitored by the watchful eyes of Chad Williams. He wanted to make sure there were no other incidents involving any of his passengers. He was also smitten with Amara, though she paid him no attention. Because of his attraction he made sure he kept his distance.

They were headed home now. Everyone was said their final goodbyes and prepared for their final lavish dining experience. Chad smiled as he watched Amara hug one of the passengers. He would have some time away from the ship soon. He might visit Seattle, he thought to himself.

Chapter 18

Myra, Jackson, Amara, and Tony walked into the house and fell into the chairs. They were all exhausted. "That was the nicest time I have ever had," said Myra dreamily. Jackson held her close and agreed. "Simply wonderful. Thank you both for such a beautiful anniversary present and for sharing your honeymoon with us," he said.

"Sharing what?" asked Tony. "We never saw you two. If you weren't locked up in your suite, you were out on a tour. We only spent the first and last days together," he said.

Myra and Jackson laughed. "Exactly! It was your honeymoon and we didn't want to crowd you. We did a lot together; we snorkeled and went horseback riding together and ate together every night!" said Myra.

Tony smiled. "That's true. It was a wonderful time," he said as he leaned his head on Amara's shoulder.

"Hey, let's get home," said Amara as she tapped on Tony's leg. Tony got up slowly and kissed Myra on the cheek and gave Jackson a hug. "See you, Mom and Dad," he said. They smiled. Amara hugged and kissed them both. Tony took Amara's hand and they walked out of the house.

Jackson leaned over to Myra and whispered in her ear. "Just because we are home, doesn't mean…." Before he could get the rest of his sentence out Myra had kissed him passionately on the lips and led him to the bedroom. "We'll unpack in the morning," she sang as Jackson followed her to the bedroom, smiling.

Tony and Amara arrived at their house and collapsed on the sofa in the den. Amara saw a note written in calligraphy by her silk flowers. She smiled as she thought about her best friend. She rubbed her own tummy and wondered if she were pregnant too.

Three months later Amara sat in the back of the crowded courtroom as sentence was passed on Michael Whitman. Amara shook her head and made a few notes on her writing pad. He would serve a long prison term of twenty years for the kidnapping, stealing one million dollars, and hiring a killer to murder her. She released her breath as Michael's brother and father wept over his fate. Maria sat stoically next to Ryan and did not shed a tear. She was large with child. She and Ryan had quietly married. It was important to her that she be married before the child was born. They already knew the baby would be a boy. Ryan had told her he had always loved her and had immediately obliged. Michael wept quietly into his hands.

Hours later, Shareese stood in front of the judge to receive her sentence for her part in the theft of the ransom money and also for hiring Duke to kill Amara. Her sentence had been lengthened due to breaking out of jail, fleeing the country, and trying to kill her yet another time; and also for shooting her late husband's best friend, nearly killing him. Amara was pleased when she heard that Mike and Amelia's sister, Dominique, had gotten together. They both seemed to need someone. Chad Williams had sent her and Tony a note telling them all about it.

She shook her head. She thought Chad had a crush on her, though he never did anything out of line. It was just the way his eyes lingered on her just a bit too long. Amara snapped out of her thoughts as the judge sentenced Shareese to twenty-five years in prison, without the possibility of parole. Shareese fainted. Amara smiled as she wrote her notes. She thought Shareese had got what she deserved, though she knew it was not her place to decide her fate.

Maria's court date had been a day earlier, and she had received a seven-year suspended sentence for her assault on Michael.

Macey had never made it to court. He had died in the infirmary from the wounds he had received in jail. Sully had died in the shootout at Michael's home.

Amara wondered if they believed that one million dollars was worth so many lost lives? She had finally gotten over the anger she felt for her biological father. She and her aunt had had a long talk and if Sarah could forgive him, then Amara would certainly try to do the same. She concluded he was a selfish man who cared only for himself. He is dead and in another place, she thought.

She thought about the Coopers. It had never come out that most of the ransom money was counterfeit. Amara was surprised Shareese's lawyer hadn't brought it out in court. I guess after the last stunt Shareese pulled, it was a moot issue, she thought.

Amara's stomach rumbled. She patted it softly and took out the small packet of crackers her mother made her carry everywhere she went. She and Tony had got their wish; she had become pregnant while on their honeymoon. She smiled as she thought about the new life coming while others had been lost. A never-ending cycle, life and death, she pondered. She jotted down some last minute notes and closed her notebook. Amara gathered her things and got ready to leave. This would be the final series of articles she would do on this case. She was glad. She was ready to work on something new and fun.

As she left the courtroom, there was a handsome man in uniform leaning against the wall, waiting for her. "Hey, good-looking, going my way?" he asked.

Amara giggled. "You'd better go away, my husband will get jealous," she teased back.

He walked up and kissed her lightly on the lips. "Let him. I can take him, I'm a cop," he teased. Amara doubled over with laughter as Tony caught her arm and took her to lunch at Sarah's.